W9-BDI-839

## TOR BOOKS BY SUSAN SHWARTZ

*Cross and Crescent*
*Empire of the Eagle* (with Andre Norton)
*The Grail of Hearts*
*Heritage of Flight*
*Hostile Takeover*
*Imperial Lady* (with Andre Norton)
*Moonsinger's Friends* (editor)
*Second Chances*
*Shards of Empire*
*Silk Roads and Shadows*
*White Wing* (with S. N. Lewitt as "Gordon Kendall")

# HOSTILE
# *TAKEOVER*

## SUSAN SHWARTZ

**TOR**®

A TOM DOHERTY ASSOCIATES BOOK
NEW YORK

This is a work of fiction. All the characters and events portrayed in this book are either products of the author's imagination or are used fictitiously.

HOSTILE TAKEOVER

A Tor Book
Published by Tom Doherty Associations, LLC
175 Fifth Avenue
New York, NY 10010

www.tor.com

Tor® is a registered trademark of Tom Doherty Associates, LLC.

ISBN 0-765-34382-7
EAN 978-0-765-34382-6

First edition: December 2004
First mass market edition: December 2005

Printed in the United States of America

0 9 8 7 6 5 4 3 2 1

To the teams in the back offices,
who know who they are,
even if no one else does

**Three months out from Earth on the asteroid run and** heading toward Vesta Colony, *Rimrunner* ceased its latest engine burn, and CC Williams began running for her life again.

As the captain's "safe to release" signal broke into programs on every screen, lights flashed and the "all clear" blared from speakers in every corridor of the ship. Except, of course, Freeze. No one there was conscious, so no one had a need to know. But the high net worth and corporate passengers, the only ones able to fill *Rimrunner*'s staterooms, thanked God and top management for key-man insurance and personnel who knew their jobs, and drew deep breaths to mask their apprehension.

It wasn't as if her life were in any immediate danger. Except for one alleged pirate sighting that turned out to be a Solar Sailor way off course, *Rimrunner* hadn't had a single incident since it boosted away from EOS—Earth Orbital Station—three months ago. Nothing succeeded like success: the last safety drill, three months ago, had been conspicuous only for the excellence of the hot hors d'oeuvres served afterward in the First Class lounge.

Just because the ship was secure, however, didn't mean its

passengers could let their fitness lapse. At the beginning of the trip, *Rimrunner*'s MedCenter had sent workout schedules to every stateroom. Meaning that CC—better known by the string of numbers on her Alpha Consultants LLC debit card than by the antiquated names Caroline and Cassandra, which she hadn't used since she'd fled her low-rent origins—knew this was part of her job, too: to report to ship's gym like a good little *shoshaman,* or salaryman, sweat alongside all the other passengers, or pay the penalty fee for missing workouts. Miss too many workouts, and it would probably show up on her next evaluation. Alpha had invested a lot of money in her training, her passage, and her life insurance: it had a right to make certain that when she landed on Vesta, she'd be able to function in what amounted to little more than zero g.

So CC ran for her life, running harder than she'd ever run back when she was struggling to escape gangs and a chronic lack of future. She had an hour to go now on her workout, and she'd be damned if she was leaving before it ended. Never mind that she was expecting a transmission from her employer, a consulting firm so powerful that it terrified other consulting firms and justified its name: *Alpha.* She could supply password, retinal scan, and timestamp an hour from now, too. The message would wait. So would her curiosity. While confidential instructions might be best practices in an audit, that level of secrecy wasn't. In fact, she'd been ordered to conceal these transmissions.

CC might have escaped a life of make-work, public support, or enforced immigration in deep Freeze; but she balanced on a scalpel's edge. Just one mistake, and she knew she'd be tossed right back into the underclass. Nightmares about landing in the discard heap still woke her at 4:00 A.M. most sleepshifts. She feared they always would, but so far, she'd managed to hide them. Exercise wasn't just mandated by ship's regs, it helped.

So, now that the ship's engines had ended their burn, CC started hers. The pun made her smile. She thought of passing it on, then paused to second-guess herself. The person next to her might consider it strange, a sign of her past as the descendant of the overeducated, underemployed tutor demographic: better not.

She glanced up over the treadmills, mini-centrifuges, and weight systems to the bulkheads. Flashing across the ceiling of the lavish gym that occupied one whole ship's bay was a narrow black zipper. Stock symbols and quotes danced across one segment; below it ran the water futures index, prices tracked against the orbiting ice chunks throughout the solar system and against challenges like the current sunspot alert.

Below the zipper, screens glowed with business news transmitted from all Earth's major exchanges and relayed by the Bloomberg Boosting Units orbiting throughout the solar system to pick up. Picked up, decrypted, cleansed of static, readjusted for Doppler shifts, recollimated, encrypted again, and sent on their way, the data gleamed gold and green. The graphics for the financial news were, appropriately, the colors of old-fashioned money.

The only flickers of red that showed up on the map lit places that most of the Non-Governmental Organizations had written off anyhow.

Next story! Chile had merged with three others to form the Republic of New Patagonia. Now that that nation had, essentially, ceased to exist, the sunset provisions of the sovereign bonds it had issued for terraforming on Mars—short term at a century—were being called. Big as New Pat was, it was still an emerging market. Compared with some NGOs, whose revenues exceed those of Africa and the Eurasiazone and were closing fast on the North American gross continental product, this new nation was a nonstarter. Still, its bonds were deeply discounted. Remained to be seen if bondos would regard that as a plus or a sign of a credit preparing to take a dive.

Next! CC listened to the latest pronouncements on last year's loss of a *Zumwalt*-class liner, a joint venture between

Cunard and EarthServ, like *Rimrunner* itself, in an explosion just outside Jupiter's orbit. The talking head on-screen opined the cause had been an undiscovered satellite on a course so eccentric that ship sensors hadn't spotted it until too late. In any event, the explosion was driving down the defense electronics sector and had caused the resignation of at least three CEOs so far. A blue-ribbon team had been assembled back on Earth to investigate.

CC stepped up her pace: by the time that team made it out to the Asteroid Belt, the real investigation would be half over.

Someone hit the remote.

The screen blanked. Then, it brightened, this time with "lite" news. Probably, after that downer story, EarthNet thought that people needed a pick-me-up—hence, this tongue-in-cheek discussion of the eleven-year Sunspot Index. Like the hemline and lipstick indices, sunspots were always good for a polite smirk, unless, of course, you were caught unshielded on the sunside of a ship. Or if you'd bet against the index and lost money.

They were in a period of maximum sunspot activity now, and the markets were reacting. So, fortunately, were *Rimrunner*'s excellent shields. Meanwhile, everyone wore badges, and kept one eye on the newsfeeds for sunspot alerts.

"State-of-the-art health and business facilities" were among *Rimrunner*'s most popular amenities, the advertorials proclaimed in living holo on all the highest-demographic nets. From bar to fresh-water showers, *Rimrunner* proved that the remaining *Zumwalt*-class ships weren't just civilian luxury liners, but safe. "Safe as houses." After all, the only people who could afford them lived in houses, or condos at the very least, even if they were subsidized by their employers.

Another reason to hang on to her job like grim death.

What's more, as the latest advertorials trumpeted every five minutes, travel on board *Rimrunner* wasn't just luxurious, it was safe. The ads had succeeded in their claims. Now, no self-respecting corporation would send executives out on anything less, especially since EarthServ was still trying to flush the last few pirates preying on the O&M, or oil and mining consortia, that had replaced Earth's "oil and natural gas bidniz" as the latest profitable frontier.

On the one long bulkhead that wasn't occupied by mirrors or Bloomberg transmissions was another of *Rimrunner*'s amenities: VR screens that displayed spectacular views of space to the passengers who cycled or ran in place, or grunted as any one of a number of high-tech racks equipped with gleaming, queeping monitors and attentive, personable trainers (available for private sessions at an additional fee, facilities and tips not included) built up their strength.

Wiping her forehead before a trainer could intervene, CC glanced at one of the VR screens. She thought she could get addicted to starlight; she'd never forget that first half-ecstatic, half-panicked moment when she first saw the stars from space. Awe, due diligence, and sheer delight danced a jig in her belly. For a moment, she thought her hollowness inside was a reaction to zero g—and she had so not wanted to be spacesick. Then, she'd shivered in pure joy as she realized the stars were another part of that heritage she hoped to reclaim—assuming she played her cards shrewdly, she wasn't fired, and she completed her audit without getting killed. Ships might be safe, but space travel on business still put you in a bad place on the actuarial tables. Now, she fought not to betray just how much she loved watching the stars.

On each exercise machine's heads-up display gleamed shipwide announcements: solar activity levels—high, not yet critical, potassium iodide available from your steward; casino night; hourly ship's tours; EVA training.

Deck-to-ceiling mirror panels showed the panting, sweating passengers. Even the retirees took time from their own modified workouts, carefully supervised by MedCenter techs in white shipsuits, that they'd had to agree to—and sign releases for—before they were allowed on board. And they too were fined for missing workouts, fined for letting their weight rise or their good cholesterol and calcium drop: disincentives to shirking that both their corporations and their insurers insisted on.

CC got a glimpse of herself, treadmilling away in sleek exercise clothing. Certainly, she was no beauty, but beauty was a disadvantage for anyone trying to climb the corporate ladder unless you played it very carefully indeed. Of middle height, she was fit and slender; medical coverage was cheaper if she kept her weight down. She'd weigh even less once she got to Vesta, whose gravity was about seven and a half times less than that of the moon, meaning that CC would weigh only about three pounds.

Before the trip, CC had cut her fairish hair short so almost-zero g wouldn't make every day a bad hair day. Now it angled smartly so that its longest strands swung beside a jawline that was just a little too stubborn for prettiness, brushing the conservative high collar of her workout suit in Alpha's discreet heraldry, differenced by logo and corporate rank on a shield of metallic navy—much like the starfield "outside."

Her eyes were dark and alert in a face she'd trained to give away as little as a blank computer screen. And she was as good an athlete as anyone who'd chosen corporate endurance tests as her lifestyle of choice. You got points for being good at team sports.

She touched the screen at "signup." On board ship, passengers had no rank, crew had told them during orientation. Never mind their corporate titles: the most junior crewmember outranked the lot of them. Assuming the passengers wanted to live to make it to Vesta or Titan or wherever, they were to obey all crewmembers as if they were CEOs.

Absolutely. Never mind that sensible salarymen, like military spouses, knew precisely where they stood in relation to other employees of any corporation in descending order of prestige. And they all knew, too, just where each company ranked in the scheme of things as measured by stock price, market cap, performance, return on invested capital, merger rumors, and pending litigation.

Three of the uniformed crew "CEOs" patrolled behind the passengers racked on their machines. As they walked, they muttered important somethings about tests or reinforcements or modifications to the Bova protective grid in preparation for solar flares.

CC paused, the better to eavesdrop the way she did in elevators back home, though she pretended she was catching her breath. The people sweating to either side of her courteously ignored her, giving her the zone of privacy they'd learned in their transitions from pens to cubes to offices and private staterooms on board ships like *Rimrunner*.

No ordinary passenger would sign up for gym time or tours until all the vice presidents had been accommodated; the rabble of ordinary vice presidents gave way to senior and executive VPs, who yielded to general partners; and partners deferred to CEOs, who knew they had to go first if anyone was ever to go anywhere at all. CC's most recent rank was comfortably high, even if "purpose of voyage" on the ship's records indicated she was just an external overseer of a compliance audit.

Even if she wasn't nearly as high status as the ranking passenger, the Honorable Everett Neave, first NGO ambassador to the United Nations, efficiently treadmilling away beside his decades-younger wife, CC knew her corporate status was what used to be called fair to middling. She ranked about level with an environmental engineer, but way above the marketing people who didn't know it yet but probably would never be able to get their trip home expensed— or at least not on a ship that was safe enough to be worth the risk of their precious butts.

*One more day of due deference,* she promised herself, *and then you can take the tour of engineering.*

The tour had proved popular among top management, some of whom had gone back for a second time. So she'd had to wait. Group activities were an acceptable way to net-

work, and if she were to hit the ground running on Vesta—
assuming you *could* run there without achieving involuntary
orbital velocity—she'd need to make friends among the engineers on board; and engineering consultants couldn't get
enough of the infrastructure that gave *Rimrunner* hot showers and haute or nouvelle cuisine heavy on sauces that stuck
to plates more than to ribs for retirees who had to be vigilant
about their plastic arteries.

She should also tour the ship's Freeze sections for passengers whose hearts were too weak to survive boost off-planet.
And then, of course, there was steerage, a cargo bay turned
into a low-maintenance freeze area where the shipsicles—
people too deep in debt or too antisocial to remain on-
planet—were stacked. Assuming the 'sicles survived the
trip, the colonies were always looking for disposable workers. If not, well, MedCenters across the Asteroid Belt always
needed more spare parts than they could culture. After all, if
the indentures had truly been productive on Earth, they
wouldn't have to be shipped out, now would they?

*There but for the grace of God—and the work ethic from
hell—go I,* CC thought, before her mind skittered away from
the fears that woke her in the wolf's hour and made her
sweat worse than this treadmill.

Run for your life.

As CC picked up the pace, her heart rate rose. She drew
deep, careful breaths, trying not to think of the nightmare
where she dashed into headquarters, pursued by the spare-
parts brokers and petty thieves who lurked in her old *insula,*
into her manager's office, where she found even more of the
same. She didn't have to be a scholar—and she wasn't, she
wasn't!—to know what that meant.

Every time she had that dream, it meant she had a new
lesson to learn. Several lessons on this most recent learning
curve, and she was damned if she wouldn't try to pick the
one she liked best. Her first outsystem assignment! It put her
on the brink now, either of success or—what time was it?
She had an hour left.

*Finish your workout, CC, before the trainers see you're slacking off. Don't let anyone see you're on edge.*

Outperform, and the rest of her life would all fall into prosperous place: job, marriage, housing, and a future for at least one licensed, carefully planned-for, and wanted child that she vowed would be far more secure than anything she'd ever had.

She could feel her body warming now from the exercise. It felt good. Warm. Like the safety she longed to give the child (or children) she would have one day.

That is, provided she didn't stumble here at the starting gate. Fall, fail, and it wasn't likely she could scramble back into the academic track from business. She'd be lucky to get make-work for the rest of her life, assuming she even got that. Screw up now, even before her assignment started, and Alpha would hear of it. It wouldn't be hard for them to discipline her in midflight and order her bumped off *Rimrunner* to a freighter before she even got to Vesta.

And if she made serious mistakes on Vesta, they might not just terminate her. They could confiscate her ticket back to Earth or call her debts. Then, she'd have no choice but to be frozen and shipped off to less-sophisticated Triton or Ganymede, like the shipsicles in *Rimrunner*'s steerage.

She'd never been in the Belt: how'd she even know if she could adapt? If she couldn't, she'd wind up as spare parts or reaction mass.

CC pumped harder, trying to build up a sweat, to get warm again. Work harder. That was the key. Harder and smarter, with an eye over her shoulder to make sure she was still safe.

She checked to see how long she'd been working out. Two minutes longer than last time she'd looked. She drained the remaining Vitabrew (TM) from the squeeze bottle embossed with the ship's logo—a holographic field of stars trampled by a gold-crowned lion—rampant guardant, she remembered automatically.

*Don't think that way!*

Ruthlessly, she suppressed the pedantry only a university

brat would know, and handed the empty bottle over to the migrating young hardbody who multitasked as steward, personal trainer, and God probably knew what after hours. That wasn't a risk she was prepared to take. And besides, she thought with a little thrill of warmth, there was David IV, her fiancé.

"Just wait till Saturn gets big enough so we can see the different rings." Even if everyone knew that Jupiter, with its constellation of moons, came first, the man's voice sounded as assured as if its owner had made the Outer Planets run countless times, even back when it was still the province of beat-up miners, not luxury liners.

But the voice was the product not of experience, but of the most agonizing, expensive speech therapy.

It belonged not just to the liaison from Alpha's client on this venture, but to her rival—and potential scapegoat if all else failed—in the god-awful game of musical chairs that survival had become for anyone wanting to escape the *insulae* and provincial academies for the "real world" where deals were done and money made.

No. Back up. She reminded herself to even think of the man by the name he'd damn near focus-grouped for how well it played in corporate culture: not plain John Sanders, but Jonathan Vinocur Sanderson, who insisted on being called "Sandy" by his intimate friends, if he still had any. Sandy wasn't just the client liaison assigned to her project, he'd been her evil twin lifelong. They'd both escaped the *insulae*, project housing for the working poor who were too high-pay (the term was relative) for the warehouses for the underemployed and the roach motels of public housing, but not nearly rich enough to qualify for the developments in the carefully manicured and guarded exurbs far away from the blue glows that were DC, Beijing, Riyadh, and Zurich, the lagoons of Old LA and New Orleans, or the DMZs of Jakarta, Tel Aviv, and Istanbul.

Sandy's luck had started even worse than hers. She'd at least had parents who had sacrificed to boost her onto a vi-able career track. She had helped support them until they died three years ago. They had taken pride in her strength, even if they had not understood her choices.

Sandy had been born off-license to two grad students who'd failed their thesis defenses and only managed, by the grace of whatever, not to have their brains repossessed when they'd defaulted on student loans. Though she and Sandy both spent their lives in the same struggle to pull themselves up by their bootstraps, *then* buy better boots, they were rivals, not allies: Sandy had never forgiven her for that early competitive edge, and he'd damn near paid her back for it several times.

It wasn't true that misery loved company. If that company represented competition, misery not only hated it, misery did its level best to sabotage it.

Sandy and CC had both been skilled at surviving the selection committees that had always reminded CC of a game of musical chairs at a children's party. In the game, there were never enough chairs. But, the day people realized that the game was for real, they started playing it for *real* toys—jobs, homes, mates, and a future.

Now that Sandy had sounded off, CC suspected it would be good tactics to keep a low profile. So she really had been smart not to pass on that bad-attitude quip about going for the burn. After all, no telling who might be listening, take offense, and flash feedback to Alpha. She truly couldn't afford complaints that Alpha's newest and lowliest consultant had spoken or behaved inappropriately, despite the company's expensive charm school on the appropriate way to use flatware, groom herself, and behave in top-level situations on her way to the hotly contested Vesta assignment.

Not that Alpha would have sent her on an older, slower ship. If Alpha wanted results, and wanted them now, its client wanted them even more. It had offered a performance bonus for good *and* fast work, and had sent Sandy out to keep an eye on operations. In other words, CC was traveling with her own personal spy. This complicated matters: if she failed, he succeeded. If she succeeded, he probably did, too—unless she was very clever indeed.

She didn't think she wanted to be *that* clever, even if it meant she never rose to managing director.

She pushed her pace. If he saw her slacking off on her exercise, he'd probably hint in his report back Home that her work ethic was slipping too. Maybe, even, her ethics, though what Sandy knew about ethics . . .

Forty minutes till she could get out of here. The trick was not letting Sandy notice how impatient she'd become.

CC glanced out. No other ships. No stations. No Bloomberg Boosting Unit that she could see. Still, there had to be a BBU out there someplace fairly close, or the stock signals from the Non-Governmental Organizations Exchange that had swallowed up the Dow, the Nasdaq, the Nikkei, the Dax, and a host of other regional and global exchanges wouldn't transmit so clearly.

For the moment, CC ignored the case studies that she would not, repeat not, think of as reserve reading, a phrase left over from her old life. She'd have time—three more months, in fact—to study up.

Sandy had been right about one thing. CC had never been out of cislunar space before. In fact, except for the trips Alpha's grueling interview process put her through to make sure she had the physical stamina for space travel, she'd never been Out. So, she might as well enjoy the ride and at least try not to look as if it were her first trip.

Letting her eyes unfocus as she pumped her legs still faster, CC indulged herself silently in a line or two of *Samson Agonistes:* "O dark, dark, dark, amid the blaze of noon." Beyond that thin barrier of life-support and metal, it was eternally noon for the faraway stars and the infinitesimally larger lights that were the outer planets, satellites, and asteroids toward which *Rimrunner* hurtled.

Beautiful. And far better than staring at the inspirational bulkhead holos from Our Sponsors, from the General Partners themselves to Singapore Transworld, Vesta Halliburton McMoRan, Bechtel Interplanetary, her own Alpha Consultants LLC, featured in a discreetly glowing pair of lines, and a host of other NGOs.

And even those holos were better than peering at the structural supports, tastefully camouflaged as columns, that could seal off sections of the bay in seconds if a meteor breached the hull. She could imagine those barriers slamming shut, then the air going and no one to help. . . .

*Run for your life.*

## 2

**Lifting her arms, CC pushed even harder. As her monitor lit,** transmitting positive feedback so everyone in the gym could see it, she grinned. Aha! Sandy played negative-sum: he couldn't win unless someone else lost. So even this minuscule success was one in his eye, wasn't it? Even if the sudden attention would make it harder for her to slip away a little early.

Maybe she'd scored physical-fitness points on Sandy today. They were still chump change compared with the knife he'd stuck in her back six years ago when, thanks to an investment-banking deal that let Halliburton McMoRan snap up a freighter fleet, he'd made EVP at Morgan Nomura about the time CC'd been restructured out of her own job there. She still suspected drive-by feedback from Sandy or praise with faint damns had contributed to her dismissal on the grounds that someone had to go, and he preferred that it be CC. Fair was fair, well sort of. All things being equal, she'd infinitely have preferred that it be Sandy.

So she owed him for the ache in her shoulders from how she'd gotten stuck serving as his ladder to a senior management position. Her stint on unemployment could well have sent her out to Vesta, not on a luxury liner, but in Freeze. It could have ended her brother's hopes for a shot at the first tenured position coming up in five years and sent her parents back to the *insula* if her funds ran out before their mortgage was paid. She'd sweated blood and redlined her EKGs by job-hunting round the clock, and managed not just to land at a premier firm before her exit package ran out, but return herself to some semblance of normal behavior when any sensible person would have had post-traumatic stress disorder from sheer uncertainty. That's the way it goes, Sandy'd said at the time. Tough luck. Nothing personal. Just business.

Hell of an epitaph. "Credit's tight," he'd added.

She'd won her chance to remain in the game, and, by Sandy's standards, it would be "just business" indeed if she took a shot at him.

Like CC, Sandy had student loans, optical repairs, and surgeries to pay off. Being Sandy, he'd practically morphed himself into a holo child for makeovers, splurging on expensive speech therapy and gene-deep blondness. Then, there was the child support he owed his ex, who'd subsidized his second degree, plus bills for the geisha or two he'd retained to impress his B-school study groups. Sandy was always trading up. And if CC judged from the fit of his workout suit, a metallic green just this much shy of flashy, he was hoping to catch an exec the next rung or so up on the corporate ladder.

Their first day out, he'd come over as she worked out and given her more than a ritual cheek-peck—not enough to create a hostile work environment, but enough so that people might wonder what in hell CC thought she was doing, given the ring, a little bigger than discreet, clearly ancestral, and bless *you,* David IV, that she wore on her engagement-ring finger. She felt her face soften as she thought of the first time he'd smiled at her, and she'd thought she'd seen the sun rise in his carefree blue eyes. When she was with him, she felt good, kind, safe—all the emotions she had had to put into Freeze to secure a future for herself and the family she hadn't seen for years.

Sandy was being just too friendly for words, wasn't he? His timing had been characteristically adroit, coming over just when she'd been coping with the aftermath of their first zero-g drill. Still, she'd managed not to throw up, and she'd stayed on guard since then. Just because Sandy and CC had grown up together, didn't mean they were on the same team. They'd been competitors for survival.

A buzzer sounded. Throughout the gym, execs glanced up. CC knew that all over Earth System, brokers, traders, and ostentatiously busy or even more ostentatiously blank-desked execs looked for the latest news, caught, decrypted, cleaned, recollimated, reencrypted, time-stamped and sent out by the Bloomberg Boosting Units until it passed the limits of the Solar System and, presumably, dissipated over the lightyears to Proxima Centauri.

Bull market. So far, so good, despite some disturbing indications from commodity indexes and the mining consortia, buried in the shiny macro picture.

CC raised a sweaty eyebrow: the screen had lit with the latest sunspot index numbers. Way up. She heard mutters of "it's overbought" behind her. But there was another reason to watch this particular index: with solar activity at the peak of its eleven-year cycle, everyone's badge was subject to at least daily checks, and ships' crews monitored their sensors until their eyes blurred as if they stared into the actual sun.

Below the news ran a quick blue scroll from *Rimrunner* Control: ship's velocity, distance and time from Earth, distance and times at the various planets and asteroids where the ship would disgorge passengers and cargo.

"We're making good time," came Sandy's voice, falling into the pedagogical intonations his expensive speech therapist never had quite feedbacked out of him. "It used to be that the blue-water luxury liners competed for a prize called the Blue Riband. Our friends up in Command seem to be reviving the tradition, don't you think?"

*Titanic* had been a White Star liner, CC thought, but bit her lip. Better not say that: no telling how superstitious ship's crew or anyone else really was. Besides, there was no point in trying to one-up the competition, let alone betray her own familiarity with historical trivia that had no bottom-line value.

Sandy was talking too much, the infallible sign of a displaced historian. If he rose to the very top, the background he'd abandoned would become exotic, distinguished in corporate circles. After all, Eurasiazone execs were a lot more cultivated than the Colorado School of Mines and A&M graduates, never mind the MIT, Caltech and Maryland info-geeks who stampeded through Thunderbird, ASEAN, Wharton, Oxbridge, and Tokyo for business degrees or EarthServ ranks, not—as the joke ran—that you could tell much difference between the military and the industrial complexes these days.

But Sandy wasn't there yet. If he didn't shut up and exercise harder, he could quite literally talk himself to career death.

*Run now, schmooze later,* she wanted to tell him. Instantly, she reminded herself not to use the old-fashioned, even common word for networking even in her own thoughts. Staying fit was every bit as much a part of his job description as it was of hers. If he chose to run his mouth rather than his legs, it was his lookout, provided she kept her own heart/lungs/bone mass indices up.

What was he doing? He'd always been such a survivor. And this was a problem of hers *how?*

In the *insulae,* as children, they'd guarded each other's backs. Then, they'd graduated to Outside and opportunity. Abruptly, backs had become something to stab, not guard. She regretted that, and not just because he'd cost her one job already.

*Keep your mind on your job, CC.* That job was working out, not career guidance. *Run for it.*

You could acclimate yourself to micro or low gravity, or risk muscular atrophy, calcium depletion, and all the other medical nightmares that could make Immigration declare you unfit to land and ship you back to Earth in a freezer box, if you hadn't already died and been turned into spare parts.

Certainly, CC didn't want premature osteoporosis, which remained a risk even two centuries after the Great Estrogen Scam. What's more, it would be a performance downcheck if she wallowed like an extinct cetacean when she debarked at Vesta. It would look unprofessional. And appearances counted as much as performance, sometimes more for people like her who weren't descended from generations of senior managers in the major NGOs that controlled every part of Earth worth investing in.

CC glanced down at her machine's readout for cardio levels, then back up at the host of glittering stars. She was sweating, but not bullets, at least not yet. As gravity dropped further on board, she'd have to wear absorbent lotions on all exposed skin so no one would have to hoover up the globules before they splashed the other execs in the gym. The sweat was scooped up by a most efficient recycling system, sanitized for the benefit of the immuno-compromised, then vitaminized and recycled. Tasted just like mineral water, chirped the overly cheerful. CC had her doubts.

Her minder went off, and she bent to her screen in time to see the *WSJ* feed replaced by a note from her fiancé. Quickly, CC compared ship's time with Earth's: how sweet of David IV to write her just before he went to bed. She smiled, savoring the corporate points as well as the closeness—a relative term three months out from Earth—to her fiancé. She'd been lucky in her choice, bagging a career-enhancing engagement to a genuine corporate scion. He was kayaking now way, way South back on Earth's Lake Shackleton.

Not for CC's David IV the six-months-each-way fact-finding trip out to Vesta to check out the "ore bidniz." It was part of his charm that he managed to make his own ferocious work ethic seem effortless. His family might have lost much of their money, but at least they'd had it once: he had no need to prove himself. If he had, he'd probably never have looked twice at her.

The ice was amazing, he wrote, the conditions challenging, and the people stimulating. CC smiled again. David was never at a loss for the appropriate adjective. He might as well be composing a résumé.

And—oh, this was nice—he'd met a partner from a rival consulting shop who'd read and liked her latest white paper and bought him brunch, and how long did they really mean to keep her out on Vesta? *Sweetie, I miss you.*

She wondered if he'd have missed her half so much if that consultant hadn't praised her paper. You're not being fair, she told herself. David IV had his values on straight, or she'd never have fallen for him.

At that thought, CC almost fell. A man, sidling toward the nearest empty sportsbot with surprising grace and one hand for the ship at all times, turned to stare at her. She blanked the screen, taking care to use her left hand where David's ring glittered like a drop of water in freefall. Her ring might be smaller than some of the trophies she'd seen at company parties that damn near required a sling to support them, but it was ancestral, therefore of higher status than mere carat-wattage.

The man shrugged and walked on by. CC scoped out the back view of the tight black and silver suit. Not bad, not bad at all, but she loved David IV, and besides, she couldn't afford to be interested. She wanted to finish this workout, take the ship's tour, and get herself to Vesta at best available speed, find her facts, and presumably pin this current wave of bad trades on someone or a bunch of someones whose fates would not be her fault.

Then, she could get home, collect her bonus, the promotion she'd damn well have earned, or a new job. In any event, she could march down the aisle in a perfectly event-planned and catered wedding and into a serene-ever-after dual career track with planned children making impeccably arranged vacations to the theme parks on Easter Island, the cofferdams surrounding Disney World, and the Gobi Dinosaur Pavilions.

A buzzer sounded and lights flashed. David's letter vanished. CC glanced up, shocked out of her daydream. Even the VR screens blanked, then flared **PLEASE STAND BY**.

*"Attention all passengers. Two-minute take-hold warning. If you require assistance, press the red square or signal on your Breitling. Thank you for your patience and cooperation."*

"And have a nice day to you too," CC muttered. She hit "More" and learned that, even though *Rimrunner* had had an engine burn just that ship's morning, she'd been ordered to brake to meet another ship.

"One-minute countdown. Stand away from freestanding objects. Take hold and strap in."

The screens went live again to treat ship's passengers to a view of the newcomer. It wasn't every day you saw another ship approach. Then, the panels flickered in a way CC knew meant either a glitch or someone pretending that meltdowns didn't happen. Maybe they wouldn't get to see the ship, after all.

Well, didn't that just suck vacuum! Despite *Rimrunner*'s impeccable soundproofing, questions bounced off the bulkheads and rose throughout the gym. From the corner of her eye, CC saw the invalids and most of the retirees ease themselves out of the corners of the gym allotted to them and head gingerly in the lighter g for their cabins, their meds, and their acceleration rests.

The screens lit, to a murmur of satisfied customers.

Gravity increased. Not pausing in her exercise routine, CC turned to watch the incomer's approach.

The screens blackened, to be filled by *Rimrunner*'s insignia.

"Show's over!" announced a steward with none of the deference the passengers had come to expect.

Ritual protests of "ridiculous" and "who's your supervisor?" echoed in the ship's bay. The screens stayed dark. For once, crew really *were* the passengers' CEOs.

CC braced and sweated as *Rimrunner* braked. She could feel the ship tremble. Gravity increased again, and she sweated more.

If the screens had stayed live, what would they have seen? A freighter? A personnel carrier, mostly pods and housing for indentured types in freeze? Or one of the ancient, rickety ships piloted by ma-and-pa rock-rat operators, either searching for the mother lode that would enable them to retire and pull their embryos out of freeze or sell out to one of the NGOs?

CC would have liked to see one of the old mining vessels. They represented a way of life that was rapidly fading. But these days, only a few independent operators kept their aging ships still working at played-out claims in hope of a bonanza that might merit a corporate buyout.

There'd been some conspicuous successes years back, including one or two unpolished elderly men now traveling on *Rimrunner*, but these days, all a corporation had to do was boost cat-or-brat insurance coverage rates. Raise the rock rats' catastrophic insurance and embryonic care insurance rates, and they had no choice but to sell out at a loss, that is, unless they wanted to bankrupt themselves to acquire healthy children or when, inevitably, the results of radiation exposure hit them as they aged.

Eventually, financial Darwinism would leave no rock rats out in space. CC had studied her business history. Past performance might be no guarantee of future results, but exploration had always been followed by consolidation. It was always the fate of pioneers to be made obsolete, if they didn't die first. With luck, they'd already made their pile, along with some interesting stories to dine out on.

There was no reason for *Rimrunner*'s command to begrudge its spoiled passengers a sight of one of the last of the old mining ships—and substantial disincentive not to brake. She ran a quick mental calculation of the average hourly rate for a top manager, multiplied it by the number of people in the gym, and shrugged as she realized she'd have to calculate how much longer the trip would take if *Rimrunner* braked every time a ship approached.

So, whatever the ship was, it had to be more important than a miner.

She glanced around. The stewards' attention was elsewhere. Leaning forward, she accessed operating level on her machine's terminal, then—with the skills she'd learned from some of her colleagues at Alpha—hacked into the exterior monitors that projected VR imaging throughout the ship.

There! Lousy resolution, but she could at least see. And what she saw made her understand.

The ship that approached wasn't ablated and scraped like a rock rat, nor unwieldy, all vanes, knobs, or welded excrescences, like a freighter or indenture transport that would never enter atmosphere. It had the sleek lines and go-to-hell beauty of one of EarthServ's latest-model ships, at a price tag greater than the net worth of a fair-to-mid-cap corporation. And it was accompanied by a wing of smaller, but equally lethal craft.

Her screen blanked a moment later.

"Hacking in once Command's blanked the screens has got to violate *some* regulation," warned a sardonic voice behind her.

## 3

**The sweat CC had worked up went cold.**

The man in black and silver who'd checked her out before had craned his neck and was staring now at her screen, in violation of the computer etiquette everyone learned in their first days at school. He slammed a hand over her keyboard. That was an even greater rudeness than just staring at someone else's console. A red light flickered, but did not light.

CC opened her mouth to complain, but the man raised a challenging eyebrow.

You think it's rude to stare at people's screens and ruder to touch them? Well, it's illegal to hack into other people's systems, the eyebrow told her.

She grimaced. He had her dead to rights on corporate misconduct, but he hadn't ratted her out.

Yet.

What *had* she been thinking of? That goddamned student-brat curiosity! If he reported it and the Captain thought she'd committed a serious enough infraction, she could spend the rest of the trip in the brig. Or a freeze-box.

Or maybe, just maybe, she could bluff this man out, then bargain her way free and clear.

"I find your behavior unacceptable," she said, the first step in formal corporate complaint. Her voice was as haughty as a top manager's and as cold as the dark side of *Rimrunner*'s hull.

"Stopping you from hacking the system? You know damn well you shouldn't be pulling a stunt like that, especially not where you're going to get stopped. Besides, what's the big deal? It's just a new-model freighter," he added.

She looked him over, trying to gauge his position on the food chain. Crew or passenger? Crew didn't work out in this gym. Too young to be a retiree, he was too old to be one of the steward/escorts. They were chosen for their looks and— it was an open secret—agility, to avoid any terminology that the paranoid or the unduly sensitive could construe as creating a hostile work environment.

A blink concealed the fact that she'd picked out some fairly good surgical reconstruction along one cheek. No surprise there: skin-cancers were always a possibility for people who went EVA a good deal or even for people who spent their lives on board ship—hence, the trend to store embryos in Freeze until you were ready to retire and decant them in areas less prone to irradiation. And a glance down at his hand showed a missing fingertip.

He caught her staring. "Industrial accident," he said, not that it was any of her business. "I'll be able to repair it next bonus."

"Industrial accident, bullshit." The words popped out of her mouth with the freedom she'd had to unlearn in her first business job. "And that's no freighter. It's a Boeing 9999XA converted to military use. I saw the holos at the '85 Paris Space Show. Modified scoops. It's built in space. And it carries armed riders. I expected we'd pick up fighter escort through the Belt, but not firepower like this. So the stories that piracy's subsided with the last mergers were prolefodder after all. Can't say I'm surprised."

She'd been at the Paris Space Show as exec assistant to a Merrill analyst at the very beginning of her corporate career, but this man didn't have need-to-know on that. She'd seen what she'd seen, and knowledge was status.

The too-well-informed man rounded on her. Involuntarily, she jolted backward and grabbed a convenient bar. He reached forward to steady her.

She could actually smell his sweat: tension added to the acrid tang of someone who spent a lot of time around equipment. Not unpleasant: merely unexpected and more *there* than she was used to. A decent salaryman would sense he needed to shower and back away, properly apologetic. This man ignored it.

DAVIDOFF, MARC flared in small letters across the black and silver workout suit that was almost a parody of early-space adventure stories. On "Davidoff, Marc," the style looked good. Accessorized with a glare, though, it was scary.

EarthServ. Deadheading en route via civilian transport to the Asteroid Belt.

How the hell did EarthServ personnel rate a chance to deadhead on board *Rimrunner*? Always assuming, of course, that he was deadheading. Those ships looked like serious defense to her.

They looked like a convoy. And here she'd thought *Rimrunner* was so fast it could outrun even the most ambitious pirates. Apparently not, if EarthServ sent ships like this out to intercept it. She shut her eyes, missing a beat in her routine and cursing herself when "Davidoff, Marc" chuckled. Her memory flicked back to Earth history: World War II. A luxury liner had turned troop transport for the duration. Accompanied by convoys partway through the North Atlantic, it was cut loose to make the dash across the stormy water by itself, rolling all the way so that they called the ship the "rolling Mary."

Not her job to reason why. *Don't even think of calculating the ransom value on board,* she scolded herself. Not if she valued her job.

Or, quite possibly, her life.

Davidoff saw her eyes flicker over him.

"Forget you ever saw that ship," he murmured at her. "Whatever you think it is, tell yourself you're wrong. You probably are, anyhow."

"Ms. Williams," he added, raising his voice, "I think you need to adjust your weights. Your ankle supports look unbalanced."

She bent to adjust it: just as she'd figured, it was just fine. But bending down explained why her face burned and gave her some time to get her composure back.

When she straightened, "Davidoff, Marc," who was probably Lieutenant or Lieutenant Commander Davidoff—he looked too young to be *Captain* Davidoff—nodded and started his own weight routine. If CC had tried to pump even half that much iron, even at lower g, she'd be on her back for the next three months on disability.

Well, she was damned if she'd let him see she was watching him. She sniffed haughtily. Or at least, she tried.

Davidoff's shoulders shook briefly. Outflanked and outmaneuvered again. Damn him.

Her monitor flashed back on. Still a bull run. A new flash complete with holo showing the latest solar activity. Sunspots were building up in size, number, and density; a major flare was projected before long.

If there was going to be a flare that required them to take cover, it better not interrupt transmission of her orders: she had a backup schedule, but management was hardly what she'd call fault-tolerant. Now, *that* was what she called ridiculous. As if a CEO's orders could delay a solar incident?

Her machine informed her she still had fifteen minutes left on her workout.

Behind her, Sandy was now protesting in official tones how "ridiculous" it was that *Rimrunner* was so "slow," that his company's executive committee had been backing banking deals to develop faster ships, let alone R&D for faster-than-light for years.

"Sounds like an excellent tax loss," Davidoff put in, deliberately intruding on the conversation. CC bent her head so no one would see her grin. The man's rudenesses were as calculated as corporate etiquette, she decided.

Just because the CEOs demanded faster-than-light didn't mean they were going to get it this quarter or next. Or maybe never, according to the scientists eking out research grants with stints as senior tutors, one step above the academic nannies like her parents who had occupied the rung below the major domo in executive households' chains of command.

Sandy was the one being ridiculous. The speed of light had never been subject to corporate chains of command.

You simply didn't mention that there was no royal road to relativity.

Until CEOs could control relativity as well as relative value, it would still take six months to go from Wall Street, all the financial districts of Earth, to Titoville, Vesta's own financial community, which—along with a gem strike or three—had helped make the asteroid Earth's most prosperous private colony. Soon, it would be spun off its parent company via IPO into corporate existence of its own.

*I'd like to get a piece of* that, CC thought.

Perform well on this trip, and maybe she might get options.

The IPO would happen, assuming a little matter of bad trades and a really odd balance of trade could be settled and blame assigned. If it wasn't, CC would take the rap. So she needed a culprit. Or a scapegoat.

Well, people did adapt to conditions in the Belt, because that was where the resources were. Ceres, at barely a thousand kilometers wide, had been the largest asteroid until the discovery of Quaoar and Vulcan, in eccentric orbit around the Pluto/Charon duo in the Kuiper belt. More accessible than Quaoar, which circled the sun once every 288 years, Vesta was also, as far as they knew, still potentially the richest. About the size of Arizona—and with a geology most like Earth's—Vesta was Earth's most prosperous private colony and the model for a host of private equity investments, many of which hadn't survived their vintage years.

Fifteen minutes more? Since CC still couldn't retreat to

her stateroom and get her messages, she might as well multitask here. She called her notes up on the screen and re-
searched while she worked out.

Like Ceres, Vesta had hundreds of millions of billions of
tons of high-grade ore. Where its advantage lay was in ca-
tastrophe. It truly was the largest distressed investment in
the Solar System. An immensity of time ago even by the
standards of the solar system, some meteor or some power
(here was where CC's flawed quantitative background really hurt her comprehension) had struck Vesta. First, it had
slashed open the asteroid's regolith. Then, it gnawed all the
way into its mantle, leaving a cyclopean bull's-eye at
Vesta's south pole, full of caves and bays that made useful
docking ports for shuttles or even bays for ships the size of
*Rimrunner.*

The basalt and olivine of Vesta's ravaged stone was tough,
but it could be blasted and sculpted into habitats that might
be stark, might be uncomfortable, but—as CC was told—
gave promise of extraordinary beauty once more funding
was approved.

It wasn't quite instant mining and habitats, but it was the
closest they had, without the treacherous seismic and vol-
canic activity of the larger moons like Titan.

By virtue of the outer space treaty of 1967, no one could
own a planetary body, or those old rivals, the United States
(part of the North American confederacy) and the Soviet
Union (vanished into the morass of the Eurasiazone like a
thousand other peoples), would have tried. However, individuals were allowed to have exclusive use of part or all of a
celestial body for the purposes of establishing human habi-
tations or extracting natural resources. And, lucky them, corporations were regarded, legally speaking, as individuals
provided they had humans living and working on the claim
sites.

Thus, an unmanned rover, like the first Martian landers,
couldn't claim a strike. But a miner could. So, there were no
conquistadores of space: just miners in their decreasing

numbers, human rats in steel cans out to gnaw away at the staggering wealth available in the asteroid belts.

Do the math.

Start with 825 quintillion tons of iron, as well as radioactive isotopes of potassium, uranium, thorium, rubidium. No point in ferrying those radioactives expensively back to Earth: much cheaper and safer to build breeder reactors in space, let them produce antimatter, assuming any decent R&D shop would fund the project, or build solar cells to tap the power of the sun, relaying it back to Earth. CC sighed, and turned her attention back to her screen. Once they'd established a beachhead, the factories followed. A carbonaceous asteroid was 20% water. It could be processed to make a mass of liquid hydrogen and liquid oxygen equal to the original mass of water. That could be used for fuel for earlier-model ships.

She paused the rapid text scroll for which a scholar's quick scan had proved to be an incredible asset and typed in "miners/East India merchants: compare." It wouldn't be hard: more or less a simple matter of drilling down from the B-school paper she'd written, comparing the NGOs with Earth's old East India Company. She remembered every word of that paper fondly: it had won her the first interview at Alpha.

It hadn't taken long for the early miners to realize there was gold, or at least venture capital, in "them thar chips." The instant the burgeoning NGOs saw that the ma-and-pa mining ships and cobbled-together fleets were showing signs of profit in the outyears, Earth's futures indices went wild, and venture capitalists knew instantly that miners would need off-Earth bases if they were to be more than fly-by-nights. And what built habitats wasn't guts, wasn't adventure: it was long-term capital.

Another problem rapidly surfaced. As some of the ma-and-pa ships scored major strikes, piracy started to become big business, just as it had in the days when Earth's oceans, not Earth's solar system, were the frontiers of exploration and commerce. And piracy required enforcement on a sys-temwide scale, a challenge costly enough to strain the bud-get of any government or NGO.

Because no one NGO, let alone one nation, had that kind of capital these days, they'd had to band together the way CC and Sandy did for this trip: allies, but with sharp knives (sonic guns would have been confiscated, and no one was stupid enough to fire projectile weapons when only hard vacuum lay outside).

Suddenly the investment bankers, with their impeccable French-cuff equivalents, found themselves replaced by an altogether different aristocracy of business-trained engi-neers. So it was their turn to retool, or join the tutors and the corpsicles. The demise of the investment banker as a class had caused a *lot* of mirth in low places. There were times when *Schadenfreude* was all you had. Even if you didn't know the word, you knew the feeling: glee at someone else's misfortune.

Given the new colony processes, someone had to oversee and monitor them. Engineering went from a cyclical field to a specialty, like computers during Y2K: someone had to make the ships, the robots, and the products, just as someone had to provide funding.

Big fleas had little fleas upon their backs to bite 'em. Lit-tle fleas had littler ones; so on ad infinitum. The old rhyme was one of the unofficial anthems of Alpha Consultancies, itself the result of a series of mergers of leading global con-sulting firms.

Alpha. Top of the food chain. And fighting like a cornered leopard to stay there. Fighting like CC herself. They were a good cultural fit.

Her monitor blazed yellow, darkening to orange. A howl like a wounded leopard—she didn't know, did leopards howl?—erupted from the speakers placed throughout the gym. Not just an unearthly, but an ungodly sound, accompa-nied by rhythmic strobings and buzzers.

The solar holo on her monitor flickered, separated from the source of its image by the lag time between the sun and

*Rimrunner*. Definitely, they were going to have problems. Solar incidents disrupted trade, not to mention securities trading. They degraded performance on the BBUs, meaning they'd have to be retuned and the parts degraded by radiation replaced. What's more, all the trades before, during, and after the solar "incident" would have to be analyzed and compared with their initiation points. A damn good thing sunspot activity peaked only every eleven years.

Was this what all the drills were for? Was CC going to have to live through a real red alert?

## 4

**"Move it!" she heard Davidoff shout. He launched himself** off his weight-training machine toward the exit.

CC paused for an announcement and further instructions.

"Do you always have to do precisely the wrong thing?" he demanded. "When they said 'move,' they meant it!"

This time, Davidoff's shout was aimed at her. His voice might carry the sting of an SEC sanction, but it bounced off the bulkheads with a lot less grace than his body, she noticed. *"This is no drill!"*

CC hurled herself toward the hatch, narrowly missing the Neave-Lovats. She bobbed her head, as much formal acknowledgment as she could muster, under the circumstances.

"Sorry, sir." She'd met the ambassador at the post-launch reception, but, playing the due-deference gambit, hadn't spoken to him or to his wife since then. And she'd given their children's tutors a *wide* berth because she could easily have known their families, and that wasn't a fact she wanted to get known.

"You saw the sunspot-activity charts," said Ambassador Neave. "Apparently, we're now in flare alert mode."

Behind her, Sandy was closing in fast: he just couldn't let CC talk all by herself to a personage like Neave, could he?

Be fair, she told herself. If Neave had received a separate briefing on flare alerts that could save him and his family a dose of potassium iodide, the trots, or worse, Sandy had a right to benefit from it, too. For that matter, so did she.

They headed down the corridors toward the lifts. Above and below the bulkheads, strip lighting flickered red/off/white/off/red/off. As they moved "inward" from the bays near *Rimrunner*'s hull, the bulkhead colors faded from colors designed to stimulate and reassure to the bare-bones austerity of polished metal on which control panels stuck out in plain sight.

The first astronauts, CC knew, hadn't fried: their voyages had been carefully calibrated for times of minimum solar turbulence. And, with the exception of astronauts on the early space stations, those twentieth- and twenty-first-century voyagers had all pretty much been short-timers.

But these long hauls out to the asteroids—sooner or later, miners ran into solar flares. They'd taken their chances—and the radiation damages that went with them. These days, even though ships were built to be as fast as possible, and launches were scheduled to limit the time people spent in space at periods of high sunspot activity, it wasn't possible to eliminate all excess radiation all the time.

So most spacers banked their genetic heritage, hostages to fortune whose cryogenic well-being was almost as expensive as ship supplies. Many didn't survive beyond a couple of years, anyhow. And radiology and oncology were and would remain growth fields in Belter hospitals.

CC flared her nostrils. What was that faint stink of ionized dust?

*Stop imagining things,* she scolded herself.

By process of elimination and some damned good R&D, ships had evolved protection during periods of maximum sunspot activities. First, there were the storm shelters, carefully shielded areas deep within the ships. Although even this morning, crew had been testing systems in the gym and it was probably safe enough to remain there, given the rising costs of legal fees—and the traditional NGO fondness for litigation of insurance claims—Captain Aquino had prudently activated the Bova grid, thin wires of exotic yttrium-based compounds wrapping the ship, especially the storm shelters. When activated, these wires became one immense superconducting magnet.

And because, in times of the highest possible activity, that *still* wasn't enough to protect fragile protoplasm against high-energy protons, the captain was also bringing the ship's electron guns on line. Quite literally, he would be giving the ship's hull a positive charge to repel protons.

Meanwhile, all passengers who weren't in Freeze were ordered to retreat to the shelters in the ship's core, please move quickly, remain calm, thank you for your cooperation, captain *out.*

Would the proton guns repel boarders too? Could they be used against pirates? CC hoped she wouldn't have the opportunity to find out. But she suspected that those electron guns could be reconfigured into weapons soon enough. The time she'd asked an analyst, the woman had developed an appointment in the direction of away as quickly as she could, and CC'd gotten an actual paper memo about "inappropriate speculation."

Which, of course, was reserved for insider traders who packed sufficient legal firepower to plea bargain.

Damn! What if those Boeings she'd seen when she wasn't supposed to be looking—what if there'd been an actual warning of a pirate sighting?

Davidoff was right. If she even hinted at it, she'd cause a panic.

"No need to panic," came Neave's voice right on cue. "It takes eight minutes for radiation to reach Earth from the Sun. We'll make it to the shelters assuming we stay calm."

The voice of reason, and top of the chain of command here. Even the language, though it translated as a very polite form of "Move it!"

Neave, top of the food chain on *Rimrunner,* would be first to be held hostage. And probably first to be ransomed.

"Take a head count!" came Davidoff's voice. "No more than ten per lift!"

If too many people jammed into the lifts, exceeding safety tolerances, the lifts would not move, and crew would have to come and pry passengers out. Unless, of course, they'd stationed guards to insure that mass restrictions were obeyed.

People stopped bouncing off bulkheads long enough to form orderly, if bobbing, ranks.

"That's better," said Neave.

Fully suited crew members came running the other way—long leaps in the low gravity. Some had their eyes fixed on monitors and were half-steered, half-carried by companions. The others were all hulking types, designated to give passengers the option: move or be carried.

Ambassador Neave glanced at the chrono woven into his left wristband and motioned his wife onto the nearest lift. "My dear, I suggest you go on ahead. I will meet you in the shelter. For now, I'll just have a brief word . . ."

Moving with the same ease as the crew, Neave poised himself against a bulkhead and tapped out first one series of numbers—probably an access code, then another.

Not much to CC's surprise, she heard a voice answer, a voice that Neave instantly muted. "Everett Neave here. Communications? Good. Sorry to disturb you during an alert, but I've got as nervous bunch of virgins here as I've seen in all my years in space."

No one dared to laugh at Neave's use of spacer argot, even if it could be construed as creating a hostile work environment if he didn't have such damn high corporate rank. CC had read his bio; he'd logged a *lot* of space time, first traveling for Alpha, then on corporate business.

A pause as Neave leaned against the panel, listening to the tiny voice.

"When will the leading edge impact?"

Neave's eyebrows went up.

"The flare's within tolerance levels? Interesting . . . May one ask why you called the alert? . . . Indeed? I see."

He turned to conceal his face, but his back muscles, the

lean, stringy muscles of an older man who'd taken expensive care of himself for decades, knotted under his bespoke shipsuit.

"No, I don't require Captain Aquino's attention; he's got his hands full. Quite literally, I should assume. Thank you, Communications. Yes, there is something you could do. My pack of virgins is bouncing off bulkheads. Literally. Highly unsightly. I realize ship's crew has its assigned stations, but if you could ask Security to spare us a guide or two to herd these good people in the right direction, I personally would much appreciate it."

Neave floated back, this time at a more leisurely pace, to a crowd of scared passengers on whom the consequences of trying to race in zero g were rapidly sinking in. Each person bobbed now at a different attitude: faces faced feet, intersected with people's arms, or more personal locations, with cries of annoyance and discomfort. Fear-stink had long since replaced the healthy smell of honest exercise.

His wife Margaret, who had disregarded Neave's instructions, rather to CC's surprise, now launched herself at her husband. CC followed as discreetly and as gracefully as she could.

"Robert just signaled. He'd been monitoring sunspot levels, and when they started to climb, he and Vi got young Elliott and Anne settled in the shelter, and they're reviewing hydroponics. More reassuring than a briefing on radiation, don't you think?"

Neave nodded approval. "Good judgment on Robert's part. A bonus is clearly in order. And a recommendation to Vesta's Botany section once we arrive."

"If this really isn't a flare . . ." Margaret Lovat began, her honey-blonde hair floating as she turned her head to one side to regard her taller husband.

"We're still in the eleventh year of the sunspot cycle, so the captain's being prudent. Commendably so. But I'm reliably informed that one of the Bloomburg Boosting Units took some damage," he said. "Its automatic distress call unit activated and *Rimrunner* was nearest. . . ."

"If you call anything 'near' at these distances," Margaret laughed. She handled herself almost as well in the ship's fluctuating gravities as her husband. Even though low or no-grav smoothed out facial lines, her skin crinkled pleasantly around her eyes and mouth. Not as young as the usual trophy, CC decided. It made her think better of Neave. Impertinence on her part to presume to judge, but what the hell.

"Precisely. Not to mention the fact that this BBU's on an exclusive lease, and Morgan's paid a premium for repairs."

Had Neave seen the EarthServ ship? Had Communications briefed him? The question hovered on the tip of CC's tongue, and she forced it back. If she blurted it out, she'd have to admit to unauthorized computer tampering, and Neave, the first NGO ambassador to the UN, was the last man she wanted to confess it to.

Emergency repairs on a Bloomberg Boosting Unit was a *fine* alibi.

Two centuries back, the BBUs, named after an entrepreneur turned politician at a crucial moment in Earth's history, had gained quasi-utility status by marketing all sorts of data to the financial services industry. Two decades after ferocious competition drove down the prices of telecom gear to the point where even the few survivors were having trouble staying solvent, a fortunate merger produced the forerunners of the BBUs. Granted, they were comsats and comsats were old tech, but, unlike the first comsats, BBUs were configured for deepspace securities trading.

When BBUs received trades, they first confirmed when buy and sell orders were initiated and where: Greenwich Time, Ares Time, Titan, or Vesta Mean Time. They were programmed to operate off a timetable that included every one of Sol System's trading centers so trades could be executed in the order they were received down to the microsecond.

Then, the BBUs decrypted each trade. Because of the immense distances that the signals had to travel—to say nothing of sunspots and other disruptions—they had to filter out degradation, before they recollimated, reencrypted, and sent the signals on their way to be time-stamped at arrival by each BBU, as well as executed and confirmed at their destination. Official confirmations returned by the same routes.

Some BBUs were retail, common to all spacefarers who wanted to invest on their own: others, like this one, were premium-grade, leased exclusively by NGOs. Servicing any BBU was a priority, but some BBUs were more equal than others.

Where there were no BBUs, there was no information. Where there was no information, there was no trade. And without trade, the worlds would falter.

Tampering with a BBU wasn't a capital offense, but some legislators, thanks to aggressive lobbying, seemed to think it should be. So there were stiff penalties for MITJI—meaconing, or transmitting energy deliberately at a receiver to knock it out; intrusions and transmissions, especially fake trades; jamming; and deliberate interference. And that was before you factored in the solar wind, solar flares, sunspot activity, and the occasional intruder from the Kuiper or Oort clouds or the Near Earth Asteroids.

The BBU that was in trouble now belonged to Sandy's company. He'd probably sweated through his shipsuit already: as the man on the spot, he would be expected to Do Something, whether or not there was a Something he could do.

And there was the man of the hour! Wedged into a corner where two bulkheads intersected, his back to a poster of instructions, Sandy was arguing with Security. Though he kept his voice low, his gestures made him bob up and down absurdly like a child's rubber bath toy.

As if Neave's approach were his cue, Sandy shoved off from his nook and leapt forward to land close, but not impudently so, to the older man.

"I'm Jonathan Vinocur Sanderson," he announced. He pulled a card out of the sweatband on his left wrist and presented it to Neave. The older man eyed it and nodded, without taking it: after all, the card was a little limp from exercise. A little damp. Not the sort of thing you should offer a man like Neave.

"Your company's hardware, I assume," said Neave.

Stiffened as if in imitation of EarthServ, Sandy went into formal-reporting mode to Ambassador Neave as if he stood at a board meeting, ready to make a presentation, but someone had tampered with his slides.

"I've just had a report from Operations," Sandy said. The didactic tone had returned to his voice. "Captain Aquino's electing to come alongside the BBU. He'll have to brake to overtake it," Sandy warmed to his subject, though Neave had probably logged more space-time than Sandy had work-years, "and he wants his unfrozen passengers where they can be strapped down and kept safe. Depending on preliminary damage control assessments, either someone's going to have to EVA or they'll have to deploy the arm to bring it inside and repair it."

CC could have told him Neave probably knew all that already.

"Nothing to worry about, my dear Mister— what did you say your name was again?"

Sandy colored. Even as far past retirement age as Ambassador Neave had to be despite the best anti-agathics developed so far by the biotech consortia, he could not have forgotten Sandy's name so quickly unless he hadn't listened or had reason to deliberately snub the younger man. There was no rudeness like that of the very polite, and Ambassador Neave was *very* polite.

Margaret Lovat frowned minutely at her husband, who seemed to ease up.

*Why, she's* kind! CC thought. It surprised her to think of a woman in her position as being kind.

"Everett, that security guard looks as if he is about to pop. That would create a terrible mess for maintenance, especially if we go to zero-g," she cut in.

"Hadn't we better move toward shelter and strap in?" she suggested just as an obnoxiously familiar voice boomed out, "All right, people, straighten up. Heads and feet all in the same directions, all right? Anyone need sick kits? Excellent. Anyone who doesn't take a kit now and sicks up gets to clean it off the bulkheads: crew's a damn sight busier than you and a hell of a lot more useful. Now that we've all gotten our heads, butts, and feet into the same attitude—one more quarter-turn there, ma'am! we're going to head toward shelter just in case. Slow and sure. Don't kick off hard, and always keep your knees flexed and one hand out to latch on, in case. But don't worry. Captain says you're not going to fry. You can take that as an order."

Sandy launched himself into Davidoff's trajectory. "Do you have any idea what damaged the BBU?"

"Stupid questions," said Davidoff. "Now, will you kindly get a move on? That is, unless you think you're going to puke. In that case, I repeat: please use the sick kits. No one wants to hoover your damn brunch off the bulkheads."

He kicked off and came to an effortless stop beside Neave.

"I don't find that man's humor acceptable," said Sandy, looking for a scapegoat.

"Tell it to the Marines," suggested Davidoff, overhearing and raising his voice. "In fact, you can consider it done. Now, haul ass or I'll pick you up by your fancy gymsuit and haul it for you."

"Let the man do his job, Marc," Neave suggested. "Mr. Sanderson's NGO has a lot riding on that satellite."

"Don't we all?" asked Davidoff. "You've already talked to Control Center, sir. What more do you need to know? The latest merger news? The impact of the sunspot activity on the capital markets? I can tell you, there's RUMINT that the British pound *finally* was phased out, but your information's probably more current than mine. Family doesn't tell me much these days."

*The family?* CC's eyebrow went up.

Was Marc Davidoff part of a financial clan? *That* financial clan? Over the centuries, the old business families had diversified into various industries, like ink diffusing in water. You were now as likely to find Lebenthals running a university as selling century bonds or Rothschilds running vineyards rather than banks or even trading water futures with the thirsty asteroid settlements—but to find a trust-fund brat running ships, not money funds or an investment bank, was new to her. Usually, the only clans that entered the military were hereditary fighters, often from what had been the United Kingdom or the southern United States, or misfits on whom therapy didn't take.

Wouldn't a family misfit be paid to change his name? And would Ambassador Neave have acknowledged a black sheep, let alone called him by his first name?

CC eyed "Davidoff, Marc." No pilot could hope to pass the rigorous screening if he couldn't squeeze himself into pods with a minimum of effort, so he wasn't tall. Instead, he was low-mass, compact, and browned in a way that had nothing to do with involuntary UV exposure: he'd been working in the sun, at some not-too-remote time in the past.

Catching her eye, Davidoff coasted back toward CC, calling out "move it along, there . . . don't push so hard . . . pull in your arms . . . there, you've got it!" and giving a sly push to stragglers.

"Alpha Consultancies, are you?" he commented. "I saw you recognize the name. Just like you recognized the ships back there. Inconvenient memory you've got there."

CC shrugged. So what if he'd opted out and into the service? It was no skin off her nose. Pilot training was grueling, but what the hell? If he washed out, he had the family business as a safety net. Must be nice.

She glanced down at her own inset chrono. Damn. Look what time it was! She had less than twenty minutes before her orders activated. Failure to open them promptly . . . well, Alpha didn't pay her to fail. She could see herself coming down with radiation sickness, cancer, whatever, but, even so, she'd read her damned timed orders before they committed her to a cost-effective deep space burial.

"I'm the family's black sheep. They say that every time. Heading Out after home leave," he added. "Wangled a chance to take a look at the Kuiper Clipper assembly plant on Mount Piazzi."

CC snorted, then regretted it. A few people with bad attitudes called Clipper—the system's most advanced vessel, designed to travel to the reaches of the solar system and make landing, if all went well, on Quaoar—the Kuiper Comet, because they expected it to shoot out beyond the Solar System and keep on going. Meanwhile, the Greeners called it the Kuiper Karma. Even though the joke had made CC inhale sparkling water at an almost disastrous moment during a reception, she'd had to pretend not to understand it.

"I could probably name names," Davidoff said, his eyes glinting. "But, never mind. I'd been digging, now that the radiation level in Ur . . . well, it's still not nominal, even after all these years, but let's say I don't have to wear lead underwear, and I'd rather run a hot ship than a hot hedge fund."

CC glanced politely away, ignoring the flippancies. "Interesting to see how the trading patterns are impacted," she observed, putting out a feeler.

"People still use that jargon?" Davidoff groaned. "That godawful misuse of language was one of the reasons I opted out of the family business!"

This time CC had to laugh. "Stop being such a curmudgeon. You don't look like Zephram Cochrane to me!" she quipped.

"Oh, and how do you know I wasn't working on an FTL drive on my home leave when I wasn't digging up cuneiform inscriptions?" She was pleased when he actually laughed back at her and didn't appear shocked at the literary reference.

"Give me a break. Ship-jockeys have a language of our own, but at least we're not candidates for broomstick-ectomies."

"I suppose I deserve that," she conceded. "Seriously," she added, "this incident is probably going to have me on wake-all for at least a week. I've got to have to examine trading patterns since the discrepancies started, plot them against this BBU's backup. Might be best to do it as close to real-time as I can before the signals dissipate, or people start covering their asses."

"Isn't that his job?" Davidoff gestured economically

with his chin at Sandy's retreating backside. For now, it was covered.

"His career path, maybe, but I've got other instructions."

"One of Alpha Scavengers' best and brightest?"

"If you know Alpha, you know we don't accept routine audits. I'm may be headed Out as an auditor, but my real job is research. Fact-finding," she said firmly. "And I am going to be in toxic waste up to—let's say it's going to be more than knee-deep, if I can't get back to my cabin and do some—"

Damned if she were going to admit it to this black sheep of a mutual-fund dynasty, but her initial briefings had warned her there were already anomalous trading patterns alarming enough for Alpha Consultancies to take an interest. Granted, at mid-career, CC was expendable enough to jettison if she screwed the pooch. At the same time, she might be seasoned enough to get to the bottom of the problem, assuming it *had* a bottom, which most things didn't in zero-g. In which case, what would be a substantial bonus would be chump credit when balanced against the revenues her work would bring in.

Apart from the fact that her future might very well hinge on what this next timed briefing contained, she was intensely curious to learn what information Alpha considered important for her to know. All of it, of course: but they had to impose some prioritizations, not to mention a bozo filter.

Davidoff, CC saw, was watching her closely. "Duty?" he asked. "What's so important you can't stay in shelter?"

"Work," she agreed.

"You make it sound like worship."

"Easy for you to talk," she snapped. "Look, how bad can it be? If it were serious, you'd have Security drag me to the nearest shelter. And I'm only one ring away."

Davidoff shrugged. "I'll call in a blue chip," he agreed. "Go to your quarters: pardon me, ma'am, to your stateroom. Do what you have to do. But if you're not in the shelter thereafter till Captain sounds the all-clear, I'll drag your sorry ass down there myself and force the potassium iodide down your throat myself."

So he was still worried about radiation. In that case, CC had better worry too, she decided.

Still, it was a major concession. In fact, it was a veritable fleet of concessions. Now, CC owed Davidoff big time, and she didn't like that at all.

He grinned at her and reached out as if to take her hand. Then, a squawk from his comm jerked him around. "Bogey?" he demanded in a mutter that wasn't low enough. "Like the last one? Shit! Okay, I'll come. You just get that cat ready for launch! I don't want to be outside any longer than I have to."

*Cat,* CC thought. Why were they readying a launch catapult? Surely they'd bring the BBU in for maintenance. Why'd Davidoff have to take a ship outside—let alone the sort hurled by catapults, when that Boeing she wasn't supposed to have seen already had riderships out?

"Get moving, Williams!" Davidoff ordered. "Fry if you want. But work or no work, if you're not in shelter, you've still got to be near a take-hold."

## 5

**Trying not to bounce off bulkheads any more gracelessly** than she could help, CC headed for her stateroom. It was tiny but luxurious in its restrained, neo-Nippon fashion, her very own floating world in palest blues. When the ship went to zero g, you felt as if you were floating in an Earth sky.

She checked her badge—still safely green. Stripping off her exercise clothes, she took a brief, begrudged shower, dressed in protective gear, and logged on. For a moment, she wished she could simply jack in, but no execs wore moddies an instant longer than they could pay to have them surgically removed. Plastic surgeons financed their retirements by removing implants (and covering the scars) from new managers who no longer needed to plug into home systems and knew that the faintest scars could damage their careers as severely as the wrong schools or the wrong accent.

She'd just paid off the cosmetic repairs to her wrists: damned if she was going to run up another bill. Besides, she just couldn't let people think she was low-rank enough still to need moddies. No matter how important her need to know was.

Two more minutes.

CC clicked on the ship's surface indicators. Radiation levels weren't anything that should net her a dose of potassium iodide, at least not yet. She spared a glance at the display for the Katz Index, which tracked the capital markets against weather patterns, economic indicators, and sunspot activity against the eleven-year sunspot cycle as far back as the recession of 1957–1958. Heavy solar activity meant droughts back on Earth, to say nothing of recessions and wars. The best example, though, intensified by millennial frenzy, had occurred in 2000. After the air fizzled out of the tech bubble, the markets had dropped more catastrophically than at any time since 1929, while wars and terrorism had made matters even worse. The more things changed . . .

Her alarm pinged. She'd deal with the geopolitical and geoeconomic macro stuff later.

Time to open Alpha's orders.

Sitting at her workstation, her spine as rigid as if she were presenting a report at a board meeting, CC activated the optical recognition system (another of *Rimrunner*'s premium amenities for business-class travelers).

If excitement weren't unprofessional, she'd have felt adrenaline prickle along her spine. Sealed instructions were like something out of ancient blue-water adventures. Above all, they indicated how far she'd come—and how far she could fall.

The file was satisfyingly huge. That couldn't all be due to encryption, either. It opened slowly, despite the excellence of her stateroom's workstation. She scanned down the menu—the visual flick of a trained, almost eidetic scan reader. Background material first: that was the sensible way to go, as well as the most congenial.

A history of Vesta Enterprises, Inc.

She'd already had that briefing before she left Earth: damn, had Alpha made a mistake? Couldn't be. Hmmm. More detail here than in any annual report she'd ever seen on how Vesta's economy really worked.

Like the other proprietary colonies, Vesta had a company-store mentality. The initial domes—like ancient Quonset huts, only vacuum-sealed—had been followed by bigger domes and preliminary excavations before better habitats were constructed. As more and more ships came, the unimaginably harsh conditions were alleviated. The colony—and its investors—had been fortunate: so far, no catastrophes. At least, none they couldn't recover from.

Vesta's population crept up. Joining the miners and engineers were pilots, scientists, a medician or two, and then finally, the adjuncts: families, bookkeepers, storekeepers, and various kinds of what were euphemistically referred to, back on Earth, as entertainers. The Colony, like any other frontier, called them by a blunter name. As the need for space mounted and population grew on Earth, the Colony also received indentures, shipped out from the inner worlds in Freeze and stacked against need.

Gradually, all of Vesta's employees, whether under contract, shareholders, full-time, or indentured, developed a community. It wasn't enough to trade labor for goods: the only way to entice many workers off Earth was to pay them well, with most of their assets held in trust on the homeworld.

Contract workers or employees at large received onsigning and performance bonuses, hazard pay, company matches, and retirement money. Indentures, once they worked off the costs of their trip Out (transit, drugs, repair after freeze, food, and housing), also were paid. Some funds were used to order goods, either shipped out from the inner system or made on Vesta or the other satellites, added to indentures' debt or deducted from employees' pay. The rest of the funds accrued. Over time, and when combined with the funds of employees on the other asteroids and outer satellites, these funds represented serious assets.

So, if you thought like an NGO or an employee who expected to return Home, those funds had to be managed.

Next, on top of the miners, engineers, scientists, and quasi-slaves, you got the chandlers, whores (read "social therapists, entertainers, and escorts"), and financial services companies—and yes, there *was* a difference.

All of these people would have accounts, and all of these accounts would have to be reviewed. The EASD—Earth Association of Securities Dealers—had strict rules for branch offices in terms of trades as well as the custody of firms' or customers' funds or securities and the acceptance of new accounts. An audit made for a good cover story, just as she'd told Davidoff.

She closed the subfile dealing with Vesta's human history and opened the subfiles marked "procedure." So. Just as they'd told her, she had an audit to perform. Overtly, it was office review. Covertly, she faced the sort of investigation that could have driven a stake into Arthur Andersen's undead corpse, assuming she believed in such things, which, of course, she didn't.

As CC read, her eyes narrowed, her processing speed slowed, and her blood pressure began to rise. Here was a surprise: Alpha hadn't been hired, as she'd thought, by Vesta Enterprises Inc., the holding company for several NGOs' private-equity development arms on the asteroid. Alpha had been hired by Earth's planetary government.

Now, CC hadn't been born yesterday. It wasn't old news that the government often worked through the NGOs, especially the financial consortia. She ran a quick check, graphing population by employee number against accounts by number. Ideally, each account should belong to someone, and each trade should match up. But there were a lot more accounts than there were Vesta employees. Either that or, like very old-style Chicago voters, back in the days of unlimited franchise, someone was creating dummy accounts for imaginary people. Trade early and often, and never mind technicalities about whether the account owner actually exists or not.

Or, what if those accounts had been created for people still on ice, awaiting the times they'd be needed and defrosted?

She could probably pin misappropriation of trust funds on someone. Fraud. Front-running. She'd definitely be able to go after the traders, not to mention the broker/dealers. Sure, Alpha could try for sympathy press from the Greeners for being nice to shipsicles. But good PR was small potatoes. Her employer was out for red meat, real, not synthesized, and plenty of it.

Procedurally, this part of her job was simple, if back-breakingly, mind-numbingly obvious. She'd have to review and re-approve customer orders over the period of the questionable trades. All of them.

It was a given that she'd find a certain percentage of mistakes: idiotic, maybe, but not criminal. Mistakes happened. In those cases, trades could be broken and clients made whole, with token fines to the people or organizations that made the mistakes. They could probably even write them off on their taxes.

None of it would make her, or Alpha, or the various financial houses particularly popular, except to the people getting reimbursed. Some frozen assets might find themselves thawed more quickly than they'd expected, which would probably be to their benefit.

But any of these transactions would probably amount only to what used to be called chump change.

The one person such a scandal would be likeliest to hurt was CC herself. She had a sane distaste for the gruntwork of tracking down trades one at a time, reviewing each transaction, and squeezing each line item until it screamed in pain and surrendered its information. That was what interns were for, assuming you had an intern you could trust without supervision, which was a stupid assumption. So CC was on her own, tough luck for her.

Still, the audit was only part of the job.

*Dear God, why me?* CC thought.

Because the project was data intensive. Because it required a maverick thinker. Because no one else of the rank to be landed with it was crazy, or desperate enough to prove herself, to take it. All of the above.

In other words, the assignment was a killer. At the same time, its sheer intellectual challenge made her adrenaline rise with the intellectual excitement of the born scan-researcher, an info-glutton addicted to high-speed data assimilation until, in a dream of intellectual indigestion, the patterns formed.

But intuition, unless it paid off, was worse than useless.

Free-range intuition made you seem like a feckless academic. A feckless female academic—fancy for "tutor" or, for those who didn't have technical skills, a "nanny." Unemployed nanny, with substantial debts outstanding, if she weren't careful. Unemployed frozen nanny, bound for the outer planetoids, but not traveling nearly as comfortably as *Rimrunner*'s biz class.

There wasn't just challenge here for her. There was temptation. Not just cheat and thrive.

Cheat and live.

People who thought that way wound up in Freeze, or in reeducation. CC would have to play it more cleverly than that: She'd have to be a weasel, but an honest one. That meant she'd have to be very, very careful, avoiding not just impropriety, but its appearance of it. Like Caesar's wife, she'd have to be above suspicion, and in a culture that made ancient Rome look like a hick town full of suckers by contrast.

But if she succeeded, she—and David IV—would be very, very rich.

Rich enough, CC realized, not to have to be grateful to her fiancé for his inherited status. And to help his family regain some of the wealth they'd lost. She'd make them proud.

Her computer screen flashed red as sirens whooped and the track lighting at deck the deck sent up its ominous faint beams. Her system flickered, but Emergency Save preserved her data.

Just in time, CC grabbed hold, as *Rimrunner* jolted hard. God *damn,* what had they run into?

A sentence she remembered from her reading made her feel sicker than she'd been since her initial exposure to zero-g. "Commander Marc Davidoff is EarthServ's representative on this fact-finding mission. He will liaise with you"—nice work if he could get it, which he couldn't—"and will afford you every cooperation. You are required to extend the same consideration, barring materials proprietary to Alpha Consultants LLC, to him."

No doubt Davidoff would dole out whatever material her own securities classification—there had to be one somewhere in all these files, didn't there?—merited, with debits for sheer snideness.

Maybe he'd explain why, after *Rimrunner* had left Earth on her own, she'd had to hook up with a convoy halfway out.

That is, if he'd made it back from outside. She'd heard him order one of the ship's catapults readied. Two minutes ago, she wouldn't have thought that was her problem, even if he had gotten her back to her quarters in time to download her instructions. Now, she understood why it was. Shit. All she needed, being dependent on a trust-funded rocket jockey with a chip on his shoulder the size of Vesta.

*"Ladies and gentlemen, please stand by for attitude adjustment."*

Well, that could mean a lot of things, mostly involving jolts, take-holds, and, at this point in the eleven-year cycle, radiation and lots of it.

Damn, if Davidoff's ship hit something, or he zigged when he should have zagged and took a systemful of radiation, there went her mission.

CC braced herself. She made herself read faster, straining even the trained speed of the eidetic scan-reader she'd been since childhood. She'd already known that Captain Aquino would have to bring *Rimrunner* alongside the BBU, maneuvering it between the sun and the satellite to protect the robot arm that brought the BBU into the ship.

Another buzz from her machine. Radiation levels were climbing, and here she was, outside the shelters. Good thing she wasn't allergic to potassium iodide.

*"Five minute warning before the next course adjustment!"* came from the bulkhead speakers.

Could she make it to shelter before radiation rose to critical?

Unsnapping herself, CC re-encrypted her files, flash-downloaded into her Breitling PDA, and flung herself down the corridor to the shelter. Micro-g and nearly deserted corridors were her friends: she made good time.

Screens glowed on the bulkheads, showing stragglers how cleverly the robot arm deployed, rising from its own bay in the ship. As she caromed off one bulkhead toward a lift, *Rimrunner* lurched again. CC grabbed for one of the handholds deployed for just such emergencies.

Surely, that was the ship deploying its catapult, getting more small craft out there, either to repair or realign the robot arm or to defend the ship against—against what? Not the riderships she'd seen, surely. Those were EarthServ, enough of a convoy to scare off any pirates unless, of course, they'd united in hopes of a rich prize—not to mention the hostages that *Rimrunner* contained. Policy was not to pay bribes or ransom. Alpha wouldn't ransom her: she suspected that others on board—Neave for example—were safer.

She fended herself off a bend in the corridor and brought herself up against the shelter hatch. Sealed.

Damnation. But predictable.

Cursing the additional seconds of exposure, CC pressed her ID against the panel next to the hatch. It clicked, edging open just enough to let her squeeze into a kind of airlock. Medicians in full decontamination gear, waiting for other latecomers, seized her, injected her with potassium iodide, and manhandled her, still clutching her Breitling, out of her shipsuit and into the emergency shower cubicle, a coffinlike structure that shot hot water and chemicals at her from sides, ceiling, and deck.

*"Take hold!"* came a metallic command from overhead. *Rimrunner* lurched yet again. CC gasped and choked, welcoming the gusts of hot air that replaced the cleansing shower. She backed herself into the nearest corner, huddling down, clutching at grips set a meter above the deck, to protect herself in case Aquino took a mind to turn what she used to think was a perfectly good liner into a pogo stick once again.

As soon as the water drained and the lock released with a ping and a green light, CC half-floated and half-staggered out of decontamination. As she shook off her PDA—good thing she'd bought herself a *real* Breitling, hardened for space travel—she wrestled herself into the slick prefab suit a medician thrust at her. It was the sort of thing you wore in infirmaries if you were too sick to be let out, but not sick enough to be confined to bed.

"Follow the instructions!" said the medician, handing her a phial of the potassium iodide that would presumably prevent her from developing radiation sickness and allow her, one of these years, to give birth to a perfect corporate trophy.

After all, didn't David IV have a right to a wife whose genotype was unimpaired? She tried to imagine them as a family, joined by the child she'd now have the money to afford. Maybe she'd even take some time off like Margaret Lovat, though she couldn't quite think macro enough to envision actually having a safety net like that. Maybe once this job was done.

Hands seized her by the collar, which gave, but didn't tear, and the puckered waist of her shipsuit, then tossed her, coughing and squawking her outrage, into the shelter.

## 6

**CC's stomach lurched as she was flung into the crowded** shelter. She starfished, then drew arms and legs into a ball as she'd been taught. When more hands grabbed her, she managed not to strike out in a way that would only have sent her flying across the shelter bay.

"CC, there you are!" came Sandy's voice. It was cordial and concerned, and CC trusted it about as far as Sandy could throw her. No, scratch that. In this environment, he could probably throw her a considerable way if she didn't crash into someone or something.

"What happened? Are you all right?"

"I had some files to secure," CC said, relishing the more-workaholic-than-thou point she was about to score, and in public, no less. "I couldn't leave them."

She clipped the Breitling to her suit and let Sandy draw her away from the hatch.

"You cut it too close, you know," he said, his voice raised and didactic as he began to talk about sunspot patterns and their impact on the capital markets.

Right. We know you know all about it, CC thought to herself. You just want to make sure people in the shelter know—

and see you towing me past them, conveniently near the Neave-Lovats so they can see what a good team player you're being.

She permitted his help. There was no denying the greater mass was helpful, even comforting, now, after the battering she'd taken. Good thing she hadn't eaten, she realized as a cough turned into gagging, and she tasted bile whether from the meds, the lack of food, or the micro-g: it hardly mattered. She flapped one hand, the universal signal in space for "give me a sick kit *now*," and held the thing up to her mouth till the spasm passed.

Sandy turned a little green. To do him credit, he kept towing her through the clusters of sleeping nets tethered to wallhooks, the foil blankets that occasionally floated up from the deck, the packets of food in uneasy suspension between deck and diner, through knots of parents, tutors, and nannies turning a red alert into a learning experience, and past the monitors that medical attendants used to check the vital functions of wealthy retirees.

CC sighted Margaret Lovat, huddled in a spot where two structural supports united to form a corner she had clearly marked as her own. Beside her were—Robert and Vi, Neave had called them. The children's tutors, who'd been so admirably proactive in getting them to shelter that they'd receive a bonus. The tutors' body language—the bright eyes, the faintly stooped posture and self-conscious awkwardness, even after months of low gravity—reminded CC of the library where she'd grown up. It would be easy, comforting, even, simply to go over and sit near them and revive her skill at academic small talk. She sighed. She knew she'd lose major face if she did anything of the sort.

She started to paddle in the air, ready to move on, but to her surprise, Margaret Lovat gestured at her.

"Over there," CC broke into Sandy's monologue, reassuring in its predictable ambition. "Yes, I know who it is. Can't you see? She's signaled to us. She wants us to join her."

The magic word "us" won first Sandy's attention, then his

help towing her over to Lovat's corner. He dropped her near the pile of bedrolls and supplies that the woman and tutors had assembled. CC breathed a sigh of relief and managed to thank him sincerely. He looked as if he wouldn't even wait for an invitation to join them, but Ms. Lovat turned her shoulder, bending to hear one of her children whisper at her. She nodded.

"Robert, why don't you and Vi see if you can't find a couple of children to form a playgroup?" she asked. How politely she phrased her order as a suggestion. CC would have to remember that for—later.

"We were thinking this would be a good time to review differentials," Vi began.

"Calculus review can wait. The children are distracted now, and we don't want to set them up for failure, now do we?"

Vi shook her head vigorously. The gesture almost launched her across the room, but she grabbed onto a tether and followed Robert.

"Thank you, Mr. Sanderson, I believe you said your name was," Ms. Lovat turned to Sandy. "I thought your colleague could do with a place to sit down."

CC bit her lower lip, concealing how pleased she was by the gesture. In the next instant, her stomach chilled. She must have looked stressed out beyond all measure. Bad move, CC. Inability to tolerate stress was the sort of thing performance evaluations, on and off the job, came down hard on.

Sandy muttered something about "the least I could do."

"It was kind of you to bring her over," Margaret Lovat added, turning away to pull the self-heating strip from a container, pull up the sip tube, and offer the cup to CC. Then Ms. Lovat sat up straight, her hands empty. She looked Sandy in the eye until he realized that he'd been dismissed.

He schooled his expression to a cordial blandness and took himself off more quickly than CC had ever managed to get rid of him at the usual networking sessions.

But then, the woman must have had plenty of experience at handling her husband's subordinates. Kind she might be, but she knew her own priorities.

CC opened her mouth on the necessary thanks. After all, Ambassador Neave had worked at Alpha years back: the culture prided itself on its alumni network, so it was logical Margaret Lovat would follow through.

"Not a word till you've drunk that. We always put some herbal tea in our emergency kits: you look like you need something to warm you up. And I was looking for someone to talk to, anyhow."

CC squeezed out a mouthful of the hot, stimulating liquid and nearly choked.

"Robert helps, that is, he helped me grow it back home," Lovat added. "His doctorate is in botany. He'll join Imperial Agronomics as soon as we get settled. I've got to decide between Schering and Vesta Bio-Pharma. It'll be good to do some bench science again. You know, I tried to keep up while the children were growing, but between their educations and the usual round of meet and greet for Elliott's business, I got rusty. I guess I'll start as a tech and work my way back up."

"But what about your staff?" CC asked, startled. She'd have thought an Ambassador's wife would have a manager, her very own miniature infrastructure to help with the entertaining.

Lovat laughed. "Oh my dear, I hope I'm done with all of that now that Everett's retired. Someone always had to supervise all those people, cope with their panic attacks and bruised egos, and that someone was always me! I hope you never know what a bore it got to be, coordinating the food to match the color of the flowers and furnishings and keep straight what dresses I wore to meet what dignitaries! I'll have other things, real things, to worry about now! And it will be nice to have friends, not just business contacts.

"Surprised, are you?" Margaret Lovat laughed, not at all put out to find that CC had underestimated her. "We're heading for the frontier. We'll all have to earn our way as well as find it. That's why I chose the children's tutors. They both have skills that will be useful on Vesta, even if you wouldn't think so at first. Robert's training, as you saw, is in botany; Vi . . . well, her training was as an art historian, so we may be able to keep her with us for at least a little while, even though I think she's been offered an internship with Muni Arcology, to make the place more livable. I tell her she might want to consult with the psych staff, too, but she wants to think about it. She isn't used to having so much choice."

Lovat awarded CC a level look. *I'm sure* you *can understand.*

CC turned to glance at the hatch and the huddled passengers and staff so the other woman wouldn't see her eyes fill. To be able to take up an offer of friendship, without the whole ship wondering how CC Williams got to suck up at that level . . .

"I saw you speaking with Marc Davidoff," said Margaret Lovat. "He was annoyed about something, which is no surprise. I've known Marc for years. He's been angry about something or other ever since he walked away from his job as a growth fund manager in the family shop to join the service. Why'd he shut down your monitor?"

CC had always had a problem keeping a straight face. Now, she could feel the blood drain from her skin.

"I'd accessed some files I wasn't cleared to use," she said. So, Davidoff had abandoned a job as a portfolio manager and joined EarthServ? That didn't make any sense. Unless, of course, he'd been tasked with watching *her.* Given the sources he probably had at his disposal, just how extensive had *his* briefing been?

Don't be paranoid, she told herself. Plays hell with your blood pressure. Davidoff's got more important things to do than spy on you.

Unless, of course, they were making him multitask. What sort of game was he playing? Whatever it was, the man had been brought up to be a player. She needed his goodwill.

"Ms. Williams!" If they'd been in normal gravity, Margaret Lovat would have tapped her toe in irritation. "My vision is excellent, even without laser surgery. You didn't have text; you had an image."

She was well and truly stuck. A small devil of mischief made CC ask, "Well, if your vision is that good, you saw the same thing I did."

"But I couldn't identify it. You clearly could, which is what got Marc so angry."

CC grinned at the Ambassador's wife, who grinned back.

"Yes, I'll have the story out of you somehow," she answered CC's unspoken thought. "Trade you, in fact. Marc joined EarthServ as . . . I believe the term used to be 'gentleman ranker.' After awhile, he realized he liked the life, and the old upward-mobility drives his parents had practically coded into his DNA kicked in. So he made a few prodigal-son-type calls back to the family, who got him sent to Officer Candidate School. Apart from that, though, he's made his own career. But now he keeps in touch, which makes everyone as happy as that lot ever gets."

Now that was more information than CC was prepared to absorb right now. She filed it away for future reference.

"I think we've got a convoy." Changing the subject, CC pitched her voice low, so only Margaret Lovat could hear it. "Do *you* know anything about pirate attacks?"

"Not much," the other woman said. Raising her head proudly, she added, "But you have to understand. I have a considerable investment in knowing that we're safe, you see. My husband filed DNRs for all of us."

DNR. Do Not Ransom.

CC whistled, a low, unladylike sound. DNRs represented a level of principle that most people talked about, but few people ever acted on, especially for their families, which were always a source of sentimental agitation in the uppermost ranks.

Again Margaret Lovat grinned. "I completely agreed with his decision. But I think we're probably safe for now. If there were an actual attack, don't you think we'd be jolted around more?" she asked.

CC nodded. Then, she gestured at the sight of Robert returning to his employer, Vi following, the children bobbing as they clung to their tutors' hands.

Margaret Lovat turned to greet her children. Ignoring Sandy's reproachful gaze, CC hunched over her Breitling, dividing her attention between its tiny, impeccably backlit screen and the shelter's hatch. She realized she was hoping to see Marc Davidoff again.

When the hatch swung open, CC almost dropped her PDA. It was only Neave, entering with considerably more aplomb and less haste than CC remembered from her own entry. He propelled himself over to his family, and held out a hand to keep CC from rising (probably far too high, given the g level). She hunched even more devotedly over her work, wondering how to ask whether she shouldn't really move on and give them the quality family time execs on Neave's level were always reported as wanting to pursue once they retired.

She supposed she could always go talk to Sandy. Now perched within eyeballing range, he had grown even more annoyed now that he saw CC within range of Neave. Points for her. But if she didn't put him out of his misery, he'd probably find a way to get back at her later on.

Neave didn't give her an opportunity to excuse herself. And she couldn't just get up and leave.

The hours ticked on, minute by eternal minute. CC had exhausted her Breitling's memory: if she were to make any progress on this case, she needed to get back to her computer.

*Dammit, Davidoff, when are you going to get your ass back in here? You're supposed to extend me every consideration: there's no consideration about this!*

Fine for him to play space pirates after a stint digging in what used to be Iraq. The minute he got tired of adventures, he could count on his family to invent a nice desk job for him or turn him into a high-tech remittance man. If she failed, nanny-work would be about all she could hope for, and it was not going to be enough to help her meet debt service. Then it would be Freeze for her, for certain, and shipment in steerage to the further asteroids or the colonized outer moons.

She tried to relax, to take advantage of the opportunity to listen to Neave and make herself look good. But her eyes kept flitting to the hatch, and she knew Neave spotted it.

She was about to try the "Sir, could I talk to you a minute" and throw herself on any corporate mercy—or Alpha alumni loyalty—he might be feeling at the moment, when he bent his head over a Breitling that made her own machine look like a 1970s calculator, smiled, and nodded to her. "I think we're about to get some answers now."

At that moment, the hatch cracked open again, and Marc Davidoff stuck his head through. The rest of him followed. Not for him the ungainly, starfishing entrance, propelled by anxious medical staff, of someone inexperienced with zero g. He launched himself into the shelter bay with one shrewd leap, fending off blankets and stray passengers with the arm he wasn't using to hold his helmet. He still wore his pressure gear, a dark suit marked with his rank and an incongruously shiny military emblem. The possibility that he might have picked up trace radiation was driving health care aides into a frenzy of protest about contamination.

Catching sight of Neave, Davidoff turned in mid-leap, and set down with enviable smoothness. With a polite nod for Margaret Lovat and an ironic lift of the eyebrow for CC herself, he handed Neave a shimmering disk. "Captain Aquino's compliments," he said.

"It would be more to the point if Captain Aquino would sound the all-clear," Neave observed.

"He's about to make the announcement," Davidoff assured him. "He just doesn't want a microgravity stampede. Think of the chaos. He's going to release people in stages: first, hardship cases. Then, by ID number."

Just wonderful. They could be here all night. And CC had work to do.

Neave chuckled. His son threw himself against his father's shoulder. Neave caught him, fielded him, listened to an urgent whisper, then said, "Why not ask him?"

Taking that as consent, the boy bobbed within range of Davidoff and reached out for his helmet. "Can I hold it?"

With a laugh, Davidoff lobbed it at him and laughed off appalled looks from the caregivers.

"I'm clean," he announced. "You think I'd skip decontamination or endanger a child? *I've* been Outside too long to be stupid. What's *your* excuse?"

He treated CC to another glare. "What did I tell you about staying out too long? Now you know better." Another stare. "I just bet they put you through the wringer, didn't they? Is decontamination any more fun now than it used to be?"

"I'll live."

*Commander Davidoff will afford you every cooperation,* her instructions had said.

*Cooperate, damn you!*

She flashed him a look. "The damn . . . Unfortunately, I've run out of things to work on," she said. "Read any good books lately?"

"I think—ah, here comes the announcement!"

*"May I please have your attention?"* Captain Aquino's voice erupted from speakers hidden in the bulkheads.

At least a tenth of the people in the shelter started, then drifted upward or were restrained by their tethers.

*"I am lowering ship's status from red alert to orange. Passenger restrictions have been lifted for the present. Ship's crew will escort you from shelter; please follow their instructions. Passengers requiring medical assistance or with young children will be released first. When your number is called, kindly untether yourself and rise slowly. If you require assistance, please activate your ID monitors."*

Neave reclaimed Davidoff's helm from his son, who protested loudly. Sending the boy over to his mother with an affectionate shove, he handed the helmet back to its owner. The two exchanged words CC couldn't hear.

*"Thank you for your cooperation,"* Captain Aquino continued. *"A digest of today's situation will be posted on ship's systems."*

"And guess who's going to have to write it!" Davidoff said. "That's *after* I give crew a hand clearing this joint. Mutualized hedge funds are looking better every day!"

Margaret Lovat rose with a slow grace that bespoke familiarity with low-g travel. "Ordinarily, I dislike taking advantage of special privilege, but I think the children have reached the ends of their tethers in more ways than one. I'll take them out myself," she told the tutors.

"Not alone, surely!" said Davidoff. "I'm sure Ms. Williams here would give you a hand."

*No one makes a nanny out of me!*

The cheerful malice in his grin showed CC that Davidoff had anticipated her reaction. That, at least, told her what she wanted to know about the depths of his briefing on her.

She rose a little too quickly, and Davidoff caught her by the wrist.

"Don't be an idiot. Give her a hand. It'll get you out and earn you points with the Lovat-Neaves," he muttered. "And it's not as if you haven't got work to do, right?"

CC could pretend to be insulted that she was reduced to waiting on a corporate trophy wife. Or she could play it as a perk from successful schmoozing. Or, rather, networking.

Stitching on her most cordial smile, a veteran of years of conferences: "I'd be delighted," she told Ms. Lovat.

"You seem to have made quite an impression," she murmured, letting her glance flick down to the ancestral grandeur of CC's engagement ring. At her nod, the tutors began to gather up the children's gear.

CC wondered what helpful passenger wouldn't be able to resist passing the word to David IV that a scion of a major financial house had singled out his fiancée for attention. She wouldn't put it past Sandy to blow the whistle, even though David disliked Sandy—along with most of the people from CC's past.

Well, that wasn't surprising: CC disliked most of them herself.

She could only hope that David IV would balance CC's apparent success in making a friend of Margaret Lovat against the "impression" she'd made on Marc Davidoff. Surely David IV would understand; he was fair by nature. He'd have to know Davidoff was simply helping out an important friend.

## 7

**CC's tiny, meticulously furnished stateroom had felt like an** escape from prison. She bought herself a quick, hot-water shower at a price she would have to rationalize later. Then, wrapping herself in a slate-blue robe coordinated with the room's décor and bearing the ship's crest in a microfiber slubbed to look like silk, she finally settled at her workstation.

Now, hours later, she felt as if she were in prison once again. Her wrists and fingers twinged in ways that made her long to return to Earth and have words with the orthopedic surgeon whose bill—her HMO at the time covered only plan-approved specialists, and she'd heard stories about the surgeons who signed on with those plans—she was still paying off.

The bulkheads' recessed lights had dimmed to nightshift, casting long, comforting shadows on the webbing that covered her bunk. More microfiber there: 750 thread-count, no less, in a tasteful shade of blue that the lights turned dusky lavender. A violet light gleamed on the netting, evidence of the captain's caution and a signal she'd be obliged to sleep strapped in tonight or risk an infraction notice.

Assuming she could sleep at all.

Careful not to dislodge herself from her chair, she arched her aching back, then rubbed her eyes.

It didn't make the data on her screen look any better. Once again, she reviewed a random sample of accounts belonging to ordinary contract employees, and shook her head. Nothing there. She'd started life as a contract worker herself, and she recognized the pattern of risk aversion that meant they'd never fight their way back from even one minor down market. When she turned to the indentured workers' accounts, though, alarms went off in her head. For one thing, where did indentures and shipsicles get that kind of money, let alone the savvy to produce a return on invested capital that solid? Just dumb luck? Dumb luck didn't product two-digit ROICs. Hell, she hadn't seen that kind of return on invested capital since the last bull market five years ago.

Maybe someone was front-running money in their accounts and rewarding them with a percentage. That wasn't just illegal, it was illogical, unless—those accounts were held in trust. Who was custodian? That was one possibility.

Another one was that someone was front-running and expecting that his or her crime would be picked up. You could be imprisoned, frozen, or barred from the industry: what fool would do that? Answer: someone who stood to gain more than he or she would lose to fines, who could fight a prison sentence—or for whom the crime was the less terrible of two alternatives.

She followed the pattern of trades, trade belonging to the colony's frozen assets—those indentures stacked in freeze until there was space and need to resurrect them. Somehow, the people still on ice, if you netted their holdings together, had managed to amass 5% of Reynolds Solar Mining, 10% of Pfizer Circum-Terra Medical Consortium, and a whopping 15% of Ariane-Grumman Enterprises. What did each of those NGOs have in common? Each one of them had an ambassador-level seat in the United Nations.

Looking more closely, CC found on file the 13D and 13G filings for the Reynolds position, but not the 13Ds for the bigger NGO holdings, which should have been filed ten days after purchase and amended. If the "owners" of these stocks hadn't been on ice, she'd have sworn that someone was preparing a takeover bid. Several takeover bids. Using other people's stocks, which was one hell of a way to abuse fiduciary responsibilities.

Now, if any of this was indeed the case, it would be her happy, happy job to put a name to the perpetrator and bring him or her or it in.

That particular spreadsheet glowed until the fine muscles at the corners of her eyes began to twitch.

She stored it and blanked the screen, staring at the soothing pattern that formed until the tiny, taut muscles at jaws and temples ceased to twinge. Quick touches of her console produced whalesong and a whiff of lavender: folk remedies for tension, if the "folk" were San Franciscan, affluent, and a little left of center.

Damn smart folk. She could feel herself begin to relax.

Then her comm beeped.

"Ms. Williams?" Oh God, she knew that voice—emphatic, efficient, and damned good at putting her on the defensive.

Just what she needed. For the first time in her life, she cursed the impulse that had made her agree to investigation so she could get a security clearance high enough to warrant her being assigned to projects like these. It got her stuck working with her very own financial apostate.

"What is it, Lieutenant Commander?"

It would be so easy and so pleasant simply to end the call, but her management would probably ask him for a report on her. He probably thought this working relationship was funny: look at how he'd managed to get her out of the shelter back to where she could do her work.

What the hell did he think she was, a nanny?

No, just another professional, the unwelcome answer came. She was being unfair, she cautioned herself. After all, Davidoff had been fast and efficient and, above all, willing in aiding her. Besides, she realized, Margaret Lovat was the sort of person she wouldn't at all mind knowing better. Not just for her position, but for her own sake.

"Just wanted to know if you were feeling any better?"

*I've got the mother of all front-running cases at the very least, a headache, an old enemy from my childhood, and a weird associate. Oh, I'm feeling just* fine.

"Thanks," she said. "I'll be fine once I get some sleep."

"Let me know if you need anything. I'm off duty in a few. I could stop by."

Was the man out of his fucking mind? CC was engaged. But she remembered Margaret Lovat's quizzical glance: maybe a shipboard romance was an unbelievable cliché in literature, but these weren't reading people; they'd accept it just fine.

Had she any right to turn down a tactic that might actually work?

*Damn. I'd like to have my life back in reasonable shape when this is over,* CC growled to herself. *All I need is for David . . . still, I've got too much on my plate to have time to worry about gossips a couple AU from home.*

"Thanks, but I'll be fine," she repeated.

He didn't end the call.

"How about I contact you if I need help?" she offered.

That got a smile from him and a nod of respect. The comm's light flickered off.

Another light blossomed: she had messages. The world could damned well end, but there would always be messages.

Damn, Sandy couldn't possibly have tracked down David IV already and squealed on her, could he?

*If you're going to be paranoid, at least do it during billable hours!* she scolded herself.

Sandy couldn't have blown the whistle on her—at least, not yet. He'd have had to justify a priority transmission, and she knew damned well that even if he did, David was probably out tracking penguins or clambering about ice floes or sleeping (she checked the chronometer) in that fur-bedded ice palace down by Lake Shackleton; he had once suggested it would make the sort of honeymoon retreat that not everyone got to do. He had such a sense of fun.

One more search, and then she'd give herself a treat: she'd reread his last message.

She turned back to her records. Question: did the numbers in the shipsicles' accounts add? Were the amounts invested the amounts that these people should have had and were they simply getting inside information? Somehow, insider trading, that scourge of the late twentieth century, struck her as almost innocent compared with the alternatives that lurked at the edges of her consciousness.

Now, this was billable paranoia, the sort Alpha paid her for. One thing was certain: her employers were definitely getting their money's worth.

CC drilled deeper, past the list of accounts, and into specific securities. For purposes of experimentation (a quick glance at ship's indicators showed radiation rising, but only slightly, so she had time), CC called up some of the extraneous accounts and their holdings. For God's sake, who was idiot enough to trade commodities in this account? And just look, she thought in mounting indignation, at those stock and bond picks . . . if this were a retirement account, or funds held for an indentured shipsicle, it was criminally insane to buy that many small-cap biotechs, not to mention the kinds of junk bonds she saw listed. And if an indentured shipsicle had participated in a private equity offering, it had to have had enough money to qualify, which meant more than enough money to have avoided Freeze in the first place!

This was more than a mistake. This was a mess. She could see the potential here for collusion, fraud, even the suspicion, which her employer clearly shared, that these accounts were being used as front-running vehicles by someone, or a bunch of someones. That was what CC would have to discover. It wouldn't be easy at all to pick out the criminals, and harder yet, if they had the sophistication to run an operation like this, to reveal them.

Where was all this money coming from? Despite the rigorous procedures to prevent money laundering, it was easy enough to do if an NGO or even a government with no scruples, a lot to gain, or both decided to do it.

Next question: who had the expertise to manage either of these operations?

If she considered every one on Earth, that could be a long list, she thought. So, for the sake of convenience, she would assume that the answer lay on or near Vesta: otherwise why send her? Well, it could be a wild-goose chase, but wild-goose chases didn't involve Alpha Consultancies, not if the person inventing them wanted to go on making money rather than being a prisoner, so she'd rule that out for now. She would not, however, rule out the possibility of an Earth-based accomplice or accomplices.

On or near Vesta. On Vesta . . . any first-year analyst had the technical skills. Any *Interplanetary Investors*–ranked analyst had the actual knowhow and influence, even without an investment bank to back him or her.

But who?

She ran a cross-check of financial-services staff, correlated them against *II,* and came up with five likely suspects. Were any in translunar space? Easy enough to check that too.

None. So much for that good idea.

She yawned. Time to get her messages, and then, she'd strip down and strap in for as much sleep as she was going to get in this gravity.

She had one message, dated and timestamped Vesta.

Mac Nofi.

CC slammed her fists down on either side of her workstation so hard that she rose into the air. She cursed in the silence, an ugly counterpoint to the restfulness of the whale songs that played serenely on.

Was there a person on Vesta qualified to do the job? Mac wasn't with any of the securities firms, at least not now. And that gave him a damn good reason for wanting to fuck with their work: revenge. And if that weren't enough, spite and a desire to show them he was still smarter than they.

Mac. Old friend. Old mentor. A superb analyst—the one, in fact, who'd taken her to the Paris Air Show. He'd been aced out of a job in the last restructuring that had parlayed three companies into one and left analyst jobs as scarce as $O_2$ in vacuum.

But Mac, ever the resourceful SOB, had used his old ore and mining bidniz (Colorado School of Mines followed by stints at A&M and Wharton) background to wangle his way into arcology management. They'd lost contact, but she seemed to remember he'd headed offworld. According to the message header, Mac was now a senior manager for the holding company that ran Vesta operations.

Mac could do it. He definitely had the know-how. He had the grudge and the mindset: analysts tended not to get over things but to get even.

But she'd always thought he was a straight arrow. In fact, he'd taught her the term.

She didn't like to think that Mac had gone over to the crooked side of the Force. She'd respected him too long to regard pitting her wits against his as a challenge from which she might come off third-best.

Best see what the man had to say.

His image formed: thin, looking younger than his years, but relaxed as he floated in Vesta's almost no-gravity.

*"CC, how's it going? RUMINT has it you're headed out to Vesta on* Rimrunner. *Captain's an old bidniz associate of mine; he'll treat you right. I'll be waiting for you when you land.*

*Mac"*

Would Mac have sent that message if he were running a scam she'd been sent out to investigate? Maybe he thought she was simply coming out, as her cover had it, to conduct the survey mandated by the Earth Association of Securities Dealers.

Yeah, right. And maybe Vesta would be terraformed into a garden spot by the time she got out there.

Mac would be a dangerous and a wily criminal.

*Anyone but him,* she muttered. *Please, anyone.*

So, did she have any other suspects in mind?

For the moment, just for the sake of argument, scratch

Mac. What about Sandy? That was a more congenial idea. After all, Sandy chronically needed money, had access to historical trading records, and was arrogant and angry enough to try a fast one. Then she sighed. The idea was unlikely, she thought. Sandy was as loyal as was in him to be to Morgan Nomura because he knew how bad life was for the un-Familied without a proper work patron.

CC pressed the heels of her palms against her eyes, setting lights off behind her eyelids. She was tired and paranoid, and that made for stupid.

How's this for a stupid idea, CC-girl?

Why not suspect Ambassador Neave himself? He had the governmental connections: for whatever reason, he might find it to his advantage—or to the advantage of any game he was playing—to want to upset the current balance between governments and NGOs.

And finally, she came to the thought-experiment she really hated. If you looked at the data from a particularly twisted viewpoint, she too could be made out to be a suspect. Granted, you'd have to really twist to make the case; still, if this blew up in her face, she could see a scenario in which CC Williams, Rogue Consultant, had set all these wheels in motion till they ground her down.

Whoever had set this scam up wouldn't hesitate to do it. After all, it wasn't as if she had family or connections other than the ones she'd made herself. She was one job—and one fiancé—away from the *insulae,* and David IV deserved so much better!

She wrung her hands. They ached. Note to self: have a word with her lawyer to have a word with that damned microsurgeon.

Time to pack it in for the day. A painstaking, if quick, encryption to embed the message in other, harmless traffic; locking the file on her computer, followed by a change of passwords, logging out, and locking up.

She fastened herself into her bunk and turned on the white noise that was guaranteed to be proof against all but red alerts. Five minutes later, she was unconscious and dreaming, not of sheep leaping fences, but of bulls and bears sur-mounting a wall of spikes. As each leaped the spikes, it snarled at her, then wheeled to drive her toward a very nar-row bridge beneath which lay a world of ice.

David IV was out there somewhere, but David IV was keeping himself to himself down in Antarctica. *He* liked the ice.

She made herself wake up. Logging in again, she began to work. A pity she wouldn't get credit for the time of night she'd started in, but one thing about translunar space: you didn't get credit for face time. At least, though, the work would get done, and she wouldn't have to try to sleep.

One more problem troubled her. Somewhere between the time she'd slept and the nightmare that waked her, an old phrase—one of the archaisms she had tried to forget she'd once learned—had crept into her thoughts. *Cui bono?* Who stood to benefit? In the trading scandals of the early twenty-first century, it had been easy to see: top management. Here, though, there were no beneficiaries she could see and lots of losers.

Including, very definitely, herself.

## 8

**Small rocks could do a hell of a lot of damage. So Captain** Aquino's crew never quite relaxed as *Rimrunner* edged its cautious way through the asteroid belt.

The Belt might be vast, but it was cluttered, relatively speaking, with everything from dust and granules to Ceres, largest of the asteroids, with a mass of 1 percent of Earth's Moon. Any rock in the wrong place at the wrong time wouldn't just ruin CC's day, but end them all for good.

Assuming she was crazy enough to call death in space good.

Yet here CC was, standing on the ship's hull, staring vacuum—and all those rocks—in the face. If that wasn't crazy, what was?

She would never get used to EVA, she realized. But suit drill, at her level, was mandatory.

Vibrations buzzed through her magnetized bootplates as the personnel airlock irised open into the vast dark. The rush of her own breathing grew louder and faster. A rush of adrenaline turned her even more giddy than each time she waited for a performance evaluation.

The promotional material for her pressure suit, a top-line

Sentry 7X1A, proclaimed it *Always On Duty!* If the damn thing ever went off-duty, though, she wouldn't live to collect damages. Still, David IV would know she had been thinking of him.

Before this, CC had always gone EVA in a well-guarded crowd. What idiot had suggested this all-but-solo excursion? Margaret Lovat? CC didn't notice *her* rushing to go Outside. Likelier it had been Neave, damned Margaret's damned influential husband. Had to have been, or CC surely would have had the brains to say she wasn't crazy, she wasn't expendable, and she wasn't going!

*Get Outside, get used to it, and wait for instructions,* she'd been told. She suspected part of the assignment was testing to see if she collapsed in an incontinent ball with screaming agoraphobia, or claustrophobia, or both of them at once.

It wasn't as if CC were physically or intellectually unprepared. She'd done the mandatory evacuation drills. She wouldn't forget any time soon how she'd raced past the retirees, their sealed bubbles pushed along by anxious caregivers who monitored their heart/lung rates and complained at the time it took for ship's crew to check out all first-time voyagers.

She'd jumped through every hoop ship's crew had thrown at her, and God knows there'd been enough of them to satisfy the most exacting insurance companies that *Rimrunner*'s passengers were well-trained.

The fact remained: more than at any time in her life, she stood now in an environment over which she had no control. She paused, waiting for courage or shame to propel her, either forward or back through the airlock into the ship.

Crew had begun to step up safety training of *Rimrunner*'s passengers from the moment the ship entered the Kirkwood Gap, a patch in the asteroid belt that Jupiter's gravitational pull kept relatively free of debris. Again, "relative" was the operational word: the Gap might be safe enough (another dubious term) to train newbies in, but it wasn't safe enough to spare you if you totally screwed the pooch or if luck or the numbers weren't on your side.

Intellectually, CC was fine. She had even developed some degree of physical competence. It was her emotions, yammering and jittering at the back of all that training, that were her enemy now, as much as the infinitesimal possibility of an even more infinitesimal micrometeorite holing her Sentry 7X1A, letting out its air and letting in her mortality.

It was all in the numbers. One day, the numbers might catch up even with Earth. Something huge would slam down, flattening the carefully reconstructed cities and probably screwing up the ecosystem, such as it was, for once and for all.

It wouldn't be the first time, as a bunch of dinosaurs could have attested if the things had had any brains. And there'd been some close shaves after that. Take, for example, Hermes, discovered in 1937 and subsequently lost. It had come within 485,000 miles of Earth. Eros, another close call, had approached within 14 million miles. And then there'd been the Panic of 2019.

That one had created popular enthusiasm for blowing up the asteroid before it hit—which it hadn't. That enthusiasm—and the funding that accompanied it—had contributed to the founding of EarthServ.

The Panic had also been, as CC had heard way off the record, a spectacular opportunity for terrorists if they'd had powerful enough ships. Thanks to some quick action against some NGOs that were powerful enough, but not quite fast or stealthy enough, the usual suspects had never quite managed to buy, build, or hijack them or the weapons that had turned the media even more paranoid than usual.

No point worrying about planet-killers, CC told herself. Weapons powerful enough to flatten asteroids before they flattened Earth were probably under development—assuming the NGO building them considered the project cost-effective. If Alpha Consultants had wanted her to worry about them, they'd have included data in her briefings. Right now, all she had to worry about was surviving this EVA.

Advanced suit drill—let alone drill with boosterpaks—was optional on board *Rimrunner*. Still, anyone with a job outside Earth's orbit learned all the skills she could. Granted, most of CC's work on Vesta would probably chain her to a workstation. Most execs would spend their entire tour in the Belt without needing to EVA. But if she had to go Outside, she'd get better training now than if she played catch-up on Vesta with the shipsicles. Assuming, in an emergency, that they didn't just stuff her in a suit and thrust her out the airlock.

Granted, labor law required hypnopedia even for shipsicles, who'd get on-the-job training after they were defrosted and their metabolisms stabilized (suits were expensive). But shipsicles tended to bad luck, CC assured herself. Why else would they be shipsicles in the first place?

*Blaming the victims, are you? Your ethics used to be better.*

*That was before I had something to lose,* CC silenced the usual reprimands.

As always, CC tried and failed not to remember the times when her financial position had been so risky she'd been close to Freeze herself. She'd managed to avoid the worst-case choice. But it left her desperate to learn all the skillsets she could. It still woke her sweating in the night. And it made her determined to see that, come what may, she and David IV had as secure a life as possible. Not that he ever worried. Things worked out for David, and he assumed they'd work out for the people he cared about. That easy disposition of his was one of the things she loved about him.

So, advanced EVA. Yet another skill in the arsenal—and on the résumé.

She wasn't the only one trying to rack up the certifications. She knew Sandy would try to log all the hull-time he could. Being Sandy, he'd probably use up the allotment covered by his ticket, then put himself further in debt to buy more—assuming he didn't try to sneak his hull-time on his Travel and Expense report.

CC's game plan was more prudent. If she played it right, she'd still reach Vesta qualified to investigate, inside the Colony habitat or outside, on the asteroid's remarkable surface. So she'd accepted Neave's preposterously generous suggestion that if Davidoff "felt like a breath of canned air," he should take CC with him on his next trip Outside as the favor he'd meant, for some inexplicable reason, to do her. The trip, of course, would be free.

Alpha loyalty again? Or maybe he'd simply appreciated her help with his children.

In any event, it was a favor she couldn't refuse, not without losing major points. Or a chance to "get her ticket punched," working off the certifications she'd need on Vesta and justifying the expense of her trip. Alpha had paid for her to have the full program, from evacuation to boosterpak, and, for all she knew, catapult training. If she skipped any even of the optional sessions, it didn't just mean she'd land on Vesta ill-equipped, but it would be reported to Alpha back on Earth that she'd sloughed off opportunities during the trip Out.

Marc offered her a chance to double her time Outside and to push her training beyond what Alpha had paid for. Besides, if Neave offered you a favor, you by God took it, even if you cursed his name.

Neave's name or God's? They weren't, CC had to remind herself, the same damn thing. Leverage be damned. Influential as Neave was, he wasn't in CC's chain of command.

At least, not the direct one.

Remembering crew's instructions from her first "field trip" in which she'd qualified for advanced EVA, CC finally got up the moral courage and forced herself to edge out of the airlock and onto *Rimrunner*'s hull.

Activating her position finder, she turned until sunlight struck her eyes an instant before her helmet could polarize. A glory of fireworks erupted behind CC's eyelids. Despite the excellence of her suit's envirosystem (which gave totally new meaning to the term "space heater"), she shivered. Until now, she hadn't realized how much she had longed for this moment all her life.

She waited a moment longer as the tears ran down her face, which itched all the worse because she could not wipe them away. When the tears and incandescent skyrockets subsided, she narrowed her eyes and looked back toward Earth, a tiny blue crescent in a corona of pure, violet light.

*My God, it's beautiful.*

That distant light held her home: her hopes as well as hatreds, the markets, the corporate retreat where she'd met David IV, seen that grin of his, and longed to be as carefree and kind as he made her feel.

That light held all her hopes. But it also held darker things: the life she'd fled, the culture she'd learned to pretend to ignore. She came from there. They all came from there, from Neave and the Captain to the shipsicles dreaming somewhere around absolute zero. And distant though Earth was, distant though the Sun itself was from CC's vantage-point, the stars that gleamed in the blackness were more distant still—and never to be reached by the likes of even a ship as fast as the one on whose hull she stood.

Compared with the immense distances through which *Rimrunner* crawled, the speed of light was a prison that trapped humanity.

CC's peripheral vision teased her as a streak of light, then another, flicked past. She ignored them to focus on the star sapphire that seemed to shrink as *Rimrunner* held its laborious course for Vesta.

Wasting a second of this beauty by regretting she could go no faster was counterproductive, she told herself. Face it: she had never expected to travel this far, let alone look back on Earth and see how far she'd come.

And if she could make it out of the *insula* and into space, who knew what else was possible?

"Dear Earth, I do salute thee with my hand," she whispered.

*"You going to stand there forever? You know you've only*

*got three hours of air, Williams."* Davidoff's voice broke her reverie.

CC flushed and heated, embarrassed that she'd spoken aloud.

*"How much of your three hours d'you plan to waste quoting Shakespeare?"* Davidoff continued. *"Cut the chat and keep moving!"*

*"Till human voices wake us and we drown."* CC couldn't remember who'd written that. It wasn't Shakespeare, and damned if she would ask Davidoff if *he* knew—because he was right. This was no time to rack her brains for the tag ends of old poems. It just wasn't cost-effective.

The usual self-reproach got her moving.

*"Well, about damn time!"* Davidoff called.

Oh shut up!

At least, she managed not to blurt that out.

Clipping her line to the ring she saw embedded in the hull plating, CC paid out her tether, then moved further from the airlock along a path marked in black and yellow with a luminescent warning sign: *Danger. Proceed at your own risk. Do not walk without a tether. Passengers may not proceed unaccompanied.*

Click-and-grip: she felt her boots release and take hold again at every deliberate step.

Davidoff turned back to meet her. He, damn the man, didn't just not-shuffle; he demagnetized his boot plates and leapt, coming in for a landing that was scarcely more than a click she felt, rather than heard.

She could see his quizzical face. His helm hadn't polarized. *"So you couldn't resist staring into the sun,"* he observed. *"Bet you won't do that again. Eyes stopped tearing yet?"*

"I didn't get a chance to look the first time I came out here. I was too busy listening to the trainers."

Davidoff snorted, a hollow, absurdly human sound in the immense emptiness that engulfed them. *"Ship's crew. 'Best bonded trainers in the system,' right. Just like your suit. Oh, the Sentry model started life as military issue, but they've prettied it up, added some shiny bells and whistles, and made it user-stupid for the tourists. And to think taxpayers accuse EarthServ of wasting gigabucks! Well, it wouldn't do to let any of Rimrunner's pedigreed passengers stupid themselves to death, now, would it?"*

"Don't tell me you didn't stop to look back your first time Outside." Even though CC kept her voice quiet, the suit's self-contained environment made it echo around her.

*"I cannot tell a lie. I stopped dead in my tracks. Damn near turned into a pillar of salt. My drill instructor caught me; and that was the last time I stopped working till I finished scrubbing the head with my toothbrush to the DI's satisfaction. My very last toothbrush, too, so my squad made damn sure I was on breath spray for the rest of the cruise. Now, come on. See if you can't pick up the pace."*

CC followed him away, clicking, on the hull. Movement didn't quite feel like the simulations on Earth, with water swirling by and light glowing gold beyond the blue waterline at the top of the tank. Out here her suit weighed nothing, but it was still cumbersome. She could smell the cleansers, the dental and skin washes she'd used that morning, and a faint clean smell of sweat that would have sent her running guiltily back to her stateroom to shower if she were back inside the ship.

CC drew a deep breath. Suited up, some passengers complained of claustrophobia and never ventured Outside again. Others glanced out into space and sank into fetal knots on the hull. Both reactions were a severe downcheck for anyone whose job required extensive travel, though usually psych profiling eliminated people likely to panic before they could be hired.

CC drew another breath and waited for her body's response. The realization came slowly, but was enough to halt her in her tracks. She was coming to like vacuum because, for the only times in her life, it let her be physically alone. But that wasn't quite right, she realized. She didn't feel as much isolated as freed.

The sensation made her want to dance in the cumbersome boots, or at least try, but Davidoff was stepping up the pace again. It grew harder to release the magnetic plates, then magnetize them again quickly enough to keep up, without feeling as if she danced a zero-g flamenco. She spared a glance to see how he managed the trick.

Why, Davidoff wasn't using the plates at all! Instead, he simply tugged himself hand over hand along the tether! She checked the tether. She was secure. Demagnetizing the plates, she pulled herself along, following her leader.

With a click of bootplates that he'd remagnetized fast, Davidoff turned and came to an abrupt halt. Of course, he'd felt the absence of vibration from her movements!

*"You damn fool!"* he snarled. His voice echoed in her helmet's speakers. CC flinched, then yelped as, in one smooth motion, he seized her tether and snapped it out so fast he flung her off the hull.

Though she couldn't feel the tether through the heavy insulation of the Sentry's gauntlets, she kept a death grip on where she thought it was in her palm as the tether whipped her out into the blackness. She starfished just as she'd done during the alert—*oh, God, if I vomit in my suit I might as well not bother coming back in!*

Then her body remembered the movements that brought her around and to a stop a couple meters away from the hull: above, below; she couldn't tell.

In space, there was no local vertical. In space, no one could hear you scream except through the comm, and she was damned if she'd give Davidoff the satisfaction.

*"A good DI would kick your ass all the way to Quaoar,"* Davidoff told her as he reeled her back to the hull.

*"Still,"* he conceded, *"the way you didn't panic was nice work. Just remember, unless you're wearing a booster— which you're not—never release your boots like that. Or, so help me, you'll clean every head in this ship with a tooth- brush if I have to make you a spare one myself."*

She felt her boots click down. Hastily, she activated her

bootplates and felt them click home just as her knees started to buckle.

She would absolutely not collapse.

Davidoff came up behind her, making her start. If her plates hadn't been magnetized, she'd have had both feet off the hull again.

"And that's why you don't demagnetize, except in emergencies," he said. This time, he didn't use the comm, but leaned helm cozily against helm.

"Here's an old trick," he added. "If your comm goes out, gives a whole new meaning to the term 'going head to head.' You still think you're going to be sick?"

CC shook her head vigorously. She'd stopped shaking. She was not going to be sick. She was *not*.

"You certainly threw me for a loop," she told him. Was that a snort of appreciation for her pun? He stifled it a second later.

"Good for you!" He paused. "You've not only got guts, you're not heaving them up. So, you win a big, big prize. We're going to let you back into the ship at the end of your lesson. Unless"—he eyed her narrowly—"you want to go back In right now?"

"Not a chance," CC made herself say. "What do we do next?"

Davidoff turned, coiling up the tether as he went. *"Now, we walk around until your heart rate slows, and then we go back In. You've had enough for this shift. I've got . . . something on . . . more damn meetings tomorrow, but the day after, I'll check you out on boosterpaks. That is, if you think you're sharp enough to try them without a herd of trainers baa-ing from the hull."*

*Assuming you have the nerve* was what he didn't say. This, not bigger and better spreadsheets or higher-level meetings, was a real challenge.

*Well, how'd I do, teacher?* Davidoff was supposed to offer her every cooperation, even if his notion of cooperation was pushing her past her groundside limits to the near side of heart failure. The idea he was evaluating her—and probably reporting on her progress to Alpha, at the very least—wasn't paranoid, it was a foregone conclusion.

*When do I get to evaluate someone?*

Maybe, if she survived this mission, Alpha would promote her to senior consultant, then to partner, and she could sit at a desk and wait for reports on the damn fools whose turn it would be to take all the risks and write reports on them. She could follow up on their projects and write feedback all over their reports. Hell, it would sure beat working for a living.

*"Well, what do you say?"*

Davidoff was waiting for her to agree to another training session.

Didn't he know it was another foregone conclusion?

"I'll be there," she promised and followed him back to the airlock's steel womb, lit by a comforting red glow around its control panels. The idea of heat, of showers, of clothing that didn't require an engineering degree to put on or take off felt like paradise regained.


*"Now, let's see you get a move on."* Davidoff started off ahead.

Along the track of ship's running lights, she trudged.

*"Soon as you pass boosters, you'll be ready for zap runs. Assuming you get authorization. We'll start with pods; work up to catapult,"* Davidoff promised, for all the worlds as if he offered a child a treat.

"I EVA'd again yesterday in preparation. Trainer said it was a good test," CC began. "Called it a high pass."

She could hear the feral grin behind his words. *"I'm a hell of a lot more demanding than those ships' nannies. You'll pass to my satisfaction, Williams, or you'll stay Inside with the rest of the flock."*

Damn right, Davidoff was harder on her than ship's trainers. She could write up unfavorable evaluations about them, which wouldn't matter a damn to Davidoff. Why'd he have to push so hard?

Because he'd been tasked with giving her every cooperation. She'd hate to meet up with Davidoff when he was being *un*cooperative.

For a moment she fantasized what it would feel like to strangle him with the tether he'd used the day before yesterday to launch her into space.

*"You wish, Williams,"* came his voice from up ahead. *"Yes, I'm a bastard, but I don't read minds. Your suit recorded your baseline, and your heart rate says you've got a mad on. Or a panic. You tell me which, but just you remember. Panic lands you right back Inside for good."*

CC forced herself to breathe deeply and steadily until the pulses in her temples stopped throbbing like ship's engines.

Davidoff had her best interests, defined as survival out here, at heart. Learning to use her suit well, to anticipate situations in vacuum and microgravity—maybe she didn't see now why those skills would be useful, but she couldn't really expect that Vesta Colony would be just like Earth.

*"Come on, pick up those feet,"* came the next order. *"You want that pod ride, don't you?"*

She had Neave to blame for that pod ride too. Senior people were always being offered ride-alongs, or zap runs as Davidoff had called them, if not by the defense contractors, then by EarthServ itself. When the question—and this dubious excursion—came up, he'd been talking about how it felt to be hurled from a catapult. Neave had been invited to ride along on another zap run now that *Rimrunner* was in the Kirkwood Gap. But he had gone on so many of these junkets he could probably log frequent flier mega-miles just on military spacecraft.

Perhaps one of the others would care to go, he'd suggested. And he'd looked straight at CC.

She sighed, resigned to the fact he'd hear that too and draw the logical conclusion. This wasn't, after all, a pleasure cruise, but work, albeit on a luxury liner. So if Neave offered less senior types his place on a zap run, you damned well joined the throng trying not to scream "me, me!" while putting oneself oh-so-discreetly forward.

At least she could have the brains to be glad she'd been the lucky one chosen. Ordinarily she'd have avoided being alone with a male colleague, especially one like Davidoff. The man had family connections as well as that don't-give-a-shit manner that lured more people than it repelled: time spent with him was time other people could turn into a hot topic at cocktails. Still, the good thing about suits was that seduction would take a can-opener.

Even so, she knew that Neave's offering her the zap run and Davidoff's offering to qualify her, solo, on EVA drill was prime gossip fodder. David IV was probably getting messages already from half the middle managers on *Rimrunner*, including Sandy.

*You know I wouldn't do anything like that! We made promises to each other. They mean something!* she thought. How long had it been since she'd told David that?

*Damn, David, I sure wish you were here.*

The time would come, she vowed silently, when they'd be able to travel together. On business as well as by themselves. And later on, they could travel as a family.

David loved spending time with her, loved going places together. And so did she.

But he had had to know how important training was for her career, didn't he? Even if Marc Davidoff was doing the training. With any luck, and some persuasive letter-writing on CC's part, her fiancé would probably just think she was doing a damn good job networking.

At least, that's what CC hoped.

And meanwhile, she had that zap run to look forward to.

If "looking forward" were the words she wanted.

## 9

**"Ready?"**

"Ready."

*"You sure? They'll get really pissed if you panic and I have to abort takeoff."*

CC's heart rate spiked not just at the coming takeoff, but the threat to her performance evaluation. She checked: still within green. Davidoff had to know precisely how nervous she was: her readings were slaved to ship's boards where he could see them.

Damn the man!

What was the old phrase she'd picked up at beer call with Marc's crew?

"Let's light this candle," she said. Her voice didn't even shake.

Beneath her vacuum suit, sweat pooled under her arms, prickled down her sides to be wicked up in the wickedly pricy fine cotton singlet Margaret Lovat recommended during after-dinner drinks three nights before.

Davidoff laughed the sardonic laugh that never failed to make her want to slug him. *"Your model of Sentry"*—he never let her forget she wore a civilian suit—*"comes with*

*tranks if you need them. Don't play iron maiden or hero,
Williams."*

"Playing hero's your job." CC tried to keep the snarl out of
her voice. She wasn't even going to dignify that crack about
iron maidens with a reply. Besides, she hadn't used tranks
once in all her EVAs, not even the first time she'd boosted
away from *Rimrunner*'s hull without tether, turned away
from the ship and seen only empty space. Her skull had
roared in the blackness, and if she hadn't tranked out then as
adrenaline flooded her system (*"Breathe,"* her trainer had
implored her, *"Ms. Williams,* breathe!"), she wouldn't now.

Davidoff was teasing her, getting her to push past her limits. Again. Promising herself she'd kill him when they got
back to the ship, *assuming* they got back to the ship, CC gritted her teeth. "Don't you have a launch window or whatever
that they get pissed off if you miss?" she asked with poisonous sweetness. She was a veteran of board meetings that felt
like guerrilla warfare. Surely, she could smart-mouth one
smartass EarthServant.

*"Where'd you learn the gallows humor, Williams?"*

"Market crash. I worked the trading desk."

It wasn't quite true. She'd been in physical danger before.
Like the time escapees from a welfare roach-motel invaded
her family's *insula* and stalked her study group on the grimy
tube transports for two of the scariest thousand K of her life.

The others in the group had been for hitting their panic
buttons for Security. CC'd not only argued their scores
couldn't afford the downcheck—not to mention the hefty
fine Outsiders got charged for cop calls—but had kept her
calm. In the end, she'd led her team out and up to the safety
of Ground Level, called in an alarm, and actually gotten the
commendation "works well under pressure" that had
clinched her first internship.

Everything counted. Everything had always counted.
Never mind if you shivered for a week, as long as you did
your shivering where no one could see.

One day, she promised herself, she'd be warm. All the

time. No more cold sweats. But for now, she had a candle to light.

*"Love the banter,"* came a third voice from *Rimrunner* Controls. *"Do you two like sounding like something out of an old vid? Either light this candle now or stand down."*

*"Just checking on passenger morale,"* Davidoff placated Controls. *"On a count of 30. Last chance, CC."*

"I'm go," she assured everyone but herself on a faint breath.

*"Your funeral,"* said Controls.

So they *were* hazing her. Bastards.

She gritted her teeth. Enough hazing, already. At every step of the trip, she'd run into some sort of juvenile ritual that was just funny enough to glaze over the hostility she'd sensed. She thought back a month or so ago to when they'd crossed Mars orbit. Smirking ship's crew had assembled the passengers and brought Mars himself on board. His old-style classic kilted armor had floated up to reveal a red balloon so small that everyone howled, except the crewman who played the part.

They'd had another ceremony when they'd actually entered the Asteroid Belt. This one involved "belting" drinks until you quit, passed out, or wished you'd done either. With brooms, mops, and brushes for those unfortunates who'd lost their drinks. That ceremony had had elements of Saturnalia, she thought, and reminded herself not to pass on that remark. In Rome, during Saturnalia, the slaves had played master. On *Rimrunner,* crew teased corporate types who could buy and sell them once their lives didn't depend on them.

The hazing had ceased being funny a long time ago. Maybe CC'd have enjoyed if more if she hadn't been playing for serious stakes her entire life.

She stared at telemetry, her suit monitors and the console in her seat module. She suspected it wasn't much more than a dumb terminal with a comm line to the pilot.

*What if those lights are the last thing I ever see?*

*Then you don't have to worry messing up your assignment*

*for Alpha,* she told herself. The thought, weirdly enough, was remarkably calming. *After all, you died in the line of duty.*

They might even cancel her debts in tribute.

On second thought, probably not.

But "line of duty" would actually be true. EarthServ ships patrolled, not just to blast the occasional rock if it was too big or too close but to warn off any ambitious pirate types who wanted to check out whether all a ship's passengers had Do Not Ransom on their files or if the ones who did hadn't lied about it.

Her hands were clammy in her gauntlets. The lights flowed and changed. Numbers streaked across her console as Davidoff readied the ship for eject. She changed her mind about the idea they'd have given her a dumb terminal. What if Davidoff actually expected her to work her passage?

Could she?

Catapult launched in three G's. She'd lasted five with only a nosebleed, then blacked out at seven. Not bad for a city girl, the other manager hopefuls said that evening as they'd rehydrated in the big hall where the ceiling zipper showed market closes in New York, Tokyo, Beijing, and Mumbai. That had been one of the last chances she'd gotten, Earthside, to trade carefully calibrated business stories and indulge in the mandatory feral industry chat over who'd bought what or gone where. She'd produced David IV's Shackleton vacation and the Amazon spa cruise they'd been on when they'd decided on a marriage contract. Grinning with pride, he'd flung his arm over her shoulders, and she thought she might break apart for sheer triumph. That one night, she had it together. She had it all. Together they could get it back and keep it, she knew that!

CC knew something else, too. If she had managed to cope all these years with the grueling social aspect of her work as well as the job itself, she could survive riding a high-tech firecracker today.

Only thing was, her gut didn't agree with her brain, and her brain was starting to skitter away in the very panic

Davidoff had warned her against. She watched the seconds tick down. No escape now. It came, actually, as a relief.

Inside had to be paid for. She'd been Inside from the moment Davidoff had started to work with her on EVA and had growled approval in the gym. Not bad shoulders, either. Quite the opposite, in fact.

Marc had even, when he was offshift and not monopolized by ship's crew, showed up at one or two of the hydration and networking sessions that followed dinner. When he'd commented that CC wasn't too incompetent at suit drill, Neave had nodded approval. In public, sealing her current state of doom.

After that, CC basked cautiously in the reflected glory of Neave's approval. Now, instead of migrating around the central points in the room, she found networkers edging up to her. Chairs were held for her, or an extra one found or vacated the instant she joined a circle. She could speak her mind—within reason. She rarely had to calibrate the length she was allowed to talk before someone more prestigious or just nervier would interrupt or before an ambitious junior fought to insert him or herself into the conversation.

There was no one junior, except caregivers and tutors, who didn't play in the same arena and who hadn't, God knows, made accommodations of their own with this game. She could pretend to be one among equals (though some were more equal than others), one among the women in their evening shipsuits, slit, glittering, and jewel-toned. A few daring souls even wore skirts that would billow revealingly upward like sea anemones in the ship's now constantly lower gravity.

CC had run out of dress clothes. Rather than attempt to remake her old clothes or camouflage them with accessories, she scoped out *Rimrunner*'s tiny, select in-flight mall and bought more, choosing the sorts of things she saw the other, more senior execs wear. Then, daringly, she put them all on her Travel and Expense account. Even if it was disallowed, she was pretty certain that her per diem would cover it.

When no one came after her, or when drinks, panic, or spreadsheets woke her in the night, she had to acknowledge it: the scent of success was as alluring as she'd dreamed long ago. She'd already given a great deal to get within striking distance. Now, if she wanted to claim it, she'd have to give more.

*Including a ride on one of these damned firecrackers.*

Sandy, of course, skirmished around the fringes of her meetings. When Captain Aquino had actually included her in a visit to the bridge and found Davidoff hovering there too, Sandy had spoken up. "Reality check," he'd called it. Feedback. It felt like an attack.

"Do you know what you're doing?" he accused. "You're making a spectacle of yourself with that man."

"I'm lucky to have the opportunity to learn EVA techniques with an expert!" she commented. "And it's not like the whole ship isn't watching."

"Do you have any idea what people are saying?"

"I'm sure you'll tell me."

"He may be a Davidoff, but he's *EarthServ*. So don't go thinking you're trading up!" Sandy told her. His face flushed so she could almost see the fine white microsurgery scars through his careful cosmetics.

"Trading up's your game," she'd retorted.

It was as much as her career, let alone this recent acceptance, was worth to hint that Davidoff's cooperation was all part of a confidential assignment. CC was a big girl. She knew how to keep her eyes on the goal. The goal was getting the job done, with Davidoff's help. That being the case, she could keep her mouth shut. Besides, the past weeks had been fun. She'd learned to counter the stares of women who looked her over, calculating the worth of her clothes—not to mention David IV's ring—with cordial poise that felt more and more natural. Gradually, most of the stares subsided. People got used to seeing her work out in the gym, attended if not by Davidoff, then by some of his friends in crew. Often, Margaret Lovat stopped by—probably the most prestigious chaperone in space history.

But now it was time to pay the piper.

*"Counting down from ten,"* said Davidoff. *"Breathe, CC."*

*"I'll kill you."* Heart-rate didn't even flicker. Talk about hostile work environments!

*". . . Eight . . . seven . . . six . . ."*

*"Other way round is far likelier. I'm the one flying this thing."*

*". . . Five . . . four . . . three . . . Enjoy the ride, Ms. Williams!"*

Just one big damn happy family.

*"Don't worry,"* Marc said. *"I've never lost a passenger yet. Or had to eject one. Don't be . . ."*

Which was more arrogant? Marc's family or his service? She didn't know. Then, as her weight, most of it on her chest, tripled, blood drained from her brain, and her harness seemed to want to cut into her through all the careful layers of her suit, she didn't give a damn.

As she'd been taught, she drew deep, careful breaths, counting them till she was sure she could breathe without heaving in her suit.

Now her body remembered the drill. It was even good at it! She had a lower center of gravity, shorter extremities for blood to drain from; no reason she couldn't . . . and then the g-forces subsided to nothing, and she had control of her own mind and body again.

Medical telemetry still showed solid greens.

*"How're you doing back there?"* Davidoff asked.

"Not dead yet. I mean, nominal," she replied. "Where're we going?"

*"To coin a phrase, thataway. Routine patrol,"* Marc said. *"I'm going to let you access geo-scan. Ignore greens, blues, and violets. They're too small to matter. You see anything orange or red, sing out. And it goes without saying, if you see anything else that doesn't look like the manuals, don't worry about distracting me. That's what we're here for."*

Marc confirmed successful launch. Then she heard the double click of optical scans and weapons-unlock, in case he had to blast some hapless chunk of rock out of *Rimrunner*'s trajectory.

*"Geo-scan's active."*

"Got it," CC said out of a mouth that was suddenly very dry. Not just a zap ride, but real responsibility.

Eagerness, anxiety, sheer fear—all the emotions she'd felt since she first held a job—crowded back, pushing her heart rate up.

*Breathe.* CC breathed.

*"Oh, and CC? Pilots have a prayer for moments like this. Want to hear it?"*

CC dropped the water tube in her helmet so quickly she splashed herself.

"Sure. What's that?"

*"Dear God, please don't let me fuck up."*

"Amen." She meant it.

She kept her eyes down, fixed on geo-scan. If she saw a rock and reported it, that would be good, wouldn't it? But in general, though, it would be better if they didn't have to fire at anything. That would mean *Rimrunner* would have to re-calculate course. All the passengers would have to spend a tedious interval strapped in. As the ship changed G's and vector, they'd probably be shipsick.

We *want* boring, CC thought. We *don't* want heroics. Right? *C'mon, boring!* she urged geo-scan.

*"CC?"*

"Yes?" Wasn't there another way to say it? Was she supposed to say "aye," like the O'Brians and Foresters she'd read before she realized she wasn't supposed to admit she could spare time for pleasure reading?

*"Breathe."*

She breathed. Then chuckled. To her surprise, Marc laughed, too.

"Marc?" she asked.

*"Got a problem?"*

"Is this ship the fastest thing we've got?"

*"Short range, yes. But you've got to remember, none of our ships are really fast. One day"*—she could hear his voice change, even through the static of the comm—*"we'll beat*

*the speed of light and then, we can start talking about real speed."* He chuckled. *"I know. 'Dream on.' That's what everyone says about it."*

He paused. *"This ship may be a turtle, but it's a lively one. Want to see what it can do?"* he asked.

Another goddamned test. Oh lord, she was going to hate herself, but if she didn't agree, he'd probably write her off.

"May as well," she agreed. "Just don't forget, this is the first time I've sat geo-scan. I don't want to screw up my concentration or mess up my suit."

*"It's already screwed,"* Marc told her, and put the ship into a steep bank that became a flip: one side, then the other. *"Ever hear of a thing called an Immelmann turn?"* he asked.

"Why do I think I'm going to regret anything you—" She couldn't control her yelp of fear and shock as everything, especially the contents of her stomach and inner ear, turned upside down. Lights exploded in front of her eyes, including the ones on scan. . . .

*Damn, if Immelmanns caused malfunctions like that, it was a wonder . . .*

It was gone.

"What's that?" she demanded. "Marc, I just saw a streak, bigger than the ones we saw when I was EVA. . . ."

She breathed, forced her eyes back to geo-scan, then breathed again. "Will you for God's sake stop playing games?" she asked. "Don't we have a . . . flight pattern to follow or something?"

He brought the ship level, whatever attitude that was. G-force pushed her back into her seat rest, so she knew they were accelerating.

A frantic study of geo-scan produced a useful touchpad labeled **REPLAY**. She captured what had streaked across her screen, attached coordinates, and shot the data to Davidoff's console.

She knew he received the input. But the silence between them seemed long, stretching out to infinite embarrassment.

She had overreacted. He had given her a responsibility, and she couldn't carry it out.

"*Shit*," said Marc Davidoff, followed by "*Rimrunner, come in, come in. We've got a bogey. I'm transmitting geo-scan. Expanding visual range to max.*"

*If I saw a meteor, a big one, aren't we supposed to go after it and shoot it out of the sky?*

That was the question CC wanted to ask, but she didn't dare. She saw boards light, heard a whine, a click, and verbal confirmation as weapons systems came on line. Another click, a flash of light—retinal scan, she told herself—and a password meant he'd triggered systems that, in ultimate necessity, would turn the small, fast ship into an extremely efficient weapon of mass destruction.

"*CC,*" he said. "*Open your seat rest. Underneath you. There's an evac module. Get into it now.*"

She thought Marc said he'd never had to eject a passenger.

Well, there was always a first time. She'd be bobbing around in space, just hoping he'd come back for her, or someone else would come out. It triggered her worst fears: she had always been expendable and, compared with an expensive ship filled with important and expensively trained people . . .

Would she have the courage to open her suit, then blow the mod apart rather than watch the clock tick down to zero on her life?

"You're wasting time." She was astonished to hear how level her voice sounded. "It'll take me 3.2 minutes to get into the pod assuming I hit my best time, which was unsuited. Then you'll have to eject me. And then, assuming you don't mean to fry me boosting away, you won't be able to accelerate. Let me come along for the ride. It'll save time."

She could hear his fingers drumming a fugue on controls. It would take even longer for him to unstrap and force her into the pod. How terrible. She'd annoyed him. But she was right.

"*This isn't a business junket anymore, CC,*" he warned her.

"I won't shriek all the way to the event horizon or the black monolith or whatever the fuck it was I saw, I promise you. I can even trank out if you tell me. But I was the one who saw the bogey. I want to see this through."

*Just don't make me sit staring into infinity while my air runs out.*

Her screens shifted. Medical telemetry doubled: now she saw his scans, too. Blood pressure, unbelievably low: heart rate, heightened. Blood chemistry? Marc was flooding his system, letting the adrenaline take over.

"Marc, your bio-signs are way up. . . ."

*"We are professionals, CC, we're used to this. I'll manage. Now, let's get down to business. I'm linking you to Control. If I say quiet, you shut up. If I say talk, you talk. I know you can talk, dammit. Rimrunner, I need to fly this thing, so I've put Williams on scan and audio. Scans are slaved to ship's systems in case. Williams will give you eyewitness. Yeah, yeah, I know . . . but she's already here, I don't want to take time dropping her, she's got a level head, you'll know that when you see the whole record. CC, talk, dammit!"*

"You saw geo-scan," CC began. She didn't stammer in board meetings, and she wouldn't stammer now. "We'd just survived an . . . Commander Davidoff called it an Immelmann turn. At first, I thought it was just my eyes playing tricks on me, but I saw a reddish streak, shading past red to violet at . . . you've got the coordinates. . . ."

She was very calm now. Every one of her evaluations had commented on her ability to take stress. Now, she had a job to do. She would do it well. And the first thing to do was transmit the data so they'd see and not have to mention on what surely wasn't an open channel but was still too open for security's sake that she'd seen that streak, too massive to be a meteorite, flame as if it traveled under its own power.

*"Moving fast,"* came *Rimrunner.* *"Whatever it was, it was a big sucker."*

Language, CC suspected, was modified for present company's tender ears. Waste of time to say she'd heard worse on the trading desk.

Did pirates get that big? She'd thought they were small,

dilapidated vessels—little more than miners adapted to carry heavy guns. This far out, though, there was no telling.

At some point, she'd have to deal with her once and future gadflies, but right now, the idea just made her tired. She watched scans, waiting for orders.

They came. *"Marc, you can't match course with that bogey. It's too damn fast. And big enough you better not try to take it."*

*"I'm going to hail it."*

"Negative, Marc, negative."

*"What is it, that's the question,"* she heard herself asking. *"Tachyons wouldn't be visible. That thing I saw was sublight. But what can move that fast?"*

She fell quiet, flushing with guilt. She'd promised not to get into the way. They had a job to do, and they didn't need a privileged civilian clamoring for attention.

*"All good questions, Ms. Williams. And we're going to do our best to answer them. With luck, you'll get to be part of the investigation."*

They sounded as if they expected her to thank them for the privilege.

CC sensed Davidoff's unwillingness to abandon his own questions by how slowly he brought the ship around.

*"We're coming home, Rimrunner,"* he said. *"Better set out the welcome mat. Heat up the oil, and get the thumbscrews ready. Or, alternatively, the tranks. I could use some."*

## 10

**The debriefing after CC's zap run lasted a good, or bad,** depending on how you looked at it, week, with time off for bathroom breaks and the occasional nap. Meals were brought in and out by uniformed personnel, not ship's stewards, along with fresh clothing.

Thereafter, Captain Aquino didn't just suspend zap runs, much to the disappointment of other mid-level management types who'd hoped the privilege would trickle down to them; he cancelled EVA training for the rest of the trip Out and doubled up on drills. RUMINT floated through the gyms, wafted through the dining rooms, and damned near got posted on the stock-market zippers in the business centers, while legends of Close Encounters, Grays, and First Contacts were murmured over during after-dinner drinks. About the only thing that didn't get whispered about was anal probes, and that was only because no one wanted to be accused of creating a hostile work environment.

CC decided she was frankly grateful for the endless debriefings. At least all Aquino and his crew did was ask question after question—or sometimes the same question, hurled at her when she least expected it to see if she'd answer it any differently this time—about the bogey she'd seen. Maybe their insistence was intimidating as well as a bit of a bore, but it was certainly better than being stared at and whispered about by the other passengers. You'd think she was a CEO awaiting indictment!

Then, abruptly as the rumor mill started, it shut down. Someone must have sent a memo. She tried finding out. The one time she hinted for information from Davidoff, he played so stupid that she decided not to speak to him for at least two weeks—or ask anyone else.

Released to her quarters, CC coded them for privacy, reviewed her orders, accessed Vesta's archived trading records, and settled down to some serious computer work.

They knew where she was. If another bogey showed up, they—whether she meant Davidoff, Aquino, *or* the bogey itself—would simply have to come and get her.

Then, *Rimrunner* began final approach to Vesta, and all bets were off.


*Rimrunner* had locked itself down to protect against impact with some of the larger chips off Vesta's four-billion-year-old block. Now Captain Aquino opened a forward viewscreen so those of his passengers who weren't shipsicles or tranked into "oh wow" levels of composure could watch final approach. As one or two pointed out, they'd paid enough for the privilege.

Along with her handmaiden asteroids and the occasional meteorite, Vesta made her 1,325 day orbit about 2.36 astronomical units out from Earth in sublime disregard of the Titius-Bode law that governed the spacing of heavenly bodies. Each of its "days" was roughly 5.34 hours.

Vesta was one of the largest asteroids at which *Rimrunner* was more or less scheduled to stop, offload shipsicles and cargo, and pick up raw materials and hardcopy mail, before the ship reached terminus at Ganymede, circling Jupiter. Possibly, Vesta had been formed as part of radioactive "shrapnel" from the supernova that might have created the solar system, giving ancient creationists crises of faith.

Wonderful thing, that zipper below the viewscreen. It spoon-fed *Rimrunner*'s passengers the usual announcements: EarthServ wanted its budget boosted in the next triennial appropriations to begin patrols; at least three NGOs had plans in incubator companies and the researchers were drooling. In envirosuits, no less.

Then, the zipper lit with a briefing about Vesta, starting with the history "factoids" about Vesta: discovered in 1807 by H.W. Olbers, mapped exhaustively by the Hubble Space Telescope, and studied in the late 1990s and in the first part of the twenty-first century from Earth by scientists such as Ben Zellner, Rudolph Albrecht, and Richard P. Binzel. NASA's Dawn mission, led by Carle Pieters, was the first of many sponsored not just by the entities that had started life as NASA, the American Geophysical Union, the United Nations, and an NGO that mated a finance holding company with the engineering/intel concern formerly known as Bechtel.

Smaller than Quaoar, Ceres, and Pallas, about neck and neck with Juno, Vesta was in the same plane as the Earth's orbit, the only asteroid whose high albedo let it be seen from Earth with the naked eye at opposition, perihelion.

With the viewscreen on magnification, Vesta resembled a flattened watermelon, if you assumed there could be such things as flattened watermelons the size of the old N.A. state of Arizona, about 325 miles, or 525 kilometers, in diameter with a surface area of 200,000 miles.

As *Rimrunner* made its careful approach, Vesta didn't so much grow larger as increase in brightness. Definitely, Neave had commented to people on open comm, a bright spot in the firmament. He had laughed at the dutiful groans that had resounded throughout the comm system, but it was true. In its odd, desolate way, Vesta was beautiful. It had a dark and a light hemisphere, formed of yellow-green basalt rich in pyroxene and feldspar, rock that formed when lava flows cool and solidify below a planet's surface. Vesta's surface was darker, but a cataclysm had exposed an upper mantle largely composed of olivine, resembling much of the mantle of Earth itself, in parts of the asteroid.

Take Olbers Crater, an immense, 285-mile-wide impact basin. It had probably been created by an accident that had blasted more than half a million cubic miles of rock into space, exposing the asteroid's molten core, and probably shifting its rotational axis so that the crater wound up near the south "pole" as the asteroid toppled.

But the crater wasn't the only astonishing thing about the asteroid. Jutting up from Olbers Crater like a giant bull's-eye was Mount Piazzi, a peak some eight miles high. On it, the colony had constructed the highest communications mast in the solar system. Naturally, it was the one from which all financial transmissions were sent. Proceeds from these transmissions financed Piazzi Observatory and the Galileo Array.

Naturally, almost the first thing humanity had done when it first reached Vesta was nearly come to blows. A dispute had broken out among the mining ships that had raced out to stake claims, the scientific vessels that were as greedy as all nonprofit organizations, and the various military vessels that had come out to watch the fun and, incidentally, to protect the other ships against suicidally ambitious pirates.

The fight was reflected back on Earth by vicious disputes about whether it was safer to build a rotating space habitat above the asteroid's surface, giving workers some reasonable gravity and letting them shuttle down to the surface each work shift, or whether it was more cost-effective to build a habitat within the asteroid itself.

Here, Vesta's unique characteristics enabled it to take precedence over Ceres and Pallas. Through the ability to bore "down" 150 miles to Vesta's long-cooled core, it was too important simply to be a scientists' nirvana. Instead, it became the gateway to all the asteroids and the bases now laboriously under development on planetary satellites like Titan and Ganymede.

Habitats built onworld had to be built as if they were ships or surface vehicles. They had to be cylindrical or spherical, and they had to be shielded with hundreds of feet of rock. Because it was easier to access Vesta's mantle, the prospector ships with their tools, their mining equipment, their mass drivers, and their smelters, chose to set up bases within Olbers Crater. Deep within it.

*Briefing completed.*

The zipper went dark, and the viewscreen blanked. *"Secure for deceleration,"* ordered Captain Aquino. The ship braked hard. For far too long, the only thing on everyone's mind was breathing despite the weight on their chests.

Switchover from atomic to chemical engines came in a shudder that rocked the ship, making passengers glad of their restraints. Now, slowed to what would be a crawl even for a groundcar, *Rimrunner* initiated final approach to its first port.

All along Mount Piazzi, lights erupted and shifted in intricate patterns that meant life itself to the ship and instructions to its navigators. As *Rimrunner* followed the welcome-home-use-this-vector pattern of Piazzi's lights, external cams came on to show passengers how the ship's own lights winked in patterns that probably sent immense streams of information to the techs and controllers staffing installations sealed deep within the rock that, geologically, was so much like Earth's.

"There's no up and down, no up and down," CC reminded herself in a whisper as the mountain slid by them in a direction she wanted to call horizontal, "only attitude."

She made a mental note to tell David IV. Even he had never seen anything like this. It was something she could do for him, even when they were this far apart.

Viewed from her acceleration rest, Mount Piazzi looked needle-thin. But scientists battled with business interests over each cubic meter of available space. Along with the laboratories and the Galileo Array of telescopes, Piazzi was the site of one of the main stations for Bloomberg Boosting

Unit transmissions from the other asteroids and the gas giants' colonized satellites to the more densely settled inner planets and Earth itself.

*Rimrunner* shuddered and twitched like the horse CC had once seen in an animal preserve with David IV when a fly landed on its flank. Past more and more of Mount Piazzi it braked, its rear jets rudely turned toward the stars.

Wouldn't this be one hell of a time for a bogey to show up? No one had mentioned bogeys for at least three days now, which made CC suspect that some poor bastards were on bogey-watch right now.

The screen blanked. When it cleared, it was filled with an image of the asteroid's surface as they moved in toward the horrific scar of Olbers Crater.

Now rock reared overhead, blotting out the stars. The ship had transited the peak and was now within the crater. More lights bloomed around them. Some of those lights, CC knew, were the Colony's camera eyes that relayed every one of *Rimrunner*'s course microcorrections to Vesta Port telemetry.

Additional lights—white, green, and red, with the occasional amber and blue—erupted on all sides of them, directing them toward a docking bay deep within what would have been the asteroid's mantle. It was like looking at the guts of an Earth from which all magma had long since cooled.

Every so often, they passed actual viewpanels, actually triple layers of one of the incredible hardened new plastics developed on the Station (CC had watched StellaPlastex's IPO with tremendous interest, wishing she could have bought in) in case of the unthinkable: a fuel explosion or a collision with an incoming ship by one of the tiny shuttles, pods, and lighters, or the more ponderous scarred miners that lumbered back and forth within the crater.

Once *Rimrunner* actually passed the lip of Olbers itself, ship's screens lit with a fabulous 360 view of what was now not so much an ancient devastation now but a high-tech pueblo. Behind those sculpted rock walls or the naked rock that jagged and jutted between lit, therefore habited, areas were the public and living spaces of Vesta Colony itself, if you didn't count the domes—those huddled masses yearning to breathe recycled air—cobbled together on the actual surface near some of the observatories and the mines.

Like a good worker bee, CC had done her homework. Once the Vesta Colony developers evolved past the domes-and-dig construction phase and could exploit the crater itself, builders turned for a model to the arcologies, invented in the twentieth century by the mad Italian architect/philosopher, Paolo Soleri, as a model for the homes they planned to build deep in the asteroid's caverns.

Vesta Colony was an incredibly sophisticated adaptation of Paolo Soleri's "Nudging Space" Arcology. It represented a fusion of two architectural forms, the Apse and the Excedra, into a structure Soleri called "Apsedra." What it looked like, in the holographic rendering she had seen, was a halved artichoke whose upper third had been sliced off and the choke removed. Its leaves were separated, but still attached to the lower center.

Soleri's original plan called for the habitat to have a solar "garment," that allowed the sun's rays to enter and trap the warm air produced both by chemicals and hydroponics. That would serve well for the inhabited parts of the crater floor once Vesta Colony grew past its cliff-dweller origins. Then, the colony would exult in large, open spaces with central common areas, sheltered by a semicircular curved dome.

Rimrunner's belly-cam showed where the first curved ribs of the apsedra were already going up. (It had been financed by century bonds, CC reminded herself, based on the 19th century railroad bonds of the western United States, though some fixed-income analysts said that even century bonds were way too short-term for successful planet-forming.)

But Vesta Colony's architects and engineers, possibly influenced by insurers, if no one else, had actually taken into account reports from psychologists. As a result, they'd hollowed out not just long tunnels but actual open spaces within the cliffs of the crater's edge. Once the entire construction was complete, several centuries from now—assuming a constant rate of inflation-adjusted funding—it would mimic the apsedral structures that would also blossom on the crater's plain. Vesta Colony would turn the ancient wonders of Earth like the Great Wall, the Pyramids, or more recently, the Vehicular Assembly Building or the third Space Station, into a child's creative playthings. She gasped to see how beautiful it was.

The ship shuddered, then stopped so suddenly CC had the sense they were still moving. Captain Aquino's voice announced that *Rimrunner* was now secured in its docking bay. Imagination brought CC the sound of an immense hatch, like a cyclops's eyelid, clanging shut behind them.

They were down. Safe.

At least for now.

## / 11

**Even before the main cargo tubes snaked out from Vesta** Landing to *Rimrunner*, techs trundled its shipsicles on float pallets offship into the Colony's hibernacula where they would sleep until needed. That had to be the only time in those poor SOBs' lives that the last would be first.

Through ship's cameras, the *real* passengers, as they regarded themselves, watched (with the occasional complaint to the bridge that landing was taking a ridiculous amount of time) while the main docking tubes were mated to the ship's hatches. Then debarkation lottery numbers were issued. Almost instantly, in-ship communications lit with more complaints of "ridiculous." Now, "outrageous" got added to the lexicon. When protests of "outrageous" didn't succeed, they were followed by special pleading and attempts at bribes and trades by people who'd spent their careers breaking into lines.

Debarkation would proceed as the captain intended. Once the shipsicles had been transferred, even before all the tubes were secured, *Rimrunner* offloaded passengers with medical challenges, sealed in protective bubbles and tended by suited attendants. She saw Davidoff, also suited, propel himself out of the ship in company with some off-shift crew. Knowing it would infuriate the passengers—probably also knowing which passengers it would infuriate most—he waved for the cameras.

Finally, the tubes were fully extended and mated to the colony. *"We are beginning debarkation. Stay in your state-rooms until your number is called. Please do not use in-ship communications unless there is an emergency."*

Outraged entitlement did *not* constitute an emergency.

Ordinarily, CC would have assumed the Neave-Lovats would be among the first to leave, trailed by their children's tutors, but Margaret Lovat had insisted she didn't want special treatment. And what she didn't want, she didn't get.

CC's own number was midway in the scheme of things. So she spent her own waiting time adjusting the weights around her waist so they were in balance with her phone, her lifesigns monitor, and the other hardware she would learn to put on as readily as a bodysuit. She glanced at the chrono woven into the sleeve of a shipsuit modified to look as much like formal corporate wear as possible. It had been one of her first "bespoke" purchases. She adjusted her hand luggage. Her Breitling PDA beckoned, but if she started to work, she'd lose track of time and possibly miss her deboarding call.

Wouldn't that be a great way to arrive in the Colony—with the crew annoyed and the passengers she'd held up furious at her? So, no messages for her.

A light flashed onscreen, accompanied by a ping on her Breitling, alerting her in case she'd actually been able to sleep. The Captain had called her number, a good fifteen minutes before she'd expected it. Either the process was remarkably efficient, or someone had jumped her to the front of the line. She could hear the rumors starting now.

Mustn't keep the crew waiting! She pulled herself up too quickly, secured herself from bumping softly into the bulkhead she had thought of all voyage as "ceiling," and headed for the hatch.

\* \* \*

"New in town, little girl? Looking for a good time?" came the questions, in a deliberately offensive dockside croon.

CC braced, instantly hostile. Then, of course, she had to save herself from a recoil that might have sent her up against the nearest wall. Of all the things she had expected, after the hand-over-hand pull through the tubes into Vesta Colony proper, she hadn't expected a street-hassler. Let alone one who chuckled as she tried to save herself.

Newbie be damned. CC didn't have to put up with harassment. The law said so. She turned, opened her mouth to read some poor fool the riot act, and found her heckler almost doubled over with laughter.

"CC Williams, by all that's unholy!" Mac Nofi, secured by thumb and forefinger circling a stanchion, pulled himself up and greeted her with the shit-eating grin he'd learned at Texas A&M. His buzz cut had receded halfway up his skull from where she remembered, but he was still the lanky beanpole she remembered, "half Jack Mormon, half Italian, and all straight arrow," as he'd always liked to say. Even here, so many hundreds of millions of miles from Earth, Mac managed to look as if he'd just ambled in off an oilfield, and his grin only added to the effect.

*Why am I not surprised? It really is a damn small solar system these days.*

Mac had been just the right height—"not to mention the right stuff" as he'd always boasted—to squeeze into a pilot's berth. He'd taken to space like a cat to cream. Wangling his way into the space program a year shy of a doctorate, he'd used his years of service to pay off his loans. When he'd finally taken his discharge, he'd been canny enough to turn his lack of a doctorate into a career plus. It let him avoid the "why do you want to leave research" whammy at interviews long enough to turn on the Texas charm and talk himself into a line of work where he could actually make serious money.

Mac had always been able to get beyond the mask of appropriate behavior CC had taught herself to wear. Now she felt her face split in an answering, spontaneous grin. "Mac, what in hell are you doing out here? Did they figure the work environment was already hostile enough that they didn't need to worry you'd screw things up?"

She caught some of the other passengers staring, started to apologize, then drew herself carefully up. All right, so she'd paused in debarkation and actually sworn at a colonist. If she was being recorded, those were downchecks. But a colonist had actually come to meet her, which had to outweigh them.

*Oh hell,* CC told herself. Fuck *the point-scoring. Mac's a* friend. CC stared into the reception bay, trying to orient herself.

"My God, will you look at that!"

"I had a bet with myself you'd say that!" Mac grinned. "People either gasp over the view, or they grab for a barf bag and want to turn around and head back home."

Reception's horizon was far closer than Earth's, but CC felt no compression, no claustrophobia. The architects and planetary engineers who'd designed this place had factored beauty as well as safety, utility, and cost-effectiveness into the equation. And dear Lord, they'd done their work well.

Mechanically driven lights floated across the vast space. Glinting off crystals in the "ceiling" hollowed out of the asteroid's rock, the movable lights cast shadow-arches of an almost Gothic shape onto lightweight, movable pavilions woven from filaments that looked white in some lights and glinted with subtle rainbow sheets in others. On each pavilion glowed signs: Customs, Medical Services, Security, and other agencies whose signs were tilted or too far away for CC to read them clearly.

A metal plaque set into a polished boulder told CC that what was now Hospitality Bay had been the site of the first settlement to migrate from Vesta's surface into Olbers Crater. She brushed her hand across the metal. Holograms shimmered, while a voice, scarcely louder than a murmur, told how the very first colonists lived in hermetically sealed versions of twentieth-century Quonset huts Outside while the demolition engineers set off carefully calibrated explosions in the caves, enlarging them, polishing them, then sealing them so that the settlers could move Inside.

For the first two generations of immigrants, the requirement had been simple: sign over all resources to the colony and receive in return a share of the construction bots, the rock, the life they were building.

But construction wasn't over. Ten years after the First Ship settlers had moved from Outside, they'd begun to cut the true apsedras that now housed most of the colony half a mile high deep within Vesta. Expansion was still going on, the plaque said. Excisions, the "nice" word for controlled explosions, were regularly scheduled for delta shift, and all Vestans were drilled (CC moaned inwardly at the pun) in how to fasten down their belongings and what to do in case of an emergency.

"Put your head between your legs and kiss your ass goodbye," said Mac, eavesdropping.

CC thought of aiming a mock-punch at him, then realized she'd probably knock herself out with the reaction.

The holographs projected by the plaque shimmered with the courtyards and central gardens of the housing complex, the sealed causeways that joined the units, the shared facilities . . . the shared future.

This housing looked like *insulae*, CC thought, flashing unpleasantly back for an instant to her own childhood in collective housing.

Only these people were free as hers had never been. Giants in the Earth. Or on Vesta.

Any of the descendants of those original settlers had to be so rich that they could cash out, return to Earth, and never, for the rest of their children's children's lives, concern themselves with meeting expenses, productivity, value-added, the bottom line, or any of the other jargon clots that regimented her life.

She sighed.

"All through with your history lesson?" Mac asked.

She sighed again. "It's really amazing," she began politely when she realized an answer was called for.

Then she realized history wasn't nearly as crucial to her as the location of the nearest toilet.

"Uh, Mac," she began, glancing frantically about for the "woman in a skirt" icon that meant toilet facilities all over the solar system even in places where skirts weren't worn.

Mac grinned wickedly. "You were the smartass who just *had* to have a history lesson before you'd even checked through Reception. Change in pressure affects everyone that way. You'll get used to it."

"Mac, dammit!"

He kept leading her forward. "Won't be long now. Wait till you see the Apsedras. That panel doesn't do them justice. And you wouldn't believe what plants can do in what passes for gravity around here. They grow like seaweed, hundreds of meters."

*I don't want to water the damn plants!* she thought, gritting her teeth.

Secured by cables, spun of metal, not rope, the pavilions resembled great sails. The way the lights and shadows flickered on them made them seem as if they were in motion, shivering in a nonexistent wind, minimizing the possibility of claustrophobia. Some people, she knew, couldn't take the sense of being enclosed and had to be drugged till the next ship arrived, then shipped out. That was the sort of corporate downcheck you never recovered from. Disability law notwithstanding, premiums on a new policy would bankrupt you for life, assuming any carrier would cover you.

"Helps not to think how many quadrillion tons of rock lie overhead," Mac commented helpfully.

CC thought of deserts, of dryness, of anything but how awful it would be if she lost bladder control out here in public. *An anxiety dream, only real.*

*Vesta's been seismically dead for eons,* she told herself. *Nothing's going to happen to you. Well, maybe something, but you don't have to worry about explosions, quakes, or collapses.*

She bared her teeth at him. "Do you haze all your visitors?"

"Just our favorites. Come on, let's get you settled. Find you a head, too," he added slyly. "Do you think you can move on your own, or shall I offer you my arm, ma'am? Don't worry, I won't make you laugh or tell you you should have gone before you left the ship."

CC batted at him. The spontaneous motion made her drift a few meters before she caught herself, while Mac yelped with laughter. Damn. She'd fallen for that newbie's trick good and proper.

The person behind her muttered "ridiculous," taking no particular pains to keep his voice down. The one behind him murmured "favoritism." Holding up lines was a severe breach of etiquette.

"Sorry," CC said, a kind of all-purpose apology such as she'd spent most of her life making. Bump into wall; apologize to wall. Hell of a life when even the walls outranked you.

She made herself start forward again. Whatever happened from now on, here was where it began. Adjusting her weights, CC took two careful steps that—dammit! She'd practiced and had a right to do better than this—extended so she was bounding toward Mac far more quickly than safety or decorum allowed.

Mac held out a hand and steadied her. The grasp turned into a bear hug.

"Welcome to Titoville."

"Titoville? How'd you ever get the naming rights?" she asked.

Either the holding company that governed Vesta Colony had gone sentimental, descendants of the first financier in space had seriously paid up, or Mac was pulling her leg. Serious money had had to change hands for assigning someone's name to any significant part of a colony—aside, of course, from memorials.

"It's what we call Vesta's financial district," Mac said. "If Dennis Tito's heirs want to slap a cease-and-desist on us for taking his name in vain, they can haul ass out here and serve it in person."

Mac pulled out his Breitling, a worn, outsize thing, so they could exchange IDs. "I'm beaming you the standard orientation. Berthing, office, maps, health center, gyms, that sort of thing," he said. "We're in Reception, right off docks. I'm the welcoming committee. Don't worry; you're not that high-visibility. This is all on my own initiative."

"Greetings," CC said, matching Mac's sarcasm. "We're from headquarters and we're here to help."

"And we're happy to see you," he completed the ritual of lies, grinning like the coyote in a holo he'd once shown her. "Now, let's let this line move along!" He took her arm and leapt deftly aside before she could yelp in surprise.

"Here come the tourists," he murmured as other passengers stumbled or floated out of the tubes. "Don't I know some of them?"

CC crossed her legs. Just a little longer, she promised herself and tried to think of something, anything, else.

Like watching how Mac and Sandy greeted each other with more reserve. They tried to calibrate each other's corporate status and, just incidentally, test each other's handgrip. Bet that wasn't all they calibrated, then cautioned herself *Don't think of toilets!*

"Try that again, mister, and I'll put axial spin on you," Mac muttered through the obligatory charm.

*I wonder how Mac would like Davidoff? Assuming he doesn't know him already.*

Mac never really had taken to Sandy. "Boy hasn't done his time," Mac had said once. And yet, Sandy'd bootstrapped himself up the same way that she had.

"Matter of attitude," he'd muttered the one time she'd gotten up the guts to ask over late night drinks. Then, he'd glared at her. Men's house things, she'd told herself, a line from an old anthropology course. She hadn't ventured to ask more.

"Let's go, CC. I know you're in a rush to get to work, not to mention the head, but I can push you up the learning curve in terms of settling in. Here. Give me some of that gear. You won't be needing most of it anyhow!"

One hand on her shoulder, her old friend propelled her

from the reception area "Seriously, it's great to see you. And will you look at that ring! Enough to weigh you down even in Vesta-g. Good hunting!

"But you know, CC"—Mac shook his head almost imperceptibly—"you really may want to take that thing off. Yes, I know it's pretty, and I know what it probably cost back on Earth if your fiancé paid retail, yes, yes, I know it's an heirloom, I was just yanking your tether. But the damn thing's big enough it could unbalance you—yes, I'm joking!"

Mac kept moving her forward. A floating lamp showered light onto her ring, which damn near exploded with a blue-white radiance.

"I know it's pretty, and God knows it's got sentimental value. But it's just that no one wears things like that around here, and if you jumped wrong, you might—it's a long shot, but Murphy rules out here—hit something you didn't want to hit. Besides, we need to get you out of the monkeysuit and into honest clothes. Tell me, who's the lucky guy? Is he one of the good ones?"

CC felt her face split into a grin that Mac instantly called goofy. Her briefing on David IV lasted long enough for Mac to propel her past the base of one of the pavilions used for immigration and processing. The structure shot up what would be at least four stories on Earth, each story consisting of a platform three-quarters open to the immense cavern. The thin fabric glinted in white and pale blue and silver whorls and volutes, held rigid by cables and wires, but quivering in the airflows of Life Support.

Shining through the fabric, set into the polished stone of the walls, were glowing screens that ran with red and green letters, charts, and symbols: Vesta's lifeblood was information. Rather like her own. She was so curious now that she forgot just how much she wanted a bathroom. That urge would come back in a rush, but right now, she was thankful for small blessings.

High overhead glittered a screen the size of a small shuttle showing markets systemwide: stocks, bonds, water futures, and cash (various currencies). Interest rates. The screen split to show ships' cargoes and the premium or loss per ship's share.

Mac guided CC to a pavilion with the Customs insignia glowing in red over the entryway. An electronic whine drew her attention. A float bearing two uniformed men angled down from a bay high in the vast reception cavern, towing several large pallets. From far off, she heard the shouts and laughter of children racing toward their homes, their leaps enormous in Vesta's near-weightlessness.

Mac gestured CC into the Customs pavilion, a lopsided pyramid divided into cubicles by panels of the same fabric that formed the exterior. CC raised an eyebrow: people were being processed in each of those cubicles, but she couldn't hear a sound. Apparently, the fabric provided excellent insulation.

"One thing, no, two things are certain," Mac said. "This David IV of yours is a lucky bastard. And you're going to have stories to tell when you get back. Hope he appreciates you."

"It's a good partnership," CC assured Mac eagerly.

"Yeah, right. That's what I told myself right up till I had to thumbprint the dissolution agreement," he grumbled. "Some agreement. Well, at least she agreed to a partial property split. She got the diamond mines. I got the shaft—and just about enough to pay off my debts."

CC seriously didn't want to go there. She remembered hearing that Mac's marriage, to a perfectly appropriate engineering manager, had been sucked into the gravity well about the time he'd accepted assignment on Vesta.

Not surprising, she supposed. Being an expat was tough. For Mac, at his seniority level, to have taken an off-Earth assignment meant he'd have had to have been desperate to keep his job. Well, she wasn't going to ask him about *that*.

At least, not now.

When had he switched from private sector to Vesta Colony management? It had to have been some time during the last few years. She was embarrassed to have lost touch.

That he'd sent her that message and bothered to look her up—well, either he was a good guy, lonelier than she wanted to believe, or he wanted something. Or, if Mac was still the man she remembered, probably both.

She murmured something he could take as comfort if he liked, then turned toward the Customs Agent. This was a woman about her own age, stocky in a blue shipsuit with the red Customs insignia over the sealed breast pocket marked "Arroyo, Lani." Her hair was long and clipped back, unlike CC's careful chin-length trim. The woman looked her over.

"This your prize newbie, Mac?" she asked with what was more a smirk than an honest smile.

*Did you expect handshakes and Welcome to Vesta? Resources are scarce out here. Anyone who's settled in has a right to know if you're going to pull your weight or be one more useless mouth.*

"Sure is, Lani. Pay no attention to the quaint native dress. CC's straight off the boat. She'll adapt. She's good at it."

CC assumed the head-down, deferential quiet that worked with bureaucrats on Earth and held out her hand baggage to be searched.

With a snort, Arroyo gestured for CC to search her own gear. When her bag was empty, the woman ran a scanner through it, then prodded it with a stick.

"You can repack now," she said and watched while CC scrambled to shove garments, disks, and toiletries back in before they drifted off into the next booth. She made no effort to help, even when a red-labeled disk started to drift walkabout. CC made a long arm, anchored herself by wrapping her leg around a table leg, and lunged, catching the disk before it drifted slowly out of range.

Damn, where was that bathroom? Or, as Mac called it, the head?

Lani shrugged. "Not bad. You're vouching for her, Mac?"

"Alpha posted the usual bond. But I'll be answerable."

CC considered calling for a supervisor. "What's that mean?" she demanded. "I take responsibility for myself. And right now, I'm holding up the line. . . ."

"Go over to the rack by workstation five," Customs Officer Arroya instructed. "There's a battery of procedures. The help icons will guide you through." She brought her palm over her screen, which blanked, then lit with another entry.

Next! It didn't seem like a good time to ask where the facilities were.

Baggage dangling from one arm impeding her motion, CC let herself coast over to the black metal seating rack Arroyo had pointed out. She secured herself in its frame by the workstation, hooked ankles around the footrests so she wouldn't drift, then accessed the menu marked "Assimilation Procedures."

And welcome to Vesta indeed, Ms. Williams. We're just *so* pleased you could join us.

Retinal scan. Application for debit account. Blood test; dear Lord, she'd been through so many of those it was a wonder they didn't prescribe—yes, here came the list of medical requirements, including vitamin supplements, schedule for full-spectrum light immersion, and centrifuge hours.

The thought of reasonable gravity started her shifting even more anxiously from one leg to the other. "That way." The Customs Official, come to check on her progress, sized her up expertly and pointed. "Mac should have set you in the right direction off the bat, but we've tightened security, and he knows it."

For a moment, the woman looked blessedly human. CC started to get up and float over "that way."

"Do yourself a favor," said the woman. "Vesta's drier than you're used to. It'll play hell with your skin, and if you've got sinus trouble, ask Medical for drops."

"Thanks," CC said and escaped before she made a public spectacle of herself.

"That way" meant a restroom attached to Customs in a small side pavilion. Even more blessedly, it was a low-g model she was familiar with. Just in time, she assumed the position, braced herself, and let reclamation whoosh.

Feeling infinitely better, CC "washed" her hands in infrared before studying herself in the polished rock that substituted for a mirror.

She looked like a perfectly appropriate, rising young consultant. *Monkeysuit. Dump the ring.* But those had been warnings Mac had given her about the culture here. It was never smart to disregard that kind of information. Vesta had its own culture, it seemed, and she'd have to learn them the way she'd learned all the others.

By the time CC emerged, Mac had secured both her completed immigration agreement, which he beamed into her PDA, and a baggage float. She took a small step that she hoped would send her soaring onto it, but lifted right past.

Damn! She'd had too much practice to make a newbie goof like that! She grabbed a stanchion and swung round, letting the micro-g buoy her as the floater coasted forward. A map lit, showing her position as a blue light with a number—her personal icon for the duration of her stay—on the Colony grid. *You Are Here*—with a vengeance.

"Past the *Challenger* Memorial," Mac said. "Intersection of MacAuliffe and Gagarin." As the float picked up speed, it beeped gently in warning and headed down a corridor whose stone sides had been smoothed over except for the occasional handgrip or some really astonishing crystal formation that reflected yet outshone the human-made lights. Display screens gleamed, embedded in the rocks, along with directional beacons. Light tracks rose from the floor. At regular intervals, red signals showed where emergency gear—vacuum bubbles, lights, and breath cylinders—was stowed.

Up ahead shone a greater light.

"You're about to see something beautiful as we head into the Apsedra itself," Mac told CC.

"Apsedra?" she asked. "The original design called for solar collectors. Aren't we kind of far out for that?"

"No, no solar collectors. We get some sun, but it's not enough. What happened is that we took the old Soleri designs as our model and made the best of a really bad blasting job. During the first years of hollowing out the area we're about to enter, one of the explosions went wrong, and we got a cave-in. Good thing Vesta's geologically dead, or we'd have had no choice in the matter and have had to abandon the whole area, and we already had cost overruns that stretched from here to Earth. So we faced a choice—either start from scratch in a different place or cover over the break. Wait till you see!"

Chatting happily, Mac led CC into the Apsedra.

"There!" Mac said proudly. "Probably the largest viewport—viewports, actually, they're composite—in the solar system."

The hair on the back of CC's neck stood up as she looked up. Words like "cave," "ceiling," "window" all failed her. Hundreds of meters overhead, a great crack, covered with clearsteel, let in the starlight. It should have been overshadowed by the lights set into the immense cavern, hanging lamps that glowed off the curves of the Apsedra, like the petals of a colossal artichoke, hollowed to enfold thousands.

Vast and intricate as the Apsedra was, that glimpse of starlight overhead overwhelmed everything else: the protective leaves of the housing units, the floats and transports that darted from leaf to leaf, the lights that glimmered deep within them, the green of the carefully maintained gardens, walks arching above them, on the cavern's floor. Vast as the structure was, many of its units were dark, waiting for people to come to fill them. And the cavern had room for twice as many additional petals. Room to grow.

She craned her neck until she swayed in the thin, dry air.

"Vertigo's normal," Mac said. "Air here's thin, as Lani said. It can play hell with your sinuses."

He eyed her narrowly, and CC realized he was scanning her for signs of agoraphobia. Another damned gatekeeper.

"I'm fine," she said. "Let's go."

A klaxon blared in the chilly air. Red lights went off, and plates slid from panels concealed within every passage leading to the Apsedra, sealing it from the rest of the Colony.

One or two of the other immigrants screamed, and CC jumped so quickly she almost fell.

Immense panels slid out from the rock ceiling and crept across the face of the immense viewscreens, clashed, paused, and ground to a halt.

## / 12

**CC shut her eyes. Quick.** *Remember the time Marc flipped you off* Rimrunner's *hull. Remember when you saw the bogey and insisted on going along for the ride? You didn't panic then, and you're not going to panic now either.*

Time stopped as she waited for whatever was going to happen to happen.

How would she go? A crack, expanding, exploding into vacuum, with air and final screams whistling into space as the last things she heard? Would the whole preposterous armature come crashing down?

Adrenaline shocked through her. Suddenly, she felt immensely strong. She'd pick up her gear and leap to safety. Now, that couldn't be right. The doors had been sealed, and she wouldn't have time to grab emergency gear and scramble into it, even assuming she could unseal the area before her air ran out.

Mac chuckled, breaking her out of fighting trance. He looked down at the timekeep woven into his shipsuit's sleeve, then showed it to her.

"Nothing like the weekly checkup for putting the fear of God into newbies," he told her. "Look up again. They've got a false roof inset in the surrounding rock. It's a blast shield made out of ship's plating, good as anything on board *Rim-runner*. It can seal off the whole cavern roof in thirty seconds, nowhere near enough time for you to start breathing vacuum."

High overhead, the immense mechanism whined, rumbled, and ground to a stop, once, twice, a third time.

"When it's working, that is," Mac said. "Assuming the gears don't jam. Or shed spokes or something."

"Damn you," CC snarled. "I'm no engineer, but I know that contraption up there doesn't have spokes. What's fucking it up?"

"Don't know," said Mac. He lifted his wrist, turned away, and spoke into his throatmic.

"They're sending maintenance floats," he said.

CC tore her eyes away from the metal plates, half extruded from the rock "ceiling" of the cave. No use fearing what would happen if the damned things came tumbling down. Focus instead on the Apsedra itself, that preposterously beautiful artichoke transplanted onto a sterile ball of rock. Focus on the Vestans, going about their business, or the other disembarking passengers, who didn't have as knowledgeable an escort as she, now being talked or tranked out of panic attacks.

"Here comes the first float," Mac said. He did a damn poor job of concealing his sigh of relief, probably just as he intended.

The float whizzed out of its bay and up into the cavern.

She heard beeping and alarms, then a banging overhead.

"Percussive maintenance?" CC asked.

"Sure," said Mac. "Even out here, sometimes, all a machine, even a big one like that, needs is a good swift kick."

Sure enough, the gears meshed. With a beeping and a sweet flash of green lights, the plates slid across the clear steel viewport, securing it.

"Three minutes. We'd have lived after all," said Mac. "Show's over. Let's move it on out."

He held up a hand, summoning another flitter that hovered close to the shining floor.

"Intersection of E&M, Edwards and MacAuliffe," he instructed its map panel.

*"Hyper Building,"* the flitter's recorded voice intoned.

"That's a hangover from the original design. No one calls it that anymore."

*"Hyper Building consists of approximately 45% residential units,"* the machine droned on over Mac's voice.

"Can't you get better vocal quality?" CC demanded.

Mac laughed. "Low priority," he said. "Besides, some of us with bad taste actually like the old Cylons, as we call them. You can look up the reference later."

*"Space includes 14% commercial space including offices and production facilities, 5% administrative, and 5% infrastructure maintenance. Hydroponic bays represent 14% of the total area. . . ."*

"What's the remaining 15%?" CC asked the flitter.

*"Cultural zones and recreational facilities. Additional office space is planned."*

"Wouldn't you just know it!" CC said.

"Cylons aren't noted for their sense of humor," Mac said. "As AIs go, they're dumb as a post."

Glancing from her perch on the flitter, CC saw many paths that sloped away from the central halls that provided "flight paths" for people who chose to leap, rather than walk in magnetic boots down to recreational facilities. Not to mention the areas Mac didn't mention, marked off by closed booths, not pavilions, and bearing red lights. That had to be Security. Other ramps led down to Vesta's fledgling maglev system for transport to facilities beyond Hyper like the solar power generation plant, docking bays, and research facilities.

"Orientation tour's required within forty-eight hours of landing," Mac said. "Once you take that, let me know what you want to see in more detail. I can get you some real guides."

"If it's all the same to you, once I figure out where I am on the grids, I'd actually enjoy taking the standard tours."

A red light flashed over her old friend's face. He shrugged.

"Once you've passed Security checks, it's your funeral. Hope you've gotten more sense than the time out by the LA reef, do you remember—"

They both laughed. CC told herself she imagined the apprehension in Mac's face.

The flitter plunged further inside the residential complex, united to other complexes by passageways at several levels.

"Anything you want to buy on Vesta, glance into the unit's beam. Payment's triggered by corneal scan, linked to your debit account. I'll give you a quick lesson: buy me a beer. I promise you, you won't like the price, but it'll give you the basics of shopping here. Local products are cheap. Imports—expect to pay through the nose. And—here we are!" he announced. "Transient quarters. I wangled you an upgrade. All the comforts of home at a tenth the cubic space!"

He beckoned CC forward to present her PDA, then "sign herself in" via optical scan. The door slid open, red lights showing the presence of emergency gear even before the cabin's main lightstrips went live.

"They do their best to make you feel as if you've got more room than you really do," Mac said. "Can't have our guests feel as if they're buried under umpteen quadrillion tons of rock. . . . You wouldn't believe how many people need tranks once realization finally sets in."

"Mac, I'm seriously trying not to think about that!"

He grinned like a wolf.

"Tranks in the facilities, not to mention exit pills in case things really go wrong. Not to worry. Well, make yourself at home."

The door slid shut. A swoop of almost sheer, glittering fabric divided the living (and eating) areas with their cushioned seating racks, table (with clips for trays), and storage/heating areas from the sleeping quarters. She gave her luggage a nudge into the sleeping area, where it stopped against an extruded ledge with mattress and straps, under which lay folded what looked like a very inadequate pillow and coverings.

"Yes," Mac laughed. "We won't say what that looks like. After a while, you'll get used to sleeping just tethered, not tied down. And if you can adjust the temperature to your liking, why do you need to get tangled up in a lot of bedclothes? It only has to be laundered or recycled anyhow and that's expensive. Unless, of course, you like hiding under the covers?"

He was hazing her again. More damned tests. Always more damned tests. She'd be glad when the door would slide shut and leave her alone, assuming this place wasn't monitored. She let her glance slide to the control panels. Her icon had already shown up on the screens.

"'Fraid so," Mac admitted. "Vital signs, check, at the very least, and there's a microphone or two about. I shouldn't say this, but you can probably find someone who can tinker with it. Meanwhile"—he pointed with his chin—"bathroom's over there. We make our own water, pun intended, but showers take power because we have to put spin on 'em. You'll get a dribble, not a spray unless Infrastructure's feeling generous, which it mostly doesn't. Smart money around here says use the ones by the centrifuges in the health center," Mac said.

CC parked her handheld in the slot designed to accommodate it. "On board *Rimrunner*, workouts were mandatory. Same here, I assume?"

"We assume our colonists and visitors are adults—unless they're not, in which case, we assume their parents are smart enough to keep their kids current on their workouts and calcium supplements. If you know what's good for you, you'll exercise. Incidentally, if anyone wants to buy your centrifuge time, don't sell it! Unless you plan on never going back, you have to keep up habituation to one g. You'll find calcium tabs in med-storage, over here. By the way, CC, if you've got a family history of osteoporosis, better speak up now, or the disability types will make your life living hell."

"My records are on file," she said. "Alpha wouldn't have sent me out here with that kind of liability."

One wall in the sleeping area held storage space, more drawers and lockers than CC thought she'd need until she opened it and discovered how much of it was occupied by emergency gear. Not that a suit, comm, torches, and a pod would make that much of a difference, but you had to try.

Work area, check. Chairs, if that's what you called the cushioned version of the seating rack she'd occupied in Customs, two. The bed's scant coverlets inflated to form pillows for additional guests. The third wall was covered by a nubbly fabric in tones of copper, beige, and blue-green designed to remind the inhabitant of Earth. When she pulled it aside, she saw that the entire wall was composed of viewscreens.

CC drifted over to controls, called up Earth Mean Time as well as Vesta Standard, and set up screens for the markets she followed.

"Smart to get on Vesta time ASAP. Nothing's more of a downcheck than missing a meeting because you were still on ship's time or Earth Mean. You can program any view you want from the library. Earth, or space. Whatever. The screens split, so you can project slides on one of them while admiring the scenery. Rumor is they monitor what views you use, and if you look like you're not adjusting well, Medical pays you a little visit."

"And finally," Mac said, "look what I got for you!"

"Looks like a blank wall to me," CC said.

"It is. But look what we have here: deluxe set of markers, just like you'd find in the very best boardrooms! You can decorate it in any way you choose in your nonexistent spare time. Shrinks probably check it out—there's no getting round the fact we live in a fishbowl, but they say painting or collages or whatever you plan to do with it can help compensate for sensory deprivation. If you don't feel like decorating, you can always use it as a whiteboard. Alpha still obsessed about flowcharts and slides, what they still called PowerPoint warriors back when we were all still Earthbound?"

"It's all gone holographic."

CC finished stowing her computer, her disk storage, and her clothing. She sized Mac up: simple shipsuit in a russet brown he'd never have worn back in an Earth office, with a deplorable plaid shirt (damn, she even thought she remembered that thing!) thrown over it. Face plumped up and unlined thanks to the negligible gravity. Her own makeup and corporate gear, even adapted for Vesta as well as the best stores on Earth could, looked all wrong! Being "all wrong" might not be the worst thing that could happen—nothing to rank up there with explosive decompression, say; but it showed you didn't understand the culture and, if you didn't take immediate steps, meant you wouldn't get information and would probably be on your way out if you didn't take immediate steps.

Mac had given her one hint she could take right away. Reluctantly, CC slipped off her ring and other jewelry and locked them carefully away. Depending on how her body reacted to Vesta's artificial ecology, she'd hate for the ring to slip off or stick into her finger and have to be cut off. David IV had smiled so happily when he gave it to her, proud it was a family piece, shy that he hadn't been able to buy her one with his own money.

"Do I have time to change before I report in?"

"Good idea. Time to get lunch too. Now, about food. We eat pretty well here. Lots of fruits and greens. We're light on meat, which shouldn't surprise you, but you can have all the tofu and lentils you want. Food's available in everything from food courts to four-star. You can even order in, but it'll cost you. And if you eat in too much, Medical will—"

CC sighed.

"So once you're changed . . . let's have some sort of meal. Vesta Standard time calls it lunch. My office. It's in your Breitling. I'll even break my own rule—I'm saving my money—and order in. I want to talk to you."

She'd never heard Mac talk so much.

*What's all this helpfulness going to cost?* she wondered.

He had to have some apprehensions. After all, she was investigating a community he helped run: the least he was likely to want would be information, probably assurances she was in no position to give because Mac, her dear old friend, might well be near the top of her Suspects list.

"Well, if I don't break my neck in the bathroom," CC called, deliberately cheerful, "I'll be with you soon as I've changed out of my monkeysuit!"

## 13

**Mac's office was in Hyper near the main Colony Management** pavilion at the intersection of Onizuko and Gagarin about half a klom from guest quarters. CC had expected him to lead her to another of the pavilions. Instead, his office was carved out of Vesta's rock. A Navajo blanket hung from one wall, shivering a little in the micro-draft that meant air was circulating just the way the Life Support gods planned.

Attached to other walls or clipped to the seating racks— no, Mac had by-God chairs, equipped with homemade seat belts—beside the extruded shelves were the other personal items Mac had smuggled "upstairs," God only knew how. His screens were live. Below a row of viewscreens showing different parts of Vesta Colony were his computers. On one, CC identified a set of curves that meant he was tracking water futures: consumption against the orbit of the ice chunks that represented frozen assets on which traders tried to lock in the best prices.

She saw him glance over what looked like a resource-consumption histogram. Vesta's infrastructure? She was immediately curious. But it was rude to stare at other people's screens. She glanced away just as he minimized the chart and brought up an image of . . .

"The Alamo?" she asked. "Mac, aren't you kind of over-doing the Texas thing?"

"Don't know, CC. I kind of like famous last stands," he told her. "Take a look at these instead. Souvenirs of a mis-spent life."

He stretched back in his chair so he was only secured by the cobbled-together seat belt, and reached for the collection of spectacularly useless baseball caps tethered to one ex-truded rock shelf. One was marked A&M, of course. Others represented his various missions, a roadshow or two from an NGO, and even one antique cap in mint condition that bore the NASA logo.

"That one must have cost you a fortune," she commented. "Assuming it's real."

"It's real, all right. Saved a man's life in EVA. A gift I couldn't refuse. One thing's certain. If I ever want to go back home, all I have to do is sell this stuff. You wouldn't be-lieve the offers I've gotten from some of the tourists."

No holo of his ex, but one of a very slender, very dark woman, her hair pulled so severely back she might as well have shaved her head. Almost sculpturally elegant, the woman's long face resembled the Ashanti masks CC had seen in museums, with some Asian admixture. She blinked at it, recording it, without seeming to notice.

"Elizabeth Inui," said Mac. "Very special lady. She's reg-istered principal here for Morgan Nomura. She wants you to sit in on meetings with the EASD examiner."

CC groaned, aimed herself at one of the chairs, and buck-led up. "Since when do you run EASD errands?"

"Consultant or not, you've got to meet the Earth Associa-tion of Securities Dealers sooner or later. She told me to ask if you could manage a breakfast meeting, tomorrow, Vesta time."

The answer to that had to be yes.

CC shrugged. "What I do for my friends. And my job. I suppose I have to meet with her some time or other. But Compliance isn't one of my favorite things. And EASD is a major pain."

"Elizabeth said she'd send you a briefing. You'll like her," Mac said. "Promise."

Was that an assurance or an order? Looking to change the subject, CC pointed. "Will you just look at all this stuff! Thought you had to sell off the clutter when you went off-world." The costs of baggage and offworld imports made Mac's collection worth a small fortune.

"I made some good trades. I know I'm a pack rat, but—" He shrugged. "All the comforts of home. Get homesick, you drop by, and instant feelgood. Now, what about lunch? Menu's in the reader on the table," said Mac. "Chinese?"

There'd probably be enough cornstarch in it that it wouldn't slosh off the bowls.

"Fine!" she said and grinned as she beat him to the debit. "I'm on expense account."

"But just remember, you still owe me that beer. Make yourself at home for a couple minutes," Mac said. "I've got a few details to tend to. 9/11 Day's coming up, and I've got to draft an invitation to your Mr. Neave to come to the market's opening. I need to make sure he's got the times straight."

Despite Vesta's five-hour rotation, its business day was standard twenty-four Earth hours, firmly tied to Greenwich Mean Time. Wouldn't do for one of the colony managers to mix the two up and invite an Earth VIP to watch the markets open at the wrong time.

His computer buzzed.

"Yeah."

"How much cubic they want?"

"Give it to them."

"Right. Not alone. No, not that, asshole!"

CC floated over to a chair and belted herself in. The crudeness of the language reminded her of her earliest days, right after her first wrist-jack surgery, doing scutwork for traders. She raised an eyebrow. More of a question than that was rude.

"Idiot down in vents," Mac said. "Had a run-in with the gardeners." He gestured, indicating on his workstation's holo just how far away the disputed territory was. Looked like the newest part of the colony's excavations.

CC nodded. The door buzzed, then opened.

"Let him pick one of the toys on the shelf against the wall," Mac said. "Trinkets, mostly lost and found or discards. He can sell it. Better than a tip."

CC occupied herself by setting out the food.

Even though the sauces were just as gluey as CC had guessed, the protein cultures and hydroponically grown vegetables were tasty, pungent with spices that were also grown in the labs. And the tea, which came in sealed bubbles, was piping hot. CC felt her stomach settle, reassured to be on a planet again, even one as small as Vesta.

"So," she asked, sopping up the last of the sauce with rice as if she suspected it might float away, "how'd a nice guy like you wind up in a place like this?"

"Not quite the career path you'd have expected?" Mac squirted tea into his mouth. "Ruth thought I was going to hell in a handbasket too so she bailed."

"I thought you two split before you went expat."

"Yeah. Career in the toilet. Company in the toilet. So out she went. Only had a five-year contract anyhow. How many years you and this David IV of yours signing on for?"

"Ten minimum," CC said proudly. Family stability was a status symbol these days. He'd wanted five years; they'd compromised on ten and a pre-nup. She took a look at Mac's face. He was staring over at the Alamo, glowing on screen.

Again, his computer buzzed.

"Commander? Sure, I can see you."

So could CC: Davidoff. He just had to turn up, didn't he? Mac turned down the volume on the com and edged his shoulder up and around in the age-old signal of "private call."

"Yeah, it's been quiet here. You were gone. Meet? How's about now? Got a fellow passenger of yours here, CC Williams."

A long pause. Probably telling Mac to get her unclassified ass out of there.

"Well, she'll probably be glad to settle in. So I'll expect you for beer call. You bring the beer. Yeah right, I was joking. Fine."

Mac was shaking his head at her. "CC, do you mind? This is security business. . . ."

"And I'm not cleared."

*I saw that bogey that made Davidoff go white around the eyes. I was in the ship when it flew chase. But I'm not cleared. All right. I know nothing, nothing. But it's all going in my report.*

There being nothing else she could do, she shrugged assent.

At some point, she'd have plenty to say to the gadfly from her past and the gadfly from *Rimrunner.* But right now, the idea of one more thing to do just made her even more tired. She'd be glad to settle in.

Even if he was weaseling, Mac had just given her the perfect out.

She apologized, unbuckled, drifted up from her seat, and aimed herself toward the door as it hissed open. And managed to get back to her quarters without losing herself or her lunch.

Home sweet home.

Light as the grav was, she was back on solid ground. She strapped herself into the strange bunk. Maybe she could actually sleep.


Too experienced with travel to let culture shock get her sick, CC squandered half an hour on a nap, lulled by the rush of air through the vents carved into Vesta's rock. It was soothing, like being back on board *Rimrunner,* but without the sensation, even at the most basic level, that her environment trembled as it rushed through space. Vesta, like Earth itself, circled the sun in a great dance, part of the larger dance of solar systems, galaxies, and a vastness she tried never to think about; but the ancients hadn't coined the term Terra Firma for no reason.

*Probably, they'd just gotten off a ship,* CC thought as her internal clock woke her. The sullen glow of the red emergency strips gave her a bad moment until she realized they were never dimmed, and she'd just have to get used to them.

Maybe she could think of them as firelight, although any fires around here were signs of deadly danger. She hadn't missed Mac's little comment about exit pills. Well, it was better than waiting for air to run out, she supposed.

In this grav, it wasn't hard to drag yourself out of bed at all. She felt rested, even exhilarated. Must be something in the air, or the fact that, finally, she was where she needed to be and could start in on the work that would either make her or break her.

She opened the port beneath her quarter's data screens. Ignoring the cables for jacking in, CC linked her machine into VestaNet, and started her first search. The screen flickered, blanked, then resolved, as she cursed under her breath. The bars of her charts flickered and expanded into red and blue fountains. Warning lights erupted and her machine squealed.

Some hacker had slipped into the Net, spotted her logon, and invaded her machine with a stripsearch that would override its firewalls, upload its data, then wipe its drive. As if it had been physically attacked, her machine squealed. Its controls and keyboard locked almost simultaneously, meaning she couldn't access the defenses she'd loaded her system with before she'd left Earth.

If she lost her data, she could kiss her job good-bye, and her return ticket was up for grabs too. Damn! Praying the stripsearch hadn't gone too far and that auto-backup still worked, CC yanked her machine simultaneously free of VestaNet and its docking port.

She hesitated over the unfamiliar control panels. Now what? If Computer could sustain an attack, what would be next? Life support? Communications buzzed, making her jump in a way she was sure simply fascinated medical telemetry.

*"Security. We're showing a computer crash."* It was one of those Cylons. The sound was not reassuring. *"Please say or press one if you require medical assistance. Say or press two if you require technical assistance. If you do not respond within thirty seconds, your account will be transferred to a live representative."*

What did they do, buy those recordings from the lowest bidder? Well, some help wouldn't come amiss. Briefly, CC considered not responding for thirty seconds. Better not get a rep for lack of cooperation her first day on Vesta. She sighed. "Two."

She heard the snap, crackle, and pop of open air, then a click that meant the alert had been transferred to higher priority.

*"Ms. Williams? We report a computer malfunction in your living quarters. Please be sure to close down systems before you remove your hardware from its docking port."*

"Is that the first thing you registered, when I pulled my machine clear of the docking port? I didn't want to yank it free," CC said, instantly defensive and resenting it. "What I got here, well, if it wasn't a stripsearch, it was a pretty good imitation thereof."

Silence from the comm. If she hadn't been interrupted, she was probably giving whatever tech she'd been assigned to new information.

"The firewall collapsed. No, I wasn't jacked in, of course not, or we wouldn't be having this conversation. No, of course, I haven't tested my system yet. And I'm certainly not going to try reentering VestaNet till someone checks out my hookup. The sooner the better. My meetings start tomorrow, and the meter's ticking."

*"We'll have someone there in fifteen minutes."*

Now that was a sign of how anomalous the stripsearch was. If Corporate Computer thought your incident was low-priority, sometimes you could wait for hours. Days, even, or longer if they lost your file, which was something they never admitted doing, but happened if you'd seriously pissed them off or were low rank, and they were busy.

CC had barely moved after she pulled her machine from its port, but she still was breathing fast. Even in the controlled environment of her quarters, she'd worked up a sweat.

She drew a deep breath, ordering herself to stop shaking!

She wasn't hurt. She had never been in any danger of being hurt. She rubbed her wrists over where her old wrist-jacks had been and allowed herself two full minutes of sitting and shivering over what might have happened. Her system might have taken a bad, even a fatal, hit. If she'd been jacked in, her brain could have been fried or at least shocked beyond the repair capabilities of an outpost this far from Earth.

With her debt levels, she'd have been spare parts, for sure.

*Playtime's over, CC. Back to work.*

Not daring to link into VestaNet, she started her system up again. It whined, ground, and took its damn time while she sweated, but systems managed to load. She ran diagnostics, found and cleaned a few bad sectors, and did a quick backup before help arrived.

Rescue showed up, a tech with a toolkit and assumptions of her idiocy around complex systems. Once she set those straight, her wall unit as well as her personal machine got a rapid and thoroughly competent checkout, followed by assurances that VestaNet was tracking the stripsearcher *and* congratulations (which would be noted in her Vesta files) for the presence of mind and speedy action that had preserved her data. Did she have backups?

CC shrugged. Of course she had backups, even though any civilized place she'd ever worked downloaded and stored in hardened offsite areas at least each hour. It wasn't the backups that mattered. It was the fact that her system held sensitive data that didn't belong in outsiders' hands.

She saw the tech out and sealed her door.

Whether or not that had been a genuine attack or a decoy, it had been altogether too easy.

A red light flashed. Messages already? She wouldn't be surprised if Mac knew she'd already fought off a stripsearch, but why would he want to expose just how good his networks were by calling her?

Not Mac after all. Locator numbers from Sandy and from Margaret Lovat. A call and a matrixed spreadsheet from Elizabeth Inui—not her assistant? You'd think a Series 24 would have at least one assistant, but Vesta seemed perpetually short of staff—to confirm their breakfast meeting once the market opened.

*"Once we're done, I'll walk you over to Security for the tour. Better sooner than later,"* this Ms. Inui added in a surprisingly pleasant voice CC liked already.

*That's one for you, Mac. If this spreadsheet's as complete as it looks, I think this friend of yours and I are going to get along just fine.*

Somewhere around the third workbook, CC's right eye was twitching from strain. She pulled out her drops, scooped a few slow globules out of the air, and was back into Inui's spreadsheets' intricacies when the comm buzzed.

She jumped, rising so far out of her rack she was sorry she hadn't used the belt. Pulling herself back down by a handhold jutting conveniently from the padded frame, she accessed messages.

*"Message received from Marc Davidoff,"* announced the Cylon.

*"How's my favorite corporate clone,"* he had the audacity to begin. *"I've got a hotel-office setup over at Hyper 4A: 12–31. You know, if you're out of practice, you forget things. So, you want to go outside for some suit practice? My kind, not yours. I'm going to be in and out, so keep trying!"*

As if she hadn't anything better to do.

Damn the man!

## 14

**CC woke in a darkness broken only by the sullen gleam of** tiny emergency lights leading to the survival gear in its locker set into a polished stone wall of her quarters. She flailed, disoriented, and felt herself almost drift above the surface of her bed.

Damn. It had been another of those nights. She unsnapped her tether. Two enormous strides took her to the shower, where she sealed herself in for nowhere nearly long enough.

Tugging on one of the drab coveralls she had seen the Vestans wear, rather than the bespoke adaptation of formal dayware she had bought on Earth, CC tapped the wall dispenser for a bubble of what tasted and hit her nerves like pure caffeine before she headed out.

She unsealed her door and propelled herself out into the corridor.

"Watch out!" Three red-jumpsuited brats on tethers bounded past her, followed anxiously by adults whose controlled leaps showed that they'd passed their free-motion tests. Clearly, children born here would have to learn the controlled leaps of Vestan movement as soon as they walked. But even the youngest children, who went tethered until they passed their free motion tests, were much less unsteady on their feet in Vesta's so-called gravity than some adults. Many visitors struggled the entire duration of their tours with tethers and weight belts.

The bounding children resembled, somewhat, the holos of children skiing that CC had sometimes seen in the offices of top managers. For that matter, David IV had skied before the market plunge that wiped out a good deal of his family capital when he was ten; he still reminisced on every appropriate occasion and some occasions where, as CC felt, it was misplaced. Networking was one thing: counting coup was counterproductive. But that was David for you. Sometimes, he simply enjoyed living in the past. With her own background, she knew just how he felt about it. He'd learn to be more self-protective, he promised.

Moving cautiously despite the extensive freefall practice that she'd been able to substitute for Vesta's free-motion test, she retraced her movements to Hyper's main hall. She looked up at the crack in the towering ceiling of the cavern, and glanced away, fighting a panic that threatened to compel her to find the nearest cave and hide, screaming. Not that caves might be any refuge: she could too easily imagine how the ground, though volcanically dead, might shudder, how rocks would topple from above, or snap upward from below, crushing bodies and her precarious illusion of safety before the darkness and the vacuum reigned once again.

Definitely, she told herself, an "Apsedrin" headache. She grimaced, then grinned. Better a bad pun than a trank. Now, if only she could remember to tell it to Mac when he was drinking something.

Well, time to get to work.

The immense screens set into the polished rock walls glowed, showing "Titoville" preparing for the formal opening of its trading day. Two men and a woman, awkward in an Earth-style suit rather than the more practical shipsuits and jackets CC noticed here, clustered around an old-style bell. She didn't even want to think of the shipping charges for lugging that thing out to Vesta. As the woman struck the bell, followed by polite applause, someone shouted "play ball," a cry echoed by the raucous traders' laughter that was a constant any place there were markets. Even though, in point of fact, the Solar System's markets, like Earth's, never closed, that didn't diminish the ceremonial importance of ringing the bell when delta shift yielded to alpha and "Titoville" officially opened for business on a Greenwich Mean Time day.

Which meant CC had better hurry. Pushing her leaps a little more than was strictly cautious, CC headed downslope to Elizabeth Inui's office.

High status; low altitude. That trend had started in the very early part of the twenty-first century after attacks on open-air high-rises had been a common fear. Vesta Colony took it one step further. Top brass tended to hole up in hardened underground lairs that state-of-the-art virtual reality technology enhanced as much as possible. After all, exposing chief executives and board members to sensory deprivation could impair their judgment.

Textured matting softened the rock floor. Lavish stands of plants camouflaged the polished walls. Stems and leaves were attenuated, more spindly in the lower g than their Earthside counterparts, but as healthy as fertilizer and full-spectrum light could make them.

Inui herself answered CC's signal. A tall, slender woman with the startlingly wide chest of a mountaineer or a third-generation Mars colonial, she wore a reddish brown jumpsuit and the matching thin-soled shoes that indicated both formal business dress on Vesta and the fact she didn't need boots or shoes with magnetic plates.

"Come in," the woman invited, reaching out to touch CC's hand, but without the pressure that might have propelled her across the room. CC glanced down, noted that Inui's wrists didn't even have the smooth marks that indicated where wrist-jack scars had been removed. Of course. If she was a Martian colonial, she'd grown up in a culture where all people were valuable, except criminals and those who refused to work (a very small number).

"I hope you're hungry?" Inui asked.

CC murmured the polite little murmur that indicated that information, not breakfast, was her reason for being there.

"I think we can do better than that," Elizabeth Inui told her. "Please sit. If you're more comfortable belted in or you want a cushion, don't hesitate."

CC launched herself at the chair her hostess indicated and belted herself in. Safely seated, she could glance about the room. One wall, as she had come to expect on Vesta, was covered with flat panels, each shimmering with cascades of numbers and mosaics of charts, changing as the Outer Planetary Markets shifted.

A zipper over the screens carried time-lagged newsfeeds from throughout the Solar System. On another wall shone a mural of First Landing on Mars, in the best NeoPolitical Realist style that turned even the Martian sand into something noble and made the animated replica of the first Voyager robot look positively heroic. It made CC, cynical after seeing too much realist art, want to snicker, so she looked away.

The room's chairs were covered in the reddish-brown of Inui's coverall: the same reddish brown of the Martian landscape. One final screen, set above the table, was filled with faces, shifting from scene to scene as newsfeeds replaced announcements throughout the Outer Planetoids.

"Mac said he'd be on the feeds this shift," Inui's voice broke into her thoughts.

There was Mac, sitting beside a woman whose resolute enthusiasm marked her as a communications drone. Her eyes glazed as Mac announced the departure of a freighter, the maintenance status of ships in port.

*"Just one minute more, Mr. Nofi,"* little Ms. Drone caroled. *"I want to patch in our latest security consultant from Earth, Lieutenant Commander Marc Davidoff, who combines military expertise with a lifetime familiarity with SCM—the sidereal capital markets."*

"That phrase really is a misnomer," Elizabeth Inui said.

"It should be 'solar system,' not 'sidereal,' but the sound bite isn't nearly effective."

Unlike Mac, Davidoff almost glowered. Must have been some beer call the night before, CC thought.

In what weren't words of one syllable but came insultingly close, he explained the security audit he'd come to Vesta to perform. He broke his sentences up into short phrases that a passerby, glancing at a nearby screen, could take away and comprehend. But terms like "security scan," "decompression," and "cave-in" didn't make for good "lite" listening, and the newscaster's face and gestures indicated she was trying her best to hurry him along.

*"Now,"* she chirped, *"I hear you traveled here on* Rimrunner *with the Lovat-Neaves. Did you have a chance to meet them?"*

Cut to official-looking portraits of people CC had seen sweating in the gym, behind the visors of pressure suits during drill, or formally dressed, but laughing like human beings, not corporate icons.

Cut back to Davidoff's face, which was no more sardonic than usual. Next time CC saw him, she'd give him full marks for not rolling his eyes at the question.

*"What about a story I heard, that you'd taken a ship out to get—do I have this right—your flying hours in? and you saw . . . well, let's say, you saw something."*

Marc Davidoff's eyes flashed quick fury.

Cut to clip of ships ejected from *Rimrunner,* a zap run from the outside, of grinning pilots carrying their helmets.

By the time the cameras returned to Davidoff, he'd gone bland. "You see lots of things in space," he observed. "But if you're asking about little green men, I hope you're not casting aspersions on EarthServ's Marines." He smiled, or at least, he lifted his upper lip to show teeth. "There is nothing *little* about us."

The interviewer managed not to squeak. Mac passed his hand casually over his mouth.

"It's easy for your eyes to play tricks on you in the dark,"

Marc Davidoff said. "That's why we have instruments. And why instruments have backups, and even backups have audits. Don't worry. It's like EarthServ itself: if we want you to worry, we'll issue you something to worry about."

The woman forced a laugh and ended the interview with what looked to CC like relief.

*Your taxes at work, boys and girls.*

"When Rita Ross tried to go all hard-driving on Commander Davidoff, I thought Mac was about to give a fine imitation of explosive decompression himself," CC remarked.

Inui shrugged. "He's really got to work on his sense of humor. Besides, there's no point in letting people know for a fact just how few real safety options we have out here," she said. She raised an eyebrow at CC's expression of surprise. "But never mind that. I'd planned to have an assistant send records to your terminal, but they're all out on audits."

Logical enough. Staffing was thin out here. Besides, expat duty was for seniors—or the unlucky. Ambitious younglings proved themselves on Earth before companies troubled themselves to go to the expense, training, and risk of shipping them offworld. And if you shipped them offworld, you had better uses for them than to dance attendance on the coffee, pastries, and whatever else passed for breakfast in a breakfast meeting out here. And you wouldn't risk putting some loser, working off both his indenture and the results of Freeze, anywhere near executive levels, with their mission-critical information systems. Not to mention life support.

"Besides," Inui added, "I understand you've had some trouble with firewalls. Good thing you came through all right. I can beam the data over now or after breakfast."

She expanded her stride into an economical flat leap that brought her to a table and unsnapped the cover off a tray of food.

"Med center sent your nutritional requirements," she said. "Your calcium supplement's in that box on the left; they always tell you to take it with food."

CC's early life had accustomed her to synthetics and short rations. As her career progressed, she'd struggled to train herself to ignore the food set out at meetings once she'd noted how its quantity, quality, and service indicated the importance of any meeting and its participants' status.

On Earth, breakfast meetings meant real coffee that rose in quality as you clambered up the chain of command; juice that improved from reconstituted to freshly squeezed; bite-sized fruit-filled pastries; and sometimes protein or substitutes.

A light flashed on the screen set above the table. Leaning forward, Elizabeth turned up the volume with a touch. Remedial emergency drills in the East Dome. Avoid if possible; if not, wear gear that was easily washed. Afternoon orientation tours.

"Are you scheduled yet?"

CC nodded, and Elizabeth turned the volume down.

CC pressed her hand to her stomach. It was starting to gurgle. Planet- or at least asteroid-bound, her system seemed to remember where "down" was and reacted with hunger.

"This isn't Earth," Elizabeth Inui told her. "Until our way of moving around here becomes automatic, you're going to be wasting a lot of energy so you'll need the calories. Besides, wasting food's an official downcheck here, not to mention a social crime."

CC handed over her Breitling PDA. The other woman mated it to her own, beaming over the promised data and politely ignoring CC's examination of the food. Juice in closed tubes. Another set of tubes that steamed temptingly and from which she thought she could smell coffee. The ritual small pastries and what looked like eggs and sausage. All the comforts of home.

"All local produce," said Inui. "The sausage is textured soy; meat animals are a nightmare to ship; we haven't bred our own out here; and I doubt we will any time soon, though ADM el-Sabah's pouring venture cap into the project of gengineering ritually clean critters."

Shaking her head at the intricacies of that deal, CC filled her plate as expected and took the calcium supplement provided for her.

Both women pulled the sip-tubes on their juice, toasted

each other, then concentrated on their meal. Table manners on Vesta: focus on the food.

As CC's plate emptied, Inui began to talk about Vesta. "Some of us go to Final Frontier for a few drinks when we're offshift," she said. "It's halfway up the needle. You get an amazing view. Or if you're up for something rowdy, there's Gorsky's Hole. Things can get kind of wild." Inui grinned.

"One time, Mac got into a card game with the purser of EarthServ's *Sheffield* and a DeBeers Amsterdam geologist who acted like he'd just crawled out of a hole in the ground—no, don't ask me who threw the first punch, Security got called, and we all got docked ten days' centrifuge time! We were gobbling calcium supplements and trying to beg, borrow, or steal MK time, but no luck! Not to mention how we all ached when we got our spin-privileges restored." She laughed, and her laughter was pleasant, even if CC didn't understand half of her references.

But no questions about Earth. No pumping CC for gossip, corporate or personal, about conditions back home.

Now that was interesting. She filed it away as "background material" for the status report she knew Alpha would want ASAP, and made mental notes of the places Inui had mentioned. David IV appreciated local color, though the idea of David, taking makeup survival training (and why would she even suspect he wouldn't pass the first time?), David tethered—no, that wasn't an image she wanted to pursue. She fidgeted in her seat.

"I'm wasting your time," Inui sighed. "You Alpha people: always so focused. Have another coffee, please do."

As CC sipped, she changed the subject to off-Earth rating actions.

"I'd expect planetary modification to require seriously long-term bonds. I mean, thirty years would practically be a note. What kind of maturity are we talking about?" CC asked.

"When Mars Colony created their original bond indentures, even century bonds were considered short-term. The first ones were general obligations of the UN, and even then, we had to write in a clause specifying who assumed responsibility in case the issuer ceased operations. Wasn't there something about it in the last *Alpha Quarterly*?"

"I remember that article," CC said. In point of fact, she'd ghost-written about half of it, coordinated the fifteen reviewers, ten lawyers, and irate B-school professors who actually had the main bylines, and counted herself lucky to work on a project that prestigious. Best not tell Elizabeth that: it was enough she'd spoken about Alpha without snapping to attention or just plain snapping.

"The sunset clauses bothered me," she said. "After all, if things fell apart, wouldn't you think people would have more important things to worry about than bond defaults?"

Like loading the survivors on whatever ships could be mustered and getting them the hell back to Earth, for starters?

"You'd think so," Inui replied. "But the bonds still had to be rated. And they were high enough risk that Mars couldn't afford to insure the first few issues. Now," she shrugged, "full faith and credit terraforming bonds are SOP for Mars, and they don't have to insure them. For Vesta, though, the holding companies have to insure them because they're deemed less safe than the UN indentures. And that goes double for bonds secured by leaseholds."

"Thank God bond ratings aren't in my job description," CC said. "I'm just responsible for sitting in on the audit. Every trade from here to Mars, God have mercy on my soul and my poor strained eyes. Who's the registered principal around here for Morgan Nomura?"

"Jamil al-Feisal," said Inui. "But he's not here; he's in transit to Mars."

CC raised an eyebrow.

"It's legal. You know Clause Fourteen."

Small offices—and even if Morgan Nomura pretty much controlled all securities trading here on Vesta, its office was small—could be in the charge of a qualified principal or manager either resident or non-resident in the area.

"Who's his sub?" CC asked.

Her opinion of Inui went up when the woman didn't go defensive. "Seat's temporarily empty. Jamil's got to come back. Mac substituted for about a month, but when Jamil tried to extend his leave on Mars, Mac said NFW, he had more important work to do than warm a seat for a lazy exec. Besides, he'd let his certifications expire anyhow."

"Has the law changed?" CC asked. "The designate doesn't need to have the examinations or the same experience."

"No change in the law. They called me in to opine, and I had to say Jamil was pushing it, and I saw a potential conflict of interests. Didn't win any hearts and minds with that," Inui flushed slightly, and CC wondered about her debt balance.

"Because you're EASD examiner."

"That's right. Mind you, I've got no desire to wind up flash-frozen and stowed in the cargo hold of the first ship bound outsystem, and neither does Mac. I play by the rules. The rules say we need a registered principal. That's Jamil. And the rules say we need annual examination by the main office. Even if you work in some wiggle room about the meaning of 'annual'—I mean, how if you count as a year not an Earth year, but how long it takes the location of each branch office to orbit round the sun—those are the rules. We run a clean ship out here, clean as *Rimrunner*. Cleaner, maybe. You'll see that when you check your records."

Not even "I think."

Inui met CC's gaze and held it. Further questions, CC clearly understood, would be a rudeness at this point.

She raised her coffee bulb and sucked down the last stimulating drops. The action let her look away without losing ground or face.

Inui did the same. Formidable woman, CC thought. Clearly, she thought she had no weaknesses, nothing to hide, and CC was willing to bet that a search of her files would confirm that.

Again the screen light glittered red. "Ms. Williams, please report to Orientation."

"I fed your morning schedule in to the Minder," said Inui. "You have ten minutes. After five more, they'll leave without you. First offense is a fine. Second, you lose centrifuge time."

CC unsnapped the seatbelt and rose as carefully as she could.

"I'm meeting Mac at 18:00," Inui volunteered. "We're heading over to the centrifuge for the p.m. workout. Then, dinner. As a matter of fact, we won reservations at Final Frontier in the last LucasNet telethon. Want to join us? You might as well get started logging in your MKs—mandatory kilometers."

Correction to first assumption: Inui did have a weakness. His name was Mac. If CC hadn't heard her laugh at the idea of a barroom brawl, she wouldn't have believed it.

Other people's weaknesses were always helpful. She'd learned that in the *insulae,* long before she'd started at Alpha.

Even if they belonged to old friends. Sometimes, especially if they belonged to old friends.

Retrieving her PDA, CC headed for the door. Broad flat steps, CC. Don't collide with the wall. At least, *try* not to.

"I'd be delighted," she said. She even made it out to the corridor without bumping into the door. Miracles happened. If they didn't, she probably wouldn't have lived this long.

## 15

**As the centrifuge built up speed, CC felt her weight building**
up. One g again, after this long, was likely to be painful unless she kept in shape. Around her, some people had shut
their eyes while others "spotted," a move drawn from bal-
let—keeping their eyes fixed on one point as they turned.
CC focused on the unfamiliar sensation of her true weight.

The centrifuge slowed, then halted. She wobbled as she
exited. A too-long stride turned into a stagger, and she was
caught and steadied by a man in offwhite pullover and
trousers stamped with the Vesta Colony holo over his sur-
name and VSN—Vesta Security Number. Another handed
her a chilled towel, good for pulling the blood up to her
head.

No, she assured the attendants, Ms. did not need to sit
down. Ms. was just fine and wanted to continue her workout,
but—seeing their anxious-to-please faces—thank you so
much all the same.

They were probably hoping she'd tip them: every little bit
helped when you had an indenture to work off. They weren't
technical staff, who frequently moved from Freeze to positions of responsibility, but if they were here, working with

the health team, they were clearly considered worthy of some trust.

She let them lead her over to the stationary treadmill and help her strap in. Yes, Ms. understood she had to work up to her full speed, whatever that was. The 'mill whirred into action, and she leaned into it, her legs extending in the long, long Vestan strides that made it easy to rack up immense distances without a whole lot of resistance. Overhead, the monitors showed news, market reports, and announcements. She chose ILMNet news for a feature on gravity research, then switched to LucasNet. This far out from Earth, it showed previews of all the System's entertainment companies. *Rimrunner*'s arrival meant fresh holos for Vesta Colony. The screen blanked to black, showed a title, and only then the words "Peter Jackson Enterprises."

She heard long-term settlers mutter approval. Nice to see the old, old studio, last of the indies, was still productive, CC thought. Maybe, if she had any time, she'd go over to the Gates Center and see the whole thing. She let the sound track draw her forward, into the action, moving faster and faster, following the Three Hunters across the grasslands of New Zealand.

She was surprised when a bell rang, indicating the end of her session. This time, she was happy to accept another chilled towel and be steered toward the shower. The water was gratifyingly hot, though she got to bask in it for too short a time.

Still, she couldn't say no one had warned her. Nevertheless, when the bell rang and water shut off thirty seconds later, she was clean, able to dress quickly and make her way out to the corridor to wait for Elizabeth and Mac.

"First elevator I've seen with seat belts," she observed, but duly strapped herself in for the ride halfway up Mount Piazzi. From time to time, their car passed clearsteel ports.

"You ought to see the view when a ship like *Rimrunner* comes into port. Spectacular," said Mac.

"I saw it from the other side," CC said. Strangely enough,

she found the thought of how her ship had maneuvered into port more unnerving now than she had before.

"Finding things a little close for comfort now that you see them from outside?" Elizabeth asked.

CC glared at Elizabeth, but found only concern. As the elevator/maglev/whatever picked up speed, CC swallowed desperately.

"Bags in the seat ahead of us," Elizabeth offered rather too helpfully. "You'll feel better in a bit."

"Worrying after the fact's pointless anyhow," said Mac. "Besides, your Captain Aquino is one of the best. And all the pilots know what they're doing. They stay in constant practice, virtual and real-time. You saw that."

CC swallowed hard and tried not to see anything further for the rest of the ride.

The car's door opened into a reception area so similar to those of expense-account four-stars back on Earth that CC was almost disappointed. But where she would have expected flowers and mirrors, Final Frontier offered stone polished until it reflected incoming guests (she had to admit she looked rather pale) and immense geodes, displayed as sculpture.

"Good evening, Mr. Nofi," a man said, striding smoothly forward to greet them. He was tall, pale, his graying hair slicked back off his face as if he wanted to make himself as inconspicuous as possible. "And congratulations on your win."

Though their host wore plain trousers and the pullover with his name and number on it, indicating that he, too, was working off his indenture, the pullover had a high neck and full sleeves. And it was made of some silvery fabric, for a sense of richness and formality to his costume.

Human service? CC raised an eyebrow. Then she realized. Out here, people were cheaper than robots. Everyone worked.

Mac grinned at the man. "Yes. And we brought a guest. On my account, please."

The maitre d', or whatever he was, presented a recorder

that flashed, smoothly accepting Mac's retinal scan before
CC could even protest, then led them forward.

The restaurant proper turned out to be a cylinder cut into
the rock and polished until it reflected itself, the severely
sculptural lights set into its ceiling and orbiting the room,
and the port that provided an extraordinary view of the space
around Vesta. Tables and seats were carved out of the same
stone, which was dark except for where the light picked out
glowing crystals. The seats were covered by silver cushions,
giving the austere space a sense of splendor.

CC rubbed her finger across one of the cushions and discovered it had been made from thermal blankets, the sort
you took on camping trips. She reached beneath the seat and
found survival gear: emergency lights glinted in patterns
from each table to the exit. It made her feel as if she sat in
the heart of an immense, beautiful grid whose lights mir-
rored the lights so far away.

Elizabeth laughed. "Waste not, want not. In the early days
of Vesta Colony everyone got so used to those blankets that
it took Jordan, who met us at the door, to wake up from
Freeze, find himself covered by one of these blankets, and
see that the fabric's really beautiful. Not to mention that we
had incredible amounts of surplus. He partnered with Ross
Engel, a retired supply officer, to create Final Frontier out of
what had been a commissary for the techs up here. I think
he's zero-balancing his debt next month. . . ."

"I am happy to correct you, Ms. Inui," came Jordan's
voice behind her. "I just made the final payment, and I hope
you will join me in a small celebration."

At his gesture, a corps of human attendants, each wearing
a glittering silver tunic cut from surplus blankets, took long
steps across the room. Each held a glowing bouquet of crystal drinking tubes already filled with a pale, sparkling wine,
and deposited one at each place.

"How do you get champagne out here?" CC gasped.

"Dammit, Jordan," Mac said. "This little gesture could put
you right back in the red."

"It's budgeted for," said Jordan, who reached out and took

a tube himself from one of the waitstaff. "Biggest part of the expense was the Reidel Corning tubes and the upgraded wine centrifuge. I've had it on order from Earth for two years. Do you know how long," he asked indignantly, "it takes for sediment to subside once a wine's lifted off-Earth?"

"I guess some wines really don't travel well," Mac observed. "I remember the bottle of vintage port you experimented with."

"Haven't cried since I realized I'd have to file Chapter Eleven and leave Earth in Freeze," said Jordan. "But I came seriously close to losing it again when I saw the gunk from that vintage bottle of Fonseca splattered all over."

"Well, good thing that, unlike some folks around here, I've only got beer tastes," said Mac. "Though, given what beer costs around here, I may have to reconsider. Sit and join us, why don't you?"

"Let me make my announcement first," the co-owner said. He raised his empty hand. The lights dimmed, except for a center spotlight occupied by a shorter, stockier man. What hair he had was almost totally gray; and even in Vesta's light gravity, he moved as if he was standing at attention. No small trick, seeing as one leg of his trousers was neatly taped above where his knee should have been. The man turned his head, as if uncomfortable with the light.

"Ladies and gentlemen, may I have your attention?" the newcomer asked. He edged forward, and CC saw his face bore scars, imperfectly repaired.

Light chatter went on.

*"Now hear this!"* he bellowed and grinned. People in the room—especially those in uniform—laughed, then fell silent.

"My partner, Peter Jordan, has an announcement to make that I think you'll all be happy to hear."

"Congratulations, you two!" shouted one of the men in uniform.

"We already made *that* announcement," Ross Engel yelled back. "Now, listen up! Tonight is the night Final Frontier loses a tax credit and gains a shareholder. Peter's zero-balanced his debt! And I can safely say, I have never been so happy to cancel a contract in my life! Peter, will you get yourself over here?"

Ross stood alone in the spotlight, grinning.

"If you please . . . partner?"

Peter Jordan joined the one-legged restaurateur in the spotlight. He took off the badge that bore his name and indenture number and handed it to his partner. Unsealing a breast pocket, Engel produced a new badge and held it up.

"It says 'Peter Jordan, co-owner, Final Frontier!' And that's *all* it says. *Congratulations, Peter!*"

He flung a hand to his forehead in a mock salute. Jordan caught him in a bear hug before he could retreat from the spotlight.

Tears glinted on both men's faces as Peter Jordan raised his glass. "Thank you, Ross! For everything! On behalf of both of us, I want to thank all of you helping us make Final Frontier a success." He laughed. "As of tonight, I am officially reborn. So, here's to freedom—at least till the tax bill comes due! And I ask you to raise a glass to my new birthday."

"Happy birthday!" the people in the room chorused. They applauded him, then drank. A few tried to sing several versions of "Happy birthday." Some were even fit for polite company.

"Just don't break the glasses to celebrate," Jordan called over the laughter and the singing. "You wouldn't believe the shipping tariff on those things. Ross swears he's going to put my old badge on display in the lobby, and I really don't fancy having to get it out again."

The room laughed, the lights rose, and menus glinted in the flatscreen embedded in each table. Jordan joined Mac's table, slipping into a seat beside CC and belting himself deftly in, just as the lights flickered in signal.

A flight of small craft darted past Mount Piazzi, their lights . . . red/white amber green/white . . . reflecting in the Final Frontier's polished black stone, surface to surface, and then gone.

"Impressive! Did you arrange the fly-by too?" Mac asked.

"Don't I wish!" Jordan laughed. "Seriously, they've stepped up patrols. Damned if I know why, and if Ross knows, he's not talking. Increased security always makes me nervous. Still, from here, it doesn't look half bad, and it impresses customers, so I guess I'll live." He drained his drinking tube.

"Now, if you'll excuse me," he said. "I really do have a restaurant to run."

And he was off.

"Think he'll ever go back to Earth?" Mac asked. "Now that he's paid off, and he's an owner here? Not a chance."

He grinned, and the lights reflected off his teeth. "Ross had some bad luck with a cave-in awhile back. Apparently, he made some sort of God-bargain that if he survived, he'd give anyone who needed it a step up. Jordan, who'd barely warmed up after resurrection, was working construction at the time and helped pull him out. As a result—well, you saw. They've made it corporate policy. Every member of Final Frontier's staff has come to Vesta in Freeze. You don't think they won't all pay it forward?"

"They can't all run restaurants," CC said. She bit her lip as she glanced around the room, with its buzzing guests and its earnest, busy staff. Once their debts were paid and they'd earned an economic stake in this new place, which needed hard workers, they'd have fresh starts. Damn. She'd never heard of anything like that.

CC blinked furiously and glanced around the room. It was almost totally full. Most of tonight's diners wore unobtrusive casual clothes that meant you couldn't tell who in the Colony had retired on investments, who was a shareholder, and who was still working his or her butt off.

Neave and Margaret Lovat sat at one table, positioned on a riser a little away from most of the others. Starlight shone down upon Margaret's fair hair and her face and gemless hands.

At it, disdaining straps or cushions, sat three men and two women, all in uniforms glittering with the anachronistic braid, the bleached white, and the primary colors of military mess dress both for EarthServ and the Marines.

Mac Nofi followed her glance. "Marc said he was buying his wing dinner. He probably stepped . . . there!"

Davidoff emerged from a drape of silver that hid a sliding door discreetly marked with an M, sketched a salute at Mac, and rejoined his table.

"Well, will you look at that?" Mac commented.

Sandy, subtly elegant in a brown coverall and jacket that shimmered from the bronze threads woven into the fabric, emerged from behind the same curtain as Davidoff and took long, drifting steps over to Lovat's and Neave's table and bowed, all without overbalancing. Neave pulled out a chair, and Sandy promptly strapped in, his face alight with his social success. CC looked away. She had started to think of them as friends, or at least people who might be friends, but not if they listened to Sandy, whose talent for putting a negative spin on competitors—and everyone who wasn't a superior or out of the game obviously was a competitor—had cost her before.

"Doesn't your friend ever stop networking?" Mac asked as Sandy nodded at Marc Davidoff's table, copying Marc's salute of a few minutes earlier.

"No," CC said curtly.

At least Davidoff had acknowledged Sandy, which was more than he'd done for her. Her eyes stung. So much for that stupid message of his, telling me to give him a call. Hyper 4A. Damn. *Why'd I have to remember his address? I don't even* like *the man.*

Looked as if she wasn't the evening's bright particular social star, didn't it? Yes, she'd hooked up with Mac and Elizabeth and met the owners of Final Frontier, but Sandy was dining with Margaret Lovat, and Marc Davidoff, who was supposed to give her "every cooperation," seemed totally involved with his wing.

Sometimes you could rescue a social disaster by faking it, she reminded herself. So she flashed as bright a smile as she had ever managed at a holiday party, praised her dinner, and promised herself she would tell David IV about Final Frontier tonight, but not about her run-in with a Vestan hacker. No point in worrying him with what he couldn't fix. And he'd want to.

"CC," Mac murmured near her ear, so that her hair drifted above the plain silver earrings she'd dared to wear, "you're overdoing it. Relax."

She picked up her drinking tube, enjoying the play of starlight and the tiny spots set into the rock ceiling on the wine. Its surface stirred, aerated by proprietary Reidel-Corning technology, so that even this far from its native vineyard, its bouquet could bloom.

"All the comforts of home," came an ironic voice. She started and damn near drifted from her chair.

Elizabeth leaned forward and caught the drinking tube.

"Would've been a tragedy to lose that wine," Marc David-off said. "They say that the wines here are worth the trip out from Earth, but I say that's marketing, and I say the hell with it."

"It certainly comes as a surprise," she found herself able to answer. Jordan took a long, unhurried step forward with a fourth chair and clicked it into place. Thanking him, Marc sat. Mess dress suited him, CC hated herself for noticing, and he managed to sit in Vesta's low gravity as if at a formal dinner back on Earth.

"Jumpy, are you?" he asked CC. "How're you settling in? I heard you had a run-in with Vesta's computer nets."

She flashed her other companions a look. No one was supposed to know about that.

Marc laughed easily. "Look, I didn't hear from you, and you don't strike me as someone who passes opportunity by. So I made inquiries."

He looked down at her wrists. No jacks. No scars, even. "That's a relief. I assumed you didn't need them, but I wasn't sure. Sorry. So, how else is Vesta treating you?"

"Elizabeth and I are starting to go over her records," she

told him, "and I had my first centrifuge session today. Got to keep those calcium levels up."

She gazed out into space. "What are you looking for?" Davidoff asked. He followed her gaze. "If you're looking for *Rimrunner*, it's docked way downbelow. And planets . . . let's see . . ." He leaned forward, as if indulgently pointing out features of the solar system to a total fool.

"Look," he said, "I did mean it. I promised you my help, or it got promised for me, and I keep those types of promises."

CC flicked her eyes from Davidoff to their table companions. He'd said all that in front of witnesses. It could mean anything from a good lie to an offer of real friendship.

Jordan showed up at their table again with two PDAs balanced on a salver so thin that light showed through the delicate whorls and veins of the stone from which it was carved. "That table would like to exchange numbers," he said, indicating Neave and Lovat.

She inclined her head, beamed her data into the PDAs, then waited while Elizabeth and Mac added their information.

"Already checked in," said Marc. "Look, I have to get back to my wing. I'm going to be in and out, up and around, just like you. But my team has beer call at a great place, Gorsky's Hole, at around 18:00 whenever we're off duty. Stop in some time."

Mac inhaled some of the ridiculously expensive wine and almost choked.

"Later," he said, gesturing with his free hand while struggling to remain in his seat. "Later."

"Not a chance," CC said. She snatched her PDA off the table and scrawled "? Gorsky's Hole."

Her screen lit blue:

**"Neil Armstrong, the first man to walk on the moon, is quoted as saying, 'Good luck, Mr. Gorsky' during his first lunar walk in 1969 on the Apollo 11 mission. Years later, Mr. Armstrong says that now that Mr. Gorsky is dead, he can tell the real story. He says that when he was a child, he overheard his neighbor, a Mr. Gorsky, being**

told by his wife that when the kid next door walks on the moon . . . that's when Mr. Gorsky will get sex."

"In my considered legal opinion," said Elizabeth, "*that is* what I'd call a seriously hostile work environment."

Marc reached out and took away CC's wineglass as, for the first time in her professional life, she laughed without restraint in a public place.

## 16

**Secure in her invitation to what seemed to be half private** club and half free-for-all, CC tapped in the private access code of Gorsky's Hole. Built at the intersection of two segments of Vesta Colony, the bar had taken advantage of the colony's hermetic security protocols to turn its door seals into a replica of an old-fashioned airlock.

Lights flickered, simulating an actual airlock's operations, before **"Pressure Equalized"** showed on a readout panel, green lights flashed **"Welcome,"** and the inner door slid aside.

As laughter, shouts, and music from Japan, Nigeria, and neogangsta from Western NA erupted, CC took a long, careful step into what looked, at first, like a spacer's graveyard for old equipment.

A pressure suit with a still-wrapped contraband cigar hanging from its open faceplate held out bar menus. In a tinny, robotized voice, it started telling her the story about Neil Armstrong and "you'll get sex when a man lands on the moon," followed by a shout of "Good luck, Mr. Gorsky!" Though CC knew the story wasn't true, she laughed anyhow, then laughed harder at the thought that she was laughing into the faceplate of an obsolete pressure suit serving as a maitre d'.

My God, she was a long, long way from Final Frontier, wasn't she? She'd earned some downtime, she told herself. At least she hadn't fallen into that tank earlier today.

The pressure suit leaned against a battered surface buggy on which dusty tanks and bottles had been stacked. CC's eye took in weapons, consoles built into the rough stone and metal tables, and, set into the bulkheads, equipment panels—wasn't that a geo-scan?

Sensors blinked on the pressure suit's chest plate, and a siren went off. Overhead, right below the ceiling, light panels erupted into a red alert.

A gleeful howl of "Hey, newbie on deck" and "Virgin alert!" went up from what had to be the direction of the bar. CC closed her eyes. She absolutely refused to check whether the seal on her coverall had opened somewhere embarrassing or whether her boot was trailing something that should have been recycled.

Time to adapt again. Every time she'd switched levels, domes, or jobs, she'd had to trade old ways for new until she wondered, sometimes, if she had anything left of whatever self she'd started out with. Adaptability might be a survival skill, but it carried a high price. It was one of the things she loved about David IV: he wore his own face. But so did some of the people she'd met since leaving Earth, and they were a lot lower maintenance.

CC suppressed a sigh. One day, maybe . . . she'd wear her own face herself, if she remembered what it looked like. But for now, once again, it was *showtime*!

She made herself grin, a big, enthusiastic one with teeth.

"That's no virgin, that's a friend of Marc's!" came a gleeful yell, shrill as chilled apples, from a woman CC remembered seeing in Final Frontier.

"Flatterer!" shouted her companion, a small, Asian man with the chest expansion that the showed high-altitude adaptation so useful in low-$O_2$ environments.

The woman laughed. "Which one am I flattering?" she demanded.

She shoved off from the bar, an immense chunk of metal that looked like it had been carved from a ship and lugged, God only knew how, into Vesta Colony. One giant loping step brought her to CC's side.

"You're Williams," she announced. Her coverall, which read Garcia-Jones, was as dark as CC's own, except for the badges of rank and time in space. (CC, badgeless except for her transient's ID, instantly felt drab, an outsider. So what else was new? She turned up the wattage on her smile.) "I'm Kate. I saw you . . ."

"Final Frontier, night before last," CC agreed.

"Marc told people you'd be coming in. Said you'd ridden with him during *Rimrunner*'s trip Out and you didn't suck. Tell me," Kate said, cheerfully propelling CC forward with a hand at the small of her back, "did you really see a bogey out there?"

The Asian man, whose coverall read Tenzing—aha, Tibetan, which accounted for the high-altitude adaptation— grinned at her and bowed over joined hands. CC copied the gesture, but carefully: a newbie's enthusiasm could send her careening across the room.

"Shut up, Kate," Tenzing said politely. "Ms. Williams hasn't even bought you a beer, and you're trying to squeeze her for RUMINT. Rule is, CC, newbies buy the first round."

CC glanced around the bar for confirmation.

"I grant you it's not the most hospitable gesture in the system," said another man who kept his head shaved and wore the globe, anchor, and helmet insignia of deepspace Marines. CC saw an old-style jack fan out right above his cervical vertebrae and glanced away: Alpha wasn't supposed to have had that report about the X-Firefox wing and she certainly shouldn't have seen it, but apparently no one in Gorsky's Hole bothered to care if she noticed or not.

"But how many newbies do we get down here? Admin mostly keeps them for themselves."

CC eyed her surroundings and took the risk. "Clear a path," she ordered, and took advantage of the bar-space to edge in and pass over her credit chip. "What's to drink here? Name brands or local booze? And will the local stuff kill me?"

Kate howled, and Tenzing patted her on the back so enthusiastically that CC nearly broke a rib from her collision with the bar.

"It won't kill you, but it'll give you one hell of a hangover and boost your $O_2$ and water consumption for about a day," he warned cheerfully.

So, she'd figured out the passwords, or at least, a password, and she was in. At least temporarily.

*I'm not a spacer though I play one on screen,* she thought. She knew these people's cheerful grins could turn grim in an instant, knew that, in that same instant, they could access skills that the likes of CC could only fake. Still, showtime was showtime.

Behind the bar, the bottles and taps that held Gorsky's Hole's trove of drinkables was awash in color—holographs and even dilapidated ancient photos of cheerful faces CC knew damn well she better not ask about, a string of jalapeño-shaped lights and even some tarnished tinsel in purple, green, and gold that looked like it had been shipped out from Earth about the time the colony was founded. The red alert lights by the ceiling had finally subsided. Now, a rainbow of gas-filled tubing pulsed from every wall: signs, advertisements, and, meticulously marked, exit routes and emergency gear.

Crowded about her were vivid faces and taut bodies in the shipsuits of various services, ranging from the old Firefox in his Marine insignia, to EarthServ pilots on flyby duty, to Vesta Security, to maintenance. Apparently, anyone who'd put in time Outside was welcome at Gorsky's Hole, at least until its groupmind decided otherwise.

So, what was CC doing here? She was a chameleon, a mountebank: in short, a corporate fraud.

The Firefox leaned over to scoop up a beer. "Where's Marc?"

That told her why she'd been let in this far. She was a guest. Once upon a time, she'd ridden fire and spotted a bogey. And they were going to squeeze that story out of her one way or the other.

"That's Lieutenant Commander to you, gunny," Tenzing shot back.

"Lieutenant Commander Marc," said the Marine. "Isn't this CC whose liquor I'm about to drink the same woman who damn near fell into hydro yesterday? I was off duty and checking out the gardens," he explained, "and this woman I'd never seen before damn near takes a header into one of the tanks. Fell or was pushed?" he asked.

Damn. She should have known she'd be noticed. But anyone could trip—right?

"Sure, I was in Hydro," CC said. "Part of my job is to get to know this place. Amazing, isn't it? I found out that Med-Center here uses citrus as a medicine. You'd think we were still back in the days of the British Navy or something." Maybe, if she tried to ignore it . . .

A woman in the blue of Vesta Security was giving her the don't-bullshit-me-lady look.

"All right," CC conceded. "I had kind of an accident. But if people hadn't crowded in, I wouldn't have tripped," she said. "As it was, I didn't fall, so no harm done," she added, hoping that would close the subject.

Contaminating Hydro was a bad thing. To say nothing of what the chemicals might do to CC herself. She'd saved herself by a swift twist in the low gravity that had let her fall free, away from the tank.

She didn't like to think about what a damn fool she'd come close to making of herself. Even if she hadn't been hurt, it would have been a downcheck. Someone was sure to say something or report it back Home. Assuming no one had done so already. Alpha didn't just do oversight; it did undersight, backup checks, and just plain spying.

Fell or was pushed, the Firefox had asked. If CC'd thought of that line, she'd have been sure she was going crazy.

Better change the subject, fast. Funny, she'd seen an "industrial incident" in her tour of DeBeers' operation, but no one commented on that. Accidents were one thing: apparently, something about her near-fall in Hydro struck these survivors as another thing altogether. Struck her too, or she wouldn't be trying so hard to block it out.

Drinks were arriving. Saved. CC pushed a heavy, translucent, pale green drinking tube filled with water toward Tenzing. "This all you wanted? Even when I'm buying? Sheesh. You've been in space too long," she told the Tibetan, carefully mimicking the speech rhythms she'd heard on board *Rimrunner* from crew and TDYs.

"Once you stand watch outside," he replied, "and everyone comes back home safe, maybe I'll let you buy me a beer. Earth beer," he specified.

"You're such a damn snob, Sherpa," came a sarcastic voice. In the flashing lights around the bar, CC's relieved flush went unnoticed. "Even if CC did fall into hydro, which she *didn't,* I'm sure she'd come up just fine and tell you it was work-related research. Like the accident she saw during her mining tour. Kept her head then, too, while tourists were puking in their suits. You should have seen her when I made her starfish during EVA training. Didn't lose control for an instant. Not her suit, not her bladder. Not anything. And don't think I didn't try."

One of the bartenders, the wiry man, not the past-middle-aged woman whose wrists still bore jack scars below her rolled-up sleeves, flipped CC's credit chip back to her in a slow, lazy arc. CC caught and palmed it, concealing the Alpha Consultancies logo that really betrayed her outsider status.

"Marc!" she said. "Good to see you. Is it all right to buy *you* a drink?"

"Dammit, CC, you don't have to ask permission to buy your host a beer," he said.

She passed back her chip to the barkeep.

"It's all right, Riley," Marc said, elbowing gingerly in next to her, one hand on the bar to keep himself in place. "The lady's safe to run a tab. At least till Travel & Expense back home gets hold of her. What about it, CC? I heard Gorsky's got in some Guinness. Your credit good for that? Flyby really gives you a thirst, just looking out there and trying not to crash into floating rocks."

Guinness wasn't cheap even back on Earth. Out here, she didn't want to think about what it would cost. Or about Marc's challenge, at least, to her expense account.

"Ah hell, Marc, why not? Two Guinnesses," she ordered. And she didn't even like the stuff. So much for sampling the local hooch.

Guinness always poured slowly; the art of pouring it well was part of the lure of the stuff. In Vesta's next-to-no-gravity, a fraction of the light g on Earth's moon, the Guinness oozed into the tubes. Just as well the asteroid had some spin: she wasn't up for a messy game of chase-the-globules. Especially globules this pricey. If she got home, she'd have a bonus. Then she could make it up to T&E, if they got nasty. And if she didn't, she'd have bigger things to worry about.

She had to admit that after the way Marc had damn near stalked her on *Rimrunner*, she was surprised she'd seen so little of him here on Vesta. The last time they'd been in the same room had been that evening in the Final Frontier.

Probably, Gorsky's Hole had rules, unwritten and therefore sacrosanct, about asking where someone had been. Maybe because some of the people here had classified assignments, maybe because every stratified culture developed its own rules that seemed idiotic to outsiders.

She could just imagine how the dialogue would go.

*Where've you been, Marc?*

*Out.*

*What'd you do?*

*Nothing.*

So, be damned if she'd ask. Not even if he wanted her to.

Spreading her elbows out to mark off her section of bar space, CC grinned, just looking around at what David IV would probably call "local color." He was getting plenty of it, and a nice healthy color at that. In his last transmission, he'd reported that he'd joined his family in the Nantucket Enclave for a long weekend.

CC hadn't quite been pleased. His parents had never invited her out for a long weekend. *"I saw our old house, the one in 'Sconset, that's Siasconset, only no one ever calls it that. We had to sell it after the crash of '09,"* he'd said.

Residence permits, even for rentals, were still quite scarce on the Enclave: you had to be sponsored, and there was at least a three years' waiting list. No one in her family had ever been able to manage more than a day trip.

She wasn't being fair, she told herself. How could her future in-laws invite her to join them when she was on the far side of the Solar System?

But still, at that point, she'd stopped reading his letter, turned off her comm, and headed to Gorsky's Hole. It might not be upscale, but it was definitely lively. And she thought she knew the rules for fitting in here.

"Hey, Ms. . . . Lady?" The bartender, who had finally filled the Guinnesses, waved a hand in front of CC to get her attention, then placed both drinks in clips set into the bar. CC propped an elbow on the cold metal and began to drink. A useful thing to remember about Vesta Colony was that it was like being at high altitude: your tolerance for alcohol went way down, at least till you were acclimated.

She wasn't acclimated. At least, not yet, and if she had anything to say about it, she'd be back on Earth before she was. But the people in Gorsky's who were happily sending her credit straight to hell were. Three of them had started some kind of dance that propelled them into the bulkheads, where they rebounded, waving their arms. Two more began singing something about an Eagle landing.

"Shut up! It's too early in the night for that one!" Kate shouted, and they switched to a raucous folksong about an historic, if legendary, ship's crew and a shore leave that was even more memorable than most.

Marc drained his Guinness and set it back down into its clips so the serving tube could be sterilized.

"CC, if you don't like that stuff, why'd you order it?" he demanded. "Here, pass it over."

Her drink, too, disappeared down the hatch way faster than the bartender had managed to pour it.

"I want to talk with you," he muttered. "Dance with me."

Marc pushed the empty tube back toward the bartender, who caught it before it fell off the edge. Then he tugged CC onto the crowded deck that passed as a dance floor, and drew her way too close.

"Don't worry. Fraternizing purely in the line of duty," he said.

"I hadn't noticed," she lied brazenly.

She wrapped her own arms around Marc's shoulders in a gesture that mimicked his. He felt good, she realized, muscled and sure. She made herself think of other things fast. Like the way she'd made life hell for everyone whose data she could beg, access, or hack for the mother of all databases she'd been building. One good thing about following up on data requests: you worked a *lot* of hostility out of your system.

"Heard about your fall in Hydro," Marc muttered against her ear. It would have been easier to understand him in vacuum, helmet to helmet. His breath tickled.

"Nothing to it," she told him. "It was crowded. I went off-balance and fell. Damn, does everyone here know about that?"

Maybe she'd felt a shove, and maybe she hadn't. She'd been so busy turning herself into a low-g human corkscrew so she didn't fall into the tank that she hadn't had time to check.

Maybe that was it. Someone else had wondered if she'd fallen or was pushed. No such worries attended the DeBeers incident.

"Nice save, Williams," Marc said. "Of course, Alpha's probably going to be annoyed they can't collect the whopping janitor's insurance policy I'm sure they've got on you."

"On me and everyone else," she agreed. He wasn't telling her what she wanted to know.

"Who told you?" she asked again.

He shrugged. "RUMINT," he said. "You're getting quite the reputation. Mac Nofi's got people going over the security records in the area. And Security's doing overtime. You saw his people are light on the ground in the Hole tonight."

"I told you, hydro was crowded. Mine wasn't the only tour group."

"Right. Maybe it was. But you watch yourself," Marc ordered and pulled her even a little closer. "You're doing all right for a newbie. And you definitely know your job. But screw up and get your insurance canceled, and Alpha will yank you home so fast . . ."

He gave her a cautionary shake that would have sent her across the room, if his arms hadn't restrained her. She knew she should pull free indignantly: he had no right to shake her, let alone draw her back in against him as if he had rights in the matter.

She didn't move.

"Look, you watch it," Marc warned. "You may know your job, but there's jobs around here you don't want to know. If I'm not around and something gets ugly, you go to Neave. Don't wait. Just move it."

"You think Neave knows?"

Fingers dug into her ribs, making her jump at least a meter. Again, Marc pulled her back. Lively idea of dancing, the man had.

"Of course not. What the hell do you think, CC?" Marc demanded. "No one on Vesta so much as farts in a pressure suit without Neave knowing it. And writing a position paper. Or, possibly, referring it to your old good buddy Mac. Stuff's coming down, CC. Stuff that makes your accident, or what we saw on that zap run, look like a staff meeting."

"Some staff meetings back at Alpha got pretty bloody," she told Marc.

"Dammit, CC, if I have to rat you out to Mac, I will. Come on. You flew with me. When we saw that bogey, you begged not to be put off the ship. You trusted me to get you safe home, and I did. I promised you my help. In front of witnesses, no less. Now, you going to trust me again?"

Mac had already told her she shouldn't be let out without a keeper. But this was Vesta. No one went Outside except in groups and on tethers.

Except maybe Marc and some of the rest of the people here in Gorsky's Hole. People who drank her booze and watched her.

And what did Mac—or Neave the omniscient—know about Marc's latest disappearance, or the bogey they'd seen? CC tried to break free, but he restrained her. Damn man's hands stuck like tangleweb during a riot. Good thing he didn't have any romantic intentions.

"I want your word," he said.

Her *word*? She wasn't aware that the word of anyone from Alpha was common currency out here. Authoritative, yes. Scary, maybe. But . . . he meant her personal word.

If anything that was even scarier. She pulled free. This time he let her.

"Come on," she said, turning back toward the crowded bar and the jalapeño lights. "I want another drink."

She'd meant to order sparkling water, which was what you did after the first drink at corporate parties. Instead, she switched to beer. Lots of beer.

"Did you know I can sing 'From the Halls of Montezuma' to the tune of 'My Darling Clementine'?" yelled a man wearing Security insignia.

"No, you can't!" Kate shouted back.

"Hell I can't," the security man said. "Why can't I?"

"Because," Marc bellowed, "you can't fucking *sing*!" He launched himself with a roar of laughter toward the singer wannabe, followed by the Firefox with gunny's insignia.

As the inevitable brawl started, CC slipped away. Tomorrow at 14:00 hours, she had a tour of Vesta's electrolysis plant. After yesterday's almost-snafu at Hydroponics, that was no place she wanted to go with a hangover and sloweddown reflexes.

She hadn't thought Marc, in the thick of what looked like overage armed bear cubs scuffling and shouting and careening across the room, had seen her go. Just as well: she hadn't expected it, and she didn't feel like talking.

But as CC headed from Gorsky's Hole back to her quarters, taking care to walk slowly, one cold hand always on a hand rail so Security wouldn't run her in, she could have sworn she saw a shadow flitting after her.

Beer and the low $O_2$ content made her want to turn around and confront her watcher. "Why Marc, I didn't know you cared."

And she didn't.

## 17

**Some damn fool with a voice that sounded like shears on** tin was trying to sing "a researcher's life is not a happy one . . . happy one."

"Whoever that is, I'm going to kill it," CC muttered as the noise woke her. Immediately, her sinuses turned into tympani, her head ached, and her bladder reminded her of her stupidities of the night before.

The idea of facing people chewing or sucking breakfast revolted her, so she grabbed a breakfast bar that was mostly strawberry flavor, this month's nutritionally approved fats, plus whole grains remarkable for their dry toughness, and sat trying to nibble it as she accessed whatever mail had come in during what someone last night had referred to as the vampire watch.

A dinner invitation from Neave. A "simple family party," as Margaret called it. And "just casual."

CC set the food bar down, revolted. Nothing short of explosive decompression or a wave of layoffs could be deadlier than a simple, casual party at top management's.

"Well, sur-fucking-prise," she muttered to herself before she thought to remember that someone might have re-bugged her quarters.

Neave. Even the name was a warning. Let CC get herself into trouble, and Neave would know. People like Neave were exempt: it was fools like CC that went to reeducation labs or prison, while the Neaves of the system paid hefty fines and turned up at all the best parties with stories to tell.

Because she had to, she accepted the invitation. Command performance. Maybe she could capital N Network. At least she'd get to see Margaret, whom she genuinely liked.

Meanwhile, David IV's letter sat in her in-box. CC could tell him about her dinner invitation. And God knows, there was enough "local color" in Gorsky's Hole to fill a library of coloring books in the fancy Montessori school she and David had picked out for when they got their child allowance. She suspected he wouldn't have liked Gorsky's Hole at all. She scrolled through his last letter once again. His family had extended their stay, and he'd taken off more time. How he always got time off on request was a mystery to CC, who'd pulled herself into work with bandages still on her wrists.

So David was still in the Nantucket Enclave. He'd met some people from this and that NGO at a farmer's market, he'd said. His entire family had been invited to whale-watch, followed by a cookout at a private beach. CC could just imagine: come as you were in Y2K, down to the period-perfect volleyball net, G&Ts, and resident athletic blond boys and girls. Even if, these days, the sunstreaks in the hair were artificially and expensively maintained. Another just-family, extravagantly casual event.

She sighed.

*"We saw what used to be the old Neave compound,"* David IV wrote. *"Didn't you say* Everett *Neave was on that ship with you?"*

It's the *Rimrunner, David,* CC thought. He didn't have a problem remembering the man he'd thought she might have met.

*"Mother thinks she's some sort of cross-cousin with this Neave, assuming he's one of the Nantucket family. If you meet him, try to say hello from her; it would be a good way to please her."*

CC would give the woman that; she never missed a trick. Pity she was out of the corporate-networking business. This way, she could climb and she didn't even have to have CC as a houseguest.

As she scanned through the letter, homesickness hit CC at seven gs, exacerbated by hangover.

David's familiar name and logo. His brief *"I really miss you, sweetie."* His smile and the feel of his arms around her. Gravity heavy enough that things, including your arms and legs, stayed where you put them and didn't move in ways you hadn't intended. Primary colors—the blues of water and air on Earth's good days; the greens of grass or careful plantations in the atrium of her office complex, not the grays and black and glittering inset crystals of polished stone. The strong tastes of food that hadn't been processed or even, God forbid, recycled.

How could she even think of food now?

Oh God.

If you upchuck here, she told herself, you'll just have to hoover it yourself.

CC got up so fast she had to fend herself off a bulkhead, and propelled herself to the bathroom. Alcodote and distilled water, lots and *lots* of distilled water. Fast.

They helped. So did a close encounter, briefer than she'd have liked, with the Oxy mask by the shower.

She must have OD'd on pure $O_2$ because she felt herself grinning. Now that she thought back over her cautious trip back from Gorsky's Hole to her quarters, she rather thought she'd been singing last night too. The same song, in fact.

It was a wonder Security hadn't run her in.

Maybe Marc had warned them off.

Or Mac. Maybe he meant well; maybe he was letting her go to hell in her own way. Old friends change. The only way she'd know if he'd looked out for her was to ask him.

She decided it was probably safer to find out on her own.

At Gorsky's Hole, she'd danced for the first time in years. She'd laughed. She'd even felt accepted by people whose respect she suspected was not easily won.

And, she realized with another jolt of happiness, she had research to do today.

Research was the part of her job she loved: as CC practiced it, "just doing my job" covered the entire asteroid. This was going to be fun.

Now that her hangover had worn off, she could hardly wait.

With the night before and the morning after buried as far back in her mind as she could sink it, CC negotiated the Apsedra, whose acoustics played hell with her hangover. Damn good thing the morning flyover didn't make a sound. She suspected her face wore an interesting pallid grin, and replaced it with a faint smile to disarm pedestrians or public health observers as she made her way to Elizabeth's office.

Certainly, she could work from her quarters, but anyone could work on spreadsheets. Where she really added value was in observing her surroundings and the people about her. Numbers could be faked. Human interactions and body language—a skilled operator could fake both, but the very attempt would provide CC with more data.

She greeted Elizabeth with a smile and ritual thanks-again-it-was-great for the evening at the Final Frontier. Yes indeed, she'd seen some of the people from the restaurant at Gorsky's Hole; yes, it was definitely an experience; and yes, she was delighted to meet Elizabeth's assistant, and thank you for the new series of return numbers.

Idly, by way of warmup, she ran a search on the new assistant, a colorless young man whose wrist-jacks still glinted. He'd been an accountant turned law student, who'd had trouble meeting student-loan payments. Rather than endure what were now truly draconian penalties for bankruptcy, he'd chosen to emigrate. At least this way he could tap out his 401(k) and travel out to Vesta without being frozen: bankruptcy left no choice, except playing the odds against freezer burn.

She ran the usual pre-work check on her own holdings.

They were holding their own, at least, and one stock was coming back. Looked as if the markets were remaining up, at least for now. If this kept up, she'd definitely have to re-balance. Thank heavens for the Sunspot Index and its eleven-year cycle.

She made a mental list of other people whose back-grounds she wanted to study. She'd only "hoteled" into this machine; it wouldn't be safe to use its notepad for any really demanding work.

Why was she bothering? A theory was beginning to form in her mind, in much the way a scientist, baffled by his data, might go to bed and dream of benzene rings.

Companies had corporate cultures. Asteroids? This was the first such colony she'd ever visited, but she was begin-ning to form an impression of a frontier society composed not just of rejects from the mainstream, but of oddballs, renegades, and the *Lumpenprofessoriat.* If her life had gone otherwise, she might well have wound up here defrosted, paying off indentures of her own. She'd conditioned herself to value the world she'd chosen, but here, in the persons of Neave, of Elizabeth, of Marc, and of Mac, she found expa-triates who valued the distance from an Earth that plagued them with feedback, followup, and increased regulation, and who'd all turned in their pinstripes.

Very interesting, CC thought. You could do a good anthro-pological—no. And no again. She was no academic; she'd given that up years ago—*like a fox in the wild, gnawing off a paw to escape a trap.*

And she would damn well have to make do.

Limp as she might on the remaining three paws, Alpha wasn't paying her to make friends or sociological analyses. Alpha was paying her to get to the bottom of a problem. And experience had taught her—and her employers—that when she investigated her doubts, she struck paydirt.

Note to self: check on friends.

Why, she was turning into just the perfect little Alpha Consultancies serf, wasn't she just?

All warmed up. CC flexed her wrists. Unless she tensed

up, they didn't hurt: neither did the muscles she'd have wrenched by her corkscrew flip yesterday in Hydro—a good thing about Vesta's gravity. And God bless beer.

For an instant, she thought of going into MedCenter and putting the minor surgery needed to reopen her old wrist ports on her expense account. Jacking in was a much quicker way to process data than just looking at a screen.

Yes, but when she went back home, that would represent another surgery, and chances were, someone in HR would decide she ought to keep the ports open. Cheaper than reimbursing the surgeon, that way; and she'd have another skill, albeit low-level, to offer.

How déclassé, David IV's mother would probably say. Well, if CC made enough money to buy back the Nantucket compound the family had lost two generations ago and still mourned as if it were yesterday, Madame could just say what she wanted and probably would. CC hadn't gotten engaged to David IV just for the privilege of having the in-laws from hell.

But David had said he missed her. Even in the place he loved more than anywhere in the world, he'd said he missed her.

And she loved him. Didn't she? They were a team, upward-bound together. Weren't they?

Quick, CC, without taking out the holo. What does David IV look like? That trick wouldn't help, she told herself. Not with her visual memory. She twisted her mouth into a socially appropriate fond smile. She knew perfectly well what David IV looked like. He was a hell of a lot better looking, if it came to that, than most of the men on Vesta, including Marc Davidoff. He hadn't even had to have the surgery that would keep coworkers like Sandy in debt for years until they paid it off and it was time to work on corporate facelifts. He'd been born that way.

By now, he'd probably bought himself a tan and sunstreaks. God, that would be worth seeing.

And after she admired it, then what?

None of anyone else's damn business, that was what. Disappear into the latest trendy bed and breakfast with him and not come out except to catch her breath, that was what, too.

She sighed and reminded herself that respect and affection underlay most productive relationships. You didn't have to be madly in love. They had interests, and abilities in common. And a work history.

Up until now.

*When are you getting back?* David IV had asked once again.

What did he want? For her to meet him at the station when he came back from a lovely family holiday of the sort to which she had never been invited?

CC shook her head and decided it might be worth a little surgery of a different sort to get her work done better and faster so she could get back to him. And off this train of thought.

Wouldn't it?

Cost-benefit time.

The benefit: if she had her wrist-jacks opened, she could process more efficiently and, probably, get her data faster. She'd never been a serious cracker of systems—she'd been too law-abiding for that; but she was resourceful and wily in pursuit of information she'd marked as her rightful prey.

The cost? *You've already had one run-in with Vesta's computers,* she told herself. "Fool me twice, shame on me." Especially if she was left with tofu for brains, or whatever they served in long-term public hospitalization wards.

She'd fought to get rid of those jacks, the province of shipsicles and students. She'd paid off the loans. Why on Earth—or Vesta—would she go back to those days? And if she ever did get invited to one of those sunlit, sports-filled vacations, she'd have to wear sweatbands on her wrists to hide the surgery, testament to her experiment in downward mobility.

Far better to get information the old fashioned ways: download, beg, borrow, or intimidate coworkers.

In other words, better not. Keep her options open.

So, covered mug of reconstituted "caffiend" clipped to her

workstation, CC sent out requests for spreadsheets—little drops of poison in the datapools that stretched across the Asteroid Belt from the Inner Offices of Mars, Luna, and Earth, drops spreading out in the offices there and causing consternation because Audit Time was even more hateful than taxes or a critical-asset drawdown cycle.

The excuses would speedily follow, to say nothing of the followups she'd send tomorrow to the people who thought that if they ignored her requests, she'd disappear as easily as they'd deleted her messages.

For now, she could review Elizabeth's records of the past years' audits. Sure, she'd amassed enough data to show front-running and fraud were definitely going on. But Alpha didn't pay her the not-so-big salary for half a job. The puzzle had a hell of a lot more pieces, she was sure of it; and it was the big picture they were looking for.

She glanced at her shipsuit's wrist. She had enough time to get started. At 13:30, she'd leave. Wouldn't do to be late for her tour of the electrolysis plant. With luck, it would go better than the tour of Hydro or some of her other adventures.

Next to the recycling plant, which didn't just hide its mistakes, but sliced, diced, and repackaged them, the electrolysis plant was potentially one of the most dangerous—and important—places in Vesta Colony.

Here, they made air.

At precisely 1400, the low-g crocodile of people touring the electrolysis plant was led in. CC grimaced at the sight of Sandy in the queue waiting for security scan. He was going to come over and try to find out whether she was invited to the Neaves' party.

Oh my God, here he came. How long had Sandy been on Vesta? Just as long as she. Yet he still had to wear a tether? For pity's sake!

CC made her face a polite blank when a security guard got into his path with "You can't go that way, sir," and steered him her way. She even mustered a smile as she gave

him news he wouldn't like. Yes, she was going to the
Neaves' party. "See you there," she said. She fended off his
various fishing expeditions, then hissed "pay attention" in a
way that reduced him to the status of a disruptive intern.

As the tourists entered, they attached themselves to
handrails with a loop that paid out into a long tether, much
like a dog's leash back home: you had room to roam, but
could, at need, be yanked back. The plant was interesting: it
wasn't necessarily safe. Precautions were in place, but precautions didn't always work, and could easily be overset by
plain bad luck, not to mention malice or stupidity.

Plenty of examples of bad luck confronted her as she ex-
plored. Working at the tanks, operating the consoles were
techs and apprentices, some wearing their indenture badges
right next to marks of rank that meant they'd soon earn
out—assuming they survived. Many of them were injured.
Some wore scars with an unconcern that had to be real, scars
that would have been repaired, if possible, with expensive
surgery or borne apologetically as a badge of insolvency.

She saw several people missing fingers, and even one man
who took a magnificent leap from one work station to the
next and landed on the one foot he had left.

Life on the frontier. People on Vesta Colony just didn't
seem to care about the things that most of CC's coworkers
spent their lives working toward. Life here was pared down,
remarkable for its lack of ostentation and its matter-of-fact
tolerance of working conditions and consequences that
would have had even the highest-level managers threatening
class-action suits back on Earth.

CC shuddered. For a moment, the guide's voice faded into
inaudibility.

Once is happenstance. Twice is coincidence. The third
time is enemy action. She was still on "twice," even if the
accident in mining was the sort of thing that just happened
out here. Abruptly, she felt as much sealed away from the
tour as if she'd put on a pressure suit and locked down the
helmet.

She might be safer that way, in any case.

The tour she'd taken—apart from the fiasco in Hydroponics—had almost made her a statistic. She'd been visiting what DeBeers Amsterdam called its "pipe"—a pit "outside" the colony, dug into the rock. Here she'd seen evidence of black diamonds of such purity and abundance that she understood why most people on Vesta didn't bother to wear any jewelry at all. Smart of DeBeers to control the supply so rigorously to keep prices high back on Earth. Back at headquarters, she'd had the chance to look at unpolished samples, then the finished gems resting against black velvet, glinting under hot lights.

Then they'd taken CC and the other dignitaries Outside where the miners worked in pressure suits. She'd remembered how her cheeks heated in her pressure helm. No matter how pretty those gems she had seen exhibited in the main offices were—and there'd been some that made her own solitaire look fake—were they really worth the risks these suited figures took each day so women like her, back on Earth, could flaunt trophies of their success on unscarred hands?

CC had stared down at her own hands, hidden by gauntlets, in a sudden flush of shame that her suit had instantly adjusted to compensate for. To think of it: when Mac had told her not to wear her ring here, she'd thought he was simply being a reverse snob.

Think of it as a learning experience, she told herself. But the irony was getting old fast.

Time to grow up, CC-girl. Values were for more than mission statements and socially responsible investment programs.

They were for real. If she had to put her life and future on the line this far from home in order to value them for the first time, it was time, and past time. First get the finances and security squared away, she'd always told herself. Then you can worry about being humane. She was more than beginning to suspect she'd had her priorities reversed.

Just as she'd reached this elevated conclusion, the clear-the-area sirens whooped and blared. The sound, confined within the close quarters of her helm, was almost sickening. She lurched and shivered, disoriented, as red lights flashed overhead, turning the shadows beneath the stars into a foretaste of hell.

A tech hurtled at her, his body almost flat as he reached her, and gave her a shove that sent her careening away from the group toward the ore-train tracks just as the heavy, robot-controlled train of carts carrying rough ore lurched, gained speed, failed to take a curve, and jumped its tracks.

*"Get back, GET THEM!"*

Something hit her at the small of her back, hurling her away from the heavy, fast little trolleys that were so deadly when they weren't controlled.

Something screamed in her earphones. Screamed, gurgled, and went silent.

Before they'd immobilized the ore train with a power surge that fused its wheels, three people's environmental suits had been holed. She'd heard one of them scream as his lungs filled. A fatality. The dead man lay near the immobilized train. Before security could stop them, his work gang had straightened his limbs and brought a thermal blanket to cover him. For the few minutes until a body bag could be brought up, they stood around his body at attention.

A miner lost two fingers. She'd been lucky; the hole hadn't been wide, and her suit had resealed in time. Now CC remembered the sudden, ugly rush of blood, a brilliant thick red in the flashing helmet lights. How quickly it froze, saving the worker's life as her suit autosealed.

MedCenter would graft fingers on. They wouldn't be pretty, but they would at least work: off-work on disability was a luxury no Vestan could afford, and mining paid better than any other heavy-labor, low-skill work.

"Don't worry about the worker," her guide reassured her when she'd asked. "If you're injured in the line of duty, worker's comp will cover the repairs. If, later on, she wants cosmetic work, well, we have a good benefits plan, and she'll be able to arrange a payment schedule."

The third person who'd been hit was Sandy. The moment

before all hell broke loose and she'd been shoved to one side, he'd been standing close to her, exchanging work-gossip in between lectures. Except for the sorts of memories that would wake him at 0400 for the rest of his life unless he had the guts to admit he needed help, he was one of the lucky ones: his suit had activated its emergency seals within seconds, and he'd managed to vomit without aspirating.

The tech who'd pushed him aside hadn't lived long enough for Sandy to thank him. He too had a blanket and an honor guard until he was carried away.

Sandy leaned against a pile of equipment. His suit was spattered with the dead man's frozen blood. If it were her, she'd be shaking, but Sandy's bulky suit concealed what he had to be feeling.

That suit, CC realized, the suit that had saved him, was a duplicate of the one she wore. What's more, they were much of a height. Had someone spotted the pair of them, not known which one to attack, and decided to take out two for the price of one? But who? That, she decided, was a thought she wouldn't share with anyone—not unless she wanted to be on a quick ship back to Earth on medical disability.

Once, happenstance. Twice, coincidence.

Maybe industrial accidents Outside are common, judging from the number of scars you've seen around here. The bunch at Gorsky's Hole seemed to gloss over it.

But there was one thing she couldn't forget. Sandy had been wearing a suit just like hers.

People shifted position around her. She edged away, not liking to be that close to strangers, strangers who could put out a casual-seeming hand and give her a—

*Stop it!*

She shivered and turned her attention back to the guide.

"All right, ladies and gentlemen, if I may have your attention, we will continue." And on they trudged.

"Now, over here . . ." The guide was pointing toward the next point of interest in DeBeers' mining operation.

Dammit, were they actually going to continue the tour? Corporate tour. It was part of the job. So of course they were.

Her mind flashed back to a story she'd heard of a board meeting in New York on September 11, 2001, a day that needed no explanation in her industry.

There'd been a meeting going on in an office building half the island away. An assistant had interrupted it, screaming about planes crashing into buildings. After her manager scolded her and sent her out of the room, he finished the meeting. Only then did he consent to be evacuated.

She could just imagine the comments in Gorsky's Hole. Damn fool. Heartless bastard. Should have dragged him out. Kicked his ass down to ground level.

But it was why the tour had to go on. Business as usual.


"Ms. Williams? Ms. Williams? Please keep up with the group."

CC nodded, coloring, and focused her attention. Her recollection of the incident Outside had been so vivid, she had to blink before remembering where she was: the electrolysis plant, safely, securely Indoors.

The faces and hands of the people in the electrolysis plant bore further evidence of working conditions—and an acceptance of imperfection—that would have had CC's Earth colleagues screaming and calling their lawyers: freezer burn, keloids, scars from tumor removal without cosmetic reconstruction.

The process conducted high-temperature gas-phase electrolysis of carbon dioxide and split $CO_2$ into carbon monoxide and an oxygen ion. Once the oxygen ions were passed through a membrane with an electrical potential difference, they emerged as pure oxygen. That, in turn, was heated with a solid catalyst to produce $CO_2$ and solid carbon.

In this part of the plant, the process was being used on water instead of $CO_2$ to make oxygen and hydrogen gas.

They'd eased down a ramp, split down the center by equipment tracks, before walking over to look at the tanks and listen to a lecture on how this process made the very air that Vesta Colony breathed.

The guide's tone, composed of equal parts delight in imparting information and slightly overdone professional goodwill, made CC suppress a smile. Even after all these years, she still had to stifle the impulse she'd had since childhood to wag her hand in the air and ask questions that would get her noticed and praised. She was, thank God, no longer in school. She didn't want to be noticed now. In fact . . .

"Watch out!"

A series of beeps quickened into an electronic howl as some sort of robot carrier—CC couldn't see it clearly—zoomed down the metal track they'd crossed. As their guide released the tethers so they wouldn't be cut, people leapt instinctively away from the runaway equipment.

That was when CC saw that the tank, which should have been securely closed so that precious water didn't evaporate into the dry air, was gaping open. And, for the second time in less than a week, she felt a hand at the small of her back, pushing her forward.

Not again! she thought. At least she was ready for it this time. She started the twist and swerve that had saved her from a ducking at Hydroponics, but the hand at her back hung on, making it impossible for her to get cleanly away. And she couldn't see her attacker's face.

You can't drown in low g! she told herself as she felt her feet leave the ground.

But you could, if you struck your head and fell into the water face down. And if someone ran a charge through that tank . . .

The hell with not being noticed.

CC opened her mouth and screamed, then closed it as water poured in. A yank on her tether jerked her back to the tank's edge, and she felt hands clamp beneath her arms, dragging her out of the water and down onto the platform into a huddle of frightened tourists, angry security, and one thoroughly alarmed consultant dripping onto the deck.

The intercom was blaring orders for a medic when CC managed to evade the people who insisted on gabbling "you've had a shock, are you all right, did you see who shoved you?" in her face while she coughed and spat water she'd probably get billed for. She'd charge it off to worker's comp, she told herself.

Once again, she hadn't seen who pushed her. But never mind that. If the thing that slid down that track had hit anyone, if the terrified guide now being stared at, almost jaw to jaw, by a furious security officer, hadn't been quick enough and cut their tethers, people might have been killed.

She'd have to see that the guide was commended. Maybe a note, on the real paper she'd brought along with the Alpha crest, might help.

As it was, only CC got a bath. On Vesta, she knew, people would pay good money to bathe in that amount of water.

The thought made her giggle. She could probably get a laugh out of that at Gorsky's Hole. If they didn't decide she was a careless bitch of a damn civilian and throw her out on her ass. In Vesta gravity, she'd probably fly a long, long way before she touched down.

"Inappropriate humor," naturally, got reported, much to her frustration, which she also showed. When the medic arrived, the first thing he did was sedate her. By the time her lips grew too rubbery to protest, he'd ordered her fastened to a gurney and delivered to her room.

"The trouble with you Earth corporates, madam," he lectured her all the way back in English accented with an Indian singsong, "is that you turn sleeplessness into a status symbol, which it is most decidedly not. Sleep deprivation is a problem, especially out here in low g, where sleep patterns can get interrupted anyhow. Tired is stupid. Stupid is unsafe. Stupid corporates become corpses."

*We can always use the reaction mass,* CC was sure that someone at the Hole would probably comment.

CC waggled one hand through the restraints. Enough feedback, her gesture meant. She was still an associate at Alpha Consulting, and the medician was only staff, getting off on the reversal, the very temporary reversal, of power.

Overriding the medician and his commands to lie quietly, CC forced words out of a throat raw from coughing.

"Do you have that passageway on camera?" she demanded.

"I ought to run you into MedCenter," the man grumbled, ignoring her. "A night or so under centrifuge, and we'd get your sleep deficit back in order."

"Do you have security cam in that passageway?" she demanded again.

"I will check, madam. But I'm telling you right now, you *will* get some rest. I'm telling Security you're locked out of your computer and locked into quarters until 0800 tomorrow, when you will be escorted to MedCenter for a thorough examination."

She had thoroughly antagonized him, she could see that now. But angry could be useful; at least, he was talking to her straight now, never mind the formal "madam."

"What you do after that's your own damn business, but, as I always say, Vesta isn't for everyone. Why they send us you damn career . . . Shit, probably shouldn't talk that way, you're still live enough to report me. . . . Oh well." The singsong accent had vanished.

He bent and adjusted something. What felt like an endorphin rush poured through her, making fear a thing of the past.

*More, dammit! More meds!*

She bit her lip against giggling, then gave it up as a bad job as her mouth went slack, first with pleasure, then with drowsiness.

Why, that sneaky bastard was going to put her out so he'd be sure she got some sleep! The "madam" corporate-deference routine had all been a scam.

CC didn't have time for this!

She fought the growing fog of sleep, but her eyelids were closing like pressure seals. The last time she'd drifted this way, she'd been tethered in zero-g. And this was so much more peaceful. Warm, with a blanket covering her even though she wasn't dead, dimming lights, soft voices . . .

Then, the lights, voices, *and* the fear, thank God, all went away.

\* \* \*

CC woke at what the chrono's green LEDs told her was six hours later with the beginnings of what she knew had to be spacer's throat—a nasty combination of a cold, a shock, dry air, and who knew what germs that had circulated since the colony went online. Emergency gear produced antibiotics and painkiller that made her start to drift again till a stray sensation in her relaxing mind brought her bolt upright, sweating not just with fear but adrenaline: Falling. Being pushed. Being held down.

Here was the real question, though. Was she meant to die, or simply be spooked so she'd exercise her panic option, pack up her stuff, and take the next ship home? Granted, she wouldn't have much to look forward to if she did that, but maybe that was the point. After all, why drown someone if you could make her commit career suicide?

It was a good question. She'd had three "incidents" in short order. That was three too many.

Even though she was safe for now, once she was released from her room and cleared by MedCenter, she'd see about getting some answers.

## / 18

**CC finished her letter to David IV and reread it carefully,**
lips moving, just the way she'd proof a memo to a managing
director.

Had she said everything she wanted and everything that
needed saying? Carefully, she had promised that, yes, she'd
certainly ask Neave if he remembered a social-climbing distant cousin—not! The ambassador probably had ambitious
relatives by the shipload. Much as she hated to deny David
IV anything because he asked so little of her, her response
contained just enough ambiguity that she'd probably be able
to weasel out of keeping it with a minimum of fallout. After
all, how likely was it that Madame would ever actually get to
meet her long-lost status symbol of a distant relation? It
wasn't as if David IV's mother made much of an effort to
meet CC either, when she was on planet.

Paying attention to the vivid verbs she'd used with such
advantage on her résumés over the years, CC gave an extra
polish to local color on Vesta, heightening how exotic she'd
found it, deleted a reference to Marc Davidoff, read the
thing again, and sent it off. Then, out of sheer boredom as
she waited to be discharged, she linked into her machine in
Elizabeth's office to check in.

Well, surprise again! Data city! Two of the spreadsheet matrices bore origination and time stamps from Phobos Center. A glance at the supplemental timestamps showed that, yes, indeed, the data had been carefully routed through the Bloomburg Boosting Units appropriate for transmissions from Mars. A matrixed spreadsheet, all the way from Luna. Once again CC noted dates, signoffs, BBU timestamps, and routing in case she needed to justify her conclusions.

Copying the data, she saved it to the data matrix she was building—a project, in its way, just as time-consuming and complex as the engineering that was gradually transforming Vesta Colony from an outpost into desirable real estate.

Then, just for good measure, she encrypted the material with one of Alpha Consultancies' proprietary lockcodes. Better wait till she had all the data before she started drawing conclusions. You could go down seriously wrong trails if you leapt before you knew all the parameters of your leap.

She was doing her followups, which included increasingly testy responses to the "What do U need this 4?" of various low-level illiterates as well as blasts to the passive-aggressives who had of course sent her half or a third of what she needed in the hope she'd go away—or at least bother someone else.

Her incomplete matrix glowed. She rotated it, observing every angle and highlighting where additional information was needed.

Go away? Just because she was already about as far away as she could get didn't mean she was out of the loop.

She saved the matrix, rubbed at the kink in her neck—even in Vesta's low gravity, she still developed muscle aches when she sat and worked for too long—and looked at the time.

Damnfool medicians. They'd promised to release her by now. Maybe it was an emergency. She hoped not: better to be mad at them than have them facing the sort of damage that an industrial accident could create. And besides, she'd only have to investigate that too, and the way her luck was running . . .

Another message. This was the third time she'd exchanged notes with the junior analyst over on Titan. What was he asking now? Couldn't he simply follow instructions and send her the damn data?

Of course she needed last year's quarterly as well as monthly statements, and she needed them year-over-year as well.

*"What did U do B4 you had this?"* he was asking in an inept version of e-bizspeak. Illiteracy squared and cubed. As if that was any of his business! If this sucker had been the one wanting data, he'd be all over her, and a whole lot less tactful.

At that, bad temper vanquished the remnants of her tact. What did she do, asked Our Man On Titan, before she'd found him to harass?

Unfortunate, potentially libelous choice of words. She'd make him pay for it.

She changed her screen to an impolite red. *"I looked at the entrails of a chicken!"* she replied, and sent the flame off before she had second thoughts. Either her mark would think she was crazy—and if he thought that, he probably had company across the solar system—or, with any luck, he'd think she was important enough to get seriously weird and testy with an underling.

Another message!

*"Now* what?" she asked herself. She wanted to slam her fist down on the keyboard, but in this damned gravity, doing that wouldn't give her enough bang for her buck, and she wouldn't hurt the keyboard anyhow.

A request for a meeting. Damn, who'd made Elizabeth or Mac that formal? She sighed and opened it.

Immediately, the message started to play "Clementine." CC found herself chuckling.

*"Yo, Jinxo!"* it greeted her. *"The Hole, 2200 tonight. That's an order!"*

No signoff. And when she doublechecked, no name on the "To" line, either.

Someone was being cute: Mac, maybe, or, given the message's theme song, Marc. Despite her thoroughly rotten mood, CC laughed aloud. Maybe it was overly cute. But it was damn funny.

As if the message—and, more probably, her laughter—broke some sort of glass ceiling, letters pinged and crawled across the bottom of her screen. Not a proper message, but an announcement from MedCenter.

Well, finally, thank God.

They were finally going to let CC go free.

She glanced over at the wall display: MedCenter gowns were shortsleeved and recyclable, no woven-in LEDs to tell the time. 2115? She'd just have time to wash, change, and haul ass, as Marc's friends would say, over to Gorsky's Hole.

"Here comes the Jinx!" Marc's raucous shout overpowered even the garish dazzle of light and the music that assaulted CC the instant she entered Gorsky's Hole.

CC laughed. "Hey, some people will do anything for a bath. Guess I'm just one of them. Don't you wish more newbies were like me?" she added, sniffing ostentatiously.

A roar went up, and CC basked in the laughter her insult had won.

Another man gave a chair a push on its clips, whirling it around to face her. "Sit down before you fall down," Marc ordered.

Beside him, crammed in at the long metal bar, two uniforms and a coverall gave snide cheers. Something edged, about the size of a buckeye, threatened to lodge in her throat. She was expected. They'd been concerned about her. And, in their own weird, ribald way, they still were.

"Yes, sir!" She took a careful meters-long stride forward, aiming for the chair and managing not to careen into the bar or drinkers before she brought herself up neatly and strapped herself in.

Almost simultaneously, Marc and another figure—Mac Nofi, of all people!—cut by three pilots relaxing after a tough day flying over rocks in vacuum to join CC at the small table she'd secured. Mac handed her a covered mug.

"What's that?" she asked, sniffing at it warily.

"You'll drink it and like it. Nutritional supplement. Your real drinks are cut off till the docs say otherwise. But your credit's still good," he wheedled. "Haven't heard anything about negative surprises in Alpha's quarterlies."

She glared at him to give it a rest.

"I don't know, Mac," said Davidoff. "Do we really want to drink with a jinx?"

"If she's buying, hell yes! Besides, I'd say she's lucky, not a jinx. Anyone else would be dead!" Nofi replied. "Don't you think so—Jinxo?" he asked her.

CC took a careful sip of the "supplement" and nearly choked. Despite Mac's helpful lies about MedCenter and no-alcohol, the covered mug held hot buttered rum.

*You better do something about that nickname right now,* she told herself. *If you get a rep as a jinx, it'll be serious bad karma in a place like this.*

"Don't call me Jinxo," she said firmly.

"Yeah, yeah, I saw that show too. Broadcast Classics of space exploration. On the History Channel a while back. But your name isn't Thomas; it's trouble!" said Marc. "I've been talking to your old friend here. Aside from the fact that you shouldn't be let out without a tether, Mac and I think you're about to find yourself in trouble that's high enough over your head to make that water you fell into look like a birdbath. So here's the deal. How long do you think it'll take you to finish up what you have to do here?"

"My initial assignment's for six months plus travel," she told Mac. "Look, you know as well as I that it's simply not economic to send me out for less time."

"Yeah, burial in space is just so cost-effective," Davidoff interrupted. "Assuming they find enough of you to bury. And if they don't turn it into reaction mass."

"Didn't know you cared!" she snapped at him. "Any . . . any newbie, what you call Vestal Virgins here . . . can run into a bad patch. If I'm not worried about it," she lied valiantly, "I don't see why it's any business of yours."

"Both of you, shut it down!" demanded Mac Nofi. "Look, CC, it's like this. You're getting a reputation as a hard worker and, from the people who really live here, well, we think you're a quick learner and a damned good sport. But you're a historian. Ever hear the old saying "once is happenstance; twice is coincidence . . ."

". . . and the third time is enemy action. Yeah-yeah," she singsonged. "But it's only two accidents so far."

"That's not quite true!" Marc echoed. "Look, your friend Sandy, that time at DeBeers? His suit looked just like yours, and he got hit. It's a wonder either of you is still alive."

"Look," CC said. "It's very sweet of you to be concerned and protective but . . ." She drew a deep, unsteady breath. No one had ever been quite this concerned, let alone quite this vehement, about the risks she'd been running her entire life. Protection had always been something other people exacted of her. She only wished she could bask in this temporary wealth of caring. . . . "But the thing is, I've got a job, an important job, to do, and I'm staying till it's done. End of story. Would you walk out on an assignment?"

"We're not talking about walking out on an assignment," Mac said. He struck the table with his fist so hard that he almost recoiled out of his chair. "Don't give me that corporate-macho crap. Elizabeth's told me you're starting to get solid data."

"Elizabeth!" CC said. "Now you're setting your girlfriend to spy on me? And she's Compliance? Mac, I don't want to begin to tell you how unprofessional, not to mention what a conflict of interests . . ."

"Look, CC, this isn't about unprofessional," said Davidoff. "It's about what you need to get the job done. You've already toured Vesta and damn near died. You've punched your ticket. So, go home. You don't need to be on-site to write your report. Elizabeth can have the data rerouted to you either on board ship or back on Earth, and I know you'll do a great job."

"You know, CC," Mac said urgently, "we've been friends a long time, and I'd rather not have to send a message to be read at your memorial service. David IV would only mumble through it anyhow. *Solar Queen*'s docking in three days. It's nothing fancy like *Rimrunner*, but it's a sound ship with a good record. What would it take to get you onto it?"

"A damn miracle!" CC snarled. "What's going on with you two? I barely see the two of you talk to each other, and suddenly, just like that, you're the famous Mac-and-Marc team that's determined to pull me off the biggest assignment of my career."

Marc clapped his hands together.

"Damn, this is what you get for calling her Jinxo. She starts talking like something out of an old vid," Mac said. "CC, I bet Marc solid money that you'd react like this. Couldn't get it through his jarhead. What the hell do you expect us to do about you?"

He waved to the bartender. "Another round over here."

The drinks arrived. She sniffed hers with deep suspicion and pushed it aside. "How do I know you won't drug it and simply dump me on board the next ship?" she asked. "Didn't they used to call that sort of thing 'shanghaiing'?"

"Look, Mac, old man," Marc Davidoff said. "I've got no problems with getting this damn fool off Vesta before she stupids herself to death. But I've got to tell you your tactics suck."

CC awarded Marc a look that reminded him that she'd had orders that had clearly specified he was supposed to help her.

"How about letting me do my damn job?" she muttered. She unstrapped herself from the chair and stood up to leave. She'd expected to enjoy herself this evening, she thought, angry at herself for the unaccountable sense of disappointment she felt.

"Fine," he said. "If you had the mass to match your guts, they'd probably draft you. Well, go and get yourself killed, if that's what it takes. But we'll be watching you. Speaking of which, have you seen the ILMnet features? The screen's huge, practically half the height of Mount Piazzi. Want to go? Tomorrow at 2100?"

"Got that dinner at the Neaves," CC said. As if he probably didn't know that. As if he weren't invited.

"So you do," he said. "Day after?"

"It's a date," she agreed. My God, it actually was, at that.

And laughed like a young girl. If it had been anyone else but Marc, with his orders to "give her every cooperation," she'd say he was hitting on her.

But he knew she was engaged to David IV. He even knew the family.

And she wasn't sure whether that reassured her or was the night's one disappointment.

## 19

**For the Neave-Lovat dinner, CC left her formal Earth-style** tunics and trousers in her quarters and wore only a clean shipsuit and jacket. She kept her ring locked up—all in deference to what she might as well call Vesta Colony etiquette, if that wasn't a contradiction in terms.

On Earth, corporate dinners were a precarious labyrinth of clothing calibrated to display not just each individual at his or her best, but to reveal current status. One was invited, after deliberations as serious as some trade treaties; one accepted after due consideration; and what one wore, ate, and drank were all matters for the utmost care.

On Earth, such dinners had been a test of Margaret Lovat's abilities, and she had all the resources and staff of a wealthy husband and a wealthy world to back her up. How would she manage here?

As the door marked Lovat/Neave (Vestans listed in alpha order, not seniority) slid open with a whoosh of well-functioning equipment and a chime that had never been part of Vestan door-signals before, Margaret Lovat was standing ready to greet her: old-fashioned Earth manners. She wore a black shipsuit. Basic black. Even though her hair was pulled back in a no-nonsense manner, the ceiling spots made its highlights glow like the jewels she wasn't wearing. High fashion, Vesta style. For a simple, casual family dinner.

"I'm glad you could come," Margaret said with a smile. "I just heard from my husband. As soon as he's done with his shift—yes, he's on the volunteer lists and his number came up for a shift in maintenance—he'll put in his time in the centrifuge, then come over."

"You'd think we hadn't left Earth," CC agreed. "We're still on call 24/7. I'm still having trouble integrating work-shifts and Earth days."

"But it's real work," said Margaret. "Mine's piling up right now, but we thought this dinner was important enough . . ."

If Vestan "society" was anything like Earth's, Margaret and Neave were already at the top of the food chain. So assuming they had no more connections they needed to make, they had to be making a point.

She shot a shrewd glance at Margaret, which was met by one equally shrewd, but considerably more serene.

She shrugged carefully. "I warned you, we're being very casual," the woman said. "If I even thought of serving half the foods we used to serve on Earth as a matter of course—you know those salads that look like little towers? Well, I was told in no uncertain terms that anything like that would probably go sailing across the room. Assuming we could manage all the ingredients, which we can't. Besides, I wanted to serve only foods produced here. Except the wines, of course." She laughed. Obediently, CC echoed her.

A hand lightly on CC's elbow, her hostess steered her into the suite she shared with her husband and children. The main living area was half again the size of hers, with cubicles leading off from it.

Nice size, CC thought, but nothing like the kind of quarters she'd have thought they could command. Track lights cast rainbows over the guests, reflecting off the beveled designs in the translucent room dividers, glamorizing them for a moment so they looked like guests at every party CC had ever attended—until the lights shifted, and you could see the scars and character lines on the faces that had not been sculpted, collagened, and botoxed away.

"What can I get you?" Margaret asked.

"Sparkling water with lime, please." The correct words came without thought.

Margaret grinned wickedly at her. "Relax, CC. Sun's over the yardarm somewhere, and we're all off the record here," she said. Her brow furrowed. No Botox, then. "Does anyone know what a yardarm is?" Margaret added plaintively.

Various guesses, mostly inaccurate except from the men and women in uniform, went up from the guests who'd already arrived. CC saw the silver jumpsuits of Final Frontier staff behind worktables, now draped with a heavy cloth and serving double duty as bar and buffet tables. Jordan and Engel, the owners, wearing the same livery, circulated freely, along with the man and woman—Robert and Vi—CC remembered from the ship, who'd been tutors to Margaret's children before they moved on to Colony jobs. Assorted military came as close as they could to relaxing, and even a few medstaff let themselves relax with wine.

Sandy was there, of course, PDA out and beaming for all his career was worth, as he circulated in the most approved Earth fashion among—"trade missions," Margaret Lovat threw the words over her shoulder. Then, clustered in a corner were three or four people whose scarred faces and hands gave evidence of long maintenance service.

"We met them while volunteering," Margaret said brightly. "At least two of that group were actually born here. You wouldn't believe how good they've been, helping us to arrange furniture swaps and scrounges. But they're a little shy."

CC followed her hostess as they drifted slowly throughout the room. Someone handed CC what looked like sparkling water, with a small wedge of lime from Hydroponics. CC raised an eyebrow. Spare no expense, it said.

"Try it!" Margaret urged her.

She sipped cautiously. "It's gin!" she said.

"Local product. We're thinking of investing in some of the local botanicals. I wonder what kind of price people on Earth might pay for Vesta-produced gin and vodka?"

"Earth." Not "home." Interesting.

"You'd have to market it as a luxury item," CC agreed. "Sell it at a premium price."

She bared her teeth amiably at Margaret and her former employee at the idea of idiots who'd pay the astronomical prices they'd no doubt charge. Would have to charge.

Robert, the botanist, shrugged. "Fools and their money," he said. Already, his speech had acquired the economic, ironic clip of a long-time colonist. "Final Frontiers just agreed to put it on the menu."

"How about Gorsky's Hole?" CC asked, to laughter only a little less raucous than at the bar.

"Not their sort of thing, they say. They're more beer than gin. Still, I haven't given up. The people at Gorsky's *drink*."

CC flushed and opened her mouth for the ritual cautions.

"Thanks," the former tutor, who'd put on weight and confidence even in his brief time on Vesta, said. "I'm not rushing into things. One of the selling points I've got in mind is that we use only materials found or grown out here. But I'm not locking in water futures yet. I'm rewriting my business plan. There's two writers, came in as shipsicles, who've agreed to edit in return for shares."

He pointed. A man and a woman whose unsteady posture as they acclimated themselves to low g hovered near around Elizabeth Inui as Sandy, of all things, bobbed at her elbow.

David IV would be astonished that Margaret Lovat and Neave, of all people, invited shipsicles to an important party. CC couldn't imagine what his mother would say.

The laughter rose, less subdued than she'd have heard at a corporate party back on Earth.

Margaret's voice, as she checked the pasta and salad stations, rose over the buzz of animated conversations. "I've reverted for tonight," she said. "I traded shifts; I'll be back on the job tomorrow. It's not as if the children need me now. Now they've passed their first-level exams, they don't need

tethers and can get around on their own— There you are!"
she called out to her husband.

Neave was wearing a jumpsuit the same color as those
worn by some of the shipsicles, though its cut, CC noted,
was considerably better.

He pushed off from the door in one long step, his practiced smile sharing itself among all the well-practiced corporate guests without leaving out the colonists.

Sandy nodded to Elizabeth. Making a good imitation of
controlling his eagerness, he headed toward Neave, picking
up a fresh drink from a silver-jumpsuited waiter. Catching
up, was he?

Smiling, Neave accepted the drink; smiling, he set it down
unobtrusively one long step later. He reached Margaret's
side in the center of the room and touched her hand to anchor himself with a smile that twisted CC's heart.

Margaret looked at the manager from Final Frontier, nodded, and raised her voice. "I'm told the wine's been cen-
trifuged, and if it breathes much longer, it'll die of anoxia. I'll
have you know it's the only import we're serving tonight!"

A cheer went up. It actually sounded sincere.

The odors of pasta and rich sauces rose in the air, so familiar that CC saw a number of people raise their eyebrows,
blink hard, and swallow. So the cheeses were local products,
some soy, some not, CC assumed. No meat: any cattle bred
out here were too valuable to be used for anything like sauce
Bolognese.

Margaret unsealed her pocket and drew out her PDA. Apparently, she'd slaved her quarters' maintenance systems to
it. The lights dimmed and music rose just as it did at every
dinner CC had ever attended. She grinned. On Earth, human
help was cheap. On Vesta, help was at a premium, and Margaret had adapted.

CC found herself tucked into a chair by cushions as she
attempted to maneuver sticky strands of pasta (local-variety
cheeses, she was told) to her mouth without wearing her dinner. For a corporate dinner on Earth, it would have been simple to the point of insult, ostentation, or political statement.

Here, however, it was a rare luxury. It wasn't just the maintenance techs who wolfed down the food, but people like Mac and Elizabeth, who had access to the best the Colony had to offer. And the trade delegations didn't seem to be displeased.

CC gazed around the room, watching groups form and reform, trying to pick up whispers. To her surprise, for this moment, the crowded room afforded her a few rare minutes of privacy. A moment longer, she promised herself, and she really would start networking again; after all, observation was also a part of her job.

She glanced around the mixed—the exceedingly mixed—crowd of guests. On Earth, if anyone had suggested that waitstaff, maintenance, techs, and corporates sit down and dine amiably together—she shook her head. No one would have suggested it. The trade delegates were avidly scanning the foods and the dishes, like slices of glittering geode, on which they were served. All produced locally, Neave was saying, in his role as an ambassador of trade. For awhile, they ignored the local people, until, again, Margaret gestured, and people rose from their seats and, just as they might on Earth, "mingled."

Preposterous as this assortment of people was, by Earth standards, here, it actually seemed to work. Was it just because the Ambassador and his lady had arranged it and the idea of feedbacking their hospitality was an even greater downcheck than eating with unsuitables? CC didn't think so. Neave and Margaret seemed to be adapting to Vesta. More than that. Margaret's serene smile looked real, not applied for the occasion like a lipstick.

Neave's face was flushed with enthusiasm. Over Hydroponics'-best salad offerings (in a dressing that adhered to the translucent stone bowl and prevented wandering greens), he shifted his seat to join a beaming Sandy and express relief that he'd survived the accident at DeBeers.

He waved his hand at CC. "I gather your fellow traveler from Earth"—one barb there, CC noted—"also has a history background," he said to Sandy, who instantly looked less comfortable. "I'd very much like to get your perspective on

204 / SUSAN SHWARTZ

this place. This evening, for example. Back on Earth, we would never have had the same freedom in dinner guests. We'd have been bound by custom. By caste, although I know that that is a word one no longer uses in polite conversation. Still, here on Vesta, I think we can abandon such customs. Although some of us have greater resources than others, we're all engaged in the same enterprise. Should the woman who oversees the quality of our air be less important than the man who heads up a company, but cannot service his own pressure suit? I don't think so. Failure in any position costs us, not just the points that seemed so important back on Earth, but our lives."

And Neave saluted with his wineglass—heavier, Vesta-produced glasses, not tubes—so enthusiastically that wine globules flew from it. One of the waiters launched himself toward Neave and caught the wine in a hoover branded with the logo of Final Frontier.

"Quite the speech, wasn't it?" came a growl at CC's elbow. She managed not to jump and send her dinner flying.

"Is it true, do you think?" she whispered to Mac, of all people.

"Don't know," he said. "But it's worth betting my life on. Don't you agree? Or are you still being risk averse?"

She saw Marc across the room. He saluted her wryly with two fingers at his forehead. Odd: he'd turned quite pale. She hoped he wasn't coming down with spacer's throat or anything like that.

Then, he turned back to Neave. A breach of corporate protocol: Marc should have focused on the senior man to the exclusion of all around him. But he'd always played by his own rules.

At least now, he was toeing the line: he and Neave turned so their backs were to everyone in the room.

CC grimaced at Mac, then angled her head toward the two men.

"Looks intense," said Mac. "Wonder why they don't take it outside. What do you think they're talking about?"

Without answering, CC rose to join him, fully aware she was playing for time.

The aroma of fine coffee—"We're calling it Piazzi Blue Mountain, but Margaret swears it's been adapted for espresso!" she heard Neave tell Sandy with a laugh—rose in the room, and steam from the Final Frontier's glittering pots was a welcome addition to the dry air.

The restaurant's staff circulated gracefully around the room, offering each guest a small covered cup that bore the Vesta Colony logo in glittering paint. Each espresso was garnished by a tiny slice of lemon rind from the hydroponics garden's precious trees.

"We'll do this in the high Roman fashion," Neave announced. CC, expecting mischief, was prepared, but Sandy almost choked on a final swallow of wine. The others, who might or might not have known what Romans were, but did know their host was sufficiently senior to get away with the obscure historical irrelevancy, arranged themselves in positions of polite attention.

"From the beginning of space exploration, one of the first technologies to benefit was the ancient ceramics industry. We would be pleased if you kept these cups as souvenirs of tonight's dinner. The spoons"—he laughed—"I'm sorry. Caterers say you have to return them!"

The laughter that rippled around the room was, again, louder than it would be on Earth, but almost wholly benevolent. Trade execs nodded to one another: whatever Romans were, they gave gifts. One man raised his PDA to scan in an image of the tiny cup.

"Don't worry," said Neave. "They're well under the maximum allowable gift. Shipping charges, however . . . let's just say we'll negotiate on them so we can make a market on these souvenirs when you get back Home. But I think my wife wishes to add something."

The lights shifted to cast a follow spot on Margaret, who had again risen from her seat between a hydroponics tech and an exec from a food NGO.

"I have learned," she said with what sounded like real happiness, "that some of our fellow guests didn't just travel with us on *Rimrunner,* but are also accomplished musicians. Some of them have been working on instruments they've built in their off-hours, and, while I apologize again for any hint that they're 'singing for their supper,' I did take it on myself to ask them to play tonight. They told me they hadn't a chance to work up much of a repertoire, but I'm sure we'll all make allowances for them—the first such group on Vesta. And so, ladies and gentlemen, I am very proud to ask you to listen to the first performance of—the Rimrunners!"

Applauding enthusiastically, but not so much so that she'd be propelled from her place, she accepted Sandy's hand and sank down into her cushions as the musicians drew themselves up, adjusted electronic sounding boards and fiber optic bows, and launched into a program that Margaret had shrewdly kept brief.

Delafold's Meditation in C Minor. It sounded much better, CC thought, in the thinner air of Vesta than it ever had on Earth. And then, to a gasp of amusement from Mac, the andante from Brahms's Sextet in B-flat major. CC shivered in pleasure. Yes, some of the bowing needed work. A great deal of work. One or two notes went awry. But she'd recently seen *Sarek* on ILMnet's classics series, and the music brought tears to her eyes. She whipped at them surreptitiously.

It wasn't the music, although Brahms was a composer CC had always loved. It was the attempt, here in what shipsicles had to consider exile from the home in which they couldn't afford to stay, to create art, to bring it out into the stars. Even in the harshest conditions known to humankind, there was music. For this alone, CC decided, it would have been worth coming to Vesta.

She glanced around the room and saw Marc, his fingers knitted over his forehead. CC's earlier unease returned. What was the matter with the man now?

As she watched him, he lowered his hands. His face had regained its normal color. Seeing her watching him, he smiled at her, and gestured.

*Welcome to my world.*

CC couldn't pretend she didn't understand the message or the temptation that it represented, regardless of his earlier warnings. *Stay. Stay here and build a life.*

Or the temptation she suddenly felt. None of this, she decided, would go into her reports to Alpha. She'd write, instead, of potential joint venture opportunities, of the Earth/Vesta balance of trade. She might even include a few warm-and-fuzzies about quality of life issues in the outer colonies, or an analysis of Vesta Colony corporate culture. But she'd say nothing about this concert or how she, like everyone else in the room, rose to their feet, weeping and cheering. Because there were no categories on any of Alpha's data matrices marked "joy."

## 20

**At least, CC thought, the recycled air in Vesta Colony's** Apsedra smelled better than MedCenter's walk-in clinic where she'd been putting in a volunteer shift in records processing. She shut her eyes, trying to remember a detail of the last file she'd worked on: something about encryption level. Volunteer or not, work was work, and she didn't fancy waking at 0400 with "Oh my God, a *mistake*!" putting her into adrenaline overdrive, as it had every day of her working life.

Naturally, she felt herself bump into someone.

She recoiled, falling back far enough that she knew she looked like a Vestal Virgin before she could rebalance. Her eyes flew open, taking in the flyover of EarthServ ships that had become at least a daily occurrence. Then, as hands caught her by the shoulders, a face entered her field of vision, and she shut her eyes again in chagrin.

Wouldn't you know it? Of all the people she hadn't expected to meet and didn't, in any event, want to meet, she would have to bump into Marc Davidoff. Literally.

"CC, I thought you'd passed your tether exam way back when," he scolded, grinning. "I can promise you this much.

Keep bumping into people and you'll be right back on the leash!"

"You wish!" she said. After all, Marc was certainly adroit enough to have dodged her. Clearly, he hadn't wished to, and he was having much too good a time at her expense.

Damn the man, where had he been?

As CC had fit into what Vesta Colony liked to call its social life, she'd gone with Davidoff a time or three to the Gates Center for Outworld Culture. He'd had a passion for historic old vids and at the slightest pretext would provide far too much information on films remastered into vids. The Gates Center had sponsored a series of First Contact vids: classics like *The Day the Earth Stood Still* and *Independence Day,* as well as more recent stories like *Black Destroyer* and an adaptation of Leinster's *First Contact.* CC might never be a fan, but his enthusiasm had been charming.

He'd also seen to it that she became a regular at Gorsky's Hole. She'd met him at the Neave-Lovats, run into him at the centrifuge, and seen him in the Apsedra from time to time. And throughout, he'd behaved, as the sayings went, like a perfect gentleman, like an officer and a gentleman—well, to the extent he could manage.

In that one thing, he reminded her of David IV and the other men she'd let herself get close to: no one pushed these days. Was it sheer good manners, fear of lawsuits, or was it her?

Damn. It wasn't as if she wanted him to . . . she lacked the words to say what she did or didn't want. But he'd become an integral part of her life here.

And then, the bastard had up and disappeared.

On assignment, the people at Gorsky's Hole had said in response to her hints. That's all they'd said. But "assignment" sounded a whole lot more ominous than "work" when it came packaged in that "I could tell you, but then I'd have to kill you, and probably everyone around me," "If I say more, it's insider trading" voice. Tenzing and Kate might like her, but when push came to shove, Marc was their friend. Marc wore the uniform. CC was a "fuckin' civilian." So she'd stopped going to Gorsky's Hole, she'd read over David IV's old letters, she'd written a few of her own that were so affectionate he'd expressed pleased surprise, and she thought she had her emotions back on track.

Just when she thought she had her arms around the situation, Marc showed up again. Her eyes and face went warm, then hot, in an instant, and she just knew the grin that had spread across her face was the size of Vesta's southern crater. God, she was an idiot.

"Good to see you," he said. "Want to go for a drink? We don't have to go back to Gorsky's Hole. In fact, I'd rather go someplace quieter."

He looked eager. Gentler, somehow, after ignoring her all these weeks. CC managed to wipe off her grin. So, it was a good thing he'd shown himself in his true colors: not a real friend.

*Friends, CC? After all these years, and you still expect to meet* friends? *Business is business. If you haven't learned that yet, you're way overdue for a refresher course. Be glad it's been no more painful than this.*

She bit her lip and told herself that Marc wasn't even a very reliable colleague. After all, he disappeared even though he'd been tasked with affording her every consideration. Just as well, really. Or she might have made the sort of mistake she'd really regret.

*You remember that, CC,* she cautioned herself. *You've set your priorities. And they're* smart *ones.*

Just because she'd been so happy to see Davidoff that she'd felt giddy from oxygen starvation was no reason to lose her grip—or the future she'd planned.

She summoned the image of David IV from her imagination. After his long vacation by the Atlantic, he'd have quite the suntan, even if it was likelier to result from cosmetics than the actual sun. David IV might be handsome; he wasn't stupid; and the ozone layer was far from repaired.

Armored now as if she stood in an emotional pressure suit, CC turned back to Marc and reduced her smile to socially polite dimensions. In response, his own smile dimmed.

"Thanks, Marc," she said. "That sounds like good fun. But I think I'd better get some more work done. These volunteer shifts—and 'mandatory volunteer work' is a contradiction in terms," she groused, "may not carry a whole lot of responsibility, but they're as tiring as my regular work, and they've really put me behind."

She was appalled at how hard it was to refuse.

Marc raised an eyebrow at her as if he knew exactly what she was thinking.

"Look," he said, "I'm sorry. But I had work to do, work I couldn't talk about. You know about security, don't you? Kind of like proprietary technology, but different?"

He grinned, inviting her to laugh at him.

CC shrugged, elaborately casual. She knew Alpha had black projects, but she didn't think—at least she hoped—that Marc wasn't referring to them.

*"He sounds like a boor, and I'm not surprised his family doesn't want him working in the business. But be nice to him, CC,"* David IV had written her. *"His family hasn't written him off, and they have Connections."*

Oh God, if she had to be nice to everyone in the worlds she knew whose families had Connections, she'd never stop being nice.

Which was probably the point.

"Nice" was rarely reciprocal. It meant she spent most of her time modeling appropriate behaviors as if they were the latest fashions, while CC herself might as well be in Freeze for all she got to say and do unmonitored.

On second thought, that was inaccurate. Shipsicles were closely monitored. Well, they were unconscious, so it probably didn't matter if their lifesigns were under constant scan, unless, of course, their dreams were evaluated too. Which they probably were.

*You haven't pretended around Margaret. Or even around*

*her husband.* That much was true, and it still scared hell out of her.

*Must be nice to have the resources, yes, and the Connections not to have to give a damn,* she thought with the usual pang of envy.

Aside from the Lovat-Neaves, who'd encouraged her . . . her friendship with Marc, what had "natural" behavior on Vesta gotten CC? Let's see: a few attempts on her life, a bad case of spacer's throat, and, because "you're fitting in so well!," she'd been assigned mandatory volunteer work just like a "real" Vestan.

Mac had been right. A smart woman like CC would finish up her work and go home. She had enough data for a report no one could fault, even if enthusiasm didn't hit orbital velocities.

She'd even gone as far as to check the schedules. *Rimrunner* was out of the question. She had no intention of staying long enough for *Rimrunner* to dock at Vesta Station again. *Solar Queen* had already fueled, taken on cargo and passengers, and departed, bound for Titan and Ganymede. Still, the number of ships making the circum-asteroid run had been picking up; it wouldn't be impossible to get a ship, maybe the *East India* or the *Buffett* in the next week or two.

"Come on, CC," Marc said. "Can't I convince you to have second thoughts?"

His coaxing tone made her turn back toward him. Anger at her own weakness made her ask crossly, "Well, what is it?"

"It'll be fun. And we need to catch up."

His eyes narrowed, reminding her. He'd been tasked to give her every possible cooperation. Maybe he was trying to make up for lost time.

She sighed. "On the off chance you're right," she conceded, "one drink. But you're buying. I've already squeezed my expense account till Headquarters is going to howl."

Marc grinned. "My treat," he agreed.

She would damn well stick to water and lime, she decided

as he took her arm and boosted her along at a speed that would have gotten her put back on tethers if she'd tried it on her own. The platforms with their Cylon guides were for newbies.

CC had reveled in her weekly water shower, a welcome respite from the chemicals and sonics the rest of the time. She should have been tired, given the additional volunteer shift she'd taken on and the "just one drink" that had turned into dinner and a long conversation with Marc on how CC was enjoying Vesta, the Neaves, her own work, and everyone at Gorsky's Hole. She'd had to admit she hadn't seen much of Tenzing and Kate. Or of Mac, which brought up that damned eyebrow of Marc's.

But his eyes had sparkled, even at her most pointed witticisms when they were aimed at him. And late in the evening, when they'd made serious inroads on Marc's credit balance and shifted from wine to brandy, to his bright particular dream, ships capable of going faster than light. He'd even walked her though the math that proved—Marc scoffed at that—that faster-than-light travel was physically impossible, trotted out tachyons, and, at the last, simply assumed such a wistful expression that CC just barely managed not to burst out laughing.

That had to be another reason he'd separated from the family business and joined the military: a man with a mission could make decisions that hurt the bottom line. If he was connected with a corporate Family, he couldn't be fired. But he could be shipped out, say, with a suitable remittance and encouraged to find an outlet for his unsuitable enthusiasms.

"I've said this before, and I'll say it again. Your drinks are cut off!" she'd told him.

"Nervy of you, seeing that I'm paying," he'd replied.

"Marc, you explained the math to me. You yourself say it's physically impossible. So you have to know you're

dreaming," she said bluntly. "You'd never get funding for
R&D, much less prototypes. Venture cap won't look at you,
and interest rates are so high, there isn't an NGO in the system that could borrow so much. You'd have to go to the . . ."

She'd fallen silent. Government agencies, she'd meant.
The ones that ran black projects that no one spoke of. Earth-
Serv might have enough funds for a co-venture, but Earth-
Serv projects definitely were black ones.

CC looked away, alarmed for him for the first time in their
acquaintance.

Had Marc told her too much? She was damned if she'd go
all supportive and womanly. Let's see, she could open with
"Oh do be careful," then move on to "I'm sure you know
what you're doing." Playing support was a whole lot like
playing middle management: at any moment, you risked
having to say contradictory things to keep your boss happy.

Not her style at all; she didn't have the right; and besides,
Marc would have laughed at her in any case.

Besides, if he'd told her too much, she'd do better to
watch out for herself. Marc's friends tended to come
equipped with weapons. CC's friends? Well, how many of
them did she really have?

Adrenaline coursed through her as it did whenever the
fear of having made a mistake woke her at 0400. Then, she
took a deep breath and adjusted her poker face. She had to
believe that, if she weren't cleared to listen to him blue-
skying, he wouldn't be saying a word.

Unless, of course, he had reasons of his own for spilling
his guts.

Maybe he was sounding her out or trying to glean data off
Alpha's capacious spreadsheets. Pumping her. Otherwise,
damned if she knew, she thought. And probably damned if
she'd let herself be drawn in.

Smart money was never on the man with the mission, unless the mission came accompanied with incredible capital-
ization levels.

She knew Marc's interests should put him on the short list

of people she should investigate. Somehow, though, she hadn't quite found the time. Or, she had to admit it, the nerve. It would be just like him to put a tracer on his own files and, next time they met, snicker at her for her curiosity.

If he didn't report her. She really didn't want to give him that advantage. But what if she didn't investigate him and something happened? Suspicion could fall on anyone else, including herself, and good-bye life, let alone lifestyle. She'd be brainwiped or reconfigured into spare parts before she could kiss her ass good-bye.

He hadn't even tried to kiss her. Not that he should, seeing as she was engaged. And not that she wanted him to. But he hadn't even tried. And he'd left her without a word of where he was going, what he was thinking, or when he would see her again.

If this went on, she was probably going to turn into a first-class paranoid. Either that, or homicidal.

Without much enthusiasm, CC turned on her workstation. If she wasn't sleepy—and she'd turned out to be one of the people for whom low g meant not insomnia but an actual physical need for less sleep—she might as well work on her report.

To her surprise, she found another letter from her fiancé. Three letters in five days: why, David IV was getting positively effusive! He'd gone back to New York, though, so he was probably missing Nantucket as well as CC herself.

*"I heard from Sandy, Jonathan Vinocur Sanderson as he's calling himself these days. Did you know he and I were interns together halfway through B school?"* David said. *"He's worried about you. Says you're all over the place, that you've been associating not just with people like Ambassador Neave, but with locals, including local military. Low-ranked ones at that. That's not like you, CC."*

Which was probably David IV's complaint. Senior military could mean connections at the policy level; CC's friends only meant cadged drinks.

*"What good can these people possibly do you? Have you lost your focus? What do you think you're playing at out in*

*the Belt? Reality-check time: You need to remember that
you're a professional woman with a bright career, not to
mention the woman I love. Remember that. You're not some
action hero off the kinds of vids only proles in the warehouses watch. And you know, you're not the only one who
cares about planning for our future."*

"*I really do wish you'd get back here,*" David IV went on
in what CC had begun to consider a well-orchestrated marketing campaign to lure her back to Earth before her work
was done. "*Since I left the Enclave, it's been boring. There's
been a few receptions; the VPs at my level are pretty much
expected to bring their partners, and it's getting hard to explain where you are.*"

"*I know you, CC. Even my father says you're one of the
best analysts he's ever seen. Haven't you got enough information yet to pin this mess on someone and come home?
Don't you want the next assignment—after our wedding? I
really do miss you. And Mother has a book of swatches she
wants to show you for the wedding and decorating our home.
Our first home together, CC.*"

Even two weeks ago, those words would have had her
dancing on air without benefit of microgravity. Now . . .
well, she supposed all that was nice to know.

For awhile, there, when all she'd heard from him was sun
on the sea, sailing, cookouts, and the people he networked
with over mojitos and G&Ts, she'd really wondered if he
still cared. It sounded as if he did. Or maybe he just wanted
a fiancée to take to receptions.

Saving the message and promising herself she'd answer it
tomorrow, *after* she'd slept off the brandy, she turned to the
rest of her messages.

There were, to her now-drowsy satisfaction, a great number of them. Surprise, surprise. So, the young lady and gentleman analysts had finally gotten around to her requests?
Who was the saint who'd insisted that the gentry out by Titan work for a living? For a welcome change.

CC ran a quick security check, then downloaded the welcome new data into her matrix. It glowed on her screen.

>>View as hologram.

*beep*

Interesting. She rotated the matrix, scrutinizing it from all angles. Now, she saw where many of her new, smaller files should go.

She assembled reports on traders, including biographies, work histories.

>>load to matrix

*beep*

>>Compile. List trades by quarter.

*beep*

>>Sort trades by traders.

*beep*

The system lit and flickered as it processed each command. CC raised her eyebrows: although past performance was no guarantee of future results, the Sunspot Index had really boosted trading volume systemwide. Well, she didn't need to be a rocket scientist to figure that out. All things being equal, she could expect to see results create a normal distribution curve.

They didn't. She saw a skew.

So far, so good. Now to pin down where the curve was skewed and how it was skewed.

If CC matched those data with her information on front-runners . . . she took a deep breath, as if she were a hunter in the Adirondacks Preserves drawing a bow on her licensed target. Once she knew how, she'd know who.

Non-linear processing, she thought with satisfaction. Computers still couldn't do it, and, though they talked about "lateral" and "out of the box" thinking in seminars on business strategy, it wasn't the sort of thing B-schools especially encouraged. Or could teach. It took a data hound with an un-tidy brain. Someone like CC.

This was where she was going to earn her bonus, her pro-motion—and her ticket to ride all the way home.

She shivered, not with cold but with anticipation. Calling up personnel lists, she red-flagged them both for suspected front-runners and for people who had displayed undue inter-est in her work.

The list formed on the screen. Not many surprises there. Mac. Marc. Even Margaret Lovat and Everett Neave. And, because she damn well meant to leave no stone unturned, she included Sandy. Interesting.

Now that she thought about it, as a suspect, her old class-mate and colleague wasn't even a sleeper. He'd always been the weasel that walked like a man. Since they'd started school and determined, within about five minutes, that they were going to escape their pasts, Sandy had always had an angle. He was especially the sort of person you tried to avoid in assignments emphasizing Working With, because he didn't so much work as coast. He'd leveraged his way through study group on old favors, mind games, and emo-tional blackmail. Back in B-school, she'd actually suspected him of having attached a datasuck to her group's network: there had to be some reason that his first-year marks had been so much better than anyone else's.

CC had always sworn she'd get to the bottom of that, and now she'd be able to.

>>Correlate traders, trades, and suspects.

There. She'd actually called the people on her list sus-pects for the first time.
*beep!*
CC sat up straight, looking at the columns as they formed, filled, and aligned.

>>Cross reference trades versus net worth.
>>Break out debt levels by individual.

*beep!*

Some bad debt levels there. No one had gone insolvent, which meant that somehow, people were managing to cover debt service.

Where were they getting the money from?

>>Matrix correlation: balance sheets/employee/attach Vesta Colony income statement.

CC whistled under her breath. Now that was interesting. More than interesting. Deadly.

For the past three years, Vesta appeared to have been importing more than it could pay for. Yet Vesta Colony's debt was in line with projections: she knew for a fact its sovereign credit rating had just been upgraded.

Where was the money coming from?

She glanced back at her list. Significant outflows from Mac's accounts into . . . why that was Marc's family's company! Those numbers were followed by disbursements in the next quarter to . . .

Oh shit.

CC nodded. Her initial instinct had been right to suspect front-running. And trading in shipsicles' accounts had been clever because very few people would be as complete and compulsive as she'd been to track them, trade by trade.

So, she knew *how*. She had a damned good idea of *who*. ("Whom," David IV would correct her in amusement. "CC, have you forgotten your grammar?" And he'd be wrong. Again.)

What about *why*?

Unless CC had forgotten the creative accounting strategies she'd had to study in order to detect cheats, someone, let's give Mac the benefit of the doubt and not use his name just yet, was laundering money through a prime broker, and feeding it back to Vesta Colony.

She knew Mac was angry and that he'd damn near gone bankrupt from his divorce.

How much was he making off these transactions? Easy

enough to turn basis points into a variety of currencies.

She came up with zero.

If indeed Mac was her name, he'd been laundering money and front-running trades, but he hadn't taken a payoff. Or, if he had, it wasn't showing up.

A non-material payoff? CC had been in business too long. She didn't believe in those any more.

Her assignment was falling into place. Mac's friendship, Elizabeth's cooperation, even Marc's help—damn, how much of this did he know?

Her system pinged with a new message.

CC felt her lips peel back from her teeth in anticipation. There was no such thing as just enough data, she decided for the nth time: it was either feast or a famine. Maybe VestaVox, too, had finally come through.

*Watch it,* she cautioned herself. The point about opening floodgates is that they let in floods.

The message came from Mac. *"I gave VV a little push. Don't say I've never given you anything. You owe me big-time, lady."*

She grinned appreciatively at the size of the VestaVox files. Big as her workstation's capacity was, they might fill it.

CC began the immense download.

Her screen flared, then flashed to the deep blue that had signaled computer disaster since the twentieth century.

Damn!

>>Emergency save.
>>Data recovery.
>>Undelete.

Would she be in time?

Whistling tensely under her breath, she watched. Why, she'd actually worked up a sweat, and her back ached.

Her screen lit again, hummed, made a grinding sound, then went black.

Every light in her quarters went out.

And the hum of air circulation, a background murmur you filtered out of your thoughts after the first few moments, ceased.

CC was alone in the dark and the silence.

Her eyes filled as she strained to see light, any light. She blinked angrily. The only lights she saw were the menacing thin red strips of emergency lights that outlined the exits, the door, and the survival gear. They were chemically treated, phosphorescent: of course they'd stay bright. Her doorseals were strong, proof against vacuum in case the Colony took a heavy meteor strike.

*Mac, you son of a bitch!* she thought. *The minute I get out of here, I am going to find you and I am going to kill you. Slowly.*

She strained to hear something, anything.

Then she heard something, all right: a faint, high whine, and her blood froze. She'd heard that sound just once, in orientation, as a warning sign: air leaking from a faulty seal.

Damn!

One terrified leap took CC in what she hoped was the direction of the door. The emergency seals had already locked it as tightly as the seals that protected the Main Concourse's skylight.

Don't panic.

Her ears were popping. The small, red-lit darkness of her quarters closed around her and spun.

Then a bell sounded and the hatch that concealed her survival gear, activated by the drop in air pressure opened.

CC hurled herself at the survival gear, clawing it open.

About time! Now the rest of the alarms were going off.

They might mean help, if anyone was alive and in shape to respond. But at this moment, they also meant an intolerable noise.

Would they ever shut up? Better question: would Security come in time? And could she get this damn bubble open before she blacked out?

The red lights seemed to be dimming, except for the ones

going off behind her eyes. She reeled, then propped herself against the open hatch and clawed at the bubble's access.

The effort left her panting and sweating. Her sweat turned cold. That wasn't just panic. The temperature was dropping fast.

Damn, what had fucked up life support?

Now the seal gave way. Quick, CC. She felt as if her freezing hands were encased in immense clown's gloves, but kept working.

Mac had access to infrastructure controls.

*Tell me he hadn't keyed a breakdown to those files,* she begged herself. *Tell me I can get through this alive!*

Thank God. The bubble was expanding now. She ducked so she could crawl into it. Lights exploded behind her eyes and in front of them, and roaring overpowered the alarms.

If she blacked out now, it would be a race between cold and anoxia to see which one would finish her off first. She wondered how long it would take David IV between "we regret to inform you" and backup plans.

*I'm not going to join you at that finish line,* she muttered to herself. Her teeth were chattering.

She tucked her robe about her, wadding it around and between her legs, and crammed herself into the personnel bubble.

Maybe she'd never been claustrophobic before, she thought, but this was a hell of a good way to start.

As epitaphs went, that was a pretty damn poor effort, she scolded herself. The lights inside her head flared, then faded.

Was this what it felt like to be a shipsicle?

Why it wasn't bad. Not bad. Not at all.

She'd be rid of her sleep deficit for once and for all. She crawled into the bubble and collapsed.

Warmed air hissed on from the bubble's built-in supply. For an instant, CC lay panting, basking in what seemed like tropical warmth and the notion that she'd managed to win herself a reprieve until the bubble's air supply ran out.

It took all the resolve she'd developed in years of fighting her way to a future she could live with to keep herself from tearing the bubble off and hurling herself at the door. Took the resolve, used it up, and spit out terror in one moment. She found more courage for the next moment, and the next . . . but it was going fast, along with her nerve.

A flick of a finger activated the medical scan. Heart and blood pressure up. Up so high CC almost sighed with relief because it would only be a matter of time until the bubble's autosystems put her out to reduce oxygen consumption.

She felt the thin rush of air along her arm, a sting, and then increasing calm.

The lights dimmed, then went away altogether.

An unspecified time later, her eyes popped open. The lights had come back on; her bubble had opened and de-flated; and she was lying on the floor.

The temptation to just lie there and let MedCenter and Se-curity find her grew almost overwhelming. They'd do a sweep of the living quarters; they'd find her, care for her—and send her home, just another casualty of a colony-wide mishap.

Assuming she hadn't been the intended victim.

Dammit, who'd set her up to fail?

CC glanced over at her workstation. Her screen was dark, except for the glowing green shield of VVDR, VestaVox's data recovery system.

Secure now in her air supply, she let herself exhale deeply, then drew in more air, luxuriating in it. At least, her files were safe and would be, at least till tomorrow.

Forcing herself to her feet, she gave a push, casting off to-ward her workstation. She'd settled herself into her chair and tethered herself by the time the shaking and nausea hit.

Computer had come up again, though distress lights were glowing like the bar at Gorsky's Hole. Even if she signaled she was all right, and she wasn't sure whether that was a lie or not, she was sure Security would make a full sweep of all living quarters.

She was determined that they'd find her quietly working.

Reported to MedCenter and Alpha, that news might end the rumors that she couldn't handle stress; reported to what she now finally had to admit herself was a potential murderer, it might allow her to pretend she wasn't half as frightened as she actually was.

*"Ms. Williams?"*

The voice from the intercom drew a gasp from her. She drew in a deep breath to steady her voice.

"Williams here."

She didn't sound nearly as frightened as she actually was: points to her.

*"Do you require immediate assistance?"*

"I'm fine," she said. The quaver in her voice was natural: too steady a tone might arouse suspicion.

*"Someone will be checking on you soon. Please stay in your quarters and remain calm."*

She heard the click that meant Security had allegedly signed off and bit her lip against a whimper of panic. It would have been nice to hear from someone who could convince her that things really would be all right and no one was trying to kill her. Someone like Marc. Or Mac. No, that wasn't right; Mac had gone bad; Mac had access to life support; Mac was definitely on her suspects list.

So, she'd have to get herself under control all by herself. After all, it wasn't as if she hadn't had plenty of practice in self-control. She was a good survivor—at least, she'd been back on Earth before an expense account and a resume stood between her, Freeze, or the work gangs.

*Fake it, CC,* she encouraged herself. *C'mon, girl. Just like in the* insulae. *At least it isn't a whole gang stalking you this time.*

Or was it?

She'd bluffed then. She could bluff now. Another good long deep breath, and thank you, God *and* Maintenance, for putting the air back. So Security would find her composedly working away.

Yes, she'd say, she had followed correct emergency procedures. Yes, she was very grateful for her training. Yes, she had been alarmed. No, thank you, officers, she didn't want to spend the night in MedCenter, and certainly she did not want to have a talk with the post-traumatic stress specialists. God knows how much of that was recorded, and her medical carriers were authorized to release data to a host of organizations that could do her no good. Thank you, she was just fine, and if they thought it was safe and did not wish her to evacuate, she thought she'd just go quietly to bed.

And all of those statements except for the last one were absolutely true.

What CC really intended to do was get back to the data she could have died for downloading. It was evidence. Once she had it organized, she was going to find Neave and talk to him. And then she was going to strangle Mac with her bare hands.

If it was the last thing she ever did. And it very well might be.

## 21

**"I'm fine!" CC insisted to Margaret Lovat, who hovered over** her with an additional blanket.

She was wedged into a corner of the Lovat-Neaves' biggest chair with pillows, cocooned with blankets. She'd thought she was over the shock of the night before. Then Everett Neave had invited her over and looked her up and down with eyes that saw too much. They must have made him a total nightmare in negotiating, if you were on the opposite side. Instantly, she'd started to shiver. Then she'd committed the unforgivable business sin of bursting into tears. An hour later, and she still couldn't stop shaking.

But she could still talk, she found. She could talk just fine, even if her teeth did chatter.

CC tucked her hands under all the fabric until they were warm enough to hold a covered mug.

"My model's too big for my Breitling," she told Neave. "Want to risk letting me onto your system?"

"I'm going to have to," he said. "Margaret, please take that cup from CC, then go over to the survival gear. If we have another episode like last night's . . ."

CC's gut twisted. If there was another life-support failure, he knew his children were in the shelters, and he'd at least make sure his wife was protected. And even now, he said "please."

You didn't learn that kind of consideration in corporate charm schools. Not so it showed in your eyes as well as what you said. *God, I wish I could afford to be a good person,* CC thought again.

"We have a guest, Ev. We can hardly abandon her."

"Of course," Neave said. "But I am going to beep the chil— No, if I . . . that could cause a panic."

Fear stamped an anxious kinship across their faces before, visibly, they suppressed it.

Margaret's fingers brushed hers as she took the hot cup, conveying reassurance. CC gulped at its contents—some sort of nutritional gunk, heated for greater comfort. In Gorsky's Hole, Mac had threatened to make her drink this stuff. But he'd given her hot buttered rum instead.

Don't think of Mac, she ordered herself. Don't think of the years of friendship, or his welcome when you landed here. Mac laundered money; he tried to kill you. He even tried to kill this colony, which had given him a fresh start. People like that don't have friends, just victims.

"I'll make this quick," she said, "so you can get to your kids in case you need to. Here goes nothing."

She accessed Neave's system and brought up her data matrix.

Neave leaned forward to study it. "Nice macro view," he said. "I like how you've compared the economic conditions in each colony with Earth, Luna, and Venus Station. It's a good cross-check and confirms the anomalies you've found."

"With respect, the macro picture's not the issue, Ambassa . . . I mean, Mr. Neave," CC broke in.

Red threads had been woven into the coverlet Margaret had wrapped around her. She drew her thumbnail down the design, trying not to focus on the ache of fear and betrayal within.

"Call me Everett, why don't you?" he asked. "After all, you call my wife Margaret."

Mind your manners, CC. A demon danced inside her brain. She was engaged to David IV, whose mother thought she was some sort of cousin to Neave. So it actually was all family.

Wasn't it?

"Thanks, sir . . . Everett," CC said instantly. "Here's the problem. Something's coming into Vesta Colony. A lot of somethings. Taken separately, nothing's particularly incriminating. Taken piece by piece, you've got a hell of a lot of commodities here that are coming in and . . . just vanishing. We've got what looks like a case of Mac Nofi's pulling an Enron on the colony's financial records. And the instant I find confirmation of my theory, systems crash all over the colony. Thousands of people could have been killed."

And the whole colony could have been written off as a bad investment. The loss could have plunged investor nations into deep recessions and what it would do to the balance sheets of the companies that were its limited partners . . . well, they'd be targets for vulture financings on a scale no one had ever seen before. Anyone with enough capital could pick them up for a fraction of their prior value. Someone would come out on top while everyone on Vesta went into a Freeze from which no resurrection was possible.

"I'd hate to think that Mac Nofi went rogue," Margaret said. She shook her head so vigorously that her whole body jolted in the light gravity. "He's been a guest in our home. But when you eliminate the impossible . . ."

Her eyes met Neave's.

"I don't want to believe it either," Neave—Everett—said. "But I have to say I'm impressed, CC. You've done the job you came out here to do, at least, you have if I understand you correctly, and your work has even turned up this . . . this . . . Yes, I think I can assure you, Alpha will be pleased. The government, too."

*I didn't think you were really retired. And now I know for sure.*

"You can leave this with me," he said. He bent over his machine and saved himself a copy.

Was that all? CC had worked her ass off when she wasn't putting it in various slings, and for what? To be told thanks, good girl, now drop it?

Not bloody likely.

Still, she knew the drill. Knew it well.

"Thank you, Everett," she said firmly.

*Accept your dismissal like a good doggie, move yourself on out, and keep on going,* she told herself.

Maybe Neave would take action: hell, even if he sent her results back to Earth, she was covered.

But by the time a decision, to say nothing of enforcers, came to Vesta, it might be too late.

After all, Alpha emphasized the ability to take the initiative.

Neatly, CC folded the wraps Margaret had heaped on her, rearranged the pillows, thanked her hosts, and escaped. She didn't think Mac would attack the colony's infrastructure again. At least, not this soon.

And she had a new idea that she was simply dying to get to work on. She'd hedge her bets, as well as her funds. That was the prudent thing to do, she decided.

Even if she knew she was rationalizing.


CC propelled herself across the Apsedra. Halfway across it, the magnificence of the starscape caught her attention, as it always did. She paused and looked up for an instant, as she always did. Had the number of fly-bys increased? She couldn't remember having seen so many small flares darting low in the dark sky.

Not her problem right now, she thought. She wanted to get back to her quarters, and her own system, and find out what had happened to the trading manifests of the ships onto which the cargoes her culprit—oh, Mac, you goddamned fool!—had bought had been loaded. What the hell had he been buying that he thought was worth ruining the economy of a place that had taken him in? That had given him a job and a future when the life he'd made on his own had crashed and burned.

Enough stargazing, she told herself, turned to go—and ran straight into Mac Nofi himself.

All her years of self-control paid off in an instant. She didn't shriek with terror. She knew that her face was perfectly, professionally composed.

"Mac," she said, in the formal cordiality you usually reserved for meetings with clients, "good to see you."

He put a hand on her arm. She flinched, then realized that this was a public place: all she had to do was scream, and Security would come.

Assuming he hadn't bought them off.

Well, if not Security, then someone. She could make it out to be a social crime. Civilians might even respond to that.

Still in formal politeness mode, CC glanced down at his hand and raised an eyebrow.

"Cut the crap, CC," Mac snarled.

"You cut the crap!" she snapped back. "Just because you've got a bug up it the size of your fist doesn't mean you've got the right to take it out on me."

To her astonishment, that won a laugh. "The bug or my god-awful mood?" he demanded.

CC had seen traders who'd gone bad led off the floor in e-cuffs, stinging them at every step and twice at every stumble. They'd always looked guilty, or angry at being caught: none of them had ever showed this sort of righteous indignation. Fear for themselves, yes. But not the kind of fear she saw in Mac's eyes.

Either he was innocent, or a very, very good actor. And he'd always prided himself on what he called his "poker face."

CC found herself able to laugh. Well, just because she'd been freaking out right, left, and center because she'd faced sudden death by drowning, sharp implements, and oxygen starvation at various times in the past months didn't mean she'd lost her own coolness in human crises.

"Yes!" she answered. "Mac, you've got a glare on you that could melt diamond. And if you don't let go of me, I'm going to have another bruise to add to the collection I picked up last night banging into things after the lights went out. What's biting you?"

Mac released the pressure on her arm, but started towing her. Where? CC's eyes tracked his line of march, picking out statues, stanchions, doorways, where she could latch on while she screamed for help, if need be. It wasn't time to make a scene. Yet.

"All these years of hard work," Mac snarled, "and they're treating me like a damned fool. Or a shipsicle transported here for petty crime."

*Not so petty, if you've done what I think, mister.*

"Let's sit down somewhere secure," he said.

"I was heading back to my quarters," CC protested. "Your office is too far out of my way. Can't we stay here?"

He bared his teeth at her. "Hell, CC, not you too! Well, why the fuck not? We can't go back to my office. It's trashed, and they've got yellow tape up to seal it. Someone broke in. What I saw before Security came and caught me—*me!*—around the collar and frog-marched me out didn't look like a break-in. It looked like a damn thorough search to me."

CC tilted her head. "Damn, Mac. Sounds as if you ticked off someone really important," she said. "Got any idea who?"

Mac eyed her narrowly. It didn't take much effort for her to look innocent. After all, she hadn't turned him in. At least, she second-guessed herself, she hadn't turned him in yet. And now his office was trashed. Had he done it himself? Security cameras might show, but he could bollix them.

CC shrugged. "Don't look at me. I haven't got the kind of contacts around here that it would take to authorize

an . . ." she could feel the black humor bubble up and erupt
". . . unauthorized search."

Not that he wouldn't trash his own office, if need be, to
cover his tracks and shift suspicion away from him.

"You're Alpha, CC," Mac said. "Some are born weasels,
some attain weasel-hood, and some have weasel-hood thrust
upon them. Don't tell me you couldn't arrange this if you
had a mind to. I've got my own tracers out, and so help me,
when I find out . . ."

This was more than righteous indignation, CC decided.
Mac wasn't just furious; she hadn't smelled that level of fear
since she'd fled the warehouse gangs.

"Have you talked to Marc?" she blurted out.

She wouldn't have thought it possible, but the fear in
Mac's eyes intensified, fear mixed with guilt.

"He's offsite," he muttered. "I suppose I shouldn't have
told you that, but hell, CC, you'd find out about it anyhow.
Look, I need a favor," he said, changing ground with the
speed that had always been one of his best survival traits.

The damn thing was, she owed Mac. Big time. He had
given her her first job in the industry. He'd taught her the beginnings of what she knew about defense industries, how to
cultivate a poker face of her own, how to talk, and how to
bluff. He was no fool; he had to know her about as well as
she'd thought she'd known him.

*No way I'm going someplace secure with you, mister,* she
thought. *I've already used up at least three of my nine lives.*

"If I can, Mac, I will," she said. Damn. Her voice sounded
too wary to conceal her suspicions.

"I can promise you, I've got my own tracers out," he said.
"And if . . . when I find out what . . ." He drew a deep breath
and collected himself, one of those dazzling switches from
full-throated rage to calculated charm she'd always admired.
"If you hear anything you can tell me, CC, I'd appreciate it.
Don't cross any lines to do it," he added.

He released her arm, nodded firmly at her, trying to smile
and reassure her the way he had when she'd been a new re-

search assistant and had screwed up a report. She knew her eyes had gotten wide as they did when she was nervous. "No harm done," he said. "Nothing that can't be fixed. Yet. But watch your back."

She'd watch her back, all right.

But she'd watch his, too. And she'd watch his hands, just in case he had any thoughts of doing unto her before she had a chance to do unto him to protect herself.

She backed away, just in case, and watched him turn to go. Five long steps away, and he was already smiling, greeting what looked like half the population of the colony, with the ready charm she'd always liked in him.

Damn!

She'd have to get some eyedrops. The Colony was too dry. Her eyes couldn't stop tearing. The whole place looked as if it was shimmering about her.

She'd been so glad to see him when she'd made planetfall here. And even now—what if he were to come clean, to promise—damn, there she went, tearing up again.

She turned and headed for her own quarters.

"CC!" She whirled back, not so fast she lost control, and stopped herself with a hand on one of the stanchions she'd marked as a thing to clutch in case Mac had showed signs of carrying her out of here.

"Sandy!" she said. Another candidate for the formal, cordial smile and voice you used, outside client meetings, when you weren't sure of the people you were talking to. "Haven't seen you for a few. When are we going to have lunch?"

"Been busy," he said. "Learning the ropes. Or tethers." He laughed at his own joke. "You know the drill."

*Yes, Sandy, I do. What do you want to know?*

"I just saw Mac Nofi stamping away. Stormed right by me. If I hadn't gotten out of his way, he'd probably have knocked me into Immigration, he was moving so fast. If this rock had normal gravity, he was so mad he'd have left holes in the floor. Deck. Whatever. Any idea what set him off?"

Sandy was smiling at her, his bonded teeth and blue eyes attempting to convey guileless charm. Yeah, right.

She smiled back.

"Haven't got a clue," she said. "I told him not to snap at *me*."

She put a hand on Sandy's arm and leaned in confidentially. "You haven't heard this from me, of course, but personally, I think he got a message from his ex. He had the divorce from hell. You know what that's like." She planted the small barb without much enthusiasm, but it was necessary to make her excuses convincing.

"Do I ever know what that's like!" Sandy agreed. "Maybe I should ask if he wants to talk."

Not bloody likely. Mac hadn't trusted Sandy when he was plain John Sanders, and he certainly didn't trust Jonathan Vinocur Sanderson.

He matched CC's long, careful strides down the corridor past workers who'd finished their shifts and were picking up children. The Apsedra echoed as boys and girls in jumpsuits and bright tethers leapt and called to each other.

"Maybe you should," CC said. "It would be really kind."

*Really kind to expose Mac to one of Sandy's inept fishing expeditions. Well, maybe the man needed a laugh. And if he was as guilty as she feared, he had more than low-level irritation coming to him.*

"You know, Mac's been acting increasingly erratic," Sandy said.

It was probably just as well that Sandy, unlike the Neave-Lovats, had never felt himself able to afford kindness. If only they could harness the gravity of his look, they wouldn't have to worry about low g, CC thought. She nodded solemnly, though she suspected Sandy of making the story up on the instant. After all, it had always worked before.

"If he isn't careful, he's going to make some serious mistakes. . . . Well, he's got shares in the Colony, hasn't he?" Sandy shrugged. "As long as they're not confiscated to pay damages, I suppose he'd be all right."

*Don't sound so disappointed. You've just made that story up. Missed your calling, Sandy. You ought to lead fishing expeditions in Alaska when the salmon are running.*

"I don't suppose he'd ever consider returning to Earth," Sandy continued. "That is, assuming he's physically able these days to take normal gravity. And he's well-known here. Any punishment he'd get hereabouts would probably be a slap on the wrist. Unless he did something really criminal, and then they'd probably space him. . . ."

*You always did like to run your mouth, didn't you, Sandy? It's one of the reasons you're not farther along in your career,* CC thought.

It had been one of Mac's maxims to her, when she'd been that young, jittery nervous research assistant in mortal terror of screwing up, that you didn't need a shovel to dig your own grave; an open mouth served the purpose even better.

Sandy pushed off the deck with too much energy, recoiled against a wall, and steadied himself with an angry hiss. He was giving himself away with every word. Talkative he might be, but he wasn't a total fool. He was capable of hard work and had probably been doing it. Like CC, he'd come up with some serious suspicions about things close to him and his interests. He paid her the compliment of not suspecting her, or at least not letting it show. And he paid her the more serious compliment of thinking that her information, her sources, were good enough to swipe.

She eyed him narrowly. What did all this concern about Mac really mean?

*Why, that son-of-a-bitch has written him off! Whatever's going down, Sandy's decided it would be safe to pin the tail on Mac.*

*Never thought you were that stupid, Sandy-boy.*

Granted, she too thought the audit trail pointed to Mac. But she owed him, and before she turned him in, she'd do just a little more research.

It occurred to her that another reason for a really thorough investigation would be to clear him. Meanwhile, if he thought she was helping him, she'd keep the access to cargo hatches and docking bays he'd given her.

"CC?" Sandy asked. "I know that look. You've got a new line of research. C'mon. Let me in on it," he coaxed. He cocked his head at her in a mannerism that had been charming when he was a boy. "After all, how many people in our present line of work really understand good, juicy research?"

If he was harking back to before they'd escaped to the NGOs, he must really want to know what she was working on. All the more reason to distrust him.

Keep up that line of attack, and it might even work—sometime next eon, CC thought.

Nevertheless, she made herself look him over, as if she was considering full disclosure, or as much disclosure as she legally could.

"I just came off a volunteer shift," she said. "Pain in the neck. And now I've got my damn MKs to do. Want to come along and do your own mandatory kilometers? Afterward, we can have lunch or something."

Just like home. Leave the office; go to the gym; go to the bar for the heavy drinking that was just a pretext for trying to stay sober while getting your colleagues drunk so you could pump them for information.

If anything, it was a game at which Sandy was better than CC. She would have to be careful.

As CC expected, Sandy actually did a decent job of concealing his eagerness to pick her brains on the way toward the centrifuge. It meant time she begrudged away from her data, but she knew she had to do her MKs; Sandy clearly wanted to talk to her, or at least be seen talking at her; and there was no way in hell she was letting him anywhere near her system.

They changed into workout clothes—for CC, the subdued, shabby shipsuits that most real Vesta Colonists wore for exercise; for Sandy, the sleek microfibers bearing his employer's logo—corporate livery that was de rigeur for Earth and *Rimrunner*, but overdone here—and stepped into the installation.

"Treadmill or centrifuge?" Sandy asked.

"Centrifuge." CC had already spent so long running in circles she really thought she deserved a change.

They stepped onto the machine and strapped in, side by side. Once every place was filled, a bell rang, and the centrifuge started to turn. CC felt the blood flow down to her extremities, felt weight return to her body as it did every day during the workouts that kept her accustomed to Earth gravity so that, one day, she could return home. As the centrifuge accelerated, the pressure built up. Like a dancer who "spots," focusing her attention on one object as she pirouettes, CC focused on the ten warning signs of gravity maladaptation posted on the centrifuge itself. Beyond it glinted the clear panel of the observation deck, lined with signs, panels fused into the stone, and Vestans, awaiting their turn at various exercise machines.

"Here's my theory," she said, bending confidentially close to Sandy. "Have you been doing your homework on trading records?"

More weight. Marc was wrong. Never mind a ship that could outrun light: what they really needed now was artificial gravity. You could get seasick—spacesick—whatever—on these damn wheels. She swallowed hard.

Sandy swallowed too as if uncomfortable at this heavier weight. Then he nodded. "Some of those trades look kind of . . ."

"That about describes it," she agreed. "Anomalous as hell. Accounts that don't qualify; trades that people, given their net worth, shouldn't be able to work."

"What about colony records?" Sandy asked.

CC drew a deep breath. They'd reached one g. Let Sandy think she was losing her ability to tolerate it. That was better than letting him know he'd hit paydirt.

"My theory is that someone's trying to get inside information on mining strikes. I haven't gotten all that far. Do you know anything that I should know?"

Sandy almost purred. "If you knew who was going to file successful claims, you could invest," he said. "Or you could sell that information, and making one hell of a killing."

So you could, CC thought coldly. You could also destabi-lize the entire sector, but that didn't seem to cross Sandy's mind. At least, not that he was letting on to her.

It was as good an argument against Mac's being guilty—aside from the little matter of front-running—as she knew. Mac had never cared for power or money for its own sake. As long as he'd had enough, he was content. If anyone threatened his notions of enough, he fought.

They were much alike in that regard, she thought.

Deprived of "enough" and a career back on Earth, Mac had emigrated. Here on Vesta, he'd made a new life, forged new allegiances. Or so she'd thought.

She had the records to incriminate him. But they didn't make emotional sense.

Sandy, now. Sandy was always angry. From his earliest days neck-and-neck with CC for various valedictorian slots from day-care on, Sandy had always thought his formidable intellectual prowess meant he was owed things. The lesson that he was the son of grad students and, unless miracles happened, he'd very likely never get out of the nanny classes had been a hard one. He didn't have connections. He didn't have entitlements. All his intellect got him was a fighting chance that, to his credit, he'd taken.

The centrifuge pressed CC against her exercise station. Either she was getting soft, or that was more than one g. 1.2, she saw on the readouts. In a little while, it would go higher: after all, what's the point of retaining the ability to tolerate one g if you can't to the point where it's normal? Accel and decel took higher gs: if you weren't in shape, you wouldn't survive the trip home.

As what felt like a person her own size landed on her, she breathed with difficulty. Her breath became a gasp as she saw, concealed by a crowd of onlookers waiting for their turn on the wheel, someone in black and silver, someone who looked like Marc Davidoff.

What the hell was he doing here?

Mac had said he was on assignment.

Well, Mac had lied before.

There was always the possibility that the heavier gs were making CC see things. The flashes of fire behind her eyes that she remembered from liftoff and acceleration were going off now, and her ribs felt as if some screw in her back were slowly being tightened, drawing them in to compress her lungs. But she was still sure that she'd seen Marc.

*I could be floating out by Charon,* CC thought, *and I'd recognize Marc even if I saw him floating by in a pressure suit.*

Sandy was gasping for breath next to her. Thank God, he had his eyes shut, focusing on his own physical struggle. That gave CC the opportunity to focus as the centrifuge whirled. Three gs. Like being tackled in a pileup and being brought down with three people kneeling on her back and the prickle of a knife at her back. At this weight, breathing became a task she had to concentrate on. But she forced herself to try, as the wheel spun around, to see Marc again.

And failed.

Then, gradually, the pressure subsided. One of the people weighing her down seemed to have disappeared, then another. As the centrifuge slowed, she felt the familiar lightness of being that meant lower gravity and sagged into it with a sense of physical well-being.

"Are you all right?" asked Sandy. "You look pale."

"I'm fine," CC protested automatically. "Just fine."

"I saw something funny," Sandy told her. He made major play of standing ready to assist her in case she had difficulty moving after the centrifuge ride.

"Thank you, I'm fine," she said. "What did you see?"

Of course, Sandy would have kept her under observation, even under 3-g conditions. Like CC, he had too much riding on this assignment to be deterred by high-gravity workouts.

"I could have sworn I saw Marc Davidoff," he said. "Didn't you?" He pointed. "That man over there?"

CC made a show of following his pointing finger. "Sure does look like him," she agreed. "But I think I heard someone say he'd gone Outside or something."

She managed to sound sufficiently indifferent that Sandy simply asked, "What do you say we clean up and grab a bite?"

Even if it was Sandy asking her, that sounded like a good offer. CC might not have moved an arm or leg on the centrifuge, but her shipsuit was sodden with sweat.

As always after a workout, Vesta's minimal gravity felt even lighter, more exhilarating. She was hungry, a sign of her acculturation: the first times she'd endured gravity this low, she had been wretchedly sick.

Sandy emerged from the men's lockers clean and dressed in Earth corporate casual, rather than a colony jumpsuit. He looked somewhat pale, but agreed that tea, at least, would settle his stomach.

Adjusting her pace to low, economic bounds, they returned to the Apsedra, browsed the food court, then belted themselves into seats beneath the skylight. Music and voices filled the great central space, muted to manageable levels by the curves and volutes of the pavilions that filled it like the sails of a blue-water ship. Lights glowed within each pavilion, directions and advertisements without— Sandy's own Merrill Nomura, Microsoft, various social service agencies, bulletins, and the omnipresent market feeds. As the lighting and the announcements changed, the pavilions' colors ebbed and deepened. All the shades of Earth paled in comparison.

A flyover streaked across their field of vision, to be replaced by the starscape that CC never ceased to be amazed at. If the skylight imploded, stars would be the last thing she saw before her eyes darkened and froze. She was horrified to realize she considered that a good bargain.

She turned her attention to the dishes they'd clipped to the stone table and fenced with Sandy. As they traded bits of data and bites of the carefully chosen curried tofu, the hydroponic stir-fry, and nut loaves with the attention they would have spent on a business lunch, CC's gaze went through the crowd, looking for a man who should not be inside Vesta Colony at all and another man who might have betrayed it.

## 22

**"You want me to get you another coffee?" Sandy asked,** with a friendly sort of malice. "See? I managed not to fall into hydro. Not like some people."

The ventilation systems released a pre-programmed gust of air. It stirred one of the broad-leaved and improbably tall plants twining about the central structural supports in the Apsedra's food court, creating a pleasant breeze as it refreshed air and spirit. Every bit of $O_2$ generation helped. Besides, the air currents produced by the HVAC team were a pleasant reminder of Earth for those few colonists who hadn't spent their lives before they'd been forced to immigrate barracked in immense, dilapidated public warehouses.

CC smiled, licked her forefinger and held it up: *point.*

Sandy laughed. "Instead," he continued, "I went exploring. And I found out something really useful. Never mind Piazzi Blue Mountain. They actually grow the real Blue Mountain here. You have to know how to ask, and you definitely have to tip, but, d'you want some? My treat."

"Provided you're paying less than the allowable maximum for a gift," CC laughed.

Why was Sandy offering to treat her to the sort of coffee

you practically had to be a CEO to afford back home? She'd had it once or twice at high-level staff meetings at Alpha, but had refused to be hooked. Predictably, that was a refusal that Sandy hadn't shared. It was a wonder his employer hadn't red-flagged him on consumer debt: financial instability made a salaryman vulnerable to bribes.

What did Sandy want now? Because he always wanted something. Maybe, right now, he didn't look as if he wanted anything but companionship, but even when he wasn't turning on the charm, he could be engaging, no matter how used to it you thought you were. She'd seen him calibrate that cordiality in accordance with each degree of the chain of command before. Yellow alert, CC.

CC nodded thanks. Sandy might be high on her A list of people she was damn well keeping an eye on, but she might as well drink the best coffee in the colony on her surveillance target's expense account.

Unfastening his seat belt, Sandy rose cautiously. Another point for the blond weasel: he'd given up expecting to have coffee fetched by subordinates, preferably those bearing double X chromosomes. No one fetched and carried for anyone on Vesta Colony unless there was an emergency or someone was hurt.

Point for Sandy. Bigger point for Vesta.

Smiling slightly, CC followed his laborious progress across the Apsedra's food court until he disappeared into a pavilion. She grinned as she imagined Sandy striking a deal for two cups of Blue Mountain—smiles, coaxing, persisting until he got the magic "yes," and applying judicious applications of credit where his victim's manager probably wouldn't see the audit trail. And if he did, well, Sandy would be long gone, and the vendor would absorb the consequences.

CC's grin widened as Sandy emerged with two covered metallic cups. He started to gesture in triumph, then caught himself. Any spontaneous move would probably send him careening into a stanchion on one side or a cluster of schoolkids all clinging to one tether. Either accident would get him written up for an infraction of the leash laws. Worse, he might spill the coffee.

Warning lights flashed *red/off red/off red/off*, making pavilions look as if they'd caught fire. A klaxon shrieked. Sandy leapt three meters straight up, accompanied by twin gouts of coffee. Damn.

CC took an unpleasant second for thanks that she hadn't been scalded. Then, the great gears that controlled the skylight's protective cover started it moving across the dome.

*"All residents please proceed to your quarters and remain calm."* Mac Nofi's voice roared from speakers placed throughout the Apsedra. *"All off-shift security personnel, report in. There is no cause for alarm. Please stand by for further instructions. Thank you for your patience."*

So, it was lockdown. And apparently not a drill.

Sandy collected himself. Abandoning the now-empty cups (a violation of the litter laws, assuming anyone was watching), he flopped around in a maneuver combining the least graceful parts of starfish and frog, then kicked off for the exit. Wasn't adrenaline a wonder? CC had never seen him move that fast in Vesta-g. Or, for that matter, on Earth.

It wasn't as if she expected him to come back and see if she needed help: she'd made it fairly obvious that she could outmaneuver him in this environment. Besides, Sandy had always made *sauve qui peut* into a lifestyle.

Time to move.

Methodically, CC unstrapped, rose, and made her way through the Apsedra. It teemed now with Security officers directing traffic and personally assisting sweating, clamorous tourists while the colonists, who had been drilled on safety procedures all their lives, wove carefully through what would otherwise have been a madhouse. Vestans skilled in maneuvering in low g helped newcomers: CC blinked as a lean woman with only one leg wrapped her arm about the waist of a larger but elderly man with the tanned look of a newcomer, kicked off sharply, and used their combined mass to propel him safely toward the exit. Older children took deep breaths, looked around, realized that they were now on the spot, just as they'd always been told they might be, and began, as they'd been drilled since their earliest moments in day-care, to shepherd younger ones toward the nearest guards.

Good order and discipline, CC thought. It was a phrase she'd heard spoken in approval in Gorsky's Hole, usually just before a bar fight broke out.

Now, it would probably get Vesta Colony through this crisis, assuming that whatever caused the lockdown was a situation that could be remedied. CC's eyes filled: she was proud of these people, of their discipline, of the way they looked out for each other.

The pride frightened her. It meant she'd have to try not to let these people down.

Trying to orient herself, she glanced up at a signpost. Rescorla Place. It was named in memory of a security chief who'd brought over three thousand people out of Old Wall Street's dying World Trade Center at the cost of seven lives, one of them his own.

Nodding salute to the man's memory, she headed for the corridor that led to her quarters. Deliberately, she closed her ears to the agitated, authoritative, or worried voices speculating about possible meteor showers, an industrial accident, even a malfunction. The voices shrilled up almost to the point of hysteria, then subsided as people got control of themselves, or Security leapt in to control them.

On Earth, that would have caused a riot that could only end in bloodshed.

Adrenaline was working on her as it always did, making her hyperaware. *Sandy,* she thought. On *Rimrunner,* he'd never been particularly skilled in their low-g training, and he hadn't been much better here, even after long practice. Maybe she'd better go looking for him, see if he needed a hand.

She admitted going out to rescue Sandy was probably not the best idea she'd ever had. So what if she'd passed her tether exam first try? That didn't make her an expert herself at Vesta-g maneuvers. Then there was what she knew for a fact: if their positions were reversed, Sandy wouldn't help her. Hadn't he just turned tail and run the instant the lock-down sounded?

All right, she told herself. All right. It was one thing to play tit for tat. But compared with the cold equations of vac-uum and low gravity, corporate combat seemed insignifi-cant. Out here, if everyone wasn't on the same team, they damned well ought to be.

CC turned carefully and headed in the direction she'd seen Sandy going. There he was! She opened her mouth to shout "Sandy, are you out of your mind?" and then shut it.

Something was different. Something was wrong. But what?

She knew where Sandy's quarters were: VIP guests. Same "cellblock" as her own. So why was the damned fool head-ing in the direction not even of the cargo holds by the Port facilities, but toward the sealed-off construction areas?

Maybe he'd panicked, she thought. Maybe he'd gotten turned around.

She caught a better glimpse of him, then, and paused. On *Rimrunner* and on Vesta colony, every time he moved, he'd either collided with something or had to rescue himself at the last moment. Now, he moved with the economic grace of . . . of Marc Davidoff.

Now that was just wrong.

She knew perfectly well what David IV would tell her: *"Nothing personal, but Sandy's no responsibility of yours, CC. Didn't you say he'd cost you a job once? Keep your eyes on your priorities, and, by the way, when are you wrapping up and coming home?"*

But then, David IV was a traditionalist. A woman's place—well, any woman with whom he'd chosen to associ-ate himself—was in their home, and as soon as she got done with work, that's where she should go and stay, preferably with a hobby like work on the board of a prestigious charity. And he'd been corresponding with Sandy, anyhow.

She could also hear Marc's sardonic *"Williams, what in hell do you think you're doing? Playing hotshot lady detec-*

*tive? Do you really want to stupid yourself to death? Get
your ass back to your quarters. Mac didn't call a lockdown
for the fun of watching the whole colony scurry."*

Overriding both voices, overriding even Mac's "Now
Hear This" alert on the loudspeakers (and crook or no crook,
he was doing a damn fine job reassuring the troops), was
CC's curiosity. It was unnatural for Sandy not to be looking
out for number one, unnatural for him to be moving with the
grace of an experienced Vesta hand, and unnatural—she
paused and hid herself—for him to be heading for what
looked like a small personal locker, opening it, and taking
out a coverall that resembled one of Marc's. And it was completely unnatural for him to pull it on, still moving with that
anomalous grace, leap away toward the docking areas, and
touch a personnel hatch with something glinting and unauthorized that he'd pulled from a sealed pouch, and slide inside—where CC couldn't follow.

She swore. Then, because there was nothing else she
could do, she headed for her quarters fast.

Damn. A man and a woman wearing Security armbands
stood outside her door, haloed in the red light that marked
the entrance and glinted in the polished black stone of the
walls. Even as she watched, the guards overrode the lock,
opening the door into the darkness of her empty room.

"I'm here!" CC called. It was futile to pretend she didn't
see them: it was a lie, and lying to Security wasn't just stupid, it was a downcheck on her file. With a lockdown in
progress, Security had so much work that any obstruction
would only make them angry. Besides, it would make Mac
even more suspicious than he usually was.

"Ms. Williams?" asked the thin Asian woman who
seemed to be leader. "We were just about to send out a Missing Person call. You've been briefed. You know that, in the
event of a lockdown, all non-essential personnel are supposed to report to their quarters and stay there."

CC prepared to lie with the absolute truth. "I was having
coffee in the Apsedra with . . . a work associate from *Rimrunner,*" she said. "He's not really very good at Vesta-g. I

mean, he passed his tether exams and all that, but . . . I went after him to see if he needed help."

*But he went somewhere I couldn't go.*

No point telling them that.

"That's public-spirited of you, Ms. Williams," said the Security officer, "but you really need to trust us to do our job. You could have gotten in the way."

CC tried to look earnest and contrite.

The two guards glanced at each other, clearly weighing CC's offense with the tremendous volume of individual checking ahead of them.

"I'd like to let you off with a warning," said the woman. "But lockdowns fall under Colony Emergency regulations. I'm going to have to write you up. I wouldn't worry about it, if this is a first offense. You'll have to attend a class on Regs and do some community service, but"—she glanced at her PDA and raised her eyebrows as if CC's entry had been flagged—"you already have a volunteer record that's commendable for a newcomer. But next time, if there is a next time, please remember that you're not part of Security and go straight to your quarters. I'm sure Mr. Nofi would tell you that himself."

CC nodded, let them hold the door for her, and seal it after her.

Sometimes, she thought, it wasn't what you knew, it was who you knew—in this case, Mac.

Even if Mac, like Sandy, was on her list of suspects.

# / 23

**Lockdown ended two hours later, just in time for the pre-**dinner buzz that usually filled the corridors as shifts changed, and workers headed home or to the centrifuge, the Gates Center, or any one of a thousand other legitimate destinations. But the Colony stayed quiet, as if people were waiting for news—or for the other shoe to drop. Too quiet altogether.

Why did Mac have the colony locked up tighter than a Chinese Wall in an investment bank with all Compliance hovering over the deal as the rest of the lawyers warned off anyone else who wanted to feed?

CC shot him a quick, friendly message that he didn't reply to, except to cancel a lunch date they'd set for the next day.

What was going on? Elizabeth wasn't talking either, but Elizabeth was Compliance, and Compliance specialized in strategic silences that outwaited and outfoxed even insiders.

Who else could give her information?

Neave? Well, CC had left a message at his quarters asking how the family had fared through the lockdown. So far they hadn't returned it. Marc was out of sight, if not out of mind. Sandy was definitely suspect, and the colonists she worked and exercised with had only rumors to go on.

She was beginning to feel like an atheist praying. What felt like an information lockdown had succeeded the lockdown of the physical site. Granted, CC was used to a life regulated by compliance, security clearances, and status based on access to information. But that was Earth. If the same culture was taking hold on Vesta, she was sorry for the loss of morale—and morality—that it represented.

To make matters worse, she saw two red-flagged messages. One was from Security: online tutorial in the Regs, just as she'd expected. Well, she'd work through it in her nonexistent spare time.

The other, more ominous, bore Alpha's logo. Once she'd stripped it of its formal bizspeak, it boiled down to: Where was her final report? Where was her report on her progress to date? Was she aware that her visa was expiring and her review was coming up? Please advise.

That was following up with a vengeance. It wasn't as if she hadn't been sending regular status reports, either. It sounded as if someone had been feeding her management a 24-carat poop-rap on the consultant that was CC, and the followups were meant to establish a chain of blame.

In other words, if CC didn't throw them a chunk of red meat real soon, they'd yank her home in a heartbeat. And that would be the best that she could expect.

Adrenaline flooded her system. It turned her hyperefficient long enough to blaze through the remedial Regs, turn back to her report, and draft the next section before it wore off, and she yawned. One ordinary day, with chaos.

A bell drew her bleary-eyed attention back to her messages: *You have been cited for an infraction of lockdown regulations and are hereby directed to perform six hours of community service. The attached list shows . . .* yeah, yeah, vacancy list. She must be coming up in the colony. She thought they just assigned the work, and be damned to you, but now, apparently, she got her choice of assignments.

So it looked as if prior efforts had paid off for her—or they'd decided not to risk putting her in Hydro or any of the

other places where she'd run into accidents. The available
options were the controller's office, immigration—and
dockside offices that processed cargo.

No sooner seen than selected. No sooner selected than
paranoia set in. It was too convenient. But it was also necessary. Her first mandatory shift started at 0100. She popped a
caffeine tab. It wasn't the Blue Mountain Sandy had promised her, but it would keep her awake.

CC rubbed her hand in slow motion across eyes that itched
as if they'd had a close encounter with hot sand. By days,
she'd worked on an ambitious chunk of her report for Alpha
and sent it off. She hoped it would propitiate the managerial
gods, but the followups had started. While they were sometimes simply a request for information, more often than not,
they were a way of documenting shortfalls. If running scared
could be translated into her mandatory kilometers, she'd
never have to worry about her health. Unfortunately . . .

Three days into her community service work by the
docks, she'd adopted the drab coveralls worn by the ex-
shipsicles now doing data entry to either side of her. At first,
they hadn't spoken to her. The thin man with scarred hands
to her right had been an artist who liked to work in wholly
impractical bronze, had been unable to pay for materials and
been forced to emigrate. He was now working off his indenture plus additional loans so he could learn how to weld in
vacuum. The woman to her left had been an accountant
whose job had been eliminated in a merger. She'd run
through her savings, been unable to repay her student and
surgical loans, and been shipped out. Now she was supervis-
ing the section and awaiting Payoff. She eyed CC like a
hawk, not wanting arrogance or a careless mistake on what
was, in all fairness, her watch. CC repaid her concern with
her best efforts, and growing respect.

Were their lives as good as some she'd seen? Hardly. But
the man at Final Frontier, the former tutors of Neave's chil-

dren: on Vesta, you could work your way out of your indenture. On Earth, it seemed, what you got was followups. And you never got free of them.

As the shifts passed, her community service and her report for Alpha blended into one exhausting whole. She gave up on going to Gorsky's Hole to relax; she gave up on clocking mandatory kilometers on the centrifuge. She took to arriving early for her volunteer work, leaving late, and spending that time prowling the docking area near where she had seen Sandy disappear. They thought she was adding value. Or maybe preparing to run for office.

Sandy must have replicated some of her own research, which showed that more cargo was flowing into Vesta Colony's holds than it could pay for.

The money had to come from somewhere. All right: she'd found outflow in Mac's accounts, as well as those of the shipsicles whose accounts someone—better not call him Mac just yet—was using. But for what?

The logical thing was to attempt to reconcile trading patterns and cargo. If the data didn't turn up on file, she'd have to get it the old-fashioned way: by conducting her very own private inventory of the "excess cargo."

She could just hear Marc's voice. *"CC, you know what happens to people who try that Nancy stupid Drew stuff? They wake up dead!"*

She didn't even bother to tell herself that Davidoff wouldn't have used language like that. The breadth of his frame of reference had always startled her. She guessed, if you were part of a Family brand, you could get away with references that weren't related to business as an eccentricity, but it wasn't universal. David IV never used a simile that didn't come out of the trade publications, and he winced whenever CC slipped, even when they'd been alone.

*"You really are going to wake up dead."* The sarcastic voice that might not have become her conscience, but was definitely a voice of caution she was trying hard not to listen to, rang in her memory. She knew she had enough data to

produce a report that would probably let her survive at Alpha. Probably.

She could show results. She had good, workmanlike evaluations of every trade in the sector, and she had hypotheses for further work—well, they would leave Mac screwed, but what was that to her? It was just business, wasn't it? Nothing personal.

Hell of a way to pay back a man who'd once taken a chance and tossed a job to a woman about to be exported as frozen goods.

*"You're being sentimental, CC,"* she'd once heard Sandy say. *"People like us can't afford the luxury."*

But there was such a thing as loyalty, even if he didn't acknowledge it. She'd seen it in Mac. She'd seen it in Neave.

*But it isn't as if they're exactly returning your messages, are they? And your manager who gave you the glowing review that got you this assignment? She's covering her own ass as fast as she can.*

This might be the last assignment of her professional life. Better make it a beaut. After all, it was the job of an analyst to gather research, and research included collecting all sorts of data. What was the point of on-site research if you didn't maximize exposure to the sites?

She didn't even have to imagine what the congress of warning voices in her head would say to that one. She knew she was rationalizing what Marc called "damnfool behavior." More than anything else off-Earth, damnfool behavior could get you killed, because vacuum didn't care.

With what caution overwork and exhaustion left her, CC tried to take steps to protect herself. She left records out in her quarters, clues that might lead Security to her if one day she failed to show up where she was supposed to be, and always assuming that Security didn't simply decide she'd done another idiotic and illegal walkabout during a lockdown.

It was the best CC could do. "Best efforts," her mission statement said, were the minimum requirement for survival in Alpha. But then, best efforts had always been the minimum requirement for survival. As a child who'd read history far too early, she'd always tried to imagine tricky situations and how she'd deal with them. Once she realized how limited her future was likely to be, that early preparation had helped her: by imagining what the worst-case scenario was, she fought her way away from the gangs, out of indentured servitude, and into what she thought was a more profitable life—then promptly ran into the dangers of that life too.

She squeezed time out of the sleep she knew she had to have to back up her data almost compulsively. She hid copies of it both in both Vesta Net and in transit to her own accounts back on Earth. She even left telltales in her quarters so that, if anyone came in, she might have some warning of unauthorized entry. From the stories Tenzing and some of the others had told her, she knew anyone skilled in tradecraft would probably laugh his ass off at her precautions, but she had to do the best she could. And, every time she left her quarters, she prepared messages to be sent to Security, to her management back on Earth, and to Margaret Lovat, who might be able to influence Everett Neave on her behalf. CC was determined not to "just" disappear.

Not without a fight. And not without leaving an audit trail from here all the way back to Earth. If it came to Titoville survivors ringing the bell for her too on 9/11 Day, she at least wanted them to know she'd solved the last problem she'd been working on.

## 24

**Tonight was definitely the night, CC told herself. The instant** her supervisor glanced aside from her screen and, hesitant at giving orders to someone who was, after all, not a former shipsicle and, ordinarily, organizationally far senior to her, said "well, we're caught up for the night; you may as well shove off," she shut down her machine and headed for the docks.

This close to the immense airlocks and bays of Vesta's docks, the corridors were chilly, an effect that neither HVAC's best efforts nor the corridors' dark stone and dulled metal, broken only by warning signs, sector markings, and the occasional graffiti onslaught, did anything to mitigate. CC shivered in the drab coverall and spacer's thermal undergarments considered appropriate for colonists and corporate visitors engaged in community service.

Not being a nocturnal animal, CC hated delta shift, which would have been the hours between midnight and dawn back on Earth. The late hours threw off her biorhythms, already shaky because of the Colony imposition of 24-hour GMT timing onto Vesta's diurnal rotation of five hours plus change.

She knew there had to be more comfortable and more productive uses for delta shift, like sleeping or even attempting to placate Alpha Consultancies. Even in these days of 24/7 business, delta was the best time for long-range transmissions. The Solar nets ran fastest (sunspot activity permitting), and the Bloomberg Boosting Units had the shortest wait times for processing. Which was why anyone with community service to perform gained mucho points by volunteering for what was still referred to as the graveyard watch.

Not that "graveyard watch" was a term anyone in the Colonies used, CC warned herself. But her shiver had nothing to do with the cold air. She was developing a spacer's superstitions. Maybe Marc had called her Jinxo once, but that was a joke she'd sat on. People who set themselves up for rotten omens frequently ran into them.

Much more prudent to call delta the cargo watch.

At first, she set herself the goal of tracking Sandy. But she'd never seen him where he wasn't supposed to be: just a good little corporate employee attempting to add value. That was his story, and he was apparently sticking to it. Maybe he'd gotten wise to her surveillance. Or maybe she'd been wrong about him all along. Delta shift, on top of chronic sleeplessness and Vesta-g, played hell with your judgment. It occurred to her that, if Sandy were as smart as she thought he was, he could be preparing a case against her. Probably was. After all, he'd sabotaged her before.

And then there was Mac, who could definitely give CC lessons in shrewdness, especially on his own turf. She really didn't want to go head-to-head with Mac, but she would if she had to.

That left CC very much on her own.

Nothing new about that.

But she had what she'd always had: survival instincts hardwired into a feral gift for research. It had been that way her entire life. She had been in primary school when she'd first realized that, while other students collected information and laboriously plowed through it, looking for linkages, her best bet would be to scan it once, go to sleep, and let her subconscious process it. She'd wake up in the morning refreshed, and with a starting point in mind. A good starting point, too—as exasperated teachers and managers who mistook all-nighters and face time for diligence had soon discovered. Starting points were easy: learning to conceal her methods and cover her ass had been harder lessons to learn.

Even now, when CC was unable to sleep and let her subconscious act as CPU, she retained that intuition and her confidence in it.

Before starting this shift, CC had checked the quarters of each person she was keeping under her distinctly unofficial surveillance. Marc was offworld, or whatever you called it, or so his message unit had said. Mac wasn't taking calls. Sandy's personnel lock was locked, and had stayed that way. If CC inquired about further, she was likely to open herself up to even more suspicion than she might have incurred: and she was damned if she wanted to be framed. She could be as right as she wanted. If she looked wrong, she was almost as screwed as if she'd been caught out in a crime. Alpha would fire consultants caught in even the appearance of impropriety so quickly that Marc could probably use it as an example of something that happened faster than light. Creating the appearance of impropriety was not only a privilege reserved for some CEOs, it was stupid, and Alpha had no place in its org chart for stupidity.

Nevertheless, just because she had to abandon the possibility of forcing her way into that tempting personnel lock she'd seen Sandy sneak into didn't mean she couldn't try to get into the cargo areas another way. Thanks to her unauthorized absence during the lockdown and her prudent choice of community service, her ID now carried the right clearances for where she wanted to be, at least for one shift longer. Just as well: a ship had docked there during Vesta Colony's prior "night"; and where there were ships, there was cargo.

Now that, she told herself, was stunningly obvious. Just the level of intellection she could expect considering how sleep-deprived she was. That too was obvious. But she could sleep later. She had better investigate now, while her ID still permitted her into this area.

Once again, CC checked the copy of the cargo manifest she'd downloaded onto her Breitling when the supervisor's back had been turned. She'd had a narrow escape getting that information. On her last shift, she had searched for that ship and brought up the bill of lading in a few shrewd keystrokes. Her sleep-deprived grimace and hiss of bewilderment might have drawn too much attention, but she'd quickly lied to cover it, even supplying a tricky bit of processing that she'd prepared for just such an eventuality.

The problem was that this cargo just didn't make much sense, given Vesta Colony's needs. Pharmaceuticals *and* herbal remedies, perfumes, cooking spices, for pity's sake, and some luxury items like chocolate and coffee. Granted, Vesta colony probably could market all these commodities, but in these quantities, and delivered together? There had to be some sort of reason for this, beside terminal incompetence on the part of Purchasing. That section reported to Mac, and Mac was hardly stupid.

So, what did spices, perfumes, drugs, chocolate, and coffee all have in common?

They were all strongly aromatic. In one way or another, they all altered moods. And they were all expensive, given the Colony's salary scales.

That still didn't explain their presence on the loading docks. Moving quietly, the way she'd dodged gangs from the roach motels when she was a girl living in not-quite-public housing, CC headed back to the cargo containers she'd seen offloaded last delta shift. Now, they were marked "Colony Supplies" and stacked on the loading docks. That was odd. Ordinarily, supplies meant for Colony use, not transshipment, would be loaded into one of the delivery monorails. If it were immensely valuable or urgent, it would, more than likely, be hand carried.

A lock opened, and CC shrank back into a side corridor, then edged around to watch. Dockworkers slammed the hatch behind them and began loading the cargo into a motorized cart. They were wearing full thermal gear, CC noticed, including hoods that covered all of their faces except their eyes.

CC hunched down as signals beeped and rang about her, and lights flashed. So, the monorails were moving. In other words, the system was operational. In that case, why were they using a cart—especially during delta shift?

The answer was obvious. Something was getting moved at a time when there'd be the fewest observers. And that something was being moved out to an area where no monorail had been built.

Now, it was possible that someone was running a scam based on chocolate and perfume, but why drag the things out to the construction perimeter to make the handoff?

Abruptly, CC's instincts woke and stood at attention. Here, she thought, was where she would find answers to the questions she knew must be asked.

No sooner decided, though, than second-guessed.

*Are you really going to go through with this?* she demanded of herself. It was risky, but she had accepted the need for risk. The higher the risk, the greater the potential for return, she reassured herself. But the amount of risk you took on depended not just on need, but comfort level. This risk might be stupid, and stupid was one thing she tried never to be.

The courage that had waked in her when she and Marc had flown away from *Rimrunner,* when she'd picked up a bogey on scan and begged to be part of the search rose again now. Or maybe it was curiosity: for CC, they had always been practically the same.

As the cart started up, CC sneaked back into the corridor. Moving quickly, she accessed the emergency locker that was always kept open for the oxygen, the inflatable pod, and light patches stored there and strapped them onto her back. Making sure her pack was balanced, she took a running start, leapt—a carefully calculated flat jump, wider and much longer than anyone but a professional athlete could have achieved back on Earth, and flopped onto the top of the cart.

Praying she hadn't been heard, she scrambled beneath a cover that, thank God, wasn't intended to withstand vacuum. Judging by the smell, she'd landed right next to the chocolate. Well, at least, she wouldn't starve to death, she told herself. She pulled the cover back over her head, and waited for the buzzers, followed by the smooth whir of well-maintained engines as the cart began to move through the cargo bay. Judging from how much colder it was getting, she thought it was headed toward the construction sites rather than the docks.

Up periscope! she told herself. With a moment of silent thanks to the denizens of Gorsky's Hole, from whom she'd picked up both the reference and the technology, CC activated a minuscule camera that she'd wired to a long, flexible stalk and linked to her Breitling, which she'd slaved to the computer back in her quarters.

Now she could see. Not just see: record. Whatever else happened—and whatever happened to her, there'd be a record.

It was a pity Neave hadn't answered her messages and that she didn't feel she could trust her manager, or she'd have had her results uplinked to them, too.

The cart's nose dipped down, hard. She turned the stalk on her improvised spy system. The cargo hands, already masked to the face, were putting on goggles. Now that was interesting! Their dark-suited figures blurred, and CC realized that they had activated what she realized was a form of stealth gear: those weren't envirosuits the dockyard workers were wearing, but the sort of low-rez suits worn by criminals. Centuries ago, they used to be called ninjas. Now that crime had gone global, they were called comrades. Or procurement associates, if you were feeling really cynical.

The cart halted, and a hiss told her that its brakes had locked on. In an instant, they'd be coming around to unload, and they'd find her.

Folding up her scanner, she slipped out of the cart. Here the stone wasn't smoothed into a reflective pavement, marked with yellow and black safety strips or with emergency exit lights. It was rocky, almost herringboned, as if a path had been cut in a hurry, with little regard for anything but utility.

They were heading her way! Maybe she could hide in the eternal shadows of Vesta's caverns. Looking wildly around for a place to hide, CC found a sort of rocky bay, protected by outcroppings that looked as if nothing had touched them since construction had blasted a hole in this part of the asteroid. Crouching, she headed for it, reaching it in a couple of bounds.

Her luck held: the bay proved to be the entrance to a cave. Snapping on the goggles she'd pulled from the emergency locker, CC followed its path. A few more meters, she promised herself. As long as the path was a straight one: maybe she could imagine worse fates than being lost here in the darkness where it might be years until the construction gangs found her body, but she tried to imagine then, she'd probably panic.

*You're not helping,* she told herself.

She hadn't the training she would need to survive on her own for any length of time, but she had her wits, and the gear she'd been prudent enough to take with her. She could map the trail on her Breitling—but risk running out of memory. She could leave light dots to mark her way for as long as the supply held out. But that trail would be clear to anyone else coming this way. Infrared and her formidable memory would be her safest course for now.

Noises grated behind her, and she shrank behind a rock spur. She folded herself up into as near a fetal position as she could manage as the cart rocked and grated past her on the rough-hewn stone. Its handlers couldn't have moved along on the rough track if they'd been in normal gravity; even now, they struggled with the inertia of the cart's mass.

At least, the racket they were making covered the sounds of any rocks CC might dislodge or her rapid breathing. Trying to control even the sound of her breathing, hoping that no one picked up the sharp smell of her sweat, CC crept out again. She traced her gloved hand along the rough-cut stone, feeling for handholds, for the cuts that indicated where cabling and structural supports would be placed.

She halted, then shivered in response to some sensitivity to the way the air was circulating in this part of the cave. Her outstretched hand no longer brushed stone, but groped into an emptiness that the way her hackles rose told her was huge. She had better see where she was going. Turning up the resolution on her goggles, she saw she'd just edged by a steep dropoff. That was one way—the way least likely to send her into a panic—of saying that she had been wandering near a great yawning gap in a part of the asteroid so isolated that construction, which had blasted through the rock here into some sort of chimney, hadn't even set barriers or warning lights to indicate the danger. Well, she supposed she could consider herself fortunate that this area even held air.

Straining her eyes even through the goggles, she hurried past, leaning as far to the side opposite the dropoff as she dared. Again, she sensed a change in the air currents and extended her hand once more. Now she felt fingers slip across smooth planes of stone that were probably crystal formations. Again, her head came up as she responded to a shift in air pressure. They were approaching another opening, another big canyon. Long before she saw a shift in the blackness, she could sense that they were approaching another cavern, a big one.

Pallid green-white lights erupted in dots and strips about the cart, as if its approach had triggered them. CC gasped and stepped back. Damn that noise. Startled as she was, frightened as she was, she wasn't so taken aback—or so intimidated—that she forgot to bring up her recorder.

Swiftly, she adjusted it for the widest possible angle and focused on . . .

My God, what was that thing? If it was a ship, it was a kind of ship she had never seen.

Though it looked like a chunk of rock battered by its passage through space, scoured by micrometeorites and dust, crystals gleamed from its skin, resembling the rock formations around it. Maybe it was just a chunk of rock blasted from the cavern when construction created the airlock that loomed up beyond it. That couldn't be right. No rock ever crouched on bowed stalks that ended in what looked like rounded skis that probably helped it balance if touched down on uneven surfaces.

The thing had stalks. It had lights. CC's mind reeled, then struggled to rationalize what she saw.

It had to be a ship.

But she'd never seen a ship like it, not at the Paris Space Show, not at Earth Station, not in her zap run away from *Rimrunner,* and not in Vesta's docking bays.

Maybe Mac or Marc might know what this thing was for. *Or where it came from.*

They'd know what to do, wouldn't they? CC desperately wanted someone to know what to do, someone to take charge and give her not just instructions, but instructions that would keep her safe. That was a luxury, like the chocolate and coffee and drugs in the cart. Even longing for it could cost her everything.

Another thought made her shiver. Maybe this . . . this ship, or another like it, was the bogey she'd seen on that rap run with Marc. They'd shut her out of the debriefings, but she'd heard enough to know what they suspected that bogey might be.

If this ship was the bogey, CC wanted to turn, to run back to the safety of the Apsedra, her quarters, perhaps the dark small space beneath her bunk. At least, she'd have the illusion of safety.

*You've already put your life on the line,* she told herself, *so you may as well get the information you came for.*

So, this thing was a ship. Where did it come from? Her eyes widened. If it wasn't a ship she'd ever seen, and didn't come from any manufacturer she knew of—would it be big enough to come from anywhere else?

She supposed that anyone would have drawn the conclusion she came to more quickly. This ship wasn't experimental, she decided. It was alien.

She shivered again, this time as much in a weird delight as in sheer terror. An alien *ship,* and here it was, squatting on its struts on a landing circle just like any other ship of its size. As if it had made an ordinary landing and would, in time, take off.

A takeoff would vent the air in this place!

CC, she told herself, you are in *deep* shit. Not to mention trouble.

She scrabbled in her pack for the survival bubble, then brought herself up short.

*None of the dock workers wore pressure suits.* You're *overreacting,* she scolded herself. She was safe from vacuum—but not from being caught. If she scrambled into the bubble, she'd probably make enough noise to draw someone's attention.

Another unwelcome thought struck her. What if this thing had scanners that could detect her, lurking out here in the dark?

*You don't know that,* she told herself. It was easier to scold herself for poor planning than for the presumptuous, catastrophic lapse of judgment that made her think she could function out here. *And if it does, it's already spotted you, so you may as well collect as much information as you can.*

The cart moved onward, nearing the unknown ship. As it approached the landing site, it moved more easily, as if someone had taken the trouble to smooth the stone.

Crouching low, CC followed. A high, keening whistle rose from the ship. CC just barely managed not to scream. "It's got to be a ship," she whispered into her Breitling's tiny microphone. "But I've never seen a ship like this. It looks like the outside of a geode. A chunk of its skin seems to be opening, it's like a hatch, but all crystal inside. Wait a minute, now, something's coming out of it, like a ladder or a ramp . . ."

Despite the chill of the asteroid's naked, dead rock, CC shuddered. As her adrenaline flooded her system, she was drenched in sweat. Each time a new air current washed over her, her face went hot, then froze. She flushed with shame at how what had started as a careful report turned into panicky free-association as she clutched at the tiny bit of precision equipment and babbled for her life.

"If this thing takes off, this whole area could be exposed to vacuum, but no, there's the airlock, it's got two chambers. . . . How did it get in? Who let it in? Where's it—oh my God, the ramp's extruding, you can barely hear it touch down, this thing's advanced. Something's coming down that ramp, no, someone, you'd have to call it people, wouldn't you? Someone's got to get down here, these aren't people we know, they're not people, tall, skinny, there's three of . . ."

Intent on not screaming as she recorded what had to be an alien ship, she didn't hear the footsteps on the rough stone until a figure—*he was hiding in the shadows, like me!*—ran out and gave her a sharp push.

CC reeled and then toppled, bounced, and dropped again, all in agonizing slow motion. No wonder construction hadn't been in a hurry to develop this area. It was riddled with pits! She scrabbled for purchase on the rock, bounced off, and fell, still clutching the Breitling she'd held up to record as long as possible. Shifting her fingers on it, she hit the red button that activated its distress call.

Would her signal penetrate the rock? Breitlings were warranted for frontier conditions, and God knows, she'd paid enough for this one.

CC screamed and knew no one would hear it except the one who'd pushed her and the men unloading that cart.

She grabbed for the rock one last time. Dammit, she missed, her hand hurt, it *hurt*, and she was toppling now, falling so slowly, slowly, she'd fall to her death in slow motion. The panic took hold, her mind gabbling at her toppling body that oh God, it was a good thing, wasn't it, that she was falling *inside* Vesta, because even if she had a pressure suit on, even at this speed, she couldn't calculate it, but it would be just her luck to reach escape velocity and become just one more little satellite, in orbit forever.

Maybe they'd name her after herself. Asteroid CC. Flying Object Williams.

Williams, you goddamned fool.

Her scream turned into hysterical laughter. Adrenaline flooded through her almost to ecstasy. Her temples swelled in sheer terror, she could feel herself blacking out. . . .

. . . and she hit bottom like a blow to the skull, an explosion of lights that ended in darkness.

## 25

**CC had company down here in the pit. Someone unpleasant.**
Someone who had serious self-control issues, or he—or
she—wouldn't be moaning.

In a little while, Security or Medical personnel or someone would have to come along and remove that person, and
CC hoped they'd tell him not to behave in that ridiculous
way. Moaning didn't accomplish a damn thing, and was seriously antisocial besides. She was surprised the moaner
hadn't learned that in preschool. *Somebody,* she singsonged
to herself as she'd learned in day-care, *has bad boundaries.*

Somebody was a seriously lousy neighbor.

CC clamped her mouth shut against the next moan with a
shock of wonder that nearly made her roll over and throw
up. Vesta-g had saved her from a fall that would have killed
her on Earth.

*I do believe in miracles. I do, I do,* she whispered to herself.
She hadn't thought of miracles since she was a child and had
realized that heaven, assuming it wasn't a wish-fulfillment
fantasy created by the underclass, helped those who helped
themselves. Maybe she really had helped herself sufficiently.

*You're not out of the woods yet,* she whispered to herself.

Every muscle aching, she brought her Breitling up to her face. Now that was strange. She seemed to have two Breitlings. Which one should she use? Really, she only needed one: when had she gotten this other one? Was that why her credit balance had fallen? Or maybe Alpha had issued it to her before she left Earth.

It didn't really matter. Both of them still glowed, showing the picture of that alien ship and the cart with its human handlers. She stared at both Breitlings till her eyes crossed. The PDAs fused into one, then split apart.

Just wonderful. If she had double vision, she probably had the mother of all concussions. What else did she have? Cautiously, she patted herself up and down, sliding her hand beneath the pack she'd worn that had somehow gotten twisted round and helped cushion her fall.

Even if CC felt as if gangs had worked over every spot on her body with electric clubs, she didn't think anything was broken. Nothing felt as if she'd torn it or strained it inside, no stabbing pain from broken ribs, no blood from her mouth, aside from a bitten lip and a nosebleed. She might be bleeding in the brain, but she didn't feel sleepy or particularly dizzy.

Just sick.

Well, that was something she could do something about. Had to.

She retched, turning her face away into the welcome coolness of the rock, then began to drag herself to a clean space.

Her First Aid training rose up to haunt her. In case of concussion or suspected neck or spine injuries, you're not supposed to move the victim. Right. Move or die.

But she'd come to a stopping point: both in terms of energy and where she could move next.

She let herself drop and stared up at the rock face.

It was way too high to climb, even if she felt 100%, had ropes, grips, *or* the knowledge of how to plant them.

"Help!"

Her voice had seemed loud enough when she thought it belonged to someone else, moaning in pain. Now, it came out quavery, futile.

Screaming, even that feeble an attempt, was counterproductive, she told herself. Someone had pushed her. If she cried out, it might be her attacker, not a rescue party, who would come down and finish her off.

Noise might kill her. But silence definitely meant death.

She remembered now that she'd sent a distress call as she fell. She'd try again. But the Breitling flickered; it might keep its charge longer than any other PDA, but ultimately, it too couldn't run on nothing. She shut it down to preserve her data.

For the first time in her life, there was nothing she could do but trust. Maybe help would come before shock, thirst, or starvation killed her.

CC yawned. She wasn't feeling quite as cold now. If she heard them, she decided sleepily, she'd turn the Breitling back on so they could find her.

Until then, she'd just have to do the best for herself she could.

She scrabbled at the straps of her pack with a sudden irritation, both at the way they cut into her through her heavy clothing and at her own concussion-induced stupidity. Her pack! She tugged it off with a violence that threatened to make her vomit again, then pulled it open. Maybe, if she moved slowly, she could get herself into the emergency bubble. It would have food, power, air, even a homing beacon. And it would have light, not the phantom flares and flickers that her brain industriously supplied to compensate for the lack of real light.

She whimpered as she struggled halfway into the bubble, then collapsed in dry heaves. At least she could activate its light and homing beacon.

*They'll find you. The ones who pushed you. The* aliens.

Maybe they would. But maybe, just maybe, it was her job to try to be found. Her duty, as her friends in Gorsky's Hole would say. It is the duty of all prisoners to try to escape. Before you punch out, steer the ship away from human habitation.

At least try, she told herself. If not for herself, then for the people from Gorsky's Hole who might even paste her picture up in that informal shrine they'd put up behind the bar.

*At any rate, you stupid bitch, make a decision, or you'll go into shock, and that will be a bad decision by default.*

The survival bubble would stay flaccid until it was sealed and inflated from within. She reached inside it and activated its light, then its homing beacon. She wished she could crawl all the way in, but she knew she didn't have the strength. Still, she could pull the bubble over her, and that would supply some sort of warmth. At least, it would collect her own body's warmth, prevent it from escaping quite as rapidly as it seemed to want to. There were med supplies inside the bubble too, but she didn't have the energy to hunt them out. Not just yet.

CC lay back against the rock, don't-sleep and just-a-little-rest quarreling in her battered skull, and stared up at the cliff face. God, that was a *long* way down.

She yawned again until her eyes watered, drying too fast. Why, she realized, that rock wall was beautiful. It was all crystals, her light striking off the facets, making them shimmer as if water ran over the ancient stone. The light was water, the light was life. She let her eyes fill with it, and let herself drift.

Now *that* was a luxury she couldn't afford.

Move, CC.

She felt, more than heard, a rumbling in the rock. Oh God, that ship was leaving. Somehow, she had to scramble into the bubble now or be vented into space!

*No,* she told herself. *You're panicking. Stop it.*

The airlock's massive hatches on the cave side would open. Then the landing circle would move, bringing the ship into the airlock proper. The hatch would seal. Only then would the outer hatches open, releasing the ship into space.

Unless, of course, it decided to blast its way through.

Assuming it could.

With an alien ship, who knew?

With the last of her strength, CC pushed herself further inside the bubble. She managed to get her head inside it, and activated the seal with the last of her consciousness.

* * *

Again, she was drifting. Drifting in space. Why had she begged Marc not to eject her? Because she hadn't wanted to scramble into the survival bubble? Stupid CC. Why, this was beautiful, so restful, like sleeping in Vesta-g.

Reality lapped at the edges of her dream.

*You're on Vesta, CC. There's been an accident. No, not an accident. There was an attack. You were the victim.*

She glanced at the bubble's readouts. There was still air outside. She wasn't thinking straight.

Abruptly, the bubble's confines made her think of coffins, confinement. She fought to crack the seal, scrambled out, and lay panting at the foot of the cliff.

When the roaring in her temples subsided, she heard it.

Scratchings along stone. Deliberate footsteps. Voices transmitted on a comm. Voices speaking to comms. Human voices. They weren't hushed, like spies, but disciplined, assured, as if the people speaking had a right to be where they were and a purpose in being there.

Her heart leapt. At this rate, she wouldn't have any adrenaline left for her old age, she told herself, and chuckled weakly. Assuming she had an old age.

Her enemies wouldn't make that much of a racket, she decided. So these people might be Security, and they were looking for her. They had gotten her message and actually come looking for her.

Tears trickled down her face at the thought that she hadn't simply been written off.

"Help . . ." she cried again.

Her mouth was dry, her voice little more than a croak. She heard feet stamp beyond the pit into which she'd fallen, head into the mouth of the cave, and exclaim over the tracks they found.

A spasm of fear brought on an attack of the dry heaves that spasmed her belly muscles. What if Security found where the ship had rested, found it and got so excited they'd race back to the Colony, and forget all about her?

Wouldn't that make sense?

Wasn't the news of an alien ship worth one troublesome outsider?

*Rescue yourself, CC. Just like you've done your whole life.*

She stripped off her gloves and rummaged in the deflated bubble. Flares, but if they hadn't seen the bubble's homing lights, they might not spot them.

Ah. Look what she had here. A spare $O_2$ canister. And an energy beam meant to serve as a cutter.

The combination ought to make some sort of explosion, shouldn't it? Damn, this was a ridiculous job for someone with her skillsets. Why'd she ever leave Earth?

Muttering and swearing to herself, CC propped the oxygen cylinder against the cliff, then propelled herself—no, that ankle was sprained, not broken—cautiously across the rock until she came to the end of the circle of light. Any further and who knew? She might fall into another damn hole.

Still, she warned herself, if this explosion idea of hers worked, she might be tossed in anyhow. She'd have to tether herself to something that would hold up. And she'd have to think carefully about how to shoot. If she used the cutter as it was intended, with a tight, focused beam on high power, it would only blow a hole in the tank, which would go flying around and maybe bash in her aching skull. But if she turned the cutter onto its lowest setting and dispersed its beam, it would heat up the tank so that it would blow up. That would probably kill her too, but it was worth trying.

Well, as they told her in Finance 101, the higher the risk, the greater the possibility of return.

*Do you have any idea how sick I am of that statement?* she asked herself.

Rhetorical question. Bad CC. No biscuit.

She dragged herself behind a substantial boulder, hitched herself to it, braced herself, and fired.

Before the explosion made the crystals in the rock too bright to bear, CC thought it was the most beautiful thing she'd ever seen. Then it flung her across the cave. Even at Vesta-g, she hit hard. She never felt her teeth sink into her tongue or the rebound that flung her against the desolate, battered rock.

## 26

**Subdued, almost pinkish light soothed CC's face in time** with soft, warm gusts of air and a humming all around her.

*The air is filled with noises.* Where was that from? *The Tempest*? Something about "still-vexed Bermoothes." She and David IV had gone to Bermuda once: pink sand, warm sun, wonderful moisture in the air, music laid on by the hotel David IV had said was the most appropriate for them to stay at. Where all the QCs—quality couples, not qualified investors—went. What a snob David IV was, she told herself, and then buried the thought.

But Bermuda didn't smell like antiseptic, and it was low-tech, kept that way on purpose, so it didn't buzz with equipment, either. On Bermuda, people in colorful shirts brought her drinks with rum in them, not whatever it was they were pumping into her here to restore her blood sugars or her electrolytes or whatever.

But it was warm here. Warm as a hearth. Well, that made sense: Vesta, for whom the asteroid and the Colony were named, had been named for the Roman goddess of the hearth. She didn't think more than three other people in the world she'd made her own knew those references, and if they did, they knew enough to keep their mouths shut.

She had survived. Survived and been brought to Vesta's MedCenter, where she was being cared for with every resource to which she was entitled, thanks to Alpha Consultancies' very expensive health insurance, which even paid off part of the time.

She relaxed and let her hands go limp. . . . Her hands. Her empty hands.

"My Breitling! Where is it?" Her voice might still be a croak across a lacerated tongue, but it was definitely a stronger croak, and it brought an instant response.

"She's awake," came a woman's voice.

Margaret Lovat? What was she doing here?

"And I think she wants to get back to work." Margaret, if that truly was her voice, sounded amused.

"No, not work . . . my Breitling! It's got pictures, my report."

Dammit, what did they do, weld her tongue back together? She tested it. No teeth lost, thank God.

"Take it easy, Ms. Williams," came another woman's voice. This one was crisp, and CC recognized Authority, at least at the level of middle management. CC had the definite sense that if she didn't take it easy, this woman would make sure she did, probably with drugs in the solution contained in the pack overhead.

Her hearing, straining and hyper-aware, heard the physician mutter, "They're brainwashed. I swear, those damned companies brainwash them. Or maybe they simply insert chips in their heads or up their asses. They send these damn-fool junior executives here half-trained, they work themselves into exhaustion, they get into trouble, and the instant we pull them out, they want to go back to work."

Anyone could sneak in and inject anything they wanted into that solution dripping into her!

CC struggled to raise herself on one elbow.

"No," she whimpered. "Where's my Breitling? I saw it, I have to report, have to tell . . ."

The physician exhaled, a sort of exasperated huff, and CC knew she was about to find a sedative. She couldn't allow that. She got one knee under her; an instant longer, and she'd be able to get up, but every muscle in her body ached so, it was hard to move, and Vesta-g was tossing her one way, then another. She'd be sick again in an instant, but she couldn't afford to be.

A well-tended hand took hers and squeezed it.

"CC, it's all right!" Margaret told her. "I was doing a volunteer shift here when they brought you in, and I've stayed with you."

She leaned over her and pitched her voice very softly. "Your distress call came through. First from your Breitling, then from the bubble you activated. They said you did a smart thing, setting off that explosion. Crazy, but it worked. They'd probably have found you. . . ." Margaret let her voice trail off as if she'd caught herself before she said something regrettable.

"But maybe not soon enough?" CC asked.

Margaret thinned her lips. "The Breitling . . . you made such a fuss about it when they brought you in that Mr. Nofi took charge of it. Colony's on modified lockdown again. You certainly have a gift for shaking things up!"

She sounded amused.

"Oh God," CC moaned. She knew what that meant. Disruptive. Not a team player. Very bad. She'd get more infractions. She'd never get out of community service, but she had to, she had to report, tell Neave or someone, anyone, about the ship she'd seen in that cave and the strange figures who'd come out of it.

Worse yet, Mac had her data. All of it.

"Relax, CC. You have plenty of time to make your report. I'll see about getting you some sort of computer access. Yes, yes, and your Breitling, too."

CC had heard Margaret use just that tone with her children. She bit back a laugh, just in time, giddy with relief. Margaret would get her back her data. She'd said so.

"Ms. Lovat, if you can't let the patient rest, I'm sure we can find other things around here for you to do." Efficiently, the physician invoked a tone of Official Reprimand.

"I'm sorry, Doctor," Margaret said instantly. "I thought she'd rest better for knowing. You can see she already seems calmer."

She rose, a glimmer of fair hair above a dark jumpsuit whose severely elegant lines meant it was probably custom-made. Gently, she smoothed the thermal sheet over CC and adjusted the light tether that would secure her to the bed in case she thrashed in her sleep.

Dimming the lights, she turned to leave, but paused at the door to say, "You'd better sleep while you can, CC."

"Now, Ms. Lovat!" cautioned the doctor.

That bitch! She must have put something in that damn pack, because CC felt the tides, like Bermuda's blue water, wash her into unconsciousness once more.


What felt like about a month later, CC finally felt herself drift up out of a sedative haze. The heat lamps and restorative air vents she remembered basking in were gone, replaced by the hushed voices, brisk steps, and clatters of equipment proper to MedCenters.

Out of intensive care, then. Good. Maybe they'd release her. If not, she was still a citizen, as far as she knew, and she would simply sign herself out.

She let herself float back to full awareness. Her tongue didn't hurt anymore. Her computer was clipped into place on the bedside table next to her Breitling. Margaret had gotten it to her! She picked it up carefully. Fully charged, too! When she accessed its screen, she saw once again the strange lines of a ship that was never native to this solar system. She blinked, taking in her surroundings.

Maybe she was out of intensive care, but she hadn't expected this. A private room, no less. With flowers. Had Sandy told David IV she'd been hurt? She hadn't liked the idea that Sandy was providing David IV with running commentary on her work here, but if Sandy had been that thoughtful and David IV that generous, she'd have to say that was such a sweet gesture and mean it!

"So, Ms. Williams, you've decided to rejoin the world?" the physician's voice asked. "Do you think you could eat breakfast?"

The answer to that had damn well better be "yes," CC realized. Despite the sugar solution and whatever else she'd been fed while she'd been out cold.

"Coffee?" she asked, testing.

"We'll get you coffee," the physician promised.

Now that was a good sign, if MedCenter staff agreed to let her have caffeine. Better push her advantage.

"So," CC asked, "am I all right?"

"Aside from exhaustion, shock, and a concussion, not to mention assorted bruises, scrapes, and sprains? I expect you to make a complete recovery. You're likely to have bad dreams, though, as your subconscious processes your experience. We can recommend a list of therapists both on Vesta and back on Earth. . . ."

The woman rattled off the litany of stress, specialists, and the other impedimenta of meticulous, privileged medical care. But her voice sounded strange, as if something was wrong. Well, if Mac had looked at CC's Breitling, seen the alien ship and put the entire colony on lockdown again, things were worse than wrong. They were terrifying.

But that wasn't the impression the physician gave CC. The woman was acting as if something was wrong with CC. Well, coffee first, and then she'd sit up and conquer the world again.

Wouldn't she?

The coffee came before she had time to do much more than start to worry. As she expected, it was weak, a little overbrewed, but it was caffeine. She felt the familiar rush of energy hit her system from the caffeine. Sitting up carefully, she pulled the arm of the bedside table over her bed, accessed her computer, and immediately wished she hadn't.

As she expected, the messages were stacked up. Alpha. Vesta Colony. David IV. A variety of names she barely recognized, including, she saw, the people from delta shift in the cargo bay where she'd done community service work. A note from Sandy.

Well, high time she got to work.

Priorities. If the Colony was on lockdown, the message was probably an announcement, maybe a briefing.

Damn. The thing was passworded. No announcements were ever passworded. And it was unexpected. That meant it was probably bad news.

CC typed in her password with fingers that felt as thick as if she wore the gloves of her pressure suit, and the message lit.

She drew in a quick, astonished breath. Her empty stomach began to churn with a level of anxiety unequalled since her layoff from Morgan Nomura.

Officialese from the Colony Manager's office, several paragraphs of it, all of which added up to: CC Williams was hereby declared persona non grata and instructed to leave Vesta Colony on the first available transport, said departure subject to delays in ship arrivals and departures, but not to be postponed beyond . . . hell, that was three days from now!

She yelped indignantly, then waved away offers of assistance.

*Mac,* she thought. *You son of a bitch.* She ran a diagnostic on her Breitling. Mac could have tampered with it: but he hadn't.

She fired off an immediate reply in her best bizspeak, appealing the decision and pressing for a hearing as soon as possible. After all, if Mac was kicking her out of the Colony, she didn't have much time.

Her system pinged. Her message had been returned. Whatever Mac had in mind, it certainly didn't seem to include communicating with her.

Her stomach, empty except for the dubious coffee, churned in a way she remembered from times when her employer had merged with another company and she had to wait to find out if she still had a job.

Speaking of which . . . CC opened the message from Alpha Consultancies.

"Is everything all right, Ms. Williams?" came the voice of a man wearing the tunic of a MedCenter volunteer aide. He had to be monitoring her life signs. She'd just bet that her blood pressure and heart rate had spiked up.

One damn thing after another.

Dated, documented, copied to what looked like half the management team and Human Resources back on Earth, the thing was a letter from her management. CC's work had been unsatisfactory, her progress sporadic. Furthermore, Alpha's partners had been receiving unfavorable feedback about her from outsiders. Accordingly, effec-tive immediately, she was suspended without pay. She was hereby instructed to turn in her identification, her final reports and expense claims, and all other property of Alpha Consultancies LLC *including her return travel vouchers* to the Vesta Colony Administrator, in lieu of senior management, pending a full review and final disposition of her status back on Earth.

As double binds went, this one was a damn work of art.

The sweat of pure panic scalded down her sides. This was worse than the fear she'd felt in the caves. There, she was at full function, straining her reason, her resourcefulness, and her courage. Here, she faced the familiar juggernaut of corporate bureaucracy. You couldn't fight the NGOs; you could either get out of their way or be run over.

This had been the world she'd fought to join. And this was what all her fighting, all her wiliness had come to.

No wonder the doctor had eyed her strangely. She was on borrowed time here, not just in the colony but in this private room. If she'd lost her insurance, how would she ever pay for this level of care? It would throw her back to the debt levels she'd fought out of after she'd gotten out of school and was trying to pay off the surgery to close her wrist-jacks. She'd just have to have them opened again, assuming Vesta Colony would let her incur that much more debt. She'd need the opened jacks so she could work harder, wherever she wound up.

What kind of assets was she carrying around? Her clothes? Her computer? Hers, not Alpha's. The Breitling? At least it was paid off.

Best thing she could do would be go back to her room, hers for now, assuming they hadn't packed up her things, charged her for the service, and dumped them into storage for which she would also be charged.

Mac hadn't gotten to be Colony Administrator by not tugging every loophole closed. And right now, those closed loopholes were the size of a noose being fitted around CC's neck. In Vesta-g, it would take a *long* time for her to choke to death. She pushed herself out of the overpriced bed.

Last time things had been this bad, all at once, shipsicle status had begun to look like upward mobility. She'd been falling through the cracks then too, but her backup plans had worked at the last minute, like a second parachute. She'd always had backup plans, even before her first job. She had always found work, or the promise of work. More recently, there had been David IV, friends, a life that was expanding quite satisfactorily. But now her world had slammed as firmly shut as the hatches of an airlock, leaving her on the outside as they pumped away the air. And she hadn't a clue of how to proceed next.

Yet.

Oh God, David IV. If CC lost her job, that would matter to him bigtime. CC wouldn't place bets—assuming she had anything left to bet with—that he hadn't already been tipped off that his fiancée was in Big Trouble. Well, she was as close to unemployed as you could get without actually getting fired: she might as well check out the bad news from David IV while she was at it.

CC raised an eyebrow as she read his letter. His father had heard. His mother said that CC seemed to be acting erratically. Didn't she care about their future? Please, could she rethink her actions and let him know so he could plan accordingly? He was certain his father could assist her.

So, so far, not as bad as it could have been: David IV had invested over a year in their relationship and positively hated change, let alone writing off that time as a bad investment. So he was still betting on her, at least for the present.

But she'd give a month's pay she was no longer entitled to find out who was responsible for the mess in which she now found herself.

A scuffle sounded in the corridor outside.

"The patient is in no condition to receive visitors," she heard the volunteer telling someone. He didn't sound particularly confident in his ability to keep out this particular someone, though.

"That's what you think!"

Marc's voice. CC sat back into the bed and pulled up the light covering. This ought to be interesting. At the very least.

Might as well get all of the trouble out of the way before she checked out and proceeded to salvage what remained of her future. If she couldn't stay here, she'd probably be blacklisted off Titan or Ganymede as well. So, it would probably be Charon or Quaoar for her. Maybe she wouldn't have to travel out to the rim of the solar system in Freeze; she'd shown herself to have good skills. Her delta shift supervisor—maybe the woman would speak for her. Pity, she couldn't take CC on: CC knew she'd worked out well down at the docks.

Well, if not on Vesta, somewhere else. Maybe, she'd be allowed to work her passage. Or maybe she could contract with a local mining consortium that would let her travel with them, a modern-day nomad.

CC supposed she had always known things would come to this point. She was running on energy now, energy and the good drugs this overpriced MedCenter had priced into her. When the stimulants wore off, she knew the truth would sink in. And she knew she'd face it, just as she'd faced every other hardship in her life. It was bearable. If she could survive the sight of an alien ship and falling down a cliff in the heart of an asteroid, she could probably bear anything.

She remembered the first time she'd coped with the threat of a mugging by standing her ground. Truth was, she'd rubbed a blister on her foot saving on public transportation, so she damned well couldn't run. Lacking any other option, she'd stared the man down. He must have thought she was crazy, or that she had backup nearby. In the end, he'd been the one to leave, swaggering a little as if to replace lost pride.

Unless Marc decided to shoot her, there wasn't much more he could do than had already hit her.

"Next!" she called.

Wearing fatigues marked only with his name and rank, Marc Davidoff entered. He looked freshly shaved. Apart from that, he looked as if he'd seen an entire fleet of ghosts. And, in an incongruous contrast, he carried a bunch of roses so dark a red they were almost black.

"I'd have gotten here earlier," he announced. "I had to convince some assholes in Security that if lockdowns don't apply to them, they don't apply to EarthServ personnel either. It took some doing; they've got hard heads. I wanted to get in here before the shit hit the fan," he told her. "I see I'm too late. I'm sorry."

"It hit a whole bunch of fans," she said, mimicking his tone.

"For what it's worth," Marc said, "the people who brought you in said you'd done an astonishing job." He pointed with his chin. "I see they made good on their word to send you some flowers."

Given the messages she'd gotten, she supposed it stood to reason the flowers couldn't have come from Sandy or David IV. Certainly, Mac, that bastard, wouldn't have sent any.

She managed a wan smile.

"Here's some more," he added, and thrust the roses awkwardly into her hands.

"I hope you like them," he said, his voice hesitant.

"My God," the words popped out before CC could stop herself. "What'd you do, liquidate your trust fund?"

"Not quite," Marc said, reverting to his usual aggravating irony. "You gave me a bad scare. Gave all of us a bad scare. Apart, of course, from your new fan club."

"Nice someone appreciates me," CC said. "Seems to me that Mac was scared I'd die before I got notified I've been made persona non grata. What did I ever do around here to get a PNG but work my butt off? He won't even take my messages."

She hated herself for the way her voice quivered.

Marc sank down in the chair beside her bed and took her hands in his.

"They're cold," he stated. "Don't people around here understand about keeping shock victims warm?" He glared out the door as if his criticism of MedCenter could bring a physician groveling in. Not a chance.

"I'm fine, Marc. I'll deal," she said. To her own surprise, she sounded like the people in Gorsky's Hole.

He shook his head. "Of course you will."

"I've got to be off this rock on the next ship. Assuming I can afford it. Alpha's impounded my travel vouchers. Guess that means Freeze. You got any ideas?"

Marc lifted her hands, still cradled, warmed now, between his. He looked her urgently in the face.

"It's not what it looks like," he told her.

"You mean it's worse?" she asked. "Short of spacing me, damned if I can see how." She bit her lip to keep it from quivering.

"CC," he said, "I know Mac's not taking your messages. Don't let that stand in your way. I know these sorts of procedures. Someone's probably told you that you've got to hand over your effects to him. That's an opportunity. If you're smart, you won't simply drop them off with an assistant. Go there yourself."

He lifted her hands again, pressing them a little.

"He'll see you," Marc whispered. "He told me."

"How come everyone knows my business before I do?" CC complained.

"Just one big happy," Marc said. "Big happy dysfunctional family. Rumors spread like spacer's throat around here. Once you get out of this place, you come down to Gorsky's Hole. People down there say they owe you an awful lot of drinks. Except for Tenzing, who says you owe him one. Earth beer, no less. They weren't looking forward one bit to posting your picture over the bar. Though I've got to say I've seen you look a hell of a lot better."

CC found herself laughing.

"Picture wasn't my best side," she said, and laughed again. It didn't hurt.

"You may not believe it," Marc nodded at her encouragingly, "but when you said you'd deal, you said nothing more than the truth. They're proud of you at the bar, CC. And so am I. You get yourself organized now. And remember what I said."

To her astonishment, he bent over her hands and kissed them. Then, he left her room before she could say a word.

She couldn't afford to stay here. She couldn't afford to stay in her current quarters either. She really should get herself discharged and start to pack.

Instead, she lay back down and cried. Cried for everything in her life, from the lost girl she'd been, to the chances she'd walked away from, the ones that were taken from her, for the long years of stress and fear, and the sharp, brilliant moments of terror when she'd come up against something no one on Earth had ever seen and managed to survive.

And then she cried for the gifts she'd received. Margaret, sitting with her when she woke. Flowers from her rescuers—a lovely cluster of tiger-lilies and daisies. Marc's incongruous unexpected roses, and even the offers of free drinks from men and women who really had no reason to take an interest in a disgraced civilian.

Marc had all but ordered her to go see Mac. Maybe that was on the level. Maybe Marc knew something she didn't: wouldn't be the first time. After all, Mac might be Colony Manager here, but even he had people he reported to. Maybe he didn't have much of a choice, until he developed some

## 27

**CC might still be a little wobbly a little on her feet, but Vesta-**g was helping her stay mobile. There was nothing wrong with her wits or her voice, so she managed to bully MedCenter's staff into letting her check out. They were probably billing by the quarter-hour, and time meant credit she didn't have.

Returning to her quarters, she took no more than half an Earth hour to pack. No point in paying exorbitant charges if she wasn't on expense account.

Now to return her ID and travel vouchers, just as Alpha had ordered. The hell with trying to fit in with Vesta Colony's conspicuous restraint. She'd go out in uniform. Peeling off the coverall they'd given her in MedCenter (and probably tacked onto her bill), she tossed it into the recycler, then dressed in one of the suits she'd brought from Earth. Defiantly, she slipped David IV's ring onto her left hand. Too bad it was a family heirloom, or she could pawn it, not that it was worth that much up here.

The ex-status symbol sparkled, but not with the luster trapped in the crystals of Vesta's caves. She hooked her Breitling to her belt, stored her computer in its monogrammed bag, then slung it over one shoulder.

Edging out the door and sealing it, she pushed the rest of her gear to the storage lockers, which were cheaper than her former quarters by at least a factor of 100 to 1. She'd worry about a place to stay later, assuming Mac didn't simply lock her up. Even so, after a night in a survival bubble, CC knew she could make do with considerably less space than she'd enjoyed. And lockup would be free. At least, she thought it might. After all, she already owed her soul to the company store.

She crossed the Apsedra in long, low steps, her Earth-style heeled boots clicking down sharply. Drawing attention. She'd put on the uniform. Now she was going to war. Or to see Mac, which felt like the same thing. Assuming Marc was right and her oldest friend in about three industries and several hundred million miles was willing to see her at all.

This new lockdown had left the Apsedra bare. A recyclable scrap drifted in the air currents across the food court, brushing against the spindly plants that grew to heights impossible on Earth. The pavilions, so filled with light and noise when the Apsedra was crowded, seemed as flaccid as an empty survival bubble.

Three long, confident leaps brought a man in a coverall branded with Security's logo to face her. "Excuse me, Ms., there's a lockdown on. Didn't you hear?"

CC showed him a thin white line of teeth, the merest sketch of a propitiating smile. "I was in MedCenter," she said.

"You'll have to return to your quarters immediately," he replied. When she started to edge past him toward the corridor leading to Marc's office, he got in her way.

"I've checked out of my quarters," she answered patiently.

"I'll have to see some ID," he said, his voice going up and angry.

She nodded. "I'm on my way to surrender it to Mr. Nofi," she said. "In case you haven't heard, I've been declared persona non grata. I have three days to leave Vesta Colony or be charged. So you see I don't want to get into more trouble by not complying with the directions I was given while I was lying in MedCenter with a concussion."

She tilted her head at him, trying not to enjoy the consternation on the man's face. She suspected that women in full corporate gear who calmly announced they were being deported were a phenomenon he had never before experienced.

"Perhaps you should accompany me," she suggested. "In case I do something else wrong."

She stepped to one side, then proceeded down the corridor, now with a Security escort, just as if she were some visiting dignitary.

Now that she was about to leave it, she realized Vesta-g left her feeling, despite the clutter of gear she'd chosen to wear, as if she were free.

What was that old song? Freedom's just a word for nothing else to lose?

Nevertheless, freedom felt good.

She realized she was about to invoke her desperation talent, the one she hadn't used in years. She had always possessed the ability to spread her hands out on the table and level with the person across from her. She told the truth. She always had.

She would tell Mac the truth too, and then she would see. Assuming Mac would let her in. Marc had told her to go see him. Admittedly, someone might be lying. The idea was stupid, but this whole mess contained so many stupidities she didn't want to count them without a computer.

With luck, formal corporate dress would look unusual enough it might give her a tactical advantage with Mac's staff so they'd let her in. Once she got in, she was going to put her cards on the table, anchor them with magnets if need be, and deal.


Perhaps the Security guard trailing behind her had called ahead, or maybe Marc had been right after all: no sooner had CC stopped at the reception area than she was admitted. It was almost an anticlimax.

Finally, she thought, something had gone right.

The doors slid aside, admitting her to Mac's office. The place had been practically the first thing she'd seen on Vesta Colony. Here she was again. The office was still cluttered with trophies of his various lives: the caps, the souvenirs left by departing tourists, certifications, and the snide sign reading AD ASTRA PER NASDAQ. Well, Mac always had been an optimist.

"CC," Mac Nofi said, rising from his chair and holding out his hand. "I'm glad you came to see me."

"Don't you CC me, dammit!" she said. "I got your message the instant I was able to sit up in the MedCenter where I was brought while tracking down . . ."

"Your unauthorized investigations?" he asked.

He didn't offer her a chair. To do him justice, he didn't sit, either. She studied the room in unobtrusive flicks. The first time she'd been in his office, Mac's computer installations glowed with views of the colony itself as well as the charts and models he'd probably used to plot illegal trades.

He had turned all of them off, and the place felt sterile without them.

*Probably doesn't want me picking up ideas,* she thought resentfully. *Bastard knows how fast I can process. But I didn't come to steal data; I came to give him enough facts to choke on.*

"My final report," she said flatly. "Seeing as I'm required by Alpha to turn it, my ID, and my travel vouchers in to you. Talk about making bricks without straw. Get off Vesta, they say, but without vouchers or ID. What do they expect me to do—walk out an airlock? So here's my damn report."

She swung her bag off her shoulder and down onto his desk, scattering the files and trinkets there halfway across the room, and pushing the comm to one side. Unsealing it, she took out her computer and opened it, settled herself in the chair across his, and unhooked her Breitling.

"Take a look," she said. "If you haven't already peeked." She activated her spreadsheet program. The hologram built itself, glowing, on his desk. Each section shone a different color as she highlighted one trading record, pension account, and cargo manifest after another, showing how each was tagged with Mac's name, identification numbers, and seal.

He nodded, taking in the evidence.

Damn the man, he'd always had a phenomenal poker face! She couldn't read him, and it infuriated her.

"Is that all you've got?" he asked.

She wanted to slap him, but the impact would send her sailing halfway across the room.

"One last thing." She touched her Breitling and displayed the pictures of that exotic spacecraft. If she hadn't been rescued, they'd have found it on her corpse.

If Mac hadn't permitted her to be rescued, she realized. If he hadn't permitted Margaret to return her Breitling.

Those realizations took some of the satisfaction out of it, she had to admit.

CC eyed him suspiciously. "That's it," she said. "You realize you don't have a legal leg to stand on, even in Vesta-g?"

"CC," Mac asked, leaning forward earnestly, "are you truly going to try to cut a deal with me?"

"Hell!" CC rose from her seat far too fast. "What kind of deal could I get? I'm PNG here. There's a kangaroo court going on back at Alpha, and I can't even go there and defend myself, because I've been ordered to turn in my ID and vouchers to you—along with my report, which contains my only hope of showing Alpha I'm not crazy. Talk about double binds. On top of that, here you are, guilty of front-running, falsifying trades, trading for unauthorized people. If we did a count, I'd bet any credit I've got left once Alpha gets through with me that you've broken every one of the Spitzer regs and then some.

"But that's not good enough. Now, I run across these weird cargoes, and that damn ship! You taught me about ships, hell, I was your assistant for three years! You know better than I do that's an alien ship.

"Mac, are you out of your fucking *mind*?" she demanded. "You've been sitting on a First Contact situation, and you haven't told anyone. Not enough, is it, to sell out every shipsicle on Vesta; now, you're screwing with the whole system? What sort of a deal do *you* think *you* can cut with aliens? Do you even know what they think is valuable? Yes, I know you can space me before they try you, maybe for treason along with securities fraud, but before you do, at least tell me what the hell is going on!"

CC paused for breath and to suppress a moment of blind fury.

Because Mac was laughing. Son of a bitch had his fingers steepled and pressed against his face. He was laughing at her. Oh, she really was going to kill him. With her bare hands. Just squeeze and squeeze . . .

But Mac was managing now to force words out over his laughter and his hands.

"You always were too curious for your own damn good, CC. What're you going to do if I don't tell? Going to blow the whistle on me? After all I've done for you, including saving your precious ass after you fell down a cliff you had no business being anywhere near!" Mac sighed. "Oh well, I suppose no good deed goes unpunished."

She was going to kill him. They might space her, but they'd space her over his dead body. Not because of the crimes he'd committed, but because he was laughing at her.

The rat bastard had set her up.

Mac grinned at her. "You've had a damn lousy run of luck. We all have. And I don't think we're out of the Belt yet."

He bent over his comm. "Elizabeth? You there? I've seen CC's report. Yes, she's sitting across from me. You're right. She's ready to chew rock she's so mad. How's her report? I think she needs some pointers on securities law. Want to come and fine-tune it? Great! How soon can you get over here? Fine! I'll tell Security to pass you along. Listen, love, will you do me a favor and pick up some lunch along the way? The lockdown's kind of brought deliveries to a standstill. Thanks!"

He leaned back. "Elizabeth's on her way over."

"I can't believe you'd involve her," CC said. "Or that she'd go along with it."

Mac shook his head. "It's not what you think. At least not totally. Sit back and shut up. Your blood sugar's probably shot to hell."

There was nothing else she could do, at least for now. And, with the possibility not just of data, but of actual food she wouldn't have to pay for (a consideration in the brave new world she faced thanks to Mac and Alpha), CC settled herself in her chair and, to save face, assumed her best "well-I'm-waiting" expression.

Balancing her own computer, her own Breitling, and a stack of containers, Elizabeth all but bounded into Mac's office as if she owned the place and the man it belonged to. Mac leapt up to kiss her cheek. Working together, they set the steaming containers out on his desk. Their whole routine, she realized, was a hell of a lot more loving than *"Please, CC, can you re-think what you're doing and let me know? Once you've got a workable contingency plan in place, I'm certain Dad will still help you."*

Compared with the affection with which Mac and Elizabeth greeted each other, even in the face of accusations that could get them locked up for life, David IV's expression of support by playing the odds seemed somewhat tepid. To say the very least.

Well, CC had no one to blame but herself. She had wanted an *appropriate* partner, and appropriate was what she got. *All* she got. And damn lucky if she could leverage it into some sort of help back home.

Mac gestured at the nearest covered dish. "I remember, CC, you like Chinese. Why don't you start while Elizabeth reviews your report?"

"You two are crazy, you know that?" CC told them. How had her grand confrontation scene turned into an informal lunch with an old friend and his fiancée? Nevertheless, the steam rising from the food made her stomach growl.

"Sorry," she muttered, and started to eat.

"Tea too," said Mac. "You're probably dehydrated, and

the coffee they give you in MedCenter really isn't fit for human consumption."

Slipping behind Mac's desk, Elizabeth brought up CC's holo spreadsheet again and started rotating it to various angles, highlighting a different sector with each move. Turning from the holo to CC's notes, she read quietly for the time it took CC to work through the last of her rice.

*Eat up, CC. Credit's scarce.*

Then she laughed.

"Not bad," said the Compliance officer. "You're right, of course, about the Spitzer regs, but if you really wanted to be complete, you should have gone all the way back to the twentieth-century precedents. For example, you might well have cited *Benton & Co.* Number 85–113 from 1985."

She raised her head. Her eyes went vacant as she pulled the citation out of memory. "The firm was found to have violated rule 406 by causing an account to be maintained on the books of another member organization in which persons other than the customers were permitted to effect transactions on their own behalf and to have violated Regulation T by allowing for the extension of credit under terms not permitted."

"Bet you can't say that three times without taking a breath," said Mac.

"Shut up, darling," Elizabeth told him. "This is serious."

"Dammit, do you think I don't know that? Here's CC all set to space us on administrivia, like violating Supervisory Requirements 411, the duty to know or approve customers. That's like nailing a pirate for failure to register his ship, or jailing a bootlegger for tax evasion! I don't know these people, I don't approve of them, but I certainly know what they're capable of doing!"

CC yelped. "So you're not just trading in other people's accounts, you've got some unauthorized accounts that belong to— You're trading with *aliens*?" Her voice went up in a way she knew was improper in meetings.

The impact of that thought hit harder than her head, when the explosion in the caves had flung her against the rock.

"Aliens," she mumbled. This had to be an aftereffect of her

concussion. Sure, she'd seen the ship, but she could never believe this, and she certainly couldn't report it to Alpha.

"This isn't real," she protested.

"You think you're crazy," Elizabeth stated. "Maybe you think this is all a hallucination, and you're back in MedCenter, in Vesta Colony's only padded cell. I wouldn't blame you if you thought that. Hell, I'd be glad to join you there. This is precisely what Mac and I've been living with for the past few years, and I assure you it's a relief, finally, to be able to admit it to someone."

CC had just had a concussion. She'd just lost her job, her position here, and probably her fiancé. She was a sick woman, but not as crazy as she'd be if she bought into this story.

"Here's the rest of the law," said Elizabeth. With incongruous precision, she accessed the proper citation on her Breitling and presented it to CC.

"'Every member, member firm, or member corporation shall use due diligence to learn the essential facts relative to every customer and to every order or account accepted. No member, member firm, or member corporation shall make any transaction for the account of or with a customer unless, prior to or promptly after the completion thereof, the member, a general partner of the member firm, or an officer of the member corporation shall specifically approve the opening of such account, provided however, that in the case of a branch office the opening of an account for a customer may be approved by the manager of such branch office but the actions of such branch office manager shall within a reasonable time be approved by a general partner of the member firm or an officer of the member corporation. The member, general partner or officer approving the opening of an account shall, prior to giving his approval, be personally informed as to the essential facts relative to the customer and to the nature of the proposed account and shall indicate his approval in writing on a document which will become part of the permanent records of his office, firm, or corporation.'"

"I approved the accounts Mac was trading in," Elizabeth

admitted quietly. "You want to bring action in district court? Go right ahead. It'll probably take a couple of years for it to come to trial. And if word gets out . . ."

"What happens if word gets out?"

"The aliens won't like it, CC," said Mac. "And frankly, I don't know what they're likely to do if they're not happy. We've both seen clients throw fits. I don't want to know how far these people can throw things. Or what they can throw."

He shook his head at her. "Look, I'd be the first one to agree I've got reasons for holding a grudge against Earth. Yes, I got screwed over by the NGOs, but that's all over. I came out here and started over, and that's all right. It's not like I'm trading for myself. If I were, I'd deserve to be led out in cuffs and tossed off the surface. Every trade I've made, I've skimmed a little off the top and left it in the accounts. Each one of those shipsicles who wakes up is going to be just a little richer, a little more secure for those trades. Always was a good stock picker, if I say so myself."

"They'll pat you on the back before they throw you out the airlock, dear," Elizabeth told him.

CC shook her head, making the room spin and threatening to bring lunch back up.

"So you're selling out Earth System, but you're telling me you're a stock-picking Robin Hood?" she snarled at her old—no, her former—friend.

Mac mimicked her headshake. His grin showed all his teeth. "Must be the bump on the head. You haven't always been this stupid, CC. Think, for God's sake. You saw that ship. You know as well as I do it doesn't come from Earth. But it has to be from somewhere. And if it's not from this system, then do the math. It had to come from outside the Solar System. And if it is from somewhere else, the people who built it, the people who're flying it have to be able to get here before they die of old age. Which, logically, means they can fly . . ."

"Faster than light," CC whispered. Awe outraced the air currents. Her hair was standing at attention on the back of her neck.

"Right. And if they can do that, *what else can they do?*"

Mac leaned forward, palms flat on his desk. "CC, if I didn't trade for them, they'd find other people to do it—at the point of a kind of gun that, frankly, I don't like to think about. What sort of fight can we put up against that? Throw rocks at them? If they're as sophisticated as I think they are, they might see our best efforts as no more than rocks and pointed sticks. So you're damned right I've been making illegal trades as a holding action.

"I knew when I saw your name on *Rimrunner*'s passenger list I was in trouble. Still, I figured I had a home-turf advantage so I could work around you. Or we could get you home. Or maybe Marc could. Hell, I didn't think you'd risk your precious job. After all, last time I'd seen you, you were doing a good impersonation of the perfect NGO serf. Down to that stupid ring. So I thought maybe you'd do your job, go home, get married. I should have realized you'd turn it into one of your damn research projects. Never did know when to quit, did you?"

CC flushed. It had taken a taste of life at the top, or as close to it as she'd ever been allowed to get, to learn there was far more to life than upward mobility.

Her tea splashed out of the container as it slipped from her shaking hands. The tears that destroyed her careful Earth-style makeup were hot, welcome. Oh God, she was coming apart.

She let out a whimper, wrapped her arms about herself, and started to curl up in a ball, just as she had when all the power failed and she thought she might die in the dark, sealed into the remains of Vesta Colony.

Then, as she fought not to come permanently apart, she felt herself held, sustained, by the very people she ought to be turning in for securities fraud and, probably, treason. But attempted murder? She didn't think so. Not anymore.

## 28

**What felt like hours later, CC hunched over in her chair and** fought for the rest of her self-control. She might still kill Mac and turn Elizabeth in to the EASD, but before she did, she had several million questions she was damned well going to get answers for.

Starting with "Why didn't you tell anyone?"

Mac looked over at his ship models, clipped to a cabinet bolted to the wall. "You know that ship you saw?" he asked. "That's just a shuttle, but even it packs more power than I like to think about. In the early stages of our . . . account negotiations, they made me come on board once. When I think of what they showed me to put the fear of—whatever into me, that was one visit too often."

"So," CC asked, "where's—I can't believe I'm having to say this—where's the mother ship?" A grin she couldn't control stretched her muscles and dry skin. "Ow!"

"Gets me that way too," said Nofi. "I still can't believe this."

"Do you remember Hermes?" Elizabeth asked. *Back to business,* her tone ordered. "Not the messenger god or the thief. In the late twentieth or early twenty-first century, I forget which now, Hermes was an asteroid that just suddenly disappeared. Well, we know now it wasn't an asteroid. It was an Ark. It entered our system on reconnaissance, then went on out again. We know now it reported back to the people who sent it."

Mac laughed. CC identified the gallows humor of equities traders. Squared, cubed, and raised to the $n^{th}$.

"About five years ago, they came back and decided to open for business. It's the old story, as you say. There's a reason some things are clichés. Their Ark had targeted this solar system as a likely acquisition. With the kind of computer power they've got, they cracked our languages in a matter of hours, then studied us and came to the conclusion we produced things they liked. They admired our trading system. Thought it would make the perfect delivery vehicle."

"So they used the tombstones in The *Wall Street Worldsnet* as Rosetta Stones and decided they wanted to make trades with the natives? For what?" CC asked. "And what did they offer?"

"You saw the contents of that cart. Chemicals. Pharmaceuticals. Some foods—luxury-type stuff, even a few gems. In return, they offered technology, information, practically a cure for the common cold. My guess is, compared to what else they've got, that's chump change."

CC shrugged. "If they're that advanced, what do they need us for? Can't they get these things in their own star system? Or is it 'systems'?"

"Definitely, it's 'systems,'" Mac admitted.

"And you're telling me you weren't seduced by the potential of gaining FTL and a cure for the common cold?" CC demanded.

Not to mention the free trip home, she thought bitterly. Disclosing information about an alien contact would have made Mac rich, secure, and famous.

"Look," said Mac, "I'm still pissed at the NGOs, but I'm not crooked. Something smelled wrong about the deal. I mean, if they simply wanted to make trades, why not contact us on the up and up? And I'm suspicious. Something about the list of things they wanted to trade for just smelled wrong. Think it through: except for the things that are merely expensive, there isn't a thing on that list that couldn't be addictive.

"So I stalled. And they started to turn up the pressure. They invited me to visit their ship. I went out there, visions of First Contact, *Klaatu barada nikto* and all that noble stuff, going off like an old-style Fourth of July in my head, and got the grand tour. They meant to make quite an impression, and they did. CC, I know weapons systems when I see them, and I've never seen anything like the installations they showed me. Even the weapons on that shuttle could punch a hole in Vesta Colony in five minutes, maybe ten. I don't even like to think about the weapons on board the Ark. My guess is that thing could melt Mount Piazzi like a candle in a cheap cafe. At that point, I couldn't go to the NGOs even if I wanted to. They'd have sent some punk hotshots swaggering out here to piss off our new clients, and we'd have all been blown up."

CC shivered, wrapping her arms about herself again.

"So this isn't a matter of crooked trades," she said. "This is a mugging. Just our luck. First Contact, and what we get is gangsters."

Mac nodded.

CC looked down at her spreadsheet, touched her keyboard, and highlighted an ascending curve. "If this curve is any indication—and yes, Elizabeth, I know past performance is no guarantee of future results—the aliens seem to be stepping up their demands without raising their levels of payment. Looks like they're not interested in just making trades so you'll bring them chocolate and drugs any more."

"That's right," said Mac. "Now they're trying to get control of the source. It's one thing to buy opium from a dealer. It's another thing to own the poppy fields. Their very own poppy patch, farmed by hicks who know enough to produce seriously good drugs, but aren't tough enough to fight them. It's classic. I may not have your background in history, but I recognize the symptoms. And they've got the biggest guns I've ever seen held to our heads."

Mac's face sagged, making him look much older. Frightened. He spread his hands out on his desk, mimicking CC's earlier gesture. "I didn't know what else to do. No one did. So I've spent the past few years trying to make one of the weirdest mergers of my life, pretty much on my own."

Talk about a hostile takeover!

CC would have bitten her tongue if it hadn't just been repaired. Instead, she bit her lip because if she started to laugh, she'd never stop.

"I couldn't figure out what else to do but play for time," said Mac. "At first, I tried to keep things secret."

He stripped open his cuffs, showing her the activated sockets in his wrists. So, he'd had them reopened so he could jack himself into the system and perform his trades himself.

"I thought I was a real wise guy, but Elizabeth saw right through me," he said. His smile at her was young, untouched, and went right to CC's heart. It would be a pity if he'd healed just in time to be incinerated by the worst trading partners in human history.

"Elizabeth convinced me I needed allies," Mac went on. "Starting with her. Then Marc."

CC nodded. "I saw you'd sent a lot of business to his family's shop. Had to wonder how much they knew."

"They know. They're cooperating. Not just with me, but with Marc and EarthServ. But mutual funds are under such tight supervision that they've had to keep a low profile so they had plausible deniability. We were still pretty much on our own. Face it, CC, so what if Earth loses Vesta? We're one colony, not even the biggest in the system. They've got other colonies. But we only have the one homeworld."

"So the idea is to—what did you call it?—fight a holding action until we could really fight back? What can we possibly throw against these people?" CC flinched away again from Mac's images: Mount Piazzi melting to a stub; aliens tearing Vesta another Olbers Crater. God, they'd split the asteroid apart.

"For a start," said Elizabeth, "we've got Neave out here now. Marc's family made the approach. As first NGO ambassador to the UN, Neave's known everyone in power for years. If anyone stands a chance of talking to these people and living, it's Neave."

"But he brought his family out here," CC protested.

"Maybe he'd figured it was better for them to go out fast than blow up, live through nuclear winter, or be peons in ET's poppy patch," said Mac. "Or Margaret told him the facts of life."

"That's cold," CC told him. "That's really cold."

"So's absolute zero, which is what we're going to face if the damn aliens punch through the rock. Marc was the one who told me Neave was retiring and looking to emigrate. He'd heard it from his father, who'd heard it on the nineteenth hole at St. Andrews. Marc told me if I could get Neave on our side, he was worth an entire Marine Expeditionary Unit. And that Margaret was probably worth two. So now Marc knows everything I do. And he started lobbying to get more ships out here—not just that pathetic flyover we have every day—even before he left Earth."

CC grimaced. "'Every man a rifleman' isn't really going to do us a hell of a lot of good," she said.

"We've had some unexpected help," Elizabeth put in. "I suppose it was something we could have expected if we'd been doing that kind of contingency planning. If we assume our visitors are criminals, we've got to assume they'll try to lie low. So, it makes sense that they'll start off by trading for what they want or trying to own the means of production. After all, vaporizing an asteroid or slagging a planet might draw attention, especially if someone out thataway's got a warrant, or the alien facsimile thereof, out for these clowns."

"If we sent out a Mayday," Mac took up Elizabeth's line of reasoning, "they'd pick it up, and you can damn well bet they'd retaliate. But we're at the height of the eleven-year sunspot cycle. There's a lot of interference. So much that we've been actually able to piggyback distress calls on some of our signals and attribute it to static."

"I was against it at the time," Elizabeth said. Incongruously, she grinned, a flash against her dark skin. "What do you expect of Compliance? We're just naturally risk-averse."

"Maybe they'll get it and, in a couple years, maybe someone else will send in an alien version of the Marines," Mac said. "Sooner, assuming they're on the lookout for these people. But I'd say that's something we can't count on. For all intents and purposes, we're on our own. Even if I wanted to tell the NGOs, you know damned well they'd overreact. Word would get out, and *wham!* Fried planet."

"So, now that we know what the problem is—and that there's no way in hell Alpha would do anything but lock me up if I presented this report—what's next?" she asked.

"We've been stepping up security. We can't take them, but maybe we can hurt them hard, or make them know that anything they do is going to be messy enough it will be spotted. And maybe," Mac added, "we'll get lucky. I'd say we were overdue for some luck. So, seeing as we haven't got enough Marines to send in, I'd say we give Neave a call and tell him it's time to deal."

# / 29

"It'll look less suspect if I call Neave," said Elizabeth. "Mac, while I'm at it, why don't you find out what meds CC's on so you know if it's safe to give her a drink? I've never seen anyone who could use a stiff belt more."

CC shut her eyes, trying to remember what she'd seen in that distant cave. She remembered three figures, tall and thin, masked like the dock workers to the eyes. As a description of Earth's first contact with aliens, that wasn't much to go on. Damn. She had so hoped . . .

To her horror, she was starting to puddle up again. Dammit, she was coming apart. She cried like a baby, like someone who'd never realized how thrilled she'd been by the archeological expeditions on Mars, the discovery of water on the gas giants' satellites. She supposed she'd always thought that solutions to every problem she'd ever seen lay out in space. She remembered an historical disk called *Independence Day*. She'd seen it at the Gates Center and found herself weeping as aliens that looked like a hideous cross between a squid and a Man-of-War told a human official who was trying to stop their attack, "You can die." They didn't even want to try to be friends. Earth had waited so long for aliens, and now they'd found only enemies.

She guessed that it looked as if these aliens—oh hell, call them Hermians after their damn Ark of an asteroid because she had to call them something and Mac hadn't given her a name—were what she had to consider Bad Aliens.

"Shit, CC, what did you expect?" Mac demanded. He reached behind him to a cabinet, unsealed it, and produced a bottle that had to have come all the way from Earth. "Something tall, dark, and greenish in robes striding off a ship and saying 'Live long and prosper'?"

*It would have been nice,* she thought.

He laughed a little wildly. "If it comes to that, our own resident aliens actually kind of like us. The way you'd like a really good dog or family retainer. *Good* boy. But this is still business. They'd shoot a dog that had outlived its usefulness. Nothing personal."

He waved the bottle at CC and poured. "Still drinking Scotch when you can afford it? Say when."

He handed her the drink. "Down the hatch, now. Yes, it's a crime to treat good Scotch that way, but if we're talking about crime, I've done worse."

The acrid burn of the Scotch felt good, all the way to her sinuses. CC mopped at her face. "Sure would have been nice to meet the good aliens," she whispered.

Mac sighed. "I believe in the tooth fairy and the Easter Bunny too. Sucks to be us."

He put the Scotch back. But then, Mac always had had a grip on essentials.

"Mac!" Elizabeth's voice had gone up a couple of tones. "I just spoke to Margaret. Neave's on his way over, she says."

Her voice brought Mac around.

"What's . . ."

*What's wrong?* CC knew he'd started to say when the doors opened so fast the warning bell pinged in discord with the comms that lit up across Mac Nofi's desk.

Carlos Montoya-Ruiz hurled himself through the doors so fast that he had to push off against the far wall. CC had seen him once or twice standing watch. Now, his features were pasty white under the normal brown of his skin, and his eyes bulged. He opened his mouth to talk. No words came out. A moment more, and he'd probably hyperventilate.

"Carlos, report!" Mac snapped.

"Turn on your screens!" the guard cried. *"Comms on speaker!"*

Outside the office, klaxons went off as if they were testing the skylight. Red lights flashed rhythmically across the polished stone walls of the corridors, the spun pavilions of the Apsedra, turning the plant life black.

"Got a hostage situation, sir," said Carlos. "Never saw a ship like that. People like that. Uh, sir, they *are* people, aren't they?"

"Oh shit," Mac whispered. It sounded like a prayer. Fear flashed across his face like the lights of Red Alert. Then he dived for the comms and activated them.

Static crackled, popped, and screamed into the room.

*". . . repeat: at 11:00 hours, a shuttle crew of unknown origin forced its way into Docking Bay 3, secured hostages and . . ."*

Static overrode the announcer's agitated voice, arcing up into painful discords.

Through the open door came the grinding and clashing of the plates dividing Vesta Colony into hermetically sealed sections. Even if there wasn't a sector breach, you had to assume one could happen. At least, the lockdown meant people were in their quarters, within reach of survival bubbles.

The bubbles could prolong their lives—how long? Maybe it would have been kinder—stop that, CC!

"Damn!" said Mac. "I thought I had the situation under control." He pounded his fist on the stone surface of his desk. "What made them pick *now* to make a move? We sent the bastards that last shipment! And we stand to win that proxy fight."

"'*Once you have paid him the Dane-geld, you* never *get rid of the Dane,*'" CC muttered under her breath. Her lips were going numb. Her hands were sheer ice. "Mac, sooner or later this was bound to happen. Tell me you weren't really stupid enough to think you could control them or give them what they wanted?"

If Elizabeth could have linked her glare to an energy weapon, Maintenance would have had to scrape charred CC off the floor.

Too damn bad.

"So they've taken hostages," CC said. "If they've got the firepower you say they do, they can take more hostages at any time. You said they could crack this place wide open, but they haven't. Why not?"

Elizabeth nodded. "They want something. Something else. That must be why Margaret sounded so strained when she said Neave had already left their quarters."

Mac sighed in relief. "At this point, he's worth his weight in black diamonds. His Earth-weight. Damn, where is he?" He drummed his fingers on the desk's polished surface, then slipped his hand out of sight. CC suspected he had a weapon cached in a drawer.

"That's far enough," came a familiar, incongruous voice just as the doorseals engaged.

What was *Sandy* doing here?

"I want to see both hands on the desk. I'm telling you: leave that gun in the drawer. Lock the drawer and put both hands on your desk, or I burn His Excellency here a second one. Think Edward the Second."

CC's hands flew to her mouth.

Sandy, arm in arm with Neave. They looked like the best of friends: an eager young man, carefully turned out and moving with caution as he assisted a distinguished elder statesman to maneuver in Vesta-g.

Then Sandy turned slightly, and CC saw the energy weapon pressed against Neave's side. A muscle jumped along the older man's jaw. It was white with what CC read as fury, not fear.

"I suggest," said Sandy, "that we all sit down. CC, I think it's your turn to get coffee. I bought last time."

CC stiffened. All these accidents, all these months of

playing CC Williams, Consultant and Galactic Spook, and now she froze when a male middle manager told her to fetch coffee. But he'd done worse, hadn't he? He'd tried to kill her. More than once. He'd even put his own life on the line. But then, Sandy always had been a risk taker. Sandy smiled, and pushed his sidearm against Neave's ribs.

"Ms. Williams," Neave broke the silence. "I can't tell you how sorry I am you've been put at risk. Marc Davidoff has given me regular updates on your extraordinary progress. Believe me, if we survive this . . ."

*You'll write a letter to Alpha? That and my travel vouchers will get me back to Earth. Assuming we live through the next five minutes.*

Still, she made herself nod at the Ambassador as if she'd just received a positive job evaluation.

"Be quiet!" Sandy snapped. "You talk when I tell you to talk."

Mac raised an eyebrow and pursed his lips. *Payback's a bitch,* he mouthed as if he and CC stood on a ship's hull, talking helmet to helmet. After years of toeing the line, Sandy had seen opportunity and grabbed it.

"In case you hadn't noticed," Mac said, pulling out his best vestiges of a good ol' boy drawl to win friends and influence people, "there's a red alert on. Security's going to be looking for me . . ."

"Oh, I'm sorry," Sandy said. "Your computer is about to fail. Catastrophically."

He fired once at Mac's computer installations. An alarm went off. "Kill it!" he ordered. His sidearm wavered across each person in the room.

Mac killed the alarm.

"Sandy," CC told him urgently, "you need to listen to Mac. He's seen the inside of that shuttle. These people could blow Earth apart and not think twice. . . ."

"Get that coffee, dammit!" Sandy said. "You haven't a clue how long I've wanted to tell you that. Your old boss isn't the only one who got inside that shuttle. What do you think I've been spending my time out here doing?"

*Selling out Earth,* she wanted to say. *Trying to murder me.* Instead, she moved toward Mac's coffeemaker, flicked it on, and asked, mimicking the tone of office ladies she'd heard back on Earth, "Would you like sugar?"

"No, thanks," Sandy replied.

If she hadn't been so terrified, the routine courtesy would have sent her into hysterics.

Sandy gestured again, this time at Carlos. "You. Disarm. Then go over to the wall and lie down, hands over your head. You"—he pointed at Elizabeth—"Away from him. Sit where I can see you. And Mac, I want you out from behind that desk."

Hands away from his body, Mac complied. Sandy nudged Neave toward Mac's seat and stood behind him.

The coffee poured itself into insulated tubes. CC clipped them onto the tray next to the machine and set them beside everyone in the room but Ruiz. A braver woman would have tried to scald Sandy and grab his weapon. But he had his firearm pressed against Neave's temple. All he had to do was tighten one finger.

Quietly setting down the tray, she took her seat.

"I know favoritism when I see it," said Sandy. "When I saw the attention you were getting on *Rimrunner,* I knew something had to be up. So I've been watching you since we landed here. You've just been getting yourself into all kinds of trouble, haven't you?"

"How much of that was your doing?" CC asked. Funny how you could grow up with someone, work with him, and never know him at all.

Sandy shrugged. "Not as much as I'd have liked. You got what meddlers deserve. The first time was a wash. I knew something was up, and I pretty much figured out that Mac was in the thick of it. But he never liked me, so I knew he wouldn't cut me in. It's not bad if you've got money to get help. I got it. He was watching me, so I had to take a risk. Damn near got myself killed. I couldn't have been happier when I caught you following me out into the docking area. I knew I had the chance to make the deal of a lifetime, if nobody interfered. I followed you out to the ship—had to admit that surprised me too. Still, a deal's a deal. So I gave you a push—"

CC kept her eyes down, not wanting to set Sandy off. He had tried to kill her. All the years of struggle, of competition: she knew he'd stabbed her in the back during their time at Morgan Nomura, and she'd never really trusted him since, but she'd thought that now that they both had enough, they could at least be colleagues.

"Once I was sure you were out of the picture, permanently or not, it didn't make much of a difference right about then, I went out and made contact with the aliens myself."

Sandy's face glowed with wonder—and greed. In the flickering lights of Mac's office, she could see the thin, thin lines of all the surgeries Sandy had had, all the expensive surgeries to tailor himself into the perfect executive. It hadn't worked; none of his strategies had gotten him the position he'd dreamed he was entitled to; and there he was with the bills.

He shook his head. "They've promised me things I can't believe even now. I'll go home, I'll make the deals, honest deals, for them just the way they want, and keep my mouth shut, and Earth will be safe. I'll be a hero even if no one else knows, but even that won't matter. I'll be *rich* and you . . . well, I'm afraid you'll be history."

"Why would they offer you anything?" Neave's voice in the silent room carried a contempt that made Sandy flinch.

"They need us," Sandy told him. "Hermes has been out of the system for years, and they're running short on resources. Might even be that their ship isn't coming back, I don't know. If it doesn't, maybe I *will* get to be a hero. Who knows?"

"Let's leave legalities aside," Elizabeth spoke up. "You'd sell out your own system? Your own people?"

Sandy nodded at her. "Sometimes, you have to make tough judgment calls," he said. "It's business. Nothing personal."

"Like the time it was you or me at Morgan, and you decided it ought to be me?" CC asked. "I landed on my feet. Just as I did when you pushed me over that cliff. Sandy, will you for crying out loud think about what you're doing? This isn't just about cutting a deal, or trying to eliminate the competition. It's about putting the entire solar system on the table. The stakes are too high!"

Let him think she couldn't handle the risk. As long as she kept him talking. Sandy had been a historian. Talking was a disease with him. A fatal one, please God.

"That's so melodramatic," he told her. "I prefer to think of this as the opportunity of a lifetime."

"If this is your notion of angel investing," Mac commented, "those people damn sure don't look like angels to me. You've seen them with their masks off; what do you think?"

Sandy shrugged. CC rolled her eyes at Mac. Not a chance they could turn him. She'd seen Sandy convince himself before that things weren't possibly as bad as other people thought and that he'd come up smelling like a rose. Maybe he even had some notion of selling out the aliens and making things right after all. It wasn't megalomania, not quite.

Neave cleared his throat, flinching only slightly when Sandy's weapon pressed against his temple this time. Slowly, deliberately, he raised his hands in the age-old gesture of surrender.

"It seems," he said, "that you've got all the bases covered. Now what? I was on my way over here to . . . ah, discuss the situation when your business associates broke into that docking bay and started taking hostages when I met you. I can assume, I suppose, you were waiting for me? Good planning."

Sandy smiled, pleased.

"Excellent," Neave went on. "Mac called me in as—I'm sure you'll pardon the expression—an honest broker with deep experience in negotiations. You've done well this far, but you're going to need someone with more seniority to take the deal from here. I suggest we go out there and talk to the aliens."

"Not a chance!" said Sandy. "I know you. All the people on your level. You let us fight like rats in a cage over the small change, but once there's a deal of any size, you come in and just scoop it up, leaving the rest of us out in the cold. So you're not going anywhere," he told Neave. "And I'm prepared to enforce that."

"So what do you have in mind?" asked Neave. "If I might make a suggestion . . ."

"Sandy," Elizabeth said urgently, "*listen* to him. If he's giving you good advice, it's your best shot at getting what you want. Advice of counsel, and all that."

Sandy glanced around a little wildly. Mac passed his hand slowly over his mouth, wiping off a purely feral grin, and CC recalled that, much as Sandy bragged about risk-taking, he had never been a trader, never proved that he could thrive on risk the way successful traders did. His hand was shaking, which didn't augur anything good for Neave's continued health.

"Go ahead," he whispered. With his free hand, he picked up the coffee CC had brought him. He gulped thirstily.

In a better world, CC thought, she'd have been able to poison it.

*Just let me survive to make do with this one,* she prayed.

"All right!" Neave said crisply. "Clearly, you've ingratiated yourself with the . . . with our visitors. Now, why don't you go out there and open negotiations on behalf of Earth itself. I will be perfectly happy to name you my attaché and, once Mr. Nofi's computer system is repaired, I am prepared to put that in writing and send it back to Earth. This not only gives you credibility, it gives you diplomatic immunity."

Elizabeth opened her mouth to object that immunity didn't hold up against felony charges, then appeared to think better of it.

"Ms. Inui is about to say that diplomatic immunity doesn't apply to felonies, but I think I can cut a deal on your behalf. If you will accept my cooperation, I think I can assure you that you will come out of this very well indeed."

"I won't spend time in prison," Sandy told him.

"You're about to cut the biggest deal in the history of this system's capital markets. I give you my word, you're not going to go to prison."

Sandy eyed him.

"Handshake agreement's binding," Neave said. "We've even got a lawyer here to witness it. Of course, she's implicated up to her eyeballs, but she's still a lawyer."

*Until she's disbarred, assuming she lives that long.*

Elizabeth inclined her head. She looked as dazed as CC felt.

"What assurance do I have that you won't go back on your word?" Sandy asked.

Neave drew himself up. "My family is here. I want them to live." He paused, waiting for that to sink in.

"Now, if I may offer you a suggestion about how to go about your business," he continued, "I'd suggest that, right now, we're at an impasse. The aliens have their hostages, and Vesta Colony has no guidance. Now's the time for someone with courage and vision to take control of the situation. Contact them," he urged.

CC cast a despairing look at the others. What did Neave think he was doing? This wasn't the language of business; it was the language of a resentful man's wish-fulfillment fantasies.

Mac narrowed his eyes. *Neave's telling him just what he wants to hear,* she realized. *Validating the scenarios he's been inventing all these years while scrabbling to keep employed.*

Though Neave was sitting, Sandy standing, if CC shut her eyes she could imagine Neave, standing at the younger man's shoulder, inspiring him, encouraging him, sending him off to war.

Sandy went absolutely motionless, as if he listened not just to Neave, but to his own thoughts.

CC held her breath while her heart pounded. She knew, as if Neave had spoken it aloud, what he feared: that sooner or later, someone would get impatient or panic.

"I'll do it!" Sandy announced. His lips all but quivered. Then he looked at the computer systems he'd disabled. Reaching into his shipsuit, he pulled out his PDA and frowned.

"It can't get through the barriers," he said.

"Take mine," Neave offered. He pulled out his own PDA. It wasn't just a high-end Breitling, but a hand-held workstation that probably represented a year's salary for the likes of Sandy. "I realize that you came out with minimal equipment, but it's always better to be prepared. You'll need to remember that in the future."

Sandy nodded, accepting the hand-held along with what was, really, very good advice.

"Good luck," said Neave. "Mr. Nofi, may we assume these doorseals have a backup mechanism? I think Mr. Sanderson wishes to go about his business."

"Right away, sir," Mac said. "If nobody minds, I'll just get these doors open for you." They unsealed with a whoosh. Outside, the whoops and klaxons of red alert still sounded. Shouts rose from the Apsedra.

Sandy paused again. This was one hell of a time for him to freeze, CC moaned inwardly.

"What are you waiting for?" Neave coaxed. "Time is credit."

"You're right," Sandy said hoarsely, squaring his shoulders in a way CC knew meant that he was searching for the appropriate sound bite, as he walked out into what he hoped was immortality.

He strode out, shedding the awkwardness that had always marked his movements in Vesta-g now that he no longer needed it.

Neave leaned forward, gesturing at CC's machine, which sat, still unnoticed on Mac's desk. "Call Davidoff," he ordered. "Now." Then, he turned to the security guard, still immobilized against the wall. "You," he said. "They'll need you outside."

Ruiz rolled over, levered himself to his feet, and propelled himself out of the room.

Mac pushed away the ruins of his computer system. Rolling up his sleeves to free his wrist-jacks, he linked into VestaNet. "This is faster," he said, and signaled Davidoff.

*"Yeah?"* came Marc Davidoff's voice after the burst of static that indicated he was Outside. *"Now you call me? You picked one hell of a bad time."*

"I didn't have a choice," Mac said. "Sanderson's pulled a power grab. He's on his way out to the shuttle. Neave told him he could handle the hostage situation."

*"Well, isn't that special? It's just a great day for double-crosses! We've got a bogey out here—big enough to be an asteroid, but moving under its own power. It's already crossed Charon's orbit, and—all right, Gamma Wing, get out there and hold your fire! We anticipate it'll come within range within . . . how should I know? We've got no idea how fast this thing can travel. An hour. Maybe two."*

"You think they're trying to double-cross their own superiors?" Mac asked Davidoff.

*"I'd bet the farm."*

"Can you hack into Neave's PDA?" Mac asked. "I want to know what Sanderson's telling them."

*"I can try,"* Marc said.

"Just a minute," said Mac. Disconnecting his jacks, he grabbed CC's machine and hooked it in. "Put it on screen," he said.

*"Hooking in Apsedra-cam 4."*

The monitor fuzzed, then resolved into Sandy's self-consciously solitary figure, trim in its shipsuit, walking across the Apsedra. His hands were conspicuously empty of everything but the PDA, and he was talking fast.

Yes, he'd heard their warnings. Yes, he was empowered now to deal with them, not as an independent contractor, but on behalf of the entire system as a diplomatic attaché. Yes, whatever terms they set, he had been instructed to meet. Let the hostages go.

It was the role of a lifetime, played by a man who'd probably imagined moments like this his entire life. Neave leaned over the screen, his eyes very bright, his lips moving in sync with every word Sandy spoke, nodding to himself.

Sandy's voice, boosted by Neave's top-quality equipment, rang out in VestaNet.

*"They're going to release the hostages,"* he said.

CC heard cheers, instantly suppressed.

*"Shifting to docks,"* said Marc.

They had a long wait. When the screen cleared, they saw that Sandy had put on a pressure suit and was making his way into the docking bay. A ragged gap marked where the shuttle had blasted its way in.

As they watched, a hatch opened, a ramp slid down, and Sandy, his shoulders squared, entered the aliens' shuttle.

"Tell your wings to stand down." Neave ordered Davidoff as the shuttle lifted. It streaked through the blasted locks.

*"It's setting course away from our bogey,"* said Marc. *"Toward the inner system."*

*"Permission to give chase . . ."* came the voice of one of his wingmen.

They could hear Davidoff drawing breath to reply.

"Denied," Neave cut in.

*"Denied?"* Davidoff questioned sharply. *"Sir, I hope you know what the hell you're doing."*

"I know, Marc. I definitely know," he said.

Neave turned to the others in Nofi's office and pointed with his chin.

"Hostages," said Mac Nofi. "Right." He leapt out the door, shouting to stand down from red alert.

"That may be somewhat premature," said Neave.

At that moment the shuttle blew up.

CC's screen blanked to white. That computer would never be the same again, she told herself. And she'd finally paid it off, too.

"I had a bomb built into that PDA," Neave explained. "Time delay of about an hour once I activated it. I'd hoped it might cause a chain reaction in whatever propulsion system the aliens used. Apparently," he added, "it performed better than I expected."

Neave sank into Mac's chair and leaned his forehead

against his hand as if he were very tired and much older than he had been only a short while ago.

"Captains of industry I will deal with," Neave said softly. "I will not tolerate jumped-up second lieutenants. A gentlemen's agreement is binding—between gentlemen. And the punishment for treason has always been death."

## 30

**CC drew herself up into her chair to avoid a shoving match** as three computer techs fought to be the first to install new monitors in Mac's command centers. The ventilation system, cossetted by another tech, panted like a trapped animal, replacing the stink of burnt silicon with Vesta Colony's usual recycled air. It no longer smelled medicinal, but wild and fresh with the promise of life—at least until the alien ship came into firing range.

*"Son of a* bitch!*"* came a cry over the comms still hooked into CC's machine. *"Sons of bitches're flying that whole damn asteroid!"*

*"Track it!"* Marc ordered. *"Keep an eye out for weapons or any ships it's carrying, but stay out of firing range. Or what you think is firing range."*

A ship the size of an asteroid.

Hadn't Mac said that Hermes, the asteroid that had come so close to Earth it had caused a panic, had been—what was his word? An Ark?

Imagine it, CC thought. Engines the size of the Apsedra, or maybe bigger, unless they'd figured out a way to micro-miniaturize them. And to think Alpha's *Quarterly* had dismissed nanotechnology as not being economic! Short-sighted idiots.

Ships that could fly faster than the speed of light, she thought. Marc would die of envy, assuming he lived that long. Weapons . . .

She wouldn't think of it. For now, Vesta was alive. Marc was alive. And as long as they survived, they had the chance to think of something that would buy them a little more life, and a little more, and a little more until they could think their way out of this—because it sure as hell looked as if they wouldn't be able to fight their way out.

And speaking of a fight . . .

CC turned to Neave, who waved away Elizabeth's offer of a drink without turning away from the monitor.

"You had a bomb in your Breitling!" CC exclaimed. "You were planning a suicide mission!"

Neave sighed. "Your late colleague was right. Sometimes you have to make the tough calls. I hadn't just agreed to co-operate with EarthServ: they reactivated a Reserve commission I'd held years ago so I'd have line authority, if need be. With that kind of authority, well, you don't give orders unless you're prepared to back them up.

"So I was prepared to take out the first hostile alien ship we encountered by any means whatsoever. I wouldn't call this a good day to die, but think it through: I'd finally gotten my wife and family out somewhere clean with a chance of decent values and a life they could make for themselves."

He snorted faintly and sagged back into his chair. "That was Margaret's final condition for the marriage, in any event: emigrate, have at least two children, or 'so long, it's been good.' God bless her, she's no mindless trophy, and she proved it again today. Margaret's a scientist; they're used to adding up facts and making tough calls. She may not have known exactly what I planned, but she knew me, she could calculate the odds, and she let me out of our quarters anyhow.

"Look," he went on, shaking his head at CC so she real-ized she must have made horrified sounds of protest. "It

made sense. I'd made my fortune. I'd had my brilliant career. If I sacrificed myself, I'd ensure I'd be remembered
with honor—maybe even a statue in the Apsedra for kids
still on their tethers to climb up on. You know, I always did
want to be an ancestor, more than a descendant."

Neave massaged his temples with long fingers. How clean
they looked.

"You know," he told Elizabeth, "if you don't mind, I think
now I would like to change my mind about that drink. Planning one's own suicide, but not having to go through with it
really does make you somewhat weak in the knees. How
very interesting."

In absolute silence, Elizabeth poured Neave a very generous double. Neave took and drained it, then looked up at her
with a cold smile. "Remember, I *was* willing. I had put all
my affairs in order. Still, when your Mr. Sanderson was kind
enough to stand in for me, I realized I'd been given a price-
less chance to see my children grow up." He paused. "I will
always be grateful to him for that. And I am profoundly relieved that Margaret will have no cause to ring the bell on
9/11 Day to begin trading."

CC tried to suppress a shiver, but Neave caught it.

"CC," he asked, "how do you ever expect to succeed in
business if you can't learn to make the really tough calls?"

She held out her tube, not giving a damn that he could see
how her hand shook.

"Your workstation, sir," said a tech. He pushed off from
the console with one long step as if heartily glad to get clear
of Neave, then turned to busy himself with the remaining
consoles. Well, it was the tech's own damn fault for listening in.

Neave whirled his chair around to face the machine. Red,
yellow, and purple lights exploded across his face from the
monitor. Not bothering with a headset, he let the chatter
from Davidoff's fighting wing fill the room and leaned back,
waiting.

So far, the alien Ark hadn't sent out any rider vessels or
fired. Maybe it was short of personnel—you couldn't really

call it manpower, could you? She couldn't begin to imagine how many people it would take to run a ship like that. Or the kind of power it could muster.

Thing was, why hadn't they used it already?

As if reading her mind, Elizabeth chuckled bleakly. "Probably trying to salvage their investment in us," she said. "I can show you the P&L. We have had a *very* profitable trading relationship with the Hermians. They may be criminal. They're not stupid."

It really was a good day for coldness all around.

*"Ten thousand kilometers and closing."*

*"Five thousand."*

"Hold your positions." Neave's voice was hoarse.

Through the open doors rasped Mac's voice. It wasn't as if he was managing to restore order to chaos. But he rated at least a performance evaluation of "Satisfactory" on attempting to plan for unknowable contingencies. Not to mention his bouts of pleading with the alien ship to stand down, send down another shuttle, the first shuttle was blown by a traitor, there were traitors on both sides, they'd traded well together. Give him E for Eloquence.

But apparently, the aliens weren't returning their calls.

Neave spoke into the silence. "I think a few loose ends on the human resources front remain to be tidied up before that ship arrives. First, I see no reason for anyone to suspect that your Mr. Sanderson was ready to sell out humanity."

CC shook her head. Regardless of what she'd thought of Sandy at the end, they'd been classmates. He was the last person she knew whose experience reflected her own struggles; from now on, anyplace she went, she went by herself.

It was like the wise guys on a trading floor. Some managers made a policy of not letting a year pass without having someone escorted off the floor in cuffs. CC never had much cared for object lessons.

"Second," said Neave, "I believe I owe you another apology, CC," he said. "I know your investigations here have put you into difficulties back on Earth. Assuming we make it out of this, I'll do what I can to make amends. And," he added, "if Alpha is foolish enough to suspend you before you finish your report, I am not. Alpha's loss will be my gain. I'm requisitioning your data and, for that matter, your services for the duration."

He smiled at her with the charm she remembered, warmth and friendship glossing over absolute zero like a slick of black ice. "Please don't worry that Alpha might decide your work is proprietary data. There are some organizations that even Alpha cannot withstand." His smile turned wry, a trifle colder if that were possible. "I recommend that you find that comforting."

"You're an optimist if you think we're going to survive two minutes after that ship enters Vesta orbit," CC said.

"So are you," he replied. "Or neither of us would have lasted this long."

She shook her head. "I can't win," she said. She shoved her machine at him. "Here's as far as I've gotten. Better make a copy now. Given the treatment that machine's getting, I don't know how long it's going to last."

Neave nodded. Lights blinked and flashed as he copied her report. "I've sent it off to Earth. Never mind fine-tuning. You can write an appendix once this is over. Or a whole new report. You've done a fine job."

*But was it enough?* It was never enough before.

It didn't matter. It was the best she could do.

For the first time in her life, she believed that.

*"Mac? Mac, you there?"* came Marc Davidoff's voice.

"Mr. Nofi is tending to business," said Neave. "Or trying to service his customers. With a conspicuous lack of success thus far. What can we do for you, Lieutenant Commander?"

*"Incoming ship's changed course. I think it saw that explosion, and man, is it pissed."*

*"One thousand K . . . 750 . . . 500 . . ."*

*"Uh-oh. It's speeding up. Looks like an attack vector, sir!"*

*"Lock on,"* Marc muttered. *"Lock on, but hold your fire!"*

"Computers are up and running, sir . . . ma'am?" Clearly not wanting to get within range of Neave, the lead tech addressed the room at large. "Someone's got to sign for this," she added.

"I will," said Elizabeth. She scrawled a signature on screen with a stylus without even looking at what she was signing.

Had to be the first time in her life she'd ever done that.

The enormous screens in Mac's office went live in fountains of schematics and color, mostly the red of incipient disaster. Sound erupted from the speakers set throughout the room.

"EarthServ issue," Neave observed, "Front-row seating."

Closing out all her files, CC began to run diagnostics on her own machine. It might be years before she could replace it.

"Look at that son of a bitch," she whispered. "It's *big*!"

Small, perhaps, for an asteroid. But, as ships went, it was a monster. An enraged monster. As it approached Vesta, an energy weapon lanced out from one of its craters, licked across a pair of irregularly shaped asteroids tumbling in its orbit, and vaporized first one, then the second in torrents of greenish-white fire.

"*I think we just got the proverbial shot across the bow,*" Marc reported. "*No-name rocks, with robot factories on them, but they want us to know they could just as easily have hit Titan or Europa. Now they're heading straight for us.*"

"*It's locking on!*" came a shout from someone in Marc's wing.

"*Steady. Keep steady. . . .*" Marc was practically chanting.

"*Not on us, on the Colony!*"

Mac flung himself back into the room and hurled himself at Neave's workstation.

"*Don't move!*" he screamed. "*Trajectory's away from any inhabited areas!*"

"No," whispered CC. She didn't want to look at the ship that would be their executioner. When she shut her eyes, she saw instead, a nightmare vision of a missile or a bomb or a lance of energy thrust into the depths of Olbers Crater. It could take the colony out in the flicker of an eye.

"*Hold position, dammit!*"

But two ships broke formation. They sped on afterburners toward the alien ship, firing as they went: energy weapons and warheads alike.

They might as well have been attacking Vesta Colony's protective rock walls with a pea shooter.

Behind CC, Mac was screaming into the comms. His voice went up and up, trembling on the edge of hysteria as he again tried to convince the incoming ship not to fire, that this was a terrible mistake, they'd see the pilots were punished, there was no point in destroying any more lives than had already been lost, they should sit down, come in, they could work out something. . . .

An unsuccessful sales call, CC thought, was one hell of a bad first contact.

Almost casually, the alien ship opened fire. One fighter from Marc's wing erupted in a brilliant firestorm. The other took a glancing hit to a wing and tumbled wing over shattered wing, to crash on the asteroid. The people inside probably hadn't even had time to scream.

Telemetry recorded the impact, then leapt almost off the scale into the red zone. A second beam erupted from a crater, almost blinding even though CC had flung her arm over her eyes. Tears poured down her face.

"Down into the mantle," Neave said.

"*Steady* . . ." Marc's voice was ragged, as if he fought back tears. That was stupid: Marc wouldn't cry if he could fight.

Neave, she saw, continued to watch the monitors as if he were studying nothing more terrible than an annual report. CC shook her head. The man had to be crazy if he still hadn't given up hope of finding someone to negotiate with.

"Give me communications," he ordered. "Let *me* see if we can raise anyone in authority. See if he, she or whatever will speak to us. *To me.* Mr. Nofi, if they're listening to you at all, tell them I am authorized to open trade negotiations on behalf of Earth," he said. "I can offer them more than the occasional trade here and there, the run on a bank, the hostile takeover of a company. I can offer them most favored nation status."

"But they're criminals!" Elizabeth cried.

"Won't be the first time," Neave said. "Dammit, Mac, make the call!"

Neave, too, was playing for time, CC thought.

At least she hoped he was. Because otherwise, what he was offering sounded damnably like surrender.

What other options did they have?

A voice she had never heard and hoped never to have to hear again boomed into the speakers. Mac gasped with relief and sagged in his chair, but only for an instant.

"It's the aliens," whispered Elizabeth. "We've got recordings."

"What does it want?" CC asked.

Neave spared a glance. "What it doesn't have. Guarantees of safety. Best I can offer them is immunity from prosecution. Earth will back me up if they cease hostilities now."

Mac leapt past them, seized Neave, and propelled him toward his own work station. "Keep talking," he said. "They've told me they'll listen. No promises beyond that. And they've got weapons lock on Vesta. This time, they say it will be the colony."

Neave freed himself from Mac's grasp, squared his shoulders, and seated himself deliberately, as if at the head of the table at a board meeting.

"Good afternoon," he began, in formal, mannered tones. "I am Everett Neave, Ambassador Emeritus from the Non-Governmental Organizations to the United Nations of Earth System, now operating without portfolio on Vesta Colony to ensure a peaceful resolution to what I am given to understand is a trade dispute. I am correctly addressed as 'Ambassador' or 'Your Excellency.' To whom have I the honor of speaking?"

"*Ambassador Neave,*" boomed the alien voice, hissing on the sibilants, twisting the syllables. "*We demand . . .*"

They were talking. Once they started talking . . .

"That's one smooth operator," Mac muttered under his breath. "You going to kiss them, or you just going to get out of bed and walk away?"

Elizabeth stroked his matted, thinning hair. "You hush and let the nice man do his job."

## 31

**The office lights cycled from "day" into delta shift's more**
subdued "night" lighting, making the violent metrics of the
hole burnt into Vesta's mantle cast vivid reflections on Mac's
workstation, littered now with the remnants of meals that
had been picked at, then pushed aside. Glare and cascades of
light from the hastily installed EarthServ screens reflected
off the table and provided one hell of a headache.

Neave's voice droned on, considerably hoarser after the
past ten hours. He had rolled up his sleeves and opened his
collar, but his hair remained smooth, and his posture impeccable as if he addressed the General Assembly, not alien
criminals with enough power to turn Olbers Crater into
magma.

Strangely enough, the situation was familiar from the earliest days of CC's career: late nights, too much bad coffee on
top of too much adrenaline contributing to an ulcer, watching or performing the occasional clerical or menial tasks
while a superior did the heavy lifting.

She spelled Mac in monitoring communications. So she
heard when Marc had to wave away the offer of EarthServ
reinforcements. *"Just stand down, dammit. We've already*

*lost two. We've got our best negotiator on it. What part of 'no fucking way' don't you understand?"*

It would probably net him a reprimand, destroy his career. If he lived to worry about such things. If he didn't, he wouldn't have to write to the families of the pilots who'd been burned down. He wouldn't have to drink to the memories of two more people whose faces grinned like spectres at the feast at Gorsky's Hole. Not to mention the ones they'd have to look for before their air ran out.

CC's eyes burned as Neave's voice droned on. She shoved documents and empty food containers away from her section of the table and put her head down on the cool stone. Her breath misted it.

Neave's voice lulled her. It would be so easy to nod off, to say she was just resting her eyes, the lie everyone pretended to believe because everyone tried it from time to time.

Wait. What was he saying now?

Those weren't conditions for trade, she realized. His voice had become careful, cautious, sympathetic, even. He was negotiating, all right, but these weren't trade negotiations.

Neave was acting as if this was still a hostage situation.

That was logical enough, but what difference would it make to an alien who had already demonstrated criminal intent in trading for addictive substances, shown an interest in taking control of an entire solar system, and now had proved willingness and ability to kill?

CC's head came up fast.

"He's grandstanding," she whispered. "He's hoping they've been tracked, that someone else is listening. You know those signals you've been piggybacking on top of routine transmissions? I think he's hoping they pan out."

Mac grinned, his features so strained with the years of tension that it looked like a death's head.

"We could use the cavalry about now," he whispered with what was left of his voice. "Neave's an old trader. He'll try to cut us the best deal he can."

\* \* \*

As the lights brightened from delta's twilight to alpha shift, CC passed out uppers and suppressed laughter that she was afraid she wouldn't be able to get back under control. Here the aliens were, trading for drugs with people who were using them to keep going. She didn't want to think of what sorts of drugs the pilots were injecting into their systems. Probably sucking 100% $O_2$ for alertness. It would cause one hell of a fire, but they wouldn't live long enough to put it out.

Now, even Neave's iron grooming had wilted. Despite the fullness created by low gravity in people's faces, sharp lines angled downward from his nose to his mouth, and his brow was furrowed. He shook his head from side to side and spread out his hands in a gesture of frustration: *I've done the best I can.*

Sometimes, though, your best just wasn't good enough. That was when you had to look for a new job, assuming you could find one. And if you couldn't, there were always the warehouses or Freeze. CC used to think those were the worst things that could happen to her. Now she knew better.

No wonder David IV had never wanted an off-planet assignment. No volleyball in space. No picnic.

She'd only thought she'd worked for rotten managers before. Now an entire system planet would learn what that was like. Well, they'd just have to build a Resistance, wouldn't they? God, she was spacing out.

She tried a few isometrics, hoping to improve her circulation. Nothing was working. Including herself.

Elizabeth appeared at Neave's elbow.

"We're getting a transmission from the Observatory on Mount Piazzi," she murmured.

"Stupid bastards wouldn't evacuate when I told them," Mac said. "What do they want now?"

"They're picking up something," Elizabeth said. Her voice, always so quiet, didn't rise, but a sound of trumpets seemed to ring beneath it. "It's not from this system."

Mac rose so quickly he lost balance. Elizabeth steadied him, then lost her grip on his arm and shoulder as the comms started to scream.

*"There's another one coming!"* Marc shouted. *"Incoming! Look at that thing run!"*

Look at it? All CC could see was a blip, a blip that grew bigger and bigger until it grew and began to resolve.

The newcomer wasn't another asteroid, but a ship, a dreadnaught from the most paranoid nightmares of historic broadcasts, books, and films. Kilometers of gleaming metal, ablated and scorched in places, gleaming in others, it streaked past the orbits of Pluto and Charon, passing the outer planets, heading in, homing in on Neave's voice with the elegant inevitable savagery of a shark.

"My God," murmured Mac. "will you look at that *ship*? It's gorgeous!"

"Only one ship?" CC murmured.

Mac cracked up, then fought to get himself back under control.

"Like the Texas Rangers," he told her. "Say a town has a problem with bandits. One gang of bandits? You get one Ranger. Just one. And here he is."

He put his hand over his mouth, suppressing another whoop. "Didn't I say we could use the cavalry?"

Neave's voice became edged, urgent as he pleaded with the aliens. "They've already seen you, there is no point in further violence, it may be possible . . ."

This time, the aliens broke. Ships rose from craters on the asteroid, rose and broke formation, trying to flee in all directions.

*"Incoming ship's not answering our hails,"* operations reported unnecessarily.

"It's busy," said Mac.

The newcomer opened fire. With surgical precision, it took out each ship until distant explosions lit the darkness.

*"It's answering now!"* came an excited voice.

"Put it on speakers," ordered Mac, who shoved Neave out of the way. CC and Elizabeth eased him out of his chair and over to a reclining seat.

Shouts came in a language that made Mac nod. "It's giving the asteroid an ultimatum. Assuming anyone's remained on board, they're to evacuate or face obliteration. They're not taking any more chances with that particular chunk of real estate, I think," he added. "But I think they want prisoners."

Three or four ships rose from the asteroid's surface and just hung there.

Again, a voice crackled through space.

"Move out of range," Mac translated. "Await pickup."

Then, the newcomer fired. CC flung her arm over her face as the asteroid blew.

"Damages?" Mac flung himself back at his workstation. "The observatory! *Piazzi* Alpha, *report!*"

"*Some damage from debris. The plating held. EMP's fried our instruments for the duration. We're on batteries now. . . .*"

"I'm telling you again, get out of there!"

"*Negative, Vesta Base, negative. You need us as eyes and ears.*"

"What are you going to see?" Mac demanded.

The ship glowed onscreen, a poisonous radioactive glow marking the incalculable power of its engines and weapons ports. It waited until the surrendering vessels approached and engulfed them.

And then, it altered course. Once again, it headed straight for Vesta.

"Maybe these are the Texas Rangers or the Marines or something from God knows where, but they don't seem to like us much either," CC said.

Again, that voice boomed over the speakers. She couldn't tell whether it was angry or not, but there was no missing the authority, the "this means business" in its undertones. This time, however, everyone on Vesta with comm access could understand it.

"*Stand down and surrender.*"

"Of course! It's completely logical," Elizabeth said. "They're arresting us as accessories to a crime."

Trust their compliance officer to figure that out fast!

But it stood to reason. These newcomers had heard first Mac, then Neave negotiating with what, clearly, they considered criminals. Mac, especially, had spoken with them, coaxed them, attempted to bribe them in such a way that these . . . these police might well think of Earth system as containing not just lowlifes, but low-tech lowlifes.

If that was the case, there was no reason why they shouldn't simply perform a curettage of the entire system, ridding themselves of criminals and primitive accomplices—except that, clearly, they considered themselves to be civilized individuals. Individuals who investigated first and shot second.

Once again, CC had that horrible mental image of Mount Piazzi melting like a cheap candle. Maybe the colonists could hide deep in the asteroid's mantle, but the aliens could follow.

The "good aliens" had arrived. But they were even scarier than the bad ones.

# / 32

**"Are you sure these really are the good guys?"** CC asked.

"They haven't slagged us yet, have they?" Mac asked. "Sure, they took out those ships and that asteroid, but they took prisoners first. My guess is they've had a warrant out for those people for a long time," Mac said. "That's what I was hoping. It's why we sent out those messages in the first place."

"You always did play the long shots," CC said. "Remind me to kill you. Once I get a good night's sleep."

Marc's voice came through. *"Get Neave on the line. Meanwhile, you'd damn well better give some thought to that order to stand down."*

Once again, CC had that nightmare image of a planet-cracking bomb lobbed into Olbers Crater, a radioactive hazard to navigation for thousands of years if you assumed it didn't crack Vesta into gravel the way it had destroyed the criminals' Ark.

"What the hell does he expect me to do?" Mac groused. "Run a white flag up Mount Piazzi? Strike our colors?"

"That's right!" CC cried. "If they've monitored us, they've got to know those idioms. Turn off all exterior lights except in the Observatory. They're already on emergency power. Have them mount lights there."

"That makes Piazzi Alpha one hell of a target," said Mac. "But we're all exposed here. Okay, we'll go with that."

CC shuddered. Now that her idea had been selected, if the aliens struck, the responsibility would be on her head, for the few seconds before they were all vaporized.

Breathe.

*"Lights coming on,"* came from the Observatory. *"Regular power's coming up. Nice and bright."*

"I think it's working," Elizabeth breathed.

No EarthServ ships rose to be destroyed with that devastating, contemptuous ease. And the ship just hung out there in space, not firing. Not speaking.

"And there was silence in Heaven for the space of half an hour," muttered Neave.

One of these days, CC thought, she was going to get tired of underestimating that man's frame of reference.

*"Neave, we need you at the docking bay. Immediate pickup,"* Marc shouted, making them all jump. *"We've been ordered to bring you out to the ship."*

"On whose authority?" Neave asked.

*"On their side? A bunch of damn nasty weapons. On ours? The joint chiefs,"* Marc replied. *"You were stupid enough to reactivate your commission. Now, haul ass. Why else do you think they've paid you the big bucks all these years?"*

Mac insisted on escorting Neave to the docking bay.

"You know," CC said, "anyone sane would take this chance to grab a shower and some sleep."

Elizabeth raised an eyebrow at her.

"I don't think I could sleep either," she said. She rummaged for Mac's liquor, the good stuff, all the way from Earth, until half her body disappeared within a cabinet.

She emerged in triumph with a bottle of cognac.

"It's even got Earth dust still on it!" she announced before starting to pour it into covered tubes.

"Hell of a thing to do to brandy," CC observed. Then she shut up and drank. The fine liquor went down like fire. By the time it finally hit, maybe she'd be asleep. She'd probably wake with one hell of a hangover, but she could always suck down oxygen.

Mac found them halfway through their third brandy. Or maybe their fourth.

"He got off safely," he said.

"We saw," CC replied. "Are our guys out there ever going to get to come back in?"

"God knows." Mac shrugged and checked his messages. "Any of that brandy left? I was saving it."

Some hours later, CC asked, "What do you suppose the investment implications of colony obliteration would have been?"

"Act of God," said Elizabeth. "Definitely act of God. We're going to be rewriting the securities code for years. There's nothing on the books about establishing offices outside the solar system. And no way you could examine their books once a year."

Her owlish composure made them laugh as if they were even drunker than they actually were.

"I hate to break this up," said Mac, "but Neave did promise a report every six hours. We all better sober up fast. We ought to be ashamed of ourselves, doing this to a fine old cognac, but . . ."

He tossed alcodote tabs at them.

CC sighed and gulped down water to counter the dehydration of exhaustion, low gravity, and far too much to drink.

"Better check my messages," she said. Ordinarily, that was a compulsion. Now? Well, she had had other things on her mind, and it wasn't as if she was expecting orders from Alpha Colony.

Her computer creaked and groaned like a living being, but finally consented to power up and display a column of messages. The usual amount of junk that got through her filters. Some housekeeping announcements from Vesta Colony, including the regulations—paragraphs of excruciating bizspeak—for filing appeals to her status as Persona Non Grata. A bill from the MedCenter.

CC blinked at them as if she gazed at them through the wrong end of a telescope. How tiny it all seemed!

Now, she thought, this was interesting, in a distant sort of way. A message from David IV.

My God, David. Her poor David! She hadn't thought of him this entire time. What a story she'd have to tell! When she returned to Earth, they could dine out on this for years.

She blinked at the message, then rubbed her eyes to see if that would change the letters that glowed at her from the screen. *"When I didn't hear from you, CC, I thought it was time to pursue other options. I have to tell you. You remember, I told you about that volleyball game and meeting. . . .*

*"She's older than I am by about fifteen years, but age is just a number, and she's very fit, very well-established in healthcare consulting—got named Managing Partner two years ago, so she's ready to settle down. Aside from that, she reminds me of you, only more focused."*

"I fucking don't believe this," CC whispered.

And she had always thought that sunny smile reflected a guileless personality. God, what an idiot she'd been. What a gullible, hard-working fool. Just what David IV wanted, until he could trade up. In his way—his casual, entitled way—David IV was an even better actor than she.

You better believe it, she told herself. She shook her head, trying to clear it. Damn, hadn't that alcodote worked?

"What's wrong?" asked Mac.

"Letter from David IV."

"You don't sound too happy," Mac observed. "What's with the Prince now?"

"It's a 'dear CC,'" she said. "He's turning me in on a richer model."

She kept reading. She felt Mac's presence as he drifted up

behind her and anchored himself with a hand on her chair, reading over her shoulder.

Well, wasn't that special? More focused. A managing partner, excuse me very much.

What else? *"We've gotten the chance to buy the old place in the Enclave. Since she's more established in her career and she's line, not staff, we've decided I should opt out and go primary caregiver . . . by the time you read this, we'll probably have gotten the result of our genetic assay . . . I do wish you luck. . . ."*

"David IV, trophy husband," Mac snickered. "Good luck to him, when he decides he wants back into the workforce. Even if she doesn't trade him in on a newer model with better abs and more . . . guts. Not to mention any other parts of his anatomy."

He eyed CC as if hoping she wouldn't cry.

She tested her emotions as if she calibrated precision equipment. How much did she hurt? A rejection this comprehensive and this poorly timed ought to hurt, she decided. After all, she'd made plans with this man, plans that would have shaped her whole life. But all she could feel was mild surprise. Maybe she was just too tired to feel devastated. After all, in the past six months, she'd now faced at least four attempts on her life. The Colony she was living in was still in mortal danger. And she was too damn far away from Earth for any of this to really matter.

Probably it had never mattered all that much. David IV, she realized, had been an accessory, like a late-model Breitling. He had been about as additive to her life as she had been to his. And when he had a chance to trade up, he had.

Nothing personal. There never had been.

She didn't *think* she'd have done the same thing.

Would she?

"CC?" asked Elizabeth. "You all right?"

"I can't feel anything. I don't know what *to* feel. Maybe once I've gotten some sleep."

"Best thing that could have happened," said Mac. "I'd

have hated to see you face the kind of breakup I did. Especially if you had any kind of assets. Wonder Boy have anything else to say?"

"There *is* more," CC said.

She glanced down the screen.

"At least, he hasn't signed it 'your friend,'" Mac commented.

CC ran her eyes over the postscript. *"I know I shouldn't have to remind you, but the engagement ring is an heirloom."*

She looked down at her left hand on which the engagement ring, forgotten all this time like the man who'd put it on her finger, glittered in its ornate setting. Then, she met Mac's eyes and started to laugh helplessly.

"You told me not to wear it around here," she reminded him. "Guess you were right all along."

Mac whooped. "That is so fuckin' *tacky!*" he yelled.

Again, CC calibrated her emotions for hurt. To her astonishment, she felt only mild guilt. She could barely remember what David IV looked like. Had she ever really known him, or had he, like the ring itself, only been an appropriate accessory, a line item on her résumé?

"How in hell do I get this thing back to him in time for the wedding?" she asked. "They're going for genetic testing now. The instant they come through with a trophy genome, I'm sure they'll get married. If he's got a chance to opt out into the landed gentry, he'd be a perfect idiot not to lock it down."

"He *is* a perfect idiot," said Mac. "Look what he's throwing away."

"Why, Mac," CC said, "I never knew you cared."

Taking off the ring, she held it up to the light, admiring the fires in the stone for the last time, then spun it around her finger. "Guess I'd better see about shipping this back to him."

Meanwhile, Ms. Managing Partner could just go and buy a bigger one for herself.

If CC knew David IV, he'd start dunning her for it, explaining how ridiculous it was that she was hanging on to it, and never mind time lags and the cost of transporting it from Vesta to Earth, if she *really* wanted to return it, she'd manage. Somehow.

"Give it to me, CC," Mac said. "I'll see His Highness gets it back in a plain brown wrapper, marked radioactive waste and tough shit on his designer genome."

That made them laugh so hard that, when Neave finally did get around to calling in with his report, it took him two tries to get through with the news that he'd convinced the aliens not to arrest them as accessories to a list of crimes ranging from trading in drugs to terminal stupidity.

And then, they laughed even harder from sheer relief.

*"I'm ordering EarthServ to stand down,"* Neave said, his voice tight with irritation. *"And I'm coming in. I've learned a few things, starting with the Hermians' real species name. They're the Maktoub. And Evander DenTen Akovey—is that an acceptable pronunciation, sir?—and his deputies are landing with me. Be ready to meet us. With a suitable escort, please. We can at least try for some decorum."*

And that, of course, only made them laugh the harder.

## 33

**How Marc and his fighting wing had managed to touch** down, shower, change into dress uniforms and line up in a formation that managed to wobble itself upright in the face of battle, exhaustion, and an alien landing, CC never knew. If Vesta hadn't been on lockdown, she'd never have managed to snatch her luggage out of storage, fling herself into temporary quarters, and dress, in time to join Mac and Elizabeth as part of the reception committee. Standing beside them was Margaret, a child holding each hand.

Mac glanced at the children, opened his mouth with "Shouldn't they really be . . ." and stepped back several meters before the force of Margaret's glare dissipated.

"If they were going to blow us up," she hissed over the children's heads, "they'd have already done so. They have a right to see their father come home. And if this is some sort of trick, better we're all together."

Through the immense screens set in the central area of the Apsedra, they watched the Maktoub shuttle come in for a landing. Piazzi Alpha's lights blazed in the Observatory. As the shuttle traversed Mount Piazzi, lights bloomed on all sides. By the time the shuttle neared Olbers Crater itself, the entire crater was bathed in rainbow lights.

The shuttle touched down in the docking bay.

*"Cycling airlock now,"* came the report.

The murmur in Hospitality Bay grew not louder, but more intense. CC dared to glance behind her. What looked like half the colony had crammed into the Apsedra. Many of the colonists looked tense, some exhausted—but all were grinning with excitement.

Maybe the Maktoub weren't robed aliens intoning "live long and prosper," but they were definitely an acceptable substitute.

Better. They were real. And, for now at least, they weren't shooting.

"So much for lockdown," came a mutter from Security.

"Discipline's shot to hell around here. Have to do something about that," Mac replied, glaring at the woman.

"First, let's just survive this meeting," Davidoff commented just as the giant doors of the airlock began to part.

"Stand back," ordered Nofi.

He paused to make certain his order was obeyed, then shook his head.

"Look at those damn fools. We trade for years with a bunch of crooks, we almost get ourselves blown out of space, and they hear 'oh, these are the good aliens,' and everyone rushes out to see. I swear, they're as sentimental as you, CC," he groused. Then he tugged at the jacket he'd fastened over his coverall. It made him look oddly formal until you saw the grin on his face.

"Does the phrase 'in a pig's eye' mean anything to you?" Elizabeth asked sweetly.

Mac managed not to snicker. He got control of himself just in time. The shuttle's landing ramp extruded, a hatch opened without even the slightest screech of metal, and Neave led the way out of the Maktoub craft.

Following him were the Maktoub. Unlike the criminals CC had seen near the mines, these aliens wore no masks. Their pallid skin gleamed with whatever they had used to treat their skin against the too-dry atmosphere. The shortest of them was easily two meters tall.

Hominid. Even if they weren't strictly what you could call human beings, they were civilized, CC told herself. Bipedal, laterally symmetrical. If they carried arms, she didn't know enough about weapons to detect them. And they all wore what looked like shipsuits or coveralls, except for one alien who had to be Evander DenTen Akovey, who had covered what had to be the equivalent of a formal shipsuit with a jacket of some metallic black fabric. Next to the EarthServ dress uniforms—worn without weapons—they looked remarkably plain.

"See," Mac whispered. "No pointed ears."

CC looked hard, just to make sure.

But then she straightened, to as close to attention as a civilian woman could, because the Maktoub were approaching. They passed in review down the lines of EarthServ soldiers and pilots, then came over to the civilians waiting to receive them.

Neave raised his head, met Margaret's eyes. His strained face, shadowed now by a day's growth of beard, lit like the lights on Mount Piazzi. She released her children's hands. They ran to their father, overbalancing in the minimal g. He caught them as they tumbled, scooped them up, and, one in either arm, stepped back among the reception committee.

*I would never have had a moment like that with David IV. I guess neither of us cared that much. Didn't know how.*

Mac stepped forward. As he opened his mouth to speak, CC flinched. She'd already suffered from the variety of greetings he'd practiced on her. Just her luck. He'd come up with some appallingly silly reference to Earth history; the Vestans would collapse with laughter, and it would be in the fan once more.

It was as if he sensed her apprehension. Tipping her and Elizabeth only the hint of a wink, he drew himself up and said only, "Welcome to Vesta. We are very pleased to see you."

It wasn't one of the solar system's most original lines. But, seeing that this Evander-whatever knew him only as the voice that had been pleading to trade with the criminals he'd taken into custody, Mac was smart to keep it short.

He bowed, then gestured the aliens past the docking bay and into the Apsedra. Seeing as Vesta was so ludicrously outgunned, Mac had ordered the skylight's shielding to be retracted. Power had been restored to the mechanically driven lights that floated across the vast space and reflected off the crystals in the vast room's "ceiling." A faint breeze from life-support made the Gothic arches of the fabric pavilions tremble slightly, causing the rainbows of lights within to shimmer. Even the glowing signs—Customs, Medical, Administrative—looked festive.

So, after all that, Mac was practically home free. Assuming Neave could deal with the aliens. Assuming Neave would cut Mac and Elizabeth deals.

Now it was time and past time for CC to look out for herself. First, she needed a job. There had to be something a successful fighter of aliens could do.

DenTen Akovey nodded gravely. As Neave's children squirmed free and dropped to the floor, he tilted his head to watch them. They were growing, CC thought, by leaps and bounds—just the way they moved. At Neave's gesture, he stepped forward, tentative in the low gravity. His hand went to his belt and pressed a small stud that lit up. Instantly, his steps became more sure.

A personal gravity field? CC understood Marc's passionate envy of the Maktoub's ships. What other tricks did he have up his sleeve, she wondered, and how could she get her hands on them?

Seeing the people crammed into the Apsedra to welcome him, he held up a hand, even if its fingers weren't parted. More to the point and better: was that an honest-to-God smile CC saw?

It was! And when a cheer went up, DenTen Akovey didn't even flinch.

## 34

**The track lights in the Lovat-Neave apartment created** warm glowing pools and deep shadows for what Margaret Lovat called "just a simple dinner among some of our closest friends."

Just a few friends: CC, Elizabeth, Marc Davidoff. Mac was missing. He had finally persuaded DenTen Akovey—and what seemed like half the alien representative's security force—to tour station operations, including the mining site where CC had spied on the alien shuttle.

"Scene of the crime," the alien representative called it. And "mending fences." DenTen Akovey still had a regrettable tendency, at least from Mac's point of view, to identify him with the Maktoub criminals now awaiting return to Maktoub Prime where they would be tried for, among other things, possession of illegal substances, theft, and economic warfare against a less-advanced species.

CC suspected Mac would spend the whole trip trying to "make nice" while dealing for anything he could get his hands on, assuming he could get the Maktoub to see him as more than a crooked trader.

Neave lounged at his wife's feet, his long legs sprawled out, his plate balanced on his lap in "one of the last chances

I'll have to really relax before the ship leaves."

That was why Margaret had invited so few people. "I won't have the place crowded with people elbowing me—politely, of course—away from my husband so they can congratulate him or give him a wish list when we don't have much time left together for who knows how long?"

But her smile was bright, and her light hair glittered over the shoulders of yet another of her basic black shipsuits.

"So DenTen Akovey's really going to let you go through with this?" CC asked.

Neave looked up at Margaret and smiled. "I've been in this business too long to try to assign emotional reactions to people I don't know, even when they're from our own species. But I'd say—"

"A witness from the species an arresting officer considers to be a plaintiff?" Margaret asked. She took a sip of wine whose bouquet of fruit subtly complemented the pasta in cheese sauce, raised her eyebrows in polite appreciation, and set the wine tube back in its clips on the low table. "I can't imagine a Maktoub falling at your feet in gratitude, Ambassador, but I'd say he was very, very pleased."

*And you're even more pleased that Mac's not being hauled off the station in cuffs, aren't you?* CC thought. At one point it looked as if both Earth and the Maktoub wanted to lock him away forever. Then Neave stepped in and imposed a compromise: he would go back to testify on Maktoub Prime, whose location was apparently still a state secret, not that people from Earth could reach it on their own power for a couple thousand years, and Mac would be banned from the securities industry and pay a hefty fine.

"Couldn't get a better plea bargain," Elizabeth had explained. "And with the potential for alien trade, Mac's colony shares are rising in value so fast he can use one as collateral, pay his fine, and zero-balance the debt in a year or two. As for me? Sure, I have to surrender my license, but plenty of lawyers don't practice. And Station Management's offered me a job."

She had smiled and put her hand over Mac's. No engagement ring, though. CC was a little sensitive on the subject. "Two jobs."

Elizabeth and Mac had started planning the biggest wedding Vesta Colony had ever seen. It would have been sickening if they weren't so transparently happy, like people twenty years younger and much, much smarter.

Good luck, nice people, CC thought. Her eyes stung. It wasn't that she missed David IV: couldn't miss what you never really knew. It was simply that she wanted something that was inalienably hers, and yes, she knew it was a pun. In a way, it was like being between jobs: you'd mourned the loss of what was past, but you hadn't started to worry yet about what was about to hit you.

"More pasta, CC?" Marc recalled her from her reverie. He'd barely spoken to her since he came in, and now here he was, turning up at her elbow as if he were the most attentive escort in the worlds. She never could figure him out—but always enjoyed trying.

She shook her head, then made herself smile as she glanced around the room. The last time she'd been here for one of Margaret's "simple" dinners, the place had been full of caterers, guests—and Sandy. She could see him now, his face bright from a social high: the skeleton at the feast. Though he had tried to kill her, she regretted his death. *Let the bastard do time,* she thought. *Look what he did to Neave.*

"So what are you going to say when you reach Maktoub Prime?" CC made herself ask brightly.

"Well," said Neave, "I'll start by reminding them that we weren't accessories to a crime, but hostages doing our damnedest to escape, which they see as a duty, too."

"Thought they'd already agreed to that," CC said.

"It's a bargaining tactic," Elizabeth told her. "If we're the injured party, compensation is clearly in order. Not just for destruction of our ships and people, which they deeply regret, but for the way the system was held hostage, for attempted destabilization of our economy. Maybe even for pain and suffering."

"Is there anything," Marc Davidoff asked cautiously, "in Maktoub financial jurisprudence about making us whole?"

Neave burst into laughter. "Got your eyes on those ships, do you, Marc?"

The EarthServ pilot shook his head, grinning.

"They'll make us whole, I'm told," Neave replied. "And once we reach agreement, then we'll have an equitable parting of the ways. I tried to get them to stay in contact with us, but the Maktoub seem to be an ethical people. They don't want to contaminate us."

"With technology we can't handle?" said Marc. "God, what a cliché! Try to see if you can't get them to give ground on that, will you, Neave?"

The older man smiled, showing a thin, shiny line of white teeth.

"I have every intention," he said. "On the upside, DenTen Akovey has already agreed that compensation in knowledge is much better than material goods. He has no way of knowing, any more than Mac did at first, what valuables in Maktoub culture could prove addictive to us—"

"Firewater, baubles, bangles, and bright, shiny beads?" Elizabeth asked ironically.

"Not to mention measles," CC went ahead and mentioned them anyhow. "Remember when Earth crashed that satellite into Jupiter, not Europa, to make sure it wouldn't infect a planetoid with water? I'd assume medical technology would be the first medium of exchange. We may finally get that cure for the common cold."

Neave held up a hand and grinned at the room. "I gather that they've been looking for this particular gang of—if you're a student of history, I suppose you could call them drug lords—for some time, and they're pleased we're helping out. My guess is that we can pretty well name our price, with some exceptions. Unfortunately, one of the exceptions is faster-than-light travel."

Marc leaned forward so fast he had to fling out a hand to balance himself. "I'm not asking them to give us a hull and a set of engines, or even some of those weapons," he said, longing in his voice. "But what about a chance to *earn* FTL? Do you think you can get them to put that on the table?"

"Let's talk about that," Neave said promptly. He steepled his fingers together in what CC recognized as negotiations mode.

"I think you could do a better job of showing we can understand the technology, as well as the science behind that drive of theirs. Want to come along and make the case?" he asked Marc. "It's a little too far to simply order you to volunteer. But I could use a military attaché," he added. "And, just maybe, a friend that far from home."

"Yes!" Marc cried and pumped his fist in the air so that people leaned forward to help restore his balance. "I thought you'd never ask."

It was the job of a lifetime. CC could see that. But it was like promotion memos: if your name wasn't on them, you got a quick rush of shit to the heart. And then you had to flash your best smile and pretend you didn't care.

She cared. And judging from the way Marc's eyes opened wide, then grew guarded, he cared too.

The hell with that, she thought. *Even if they make it back here, I'll never see him again!* she told herself.

That was *worse* than no promotion. By several orders of magnitude.

Sur-fucking-*prise* again. Well, emotional intelligence never really had been her lead skillset.

*Marc really wants to go out there. He really really wants to go out there. Don't you* dare *let him see you mind it!* she warned herself.

"All right," said Neave. "In that case, your first order is to get some sleep. After you send in the paperwork."

"Way ahead of you," Marc assured him. "All it needs is your approval."

He was no longer looking CC's way.

*"It is a far, far better thing . . ."*

Oh *crap*.

Margaret rose from her chair. "I think this calls for champagne," she said. "I have three bottles that survived the trip from Earth. But I want to save one of them for your wedding, Elizabeth."

"I'm only sorry I won't be able to see the wedding," Neave said. "I'd even offer to give you away. Anachronistic as the offer is."

"I've already taken care of it," Elizabeth told him. "Margaret will represent you. I think you already know she's agreed to ring the bell on 9/11 Day?"

Neave flashed his wife a look. "My dear, this is the place where a superstitious man might say 'knock wood.' Do we have any wood around here?"

Margaret turned, the champagne bottle in her hands. "I've always wanted to see how champagne reacts to Vesta-g," she said. "Even if it would be a criminal waste. No, Everett, my mind is made up. I'm ringing the bell because I think it's high time to use 9/11 as a day not of mourning, but of looking toward the future."

She unpeeled the foil from the bottle and braced herself so the opened bottle wouldn't send her flying. "Now," she said, "stand back!"

The cork erupted from the bottle and ricocheted around the room as people laughed, applauded, and held up opened glasses to catch the iridescent, frothing wine.

CC laughed with the best of them. Catching Neave's eye, she raised her glass to him.

*Now what?* She thought. *You've gotten Mac and Elizabeth off light. You're getting Marc out of the picture. Sandy's dead. What's the nothing I get?*

He already had her report, and just this morning, she'd received an "all is forgiven, here's your bonus and a nice raise" memo from Alpha. Financial security at least, or for at least the next four quarters, she supposed.

It felt slightly anticlimactic.

Sandy, she realized, wasn't the only skeleton at this particular feast.

## / 35

"What do you *mean,* Mac's in a conference call, you'll signal him?" CC asked the assistant now ensconced outside the Colony Manager's office. The woman wore a heavy jacket over her coverall, and her badge carried her name, Saito, Yoshiko, and the markings CC had seen in Final Frontier that designated an indentured worker. Practically right off the boat, judging from the time stamp on the badge. Her skin was still sallow, almost fragile, from her time in Freeze.

"Those were my instructions, Ms. Williams," the woman said, her voice high-pitched with the most formal courtesy from her native country. She glanced down and away, clearly not wanting to offend by a direct refusal. CC caught the appeal in her eyes. If this were the woman's first job out of Freeze, she'd be desperately anxious to make good.

CC drew in her breath. "Thank you, Ms. Saito," she said. "Please let me know when Mr. Nofi is able to see me."

Yoshiko Saito bowed. CC, as the organizational senior, inclined her head and took a seat in the newly organized reception area. One large chrysanthemum and some leaves, two pebbles, and a twig were arranged in the unevenly shaped dish on the table.

Refusing the receptionist's offer of tea, coffee, or the local newsletter, CC forced herself to sit immobile until Mac's door slid aside and Mac appeared on the threshold.

He nodded kindly at Yoshiko Saito, who had bobbed to her feet. "Ms. Williams is a personal friend," he told her.

Fear flickered in the woman's eyes. "I much regret . . ."

"Mac, if she was following your instructions, she made absolutely the correct choices," CC said.

He nodded and stood aside for CC to enter.

The door slid shut.

"Staffing up, I see?"

He nodded. "I suspect there'll be plenty of opportunity out here. I mean to get my infrastructure in place before the next wave of colonists arrives. This one'll whip me into shape in no time," he added. "Come on in. I take it Yoshiko-san offered you tea, coffee, and everything else in the house?"

CC laughed and made as if to fling herself into a chair, but something in Mac's posture as he headed for the seat behind his desk, not the seating area where they'd had so many casual meals, halted her.

"Please be seated," he said.

His voice took on the intonations of business, not casual, speech. Because, once upon a time, he had been her line manager and he now managed Vesta itself, CC complied. She seated herself with the precision she would bring to an interview and waited for him to speak. After all, if he were playing manager-to-subordinate vocal games, he could damned well tell her the topic of conversation.

Mac rested his hands on his desk and leaned forward.

"As colony manager—and as a friend," he added, "I think I ought to ask what you're planning to do with yourself now."

"I thought I'd take some time off," CC said. "It's been a tough few months, and I don't know when I've last had a break. So I've been working out. Doing social things. Helping Elizabeth with the wedding."

"How do you mean to support yourself?"

"I'm not penniless. I've savings. And my bonus and severance from Alpha . . ."

"It was my understanding that Alpha rescinded your suspension," Mac said.

"Mac," CC interrupted him, "that transmission was private!"

"CC," he mimicked her tone, "this was practically a war zone. And that message came through on a proprietary BBU to which Vesta Colony has access."

She huffed. "Well, if you know that, then you know I sent Alpha a 'fuck you very much' message. They were quick enough to suspend me on the basis of rumor, and believe me, I know where the poop-rap came from, but when Neave yelled 'jump,' they were quick enough to ask 'how high.'"

"Station records reveal you've resettled yourself, and you're burning cash at a tidy rate. So once you go through your savings, your back pay, and bonus, then what?"

CC got up. In defiance of Meeting Protocol, she turned her back to Nofi, and busied herself making a cup of coffee.

"You want any?" she asked.

"I want to know what you plan to do when your assets run out. I don't suppose you plan to return to Earth?"

"What would be the point?" she asked. "Even if I did go back to Alpha, I'd be empty-handed. Neave's got my report, and I'm guessing it's going to be classified till the heat death of the universe. And you know as well as I do that David IV and his new wife will probably do such a good job of praising me with faint damns that no one else will want to even take my calls. Why go back to Earth if I'll only have to come back out here in Freeze?"

It all sounded reasonable enough until she listened to the anger and hurt in her own voice. Everyone else had a future to go to. Neave was going out to Maktoub Prime, Marc with him. Margaret, if CC were any judge, would probably wind up owning the half of Vesta that Mac and Elizabeth didn't.

CC recalled the last time she'd discussed her alleged prospects with Mac Nofi. She'd come in here, dressed in corporate combat gear, spread her hands on the table, and hit him with the level truth.

And it had worked.

Time, then, to try it again.

Drawing a deep breath, CC asked, "You got any suggestions?"

Mac let out a deep breath. "You stubborn bitch. I thought you'd never get hit hard enough that you'd ask."

Games. Always games. Now that the emergency was over, was it back to business as usual? The whole idea made her tired.

"Why not stay here?" Mac added. "When I came out here, I did it because I had a job waiting for me here, and it was that or come out here in an icebox. Believe me, I spent years pissing and moaning about being on Vesta, but now, when I think about it, I realize this is home to me. Oh, I do the mandatory kilometers just in case, and because it's good cardiovascular exercise, but if I never see Earth again, hey, I can live with it.

"So, why don't we assume that Alpha's loss is Vesta's gain. You've got your savings and your salary. Severance. Bonus. Assume you cash in your ticket, too." He leaned forward, tapping on his keypad. "That could add up to a pretty good stake, enough to buy Colony shares. We could probably discount them, too, all right, a *deep* discount, in return for your good work here. So you might find yourself with quite a considerable chunk of the rock."

He grinned at her. "You're the kind we want out here, you know. From everything I've heard, you've fit in well. And God knows, after the way you've been nosing about, you know the place from top to bottom.

"It's not as if you fit in back on Earth," he went on. "Think of the gentlemen adventurers who went to the New World. Some were too stupid or too lazy to adapt, so they went back, starved to death, or got themselves killed. The rest, though: the rest adapted, and some even made it into history.

"Want to be a pioneer woman, CC?" Mac asked ironically.

"Hell no!" were the first words out of her mouth.

They both laughed.

Sure, CC could stay on Vesta. Be Elizabeth's maid of

honor. Fill some useful position. Hell, maybe Margaret needed an executive assistant. She'd find something. As Mac said, she'd adapted well. She might only have a little bit of a life, but, for the first time in her life, she'd have equity in something.

Why did it all sound so damned dull?

"Doesn't sound very good, does it?" Mac asked. "But I remember times when you'd have jumped at the chance. Times when you didn't feel quite so sorry for yourself. Well, I told Neave that I wanted to make my pitch before I made his. Hell, bad enough I'm banned from the securities industry; now he wants me to play headhunter. How much lower do they expect me to sink?

"Neave asked me to talk to you about a job he's got in mind. It's kind of like the one you came out here to do—but much more responsible. It isn't the next step up; it's the next couple of steps. Maybe a great big jump."

Mac got kind of a sly look. "Or maybe a giant leap for mankind. CC, Neave wants you to go with him. All the way thataway?" He laughed at CC. "Think of it as First Contact for Dummies."

"Besides," Mac added, "even if you're not interested in what's likely to be one of the highest-profile jobs of the century, Neave says it's a morale issue. Says he's damned if he wants his military attaché sulking all the way to Maktoub Prime and back again."

CC stood up so quickly that she almost fell, a newbie's idiot mistake she hadn't made for weeks. Mac steadied her, pulling her back down. Not down to Earth, but to Vesta. She had never realized Vesta-g could feel so reassuring, or maybe it was Mac's hands on her shoulders.

"But I'm not equipped for a trip like that," she protested.

"Aren't you?" Mac asked. "You've been helping Elizabeth shop, getting fitted yourself, haven't you? Well, Margaret's been in on the secret. Aside from the fact that we needed her to help out, Neave blabbed. That man's never been able to keep a damn thing away from her. Not as if I've got any right to talk.

"Did you try to call either of them today?" Mac asked.

"They're nowhere to be found," CC muttered.

"Of course not! They've been packing your things all day. If you went to your quarters now and shouted 'boo!,' I bet they'd damn near achieve orbital velocity. What's worse, I don't think either of them was able to resist adding a few things. Like Margaret's last bottle of Earthside vintage champagne. And an honest-to-God white wedding dress."

Mac hugged CC, then gave her a smacking kiss.

"I get to be the first one to kiss the bride!" he announced.

"What bride?" CC wailed.

"Oh for God's sake, CC, how stupid can you be?" Nofi snapped. "It isn't as if everyone on Vesta, not to mention the EarthServ types at Gorsky's Hole, couldn't see that you and Marc have been crazy about each other for ages! David IV indeed. That guy was such a lightweight I'm surprised he didn't float even in Earth gravity."

*"Bride?"* CC's voice squeaked on the word. A bubble seemed to be expanding inside her. When it finally exploded, she thought it would effervesce like Margaret's champagne, until it bubbled over into something intoxicating.

Something, she realized, she wanted more than she'd ever wanted anything in her life.

"My God, she's speechless," Mac commented. "Never thought I'd see the day. Among Neave's many other accomplishments—man's got a résumé about as long as Halley's comet—he's a justice of the peace. He can perform the ceremony. Looking forward to it. For some damn reason, he thinks he owes you. But . . ."

The bubble was getting bigger and bigger. The last time she'd really been drunk, her face had gone all numb. It was numb now as the bubble grew, occupying more and more of her attention. She thought she understood the word "bride." The word "wife," though, escaped her comprehension.

*You'll have years to figure that one out.*

Mac looked at his screen. "CC, if you're leaving, you haven't got much time!" he said. "Margaret's at the docking port, seeing her husband off even as we speak. I'm supposed to manage the release myself in . . . you've got maybe five, ten minutes to get there. You can make it if you run for it."

The numbness was going away now. Hot and cold washed over her. The lights in the room seemed to have acquired a rainbow shimmer.

"What do you say?" Mac asked.

The bubble burst, and with it, the unnatural silence that had gripped her while she tried to sort through her thoughts and feelings.

"Yes!" she erupted in a yell of pure joy.

My God, she thought in wonder, she sounded just like Marc, when Neave had asked him to go with him on the Maktoub ship and plead for ships of their own. Tears poured down her face.

And the last memories of Earth, of David IV, and Alpha Consultancies faded like bubbles, losing their sheen, then popping out of existence.

With a whoop, Mac caught her in a bear hug and spun her around. Still holding her, he turned her toward the door and shoved her through.

His receptionist put a hand over her mouth, stifling high-pitched laughter.

"Get the hell out of here, CC. Run for your life! And don't take any wooden dilithium crystals!"

CC ran. She bounded through the Apsedra and down the passageways like a kid who'd grown up in Vesta-g.

And there was Marc, standing on the ramp that led into the Maktoub shuttle. He was alone.

Was he looking for her? Hoping she'd come but beginning to give up?

Damn, what if the damn thing retracted and she missed her chance? She'd have missed the whole rest of her life.

That was a risk CC couldn't take. She panicked. She'd never be able to run fast enough to reach Marc in time. He'd think she hadn't wanted to come, and he'd leave, taking their future with him. She couldn't let that happen.

"Marc!" CC screamed. "Marc, wait!"

He saw her. Even at this distance, his eyes lit, and he started forward.

Would there be time?

She'd make damn sure there was. Taking a deep breath, CC launched herself into full flight, aiming herself at the Maktoub shuttle.

Touching down on the ramp, she sprawled, then pushed up again just as it began to retract and the doors to the docking bay began to rumble shut.

Marc took one long, *long* step, bent down, and caught her in his arms. Was that full-g she felt on the landing ramp? Or was it simply that for the first time in her life, CC felt grounded. Anchored. At home.

Marc grinned into her face. "I knew you'd come!" he exulted. "I knew it! Your baggage is on board. Once we pull away from Vesta, Neave says he can perform a civil ceremony. He's already clued in the Maktoub. DenTen Akovey told Neave he and his team want to watch. The ceremony, that is."

"I'll get you for that!" CC announced. She tried to jab him in the ribs, but he hugged her and she couldn't move. Not that she really wanted to right about then.

But then, he was guiding her, still under one-g, into the alien ship. She tore her eyes from Marc's face to her surroundings.

"Oh my," she breathed, and saw him grin.

Strange installations glittered on bulkheads the color of polished bronze. The deck was soft, cushioned, although it shone. The place smelled faintly of cinnamon and sandalwood, and it was blessedly warm.

She'd have the chance to learn this particular ship's ropes, she told herself; at least, she hoped she would. For now, however, what she really wanted to do was swat Marc the one he deserved for that remark.

Then she discovered that kissing him was much more important, and considerably more fun.

"I'll get you," she promised.

"We have a long trip ahead of us. You can try." He kissed her back. "Besides," he said, "you've already got me."

She already knew what their smiles looked like. Was the sound she heard from behind them an honest-to-goodness alien laugh?

She'd find that out too, she promised herself. She'd find out everything. She'd write her reports, make her business assessments, and when they returned to Earth, she'd sell them for all they were worth.

Not that they'd need the money. But because that was how the game was played. She'd always played to win, and now she'd won, bigger and better than she'd ever dreamed.

Marc whirled CC around and around until her head spun. Taking her hand, he led her deeper into the Maktoub ship.

"You know," he said, "this is going to be one hell of a honeymoon."